Shores of Okinawa
Patrick Greenwood

Quill Hawk Publishing

CyclewriterLLC.com

ISBN Number - 979-8-9850905-9-8 (Paperback)

ISBN Number – 979-8-9869102-0-8 (Hardback)

Library of Congress LCCN: 2024915971

This novel, "Shores of Okinawa," is dedicated to my parents, John M. and Eileen Gormally, Ken, Nancy, and Michael Gormally. Even after 60 years, my family is still a great source of inspiration.

I truly thank my father for taking me to his office at a young age to see how the world of engineering has helped to shape my present and my future.

To my mother for stuffing newspapers in her shoes on a cold Virginia day to cheer me on while I played football.

To my oldest brother, Ken, for giving me his shortwave radio, which changed my life forever.

A loving hug to my sister, Nancy Meshell, for her reviewing, editing, and creativity!

And to my brother Michael for always being there for me my whole life.

Our Benefactor

HelpOki's Story: Action in Compassion

"Our story at HelpOki is one of compassion, unity, and resilience. Founded in 2011 after an encounter with homelessness, our mission has always been to end poverty in Okinawa and uplift those in need. We work relentlessly through dedicated volunteer efforts, community development initiatives, and inspired philanthropy to bridge the divide between the international and Japanese communities. As we continue to write the story of HelpOki, we remain committed to transforming lives, fostering hope, and creating a brighter, more inclusive future for all members of the Okinawan community."

Proceeds from the sale of the novel, "Shores of Okinawa," will help end poverty on the island.

HelpOki Community Center

Address: 2 Chrome 13-3 Misato Okinawa, Japan

Phone: 080-4403-9855

Email: helpoki@yahoo.com

Website: www.helpoki.org

Contents

Cast of Characters

Jack Kendall: Gritty, handsome former U.S. Marine, now head troubleshooter for Techline, chasing his arch nemesis Travis Jones in Taiwan and Okinawa. While pursuing his nemesis, Jack suspects Travis Jones is plotting a global cyber-attack against strategic partners of the U.S.

Travis Jones: Arch nemesis of Jack Kendall and CEO of Trans World Global, LLC, a global advisors firm that specializes in corrupt deals. A Canadian former UN Peacekeeper with connections to organized crime groups, including the Fong Gao Triads in Taiwan, Japanese Yakuza, and Gorky Park Russian hacker group. Travis is plotting a global cyber attack in partnership with the Chinese government and a rogue Vietnamese hacking team.

Forest Adams: CIA station chief in Vietnam and former ex-Marine stationed in Saigon during 1975. Forest is Jack's guardian and mentor, providing intelligence information about Travis Jones and the Chinese PLA hackers.

Lilian Tang: Codename: Vulturess on Darknet. One of the most violent hackers in the world, known to kill in the blink of an eye. She has no limits to cyber hacking skills. Raised as the stepdaughter to BOSS-Snakehead, head of the Fong Gao Chinese Triads, she kills on his orders.

<u>Poppy Ledger:</u> Australian expat, global hacker, and freelance investigative reporter, for the New China News Agency.

<u>Dimi Zosh:</u> Ex-Russian Spetsnaz. One of the deadliest hackers in the world. His cyber outfit, Gorky Park, is notorious for targeting global banks and foreign governments and killing off their rivals.

<u>Regina Kendall:</u> Daughter of Jack Kendall. Former U.S. Coast Guard special ops responsible for the capture of several Mexican and Columbian cartel members. Upon graduating from Harvard Law, she is seduced into joining a global law firm secretly funded by Travis Jones.

<u>William Kendall:</u> Son of Jack Kendall and brother of Regina Kendall. William's technological advancements in developing high-speed internet communications are expected to dominate the market for years to come. However, this innovation also has made him a target for Travis Jones and Poppy Ledger.

Foreword

Thank you, Patrick Greenwood, for the enlightenment of what might be, what can be, what is. "Shores of Okinawa," a sequel to Patrick's debut novel "Forever Our Sunrise in Saigon," follows protagonist Jack Kendell and Forest Adams on the hunt through Taiwan and Okinawa to stop their nemesis, Travis Jones, from pulling off the cyber attack of the century.

A truly complex story linking together several powerful events into an unexpected climatic moment.

While reading this sequel, I continued to question which parts of the book were fiction or nonfiction.

The level of detail Patrick provides in his story is phenomenal. The plot line roller coasters from the Chinese government wanting to invade Taiwan without firing a single shot; the use of cyber hacking to create a blood rivalry between the Fong Gao Triads and the Japanese Yakuza~ then systematically provoking a cyberspace battle that was beyond comprehension.

How does a reader know the difference between fiction and non-fiction? Is the romance and level of violence more art imitating life or the other way around?

Patrick's description of intense tragedy, soulless murder, evil threats, and raw violence landscapes his book, creating layered multiple subplots. Greenwood's Character Development is complex. His characters: Lilian Tang, General Ho, and Poppy Ledger are manifested as super arch villains, but the reader reluctantly develops a sense of compassion for them as much as the reader emotionally responds to storylines for Regina, William, and Tricia.

Patrick Greenwood knows the ins and outs of cyber hacking in the real world. The extremes of hacking, the ultimate corruption of power, and the radical cyber terrorism held in the clutches of state-sponsored countries like China, Russia, and North Korea.

"Shores of Okinawa" gives a glimpse into the world of hacker outfits against hacker outfits, state-sponsored cyber-attacks, and individual greed mirroring many global leaders, globalist business executives, and corrupt politicians of our day.

The book sheds light on a world that very few see and as a reader, I only hope this is more fictional than not.

R. Janet Walraven, M.Ed.
International Award-Winning Author

BOOK ONE

Deception

"Deception's seduction ignites devastation.
Arrogance and ignorance become lovers.
Giving birth to destruction with all extreme prejudice.
While darkness ascends."

Gigi Kim Peeling

Prologue

Is China Waging a Cyber War with Taiwan?

"Nation-state hacking groups based in China have sharply ramped up cyberattacks against Taiwan this year, according to multiple reports. With geopolitical tensions and a trade war acting as a backdrop, China-led cyberattacks in Taiwan are rising sharply, according to multiple security reports. In the latest report about alleged China-sponsored cyberattacks on Taiwan, Kate Morgan, a senior engineering manager in Google's Threat Analysis Division, told Bloomberg that Google is tracking close to 100 hacking groups out of China. The malicious groups are attacking a wide spectrum of organizations, including the government, private industry players and defense organizations."

Source: https://www.csoonline.com/article/1250513/is-china-waging-a-cyber-war-with-taiwan.html

Message from the Author, Patrick Greenwood:

"Shores of Okinawa" is a fictional novel based on actual events. The events described in this novel are a work of pure fiction including the associated characters."

This Novel is a Work of Fiction...Or is It?

Chapter 1
Reciprocity

"Mr. Jones, line four please, Bao Xu is holding," Ms. Vingle called.

Travis, the Canadian former UN Peacekeeper turned CEO of the global advisor firm, Trans Global, braced himself for a critical phone call from the most powerful terrorist broker in Asia. "Travis here, Bao, what can I do for you today?"

Bao Xu was not in a good mood.

"Travis, interesting development with the Vietnam project."

Travis chose his words wisely. "Yes, Bao, a setback, but the project is going to come to us."

Hearing Bao breathe over the phone, Travis continued with the hope of pacifying the broker. "Bao, please ensure all parties that are involved, Techline only bought themselves time to hang themselves. We will increase all resources, gain access to the World Bank funds, and continue with the next phase of Operation Dragon Vault."

Bao Xu, a stealthy powerful global lawyer, represented several criminal clients. Bao's clients included the Fong Gao Triads criminal organization in Taiwan.

"Jones, you are getting ahead of yourself. Our friends in China want the Vietnam project back on now before our mutual clients will consider anything else on the table. The general is displeased with you, Jones."

Travis considered his near-term fate. "Okay, Bao, you tell whoever you are working for to take their share and stick it up their ass. The Vietnamese project will not happen without exposing their names and bank account information to the World Bank."

There was a pause while Bao took a moment to consider Jones's assessment of the situation. "Jones, our investors are not hiding in the shadows. This Kendall guy outdid you. I suggest you make it work before someone comes by for a wet refreshment." Bao slammed the phone down before Travis had a moment to respond.

Travis knew how deep Bao was with the Fong Gao Triads. This made Travis carefully consider what more danger he could be in. "Vingle, bring me the Kendall file."

Bao, dissatisfied with the direction Jones was going with the Vietnamese takeover project, murmured to himself, "Kendall, I wonder what you said to spook Jones?"

Bao reached over to his laptop to access the hidden video feed from Travis Jones's office. "Let's see what happened here." Bao played back the conversation between Kendall and Jones from two days ago. "Hmm, this guy has some guts. CIA?" Bao dialed his phone to make an inquiry into Jack Kendall. "Central Security, yes, please bring me what you have on an American, Jack Kendall."

Bao searched his secret files of American spies. "Oh, that is interesting," he mumbled to himself.

"Jack Kendall was born on February 20, 1964. He is an accomplished technology troubleshooter, divorced, has two kids, and served in the United States Marine Corps. His tours of duty included Japan, Okinawa, Korea, Thailand, and Beirut. Kendall recently spent time in Vietnam and Taiwan." Bao thought to himself, *a real American hero.*

After reading more data about Jack, Bao picked up the phone and called his assistant. "Please have Lilian Tang come see me." Bao hung up the phone with a smirk. "Okay, Jack, let's see what you are really up to."

Travis received a second call from Bao.

"Okay, Jones, I read the Kendall file. Did you know he travels frequently here in Asia?"

Jones, not knowing a great deal about Jack, replied, "Not really. I only met the guy two days ago. From what I read, he works for some small technology firm in California and somehow had access to our global compliance documents."

Bao replied quickly, "Yes, he clearly knew more about you than you knew about him."

Travis knew he was on borrowed time with Bao and the Triads. "Yes, I probably should have dug deeper into Kendall's background."

"What do you plan to do about it?" Bao sensed that he had Travis concerned.

"I will handle it." Travis contemplated his fate as he disconnected the call.

Bao had spooked Travis into handling the Kendall problem. He also must consider his fate with his client—the Chinese People's Liberation Army (PLA) cyber security group. Bao served as legal counsel for the Chinese Fong Gao Triads while maintaining deep connections with Chinese cyber groups.

He carefully weighed what he should share with his Chinese client, General Tsai Vo, commander of all Chinese Cyber Defense forces. He received a call from the general.

"General, most honored, sir," Bao proclaimed.

The general, not one for social calls, went on a tirade. "Xu, what happened to my project in Vietnam? I hope you are handling this minor setback as a priority. I need to get my cyber hacker forces in that region. Without that project, the Vietnamese will continue to block my efforts!"

Bao chose his words carefully. "Yes, General. I spoke to our Canadian friend. He will make the needed course correction in due time to get this project back on track."

The general, not taking anything from Bao at face value, said, "What do you mean, Xu? I am a busy man," the general shouted.

Bao replied with deference. "Project Dragon Vault, honored sir, has accelerated towards Phase Two!"

The general seemed somewhat impressed with Bao's initiative. "How marvelous! You have secured the fiber vault in Kaohsiung?"

"Actually, Trans World Global has the full title and deed now," Bao replied.

"Oh, they do? Well, I guess we need to keep them around longer than I anticipated."

"Yes, General. I will monitor the situation closely. I will send someone over to make an assessment to ensure we have no more setbacks."

The general agreed. Bao gave a sigh of relief, pleased with his positioning as a middleman.

"Yes, General, we will also keep you around longer."

General Vo was a twenty-year veteran of the Chinese army. He knew if he could somehow secretly connect his hackers to the backbone network, which served as the core infrastructure for all modern telecommunications, internet, and data transmission within Taiwan, he could bring this rogue island fully under Beijing control once again.

"I will be a hero in the eyes of China forever," he thought proudly.

Travis spent several hours reviewing the Kendall files and took notes of the things he would later act on.

"Regina Kendall, recent Harvard law student graduate with six years in the Coast Guard." Travis saw a plan beginning to take shape. "Regina, I bet you need to pay off those student loans." He considered his next move. "Vingle, get me Noah on the phone. Now!"

Chapter 2

Gratification

Regina looked at herself in the mirror and saw the few scars from her Coast Guard service. "Girl, you have made it."

Her scars came from years of chasing drug boats off the coast of Florida. Regina took her share of bullets in her chest and legs. She was ready for her transition into a calmer, more peaceful life as a lawyer.

Graduating from Harvard Law was Regina's lifetime dream. However, $200,000 in student debt was not part of the original plan. Thanks to the Coast Guard and the U.S. government education program, forty-five percent of her educational expenses were covered. However, she still ended up with $110,000 of outstanding debt.

"I need to go find a real job," she muttered under her breath turning from the mirror.

In the interim, Regina was clerking at a small Boston law firm, while waiting to obtain a full-time first-year associates' program. Being a Harvard graduate, she believed this phase of her career would be a smooth transition. However, she soon discovered the stark reality of the legal job market, where opportunities for young lawyers were very competitive. A surplus of newly minted attorneys vied for highly desirable positions in prestigious law firms, presenting Regina with a formidable challenge.

Regina began tidying up her small kitchen. While sorting her mail, she found a letter from a local Boston-based law firm.

Dear Ms. Kendall,

The Offices of Blake, Wilson, and Todd, offer you an invitation to interview for our firm. Please contact Mr. Wilson Yu, our managing partner, to help set up a convenient interview time.

"What!" Regina could not believe one of the top law firms in the world wanted to interview her.

Holy shit, I can't believe this. After she composed herself, Regina researched the law office in preparation for her interview with Mr. Yu.

She discovered that the Offices of Blake, Wilson, and Todd had 250 lawyers, 120 partners, and global clients including Shell Oil, Microsoft, BT, China Mobile, and Fiberex-Xiamen. The law firm specialized in mergers and acquisitions, as well as hostile takeover resolutions. Their partners included two former senators, one Supreme Court justice, and several members of legal firms from the UK, France, Russia, Taiwan, Vietnam, and China.

This is a dream job. She assured herself and took a moment to let the excitement set in. "Okay, I need to write the perfect acceptance letter now."

Dear Mr. Yu,

Thank you for your consideration in reviewing my credentials. I welcome the opportunity to meet with you and discuss joining your Law Offices; I am currently clerking here in Boston. Please let me know what day and time would work for you.

Respectfully yours,

Regina Kendall,

Attorney at Law.

Brimming with excitement, Regina called her brother, "William, you would not believe who invited me for an interview!"

William listened to the jubilation in his older sister's voice and responded, "Sis, I am so proud of you. I am sure Dad and Mom are as well."

"Thanks. Until I get an actual offer, I'm not going to tell our parents. Are you coming out for my graduation?"

William considered everything he had going on in his life—marriage to Tricia, a new baby on the way, and his work at Cybercom Systems. "Sis, of course, I will be there." He smiled as they hung up. William took a moment to make another source code revision before letting his wife, Tricia, know about Regina's interview. "Regina got an interview with some huge global firm. She wanted to know if we are attending her graduation next week."

Tricia put a hand on her growing belly. She was nearly seven months pregnant and thought it might be better to stay at home. She said as much to William, sad she wouldn't be there to support her sister-in-law.

After he finished his last round of code changes, William uploaded the source code he'd been working on for the new fiber optic quality of service (QoS) software for long-range underwater internet connectivity. William and his engineering company had been covertly working with the American Navy to provide an improved solution for greater internet and telecommunications speeds using underwater cabling.

If this project continued to be successful, William could expect several billion-dollar contracts from governments all over the world. William logged into a secured portal to send the source code to the other developers. After several minutes of continued loading, the files were successfully transferred. William received an encrypted communication verifying the files sent. He closed his laptop with a great sense of satisfaction and headed off for dinner with Tricia.

Unbeknownst to him, a second computer in Shanghai, China was also pinged with the same notification.

"Yes, thank you, William, for the most recent code revisions." The entity on the other end of the rogue computer smirked with great satisfaction.

Chapter 3
Sea Turtles

Lilian Tang reached for her phone, only to see Bao Xu calling her for the fifth time today.

"Bao, I was busy interrogating that software engineer geek."

"Let me guess, the only thing you got out of him was his GPA?" Bao asked.

Lilian replied, "Ha, I got nothing!" Lilian was not amused anymore by the lawyer for the Triads. "What do you want, asshole? I'm busy."

"I need you in Taipei. We have something in motion that may be coming your way soon. I need to brief you and pass along instructions from the general," Bao replied.

"Okay, let me freshen up, dump the body, and I will be on the first train in the morning," Lilian responded.

Bao always trusted the top hacker for his organization. "See you soon!"

Lilian observed her reflection in the shower mirror and wondered to herself how she became the woman staring back at her. Born in 1975, she was placed in an orphanage at the age of two, never having known her biological parents and often pondering if she looked like them. Eventually, she was adopted by a couple who were high-ranking members of the Fong Gao Triads based in Taipei.

For centuries the Triads were comprised of several groups within Chinese society. Each group controlled both criminal and normal business life. In the latter part of the 20th century, the Triads focused on global drug running, human trafficking, and money laundering. The Triads, known to be ruthless killers, had many victims in over eighty countries. In the early 1980s, the Fong Gao Triad group left Hong Kong and settled in Taiwan. This move gave them access to more criminal activities, including gambling, murder for hire, and shipping drugs to America. In 1996, the Triads invested in internet technology. This expanded their global reach into the narcotics and human trafficking rings.

Growing up as a member of a global criminal organization, Lillian started young by pick-pocketing tourists in Taiwan. Eventually, she moved up to armed robbery at the age of fifteen. After spending two years in youth corrections, Lilian emerged as a hardened member of the Triads group.

At that time, Bao Xu was a rising star within the Triads. He presented a plan to the leadership to send Lilian to America to further her education skills and tradecraft.

Showing great promise in computer science, Lilian attended UCLA for her ungraduated studies, and then Stanford University for her master's degree in advanced computer engineering and software design. While she attended college, Lilian performed low-impacting hacks against several key US firms, including Wells Fargo Bank and Disney Studios. Her online reputation grew, along with her hacker handle, "Vulturess."

The sheer mention of her name on the internet struck fear in many cybersecurity firms and government agencies. Being "Vulturess" gave Lilian a deep sense of power over others. Her quest for control and lust for success fed Lillian's ambitions. She realized that there were no limits to her potential or desires.

After finishing school at Stanford, Lilian was highly sought after by many firms. She accepted an engineering position at Binarycore, a technology company specializing in artificial intelligence. While she had a choice of several firms, the leadership within the Triads needed a source inside of Binarycore to feed their proprietary data and software code to the Chinese cyber security forces within the PLA.

A young captain at the time, Tsai Vo, covertly developed a relationship with the Triads. He funded the placement of Lilian in America. During her time at Binarycore, Lilian excelled in software development and product engineering. Her leadership skills and abundant confidence manifested in rapid advancement within the company.

Lilian sensed the male chauvinistic tendencies within Binarycore and confronted the executive partners, specifically those responsible for promotions.

"Jerry, why do I continue to be passed up for promotions?" Lilian asked.

Jerry, a senior manager for Binarycore, dating back to the start of the company, responded, "Well Lilian, you are not performing on all cylinders. Other developers are showing great promise inside and outside of the company."

Lilian, totally confused by her boss's comments, approached human resources to ask for help. "I don't understand what Jerry means when he says I'm not showing promise outside of work," Lillian said to the HR coordinator.

"Lilian, you need to ask Jerry out for dinner. Have some one-on-one time to talk more about what kind of growth he wants to see from you."

Completely shocked by the mere suggestion of using a date, or worse, a means to climb the corporate ladder, Lillian stormed out of the HR office. She ran outside to her car in the parking lot.

As she was leaning against her car, Lilian noticed a couple getting cozy in the backseat of a car. She squinted across the parking lot at them. It was her old schoolmate, Ellen, from UCLA who had also interviewed for Binarycore with Lilian. She was with one of the C-level executives. He had to have twenty-five years on her at least! She had been wondering how Ellen, who she had been able to run laps around in school, was snagging promotions so quickly.

"Oh my God, that bitch. We started here together," Lilian cried.

As she tried to compose herself, Lilian walked over to the car, pulled out her phone, and began recording her UCLA classmate and the senior executive as they engaged in inappropriate activities. Within a matter of hours, the video leaked on YouTube and several other outlets from a myriad of anonymous accounts. The video explicitly showed the guy throwing his head back and the girl looking up, smiling with pleasure. The video caption read, "Promotion board at Binarycore."

News feeds from all over the world picked up the caption and video. YouTube attempted to take down the video, only to have it appear under multiple anonymous accounts with nods to Lilian's digital persona, Vulturess. Lilian created an automated video uploading program to re-upload the video every fifteen minutes, staying one step ahead of Binarycore and YouTube content controllers. Within hours, the video, viewed by millions on the internet, had gone viral. The legend of Vulturess exploded.

Binarycore, reeling from the public embarrassment, hired an entire team to uncover the source of the video uploads. After weeks of a dedicated team working directly with YouTube, they traced the upload back to a Binarycore laptop belonging to Lilian. After uncovering who Vulturess was, the company offered Lilian millions to walk away, never say another word about the video, and delete all evidence. Lilian chose the package and walked away then and there with a seven-figure paycheck, complete with stock options. Once her belongings were packed, she was immediately escorted off company property and told she would be heavily fined if she ever returned to any Binarycore property.

Lilian spent the summer back in Taipei with her newfound wealth and her ever-increasing sexual appetite for both men and women. While she reveled in her freedom, she used her time off to discover her hidden talents. She kept tabs on executive-level Binarycore employees and made their lives just a little bit harder, with minor data leaks here and instances of malware attacks there... all via untraceable IP addresses, of course. Bao and the Triads continued to monitor their rising star and were impressed with her steadily growing skills. The mystery and intrigue surrounding Vulturess's cyber persona excited their imaginations for future projects.

Bao stayed in touch with Lilian via secured chat. He occasionally asked his young cyber warrior to handle a few issues with rival firms, including dealing with the Yakuza crime group in Japan.

The Japanese Yakuza were known globally to be as ruthless as the Chinese Triads. The Yakuza maintained a substantial stock of cyber hacking resources. Many students recently graduated from Tokyo University found themselves deep in debt. Most graduates needed to make money fast to avoid years of poverty. They often signed on with the Yakuza to help pay off their college loans and support their aging parents.

On rare occasions, the Triads and Yakuza would attempt to hack each other. Stealing cryptocurrency in the form of bitcoins, downloading gambler information, and locations of human traffic resources, became the favorite targets for these cyberattacks. The Yakuza was heavily invested in the Japanese porn industry. They partnered with the Triads to distribute adult content on the internet throughout China and the U.S.

Bao maintained a secret rolodex with sensitive information on his counterparts and lawyers within the Yakuza. The Yakuza had heard about the legacy of Vulturess and for years attempted to find out who this person was. Bao continued to feed bogus information to the Yakuza about Vulturess. He hoped to confuse and distract them from discovering the identity of one of his most important hackers.

Lilian began to receive a growing list of assignments from Bao during her time in Taipei including encrypting Triads. The files ranged from video content, financial statements, and articles of incorporation. Sensing the importance of these arrangements, Lilian cloned these files into an encrypted vault within an offline server at UCLA that only she and a handful of other people knew about.

One day her curiosity got the best of her. She started watching these videos and discovered why they were so important to these crime groups. Many of the videos were showing pornographic images of high-level government officials engaging in sexual escapades with young girls, perhaps too young. In many of these films, several officials had sex with multiple girls at one time while ingesting illicit drugs like cocaine and ecstasy. When the films were over, the Triads brutally beat the girls to the point of certain death. She knew the videos would send a message to anyone contemplating a betrayal of the Japanese crime syndicate in any form. She was sickened by what she saw but did not let it stop her from continuing her relationship with the Triads. Her money was starting to run out and she knew what she had to do. Lilian showed up at Bao's office in Taipei for more assignments.

"Bao, I am bored. Give me something that will take me to a higher level in this place."

Bao sensed a new side to his seasoned asset. "Come take a seat and let's discuss your future," Bao said. After the discussion with Lilian, Bao dropped an email to a newly promoted Major Vo.

"Major, we have an asset developed here in Taipei. We recommend keeping her here at home and not reassigning her to America." Bao mumbled to himself, "Welcome home, Sea Turtle."

Lilian returned home to her penthouse ready for whatever changes her discussion with Bao would bring. She undressed looking out over her city of Taipei. She stepped into the deliciously hot water of her rain shower and Lilian reflected on her life, how she came from almost nothing to live in a penthouse suite. She stepped out of the luxurious spa shower glistening and wrapped herself in a plush towel. As she dried herself off, she checked the messages on her phone.

"Vulturess, welcome home. Stand by for a new bio and cover story, signed Vo."

Lilian took a deep breath and typed back. "Absolutely, Major Vo, this is my time now."

Chapter 4

Deception

While he read his emails, Thomas Wilson, CEO of Techline in Pasadena, California, for the first time, was about to try a triple espresso; highly recommended by his troubleshooter, Jack Kendall. After taking one taste, Thomas spat out the coffee back into his cup.

"Jack, how can you stand these?" Thomas uttered with disgust.

Thomas had grown fond of Jack. Being Thomas's top deal maker and troubleshooter, he relied on Jack for so many things for the company. The CEO opened his emails and recognized a secured encrypted message from the World Bank.

Dear Mr. Wilson,

Thank you very much for your bid proposal. Our organization reviewed your offer and investment strategy. While your bid meets all our require-ments, our committee felt that your organization lacked global recognition or experience. We required a company to be at a certain professional level to support this project. We thank you again for taking the time to network with us. However, we extended the offer to another firm.

Signed,

Pedro C. Gomez

World Bank, Project Manager

This news caught Thomas off guard. His entire firm's financial projects for the coming year revolved around the Vietnam project. Techline had spent thousands of dollars on research and proposal development. Without this project and yearly management fees, Techline would not have a new support project in the coming year.

Over his office intercom, Thomas shouted, "Ronald, in my office—ASAP!"

"Yes, sir," Ronald, a junior partner in the firm, answered.

"Ronald, we lost the Vietnam project to an unknown firm. Please check the proposed legal language to see if we can challenge this determination."

Ronald paled and quivered as he replied, "Yes, sir."

"Jack, I wish you were here," Thomas mumbled. "This must have been a state-sponsored global terrorist organization to pull this off."

Several thousand miles away in China, newly promoted to a two-star general, Tsai Vo read a similar encrypted message from the World Bank.

General Vo,

Thank you for your recommendation concerning the Dragon Vault LLC firm.

Based on the information you provided along with the vault leadership, we have determined the Dragon Vault LLC has the winning bid for the Vietnam project. Congratulations to you and your team. We look forward to a very enriching long-term relationship.

Signed,

Pedro Gomez

World Bank Project Manager

As he sat back in this new office overlooking the Forbidden City in Beijing, General Vo smiled with a great sense of pride. "Now, we have a base for our cyber resources in Vietnam. Excellent."

After a few moments of private celebration, the general reached for his phone. "Bao, I need to see you and Tang in my office. We have a lot to discuss."

Bao recognized the urgency in the general's voice. "Yes, General, I will get Tang on a plane within the hour."

General Vo replied, "Good."

The general started pacing around this office, deciding on the next course of action, now that the Vietnam "distraction plan" was underway. He reached for the intercom. "Major, have Poppy Ledger report to my office immediately."

"Yes, sir!" Major Vonn replied.

Today, just like most days within the People's Liberation Army, the cyber security group, codenamed Dragon Vault, was a hive of great activity cloaked in total secrecy. Several team members spent long hours hacking into American, British, Russian, and French data information networks.

The Dragon Vault team members were selected by General Vo himself. All applicants were classified as Sea Turtles. The team members needed to be educated in the United States and must have spent a minimum of five years working in cutting-edge technology companies, such as Apple, Binarycore, Cisco, Microsoft, and Oracle.

The Sea Turtles, after proving to the Chinese PLA leaders their ability to steal data from within these companies while avoiding detection, earned the opportunity to apply to be a Dragon Vault team member.

Poppy Ledger, a well-known freelance writer from Australia and a covert hacker consultant, worked for General Vo. Educated at the University of Southern California, Poppy spent five years at Facebook as a security engineer. During her time, she successfully set up a trash file data dump of all Facebook users globally into the Chinese PLA's mainframe farm in a secret data center in Las Vegas, Nevada.

Even with the most advanced technology in the world, the Americans still had not discovered how many data centers the Chinese government controlled within the United States.

"Poppy, report to General Vo's office immediately," Major Vonn ordered.

"Yes, sir," Poppy replied.

The subway rumbled under the streets of Beijing as the train arrived at General Vo's office in Tiananmen Square. Poppy could not believe how many tourists left their phones in their bags, making them an easy target for pickpockets.

What they don't know will hurt them someday, Poppy thought.

She arrived at the Chinese PLA forward operating headquarters in Beijing. Poppy walked through the secured glass doors and presented her ID to the guard. The security guard scanned Poppy's badge, only to find she did not exist in their security system. The young soldier panicked and drew his weapon on Poppy.

"Freeze, traitor, you are not in the system," the young soldier yelled. "You are a spy!"

Poppy remained very calm. "Soldier, I am Poppy Ledger, a reporter for the New China News. Please, take a moment and phone General Vo's office. My clearance code is Dragon Vault."

The soldier was not convinced. He reached for the phone and called his superiors. Within minutes, several armed personnel arrived at the desk.

"Who are you? Keep your hands up!"

"I am Poppy Ledger, here to report to General Vo, by his order."

The security officer, while keeping his sidearm at the ready, phoned General Vo's office. "General Vo, we have a traitor in the lobby claiming to be from a secure PLA cyber group, Codename Dragon Vault."

General Vo became outraged. "Captain, I will put a bullet in you if you do not release her now."

The captain suddenly realized that the secure cyber team would not show up in the central search file. The captain replied rapidly, "Of course, sir."

"Miss, you are free to go. The general's office is on the eleventh floor."

Poppy knew this was probably the last time she would see the captain alive. "Thank you, Captain." Poppy exited the elevator and walked into the outer area of General Vo's office. "Poppy Ledger reporting to the General."

Major Vonn recognized Poppy. "Ah, Poppy, good to see you again. Go in. The general is expecting you."

Poppy nodded and entered the general's office. "General Vo, Poppy Ledger reporting, sir."

General Vo nodded and pointed to a seat across from him, acting as if she had not just been held at gunpoint. "Sit. Well done on your data exfiltration of Techline. The data you scrubbed from their emails gave us a competitive advantage in the Vietnam project."

Poppy replied, "Thank you, sir."

As Poppy moved to sit across from the general, he noticed how attractive the Australian was and didn't make an attempt to conceal his roving gaze. "Are you married? Boyfriend? Girlfriend?"

Poppy replied, "No, sir, I live alone."

Pity, the general thought. "Poppy, I am sending you on a new assignment."

The general's declaration stunned Poppy. "Thank you, sir."

The general nodded. "Yes, well, we are ready for phases one and two of Operation Dragon Vault and the new team needs a proven leader. Our entire operation will virtually take control of Taiwan's cyber networks."

Poppy nodded. She only heard about this new project recently.

The general continued. "With the Vietnam distraction project underway, we can quietly disguise our cyber resources headed to Vietnam to help with the Operation Dragon Vault cyberattack."

Poppy, not totally sure what the Taiwan project entailed, wisely decided to listen instead of questioning her superior officer. "Yes, sir, I am ready for the task."

General Vo smiled. "Well, come back tomorrow. You will meet the additional assets that we have assembled to help with this mission."

Poppy rose, thanked the general, and departed his office. She entered the elevator and noticed the captain of security in handcuffs, his face bloodied from a recent beating.

"See you around, Captain," Poppy said with a smirk.

Chapter 5
Deceit

While sitting in the lobby of the law firm of Blake, Wilson, and Todd, Regina reflected on her dream of joining a global law firm. Fresh out of law school, she had received several offers to join smaller firms. Yet, in her heart, she wanted to be a global player in the legal community.

"Regina Kendall? Glad you made it," Noah said.

Regina rose quickly from the couch. "Yes, Mr. Blake, it's a great honor to meet you, sir."

Noah smiled. "No, the pleasure is all mine. By the way, thank you for your service," he said, referring to her years spent in the Coast Guard.

Regina smiled. She always exuded confidence, this was gleaned from her years in the Coast Guard, going toe to toe with international terrorists and drug kingpins.

"Thank You, Mr. Blake, for the acknowledgment, sir."

Noah walked Regina to his office. His floor-to-ceiling view of downtown Boston was breathtaking. Regina complimented Noah on the magnificent view.

"Regina, have a seat please," Noah requested. "Look, let's cut to the chase. We want you here at the firm, plain and simple. You are a Harvard graduate with honors, a military hero with several accommodations from the Coast Guard, and a compilation of excellent clerk assignments with a solid local law firm. You are exactly what our firm needs."

Regina took a deep breath, a surge of pride rushed through her, and she worked to remain composed. She was thrilled by how quickly this interview was progressing in her favor.

"Well, Mr. Blake, thank you. I am looking forward to a long, successful relationship with this esteemed law office."

Noah could sense he had Regina hooked. "Okay, let's get to it then. We will offer you a salary of $120,000 per year plus a bonus program. Our firm will pay off your student loans, with no requirement to pay back, unless you leave the firm within three years. Questions?"

Regina was stunned and almost speechless. "In summary, counselor, the firm will pay off my loans, and pay me a salary with a bonus program," she confirmed.

Noah prepared to close the deal. "Yes, and after your first year, you will be eligible to become a partner in the firm," he replied.

Regina may not have had much professional experience, but from her schoolmates, she thought his offer seemed almost too good to be true. Everything seemed to be falling into place perfectly for her.

"Mr. Blake, I am completely honored, sir. I hope to prove worthy of this generous offer. May I ask, what role would I play in the firm?"

Noah got up from his chair and walked over to the portrait of the founder of the firm, Ernest Todd.

"Mr. Todd, our founding partner, made his bones from his very first day by getting deals done in China. Mr. Todd will retire next year, and we are looking for someone to head up the Chinese operations. Based on your military and global experience, you would be the perfect candidate for that role."

Regina processed the generous salary and benefits. She felt overwhelmed by the whole offer. She asked, "Mr. Blake, may I have a glass of water, please?"

Noah replied, "Yes, let me show you to what will be your office and we will have some water brought in."

Regina rose from the couch and followed Noah down the hall to an office that was almost as grand as Noah's. As she entered the space, Regina was astonished at the view. While maintaining her professional composure, Regina calmly remarked, "What an incredible view of the Charles River!"

Noah replied, "I believe you live just over the bridge, yes?"

Regina smiled back at her new boss. "Well, Mr. Blake, when do I sign?"

Noah already congratulated himself for a job well done. "How about tomorrow? I will have all your paperwork ready. Let's meet at 9:00 am sharp and get you settled in. I know you have the bar exam coming up soon. Not to worry, you will have time to study."

Regina shook Noah's hand with a firm grasp. "Yes, sir. I will see you tomorrow."

Noah walked Regina out of the building and thanked her again. Unknown to Regina, her recruitment and hiring at the firm was an integral piece of a meticulously planned puzzle being crafted from the other side of the world. After seeing Regina out, Noah reached for his phone.

"Travis, it's Noah. She is in. Starts tomorrow."

Travis Jones could not contain himself. "Did you screw her?"

Noah, not one to discuss those matters with Travis, said, "Dude, I don't screw and tell."

Travis laughed. "Well done. I will let the powers that be know that you held up your end of the bargain." Noah knew that the entire project had elements he was not in the loop on.

Travis continued. "Keep me updated on her movements."

Travis hung up with Noah. He thought to himself, *Kendall, I am not done yet, my friend. Not even close.*

Travis, never hesitant to seize a moment of self-glory, congratulated himself. "Trav, you are a rock star." Travis reached for his phone. "Bao, Travis Jones. Regina Kendall is in the fold now. When can I meet the general?"

Bao, now not wanting to expose Travis directly to General Vo, answered, "Ah yes, Jones, I will see if the general is available. If not, please continue to update me on your progress. We are most interested in the next task at hand."

Travis replied angrily, "Look, Bao! The deal was that if we flip the Vietnam project to your people and get the Kendall girl in the loop, we will have access to the general."

Bao knew Jones could be a loose cannon and become a liability.

"The general appreciates your teamwork, Jones. Let me ask him in the morning."

Jones felt more empowered and replied, "Now, that is what I am talking about. Make it so!"

Bao hung up the phone with Travis. "That man has to go," he declared with resolve.

Contemplating his next move, Bao searched through his secured file storage to retrieve the Dragon Vault file.

"Let's see. What's next on the list?" Bao realized the Taiwan cyberattack was moving according to the general's timeline. He needed to update the Triad leadership on the progress.

He pondered for a moment. *If this plan is to become operational, the Chinese PLA and the Fong Gao Triads will elevate my status in the criminal organization.* Bao drafted an email to the chairman of Fiberex, a major backhaul fiber optics company based in Xiamen, China.

Dear Yung,

I believe it is time for us to finally meet. The project we spoke about is becoming a reality sooner rather than later. I ask that we treat this project with the highest levels of sensitivity and confidentiality. We are moving rapidly into Phase I and Phase II. We welcome your counsel and resources to make Dragon Vault a reality. The direct success of this project will have crushing effects on the people and infrastructure in Taiwan. We will suppress and destroy any separatist mindset. Your company is on the verge of historic importance to our people and our way of life. China will forever become the sole superpower. China will control all elements of communications, healthcare, and components of everyday life throughout Taiwan.

I look forward to meeting you in person and discussing the next phases.

Regards,

Bao

Savoring the glorious prospects of his success, Bao joyously reflected. *I couldn't be in a better place, being the captain of the ship that is going to crush Taiwan for good.*

"Everyone! Keep it down," Abe Yung, CEO of Fiberex, said. "Today we received a secured message from our partner. Operation Dragon Vault is moving ahead as planned. I need all fiber maps, connector resources, and scale models on my desk no later than next Tuesday. Questions?" He surveyed the room and video-conferencing screens of employees from around the world. Every team member shook their head, acknowledging no further questions. "Good," Abe said. "Meeting adjourned."

Abe Yung guided the company to its most impressive growth. Since his tenure as company leader, the company had grown at a massive 450% year-over-year. Abe, like many Sea Turtles, received his education in the United States at UCLA. An excellent optics engineer, Abe spent most of his working life at Cisco Systems, Inc., a global leader in networking and security. Abe became an expert on backhaul fiber and optical communications. A significant part of Fiberex's technology came from many of Cisco's product lines.

"Comrade Yung, you have a call," Yuli said.

"Yung here," Abe replied, picking up the desk phone.

"Go secure," the general said.

"Secure red over yellow," Abe replied.

"Good. This is General Vo. I need you in my office in the morning. I have a few members of the team flying in, and we need to discuss a few things."

Abe understood the significance of General Vo and the authority his commands held. "Yes, General, see you in the morning." When Abe hung up, he headed to the bathroom, trying to keep his face blank. Once inside he ran to the toilet, retching uncontrollably, tears stinging his eyes.

"I can't do this," Abe cried, resting his face against the cool porcelain.

Chapter 6
Unveiling

February in Beijing was usually freezing, so rarely did people hold meetings outside. However, on this Friday morning, a small group would gather in Tiananmen Square. General Vo, while he admired the view of Chairman Mao's tomb, had moved the all-important Dragon Vault team briefing outside and into the middle of Tiananmen Square.

"Major Vonn, signal to all Dragon Vault personnel that the meeting will be moved to the northeast corner of the square, assemble at 10:00 am sharp," the general commanded.

"Yes sir," Vonn replied.

Lilian, Abe, Poppy, and Bao all received a secured text to meet at the new location and to be on time.

Bao replied, "Is that man crazy? It's minus four Celsius!"

The general instructed each team member to enter Tiananmen Square from different entrances. Major Vonn had a team set up ten chairs, six feet apart from each other. As the clock moved towards 10:00 am, the Dragon Vault members assembled at the meeting location and took their respective seats.

Major Vonn instructed them to wear dark sunglasses and not speak to anyone at the meeting. While each team member took their place, the general, standing off in the distance, smiled with amusement at his team shivering. Vo, dressed as a peasant factory worker, walked slowly up to the meeting place within the square and sat down. Each Dragon Vault member inserted a sub-vocal earpiece to hear their leader. The wearer could silently articulate words without vocalizing them aloud. This technology picks up the subtle muscle movements associated with speech and converts them into signals that can be transmitted or interpreted as spoken words. The general controlled the earpieces from a Huawei computer tablet.

"Good morning. I am General Vo. Many of you have never met me in person before. Welcome to our lovely capital city." Each team member nodded and tried to focus on the matter at hand while contending with the freezing temperatures.

"I am in control of your earpiece. Don't speak unless I have addressed you. You are not to speak to other team members ever while in person, only via secured chat and emails," the general said.

"I have chosen you for various reasons. Our leadership, including the President of the People's Liberation Party, The Central Committee, and regional governors, have grown weary of Taiwan. For several years, our government has used every means at its disposal to control Taipei. With each step towards dismantling the separatists, Taipei has only become closer to independence. While we have considered all the military options on the table, our president fears the United States will come to Taiwan's aid in a time of war. The president has empowered me to use whatever cyber warfare resources available to convince Taipei to dissolve its government and assume the status of a regional province."

The general paused to assess the reaction from his team.

"Operation Dragon Vault charter is to bring down the Taipei government once and for all, without firing a single missile or gun. Each of you has a specific skill set or access to resources that will help make this mission a success."

While adjusting his seat, the general began to lay out the plan for the team.

"Our mission will be to connect a backhaul fiber optic cable from Xiamen, China, to Kaohsiung, Taiwan. We have gained access to an undisclosed fiber vault that has proximity access to Taiwan's central network codename: TAINET backbone. Once the fiber connections are in the fiber vault, our team will connect the cable to an optical connection router within the Taiwan regional command-and-control network. The network already has several hidden routes and access control to the management network within TAINET. Once we have successfully connected, a hacker group, code name Emerald Forest in Vietnam, will deploy multiple application bots across 5G radio cell towers and Internet of Things sensors distributed throughout Taiwan."

As she took in the plan laid out to the team, Lilian took a long deep breath and said, "Holy shit."

The general paused to communicate via a secured channel to Lilian, "Tang, do you have a question?"

Lilian, not realizing she'd spoken aloud, quickly replied to the general. "No, sir."

Using his tablet, the general selected all the earpiece communications and continued to discuss the project details.

"Within weeks our cyber forces will be in control of power stations, medical hospitals, traffic lights, banking systems, waterways, and military assets. The Taiwanese cyber forces will view the new fiber optics connections as nothing more than a maintenance node on their remote network."

Bao, absorbing everything that the general mapped out, considered that this stolen information from Taiwan to Mainland China could also be very useful to the Fong Gao Triads.

The general selected each team member to brief them on their specific assignment.

"Each of you has received $10,000,000 in Bitcoin to your secured vaults along with your new identity, assignments, and task lists. If you succeed, there will be another $50,000,000 in Bitcoin deposited in your vault. Anyone who fails in their primary duty will find a very painful end to your life and to your family's lives."

The general already had hit squads throughout China and Taiwan ready to execute anyone on his order.

"Tang?"

"Yes, General," Lilian replied.

"We need your services immediately. In the morning, you have an interview with Sunny Ho, CEO of ADConnect, in Taipei. His firm is the chief architect for TAINET, including providing all services and security for the Taiwan government. Our operatives have presented your credentials and work history to them. It is very critical that you get hired by that firm and begin the covert optics hookup."

Lilian recognized the importance of her assignment. "Yes, General."

Before Vo briefed the next team member, he made a calculated decision to have Travis Jones address the group.

"Listen up. I am going to bring an asset on the line. He is the one that helped with the Vietnam project's redirection of funding along with obtaining the fiber vault in Taiwan."

The general ordered Travis over his earpiece. "Mr. Jones, go ahead."

Travis seized his moment of glory and exclaimed, "Okay everyone, just as the general has said, I own the Vault. This is my project! The master plan is simple. You techies are going to run your fiber optic cable straight into Taiwan's digital network and implant your malware and rootkits into the heart of their military, civilian, and Internet of Things networks. Once your stealthware has been enabled, we will have access to every secret file and data source in Taiwan. Thanks to me, you guys will be able to fuck them for years to come."

The entire team cringed, showing their disdain for how their teammate presented himself, even evident behind their dark sunglasses.

"Thank you, Mr. Jones," the general said. He continued to brief the shivering team members. "Poppy, I understand you have access in real-time to the backhaul QoS code, correct?"

Poppy replied, "Yes, sir, I have an active, secured rootkit connected to the chief developer himself."

The general smiled. "Good. Once you have the correct, updated version of their source code, please send this to Fiberex for testing and validation. The fiber optic cabling will be over 356 kilometers from Xiamen to the hidden vault in Taiwan. We need that code to work!"

Poppy understood the urgency in the general's order and said, "Yes, sir, I will head off to America and gain access to the source code crypto keys."

The general disclosed to the group that Fiberex had already started repairing the underwater cable weeks ago. Next, the general addressed Bao directly over the earpiece. "Bao, have we secured a law firm to establish Dragon Vault, LLC, as a formal global technology offshore firm?"

Bao took a moment to shake off the feeling of cold. "Yes, General. Blake, Wilson, and Todd Law Offices have already prepared the documentation for the World Bank. Funding should be available for the Vietnam project next week. We have siphoned off $50,000,000 to help cover the cost of the fiber cabling."

The general was pleased with Bao's work and replied, "Excellent. Please keep me informed." As the general rose, each team member rose and bowed to their leader.

"Meeting over. Go in the name of China," the general proclaimed.

Chapter 7
Sneakers

Red Line Subway Station (Beijing, China)

Once they departed from the meeting, Lilian and Poppy coincidentally met up at the Beijing subway station. Each woman knew their respective assignment, not anyone else's. Lilian gave Poppy a nod of respect, knowing that she would never see her again. Poppy, intrigued by Lilian's looks, smiled, and blew her a goodbye kiss. One was headed to Taiwan and the other to America. Both served the same mission for a common cause.

Lilian boarded the Evergreen Airlines flight 101 to Taipei later that day at 7:00 pm. Her interview with Sunny Ho, CEO of ADConnect, was scheduled for the next morning. While she enjoyed the free cocktail in first class, Lilian read up on Ho's background.

"Hmm. Single, no kids, rich, educated in America, CEO, net worth $1.5 billion US."

Lilian considered all the possibilities. As she read through her newly created cover identity developed by the Chinese PLA, she noticed the intelligence team had her posing as a single mother with two children living in America. She then continued reading more about Sunny Ho's company.

"Interesting. ADConnect oversees ninety-five percent of fiber cross-connections in Taiwan, including all dark fiber, short and long haul along with backhaul service controllers, all controlled by them." Lilian realized the opportunity to hide a new fiber optic node with TAINET may be a lot easier than expected.

Let's see the distance between the vault in Kaohsiung and the regional command... 1.6 kilometers... perfect, thought Lilian.

She knew that with the additional dark fiber connector, this would give her access to several single and multi-mode fiber strains to hide her rogue connections.

Lilian continued to brainstorm. "ADConnect has access to the entire spectrum of fiber connectors on the island. This should be easy if I can get someone to run a home-run fiber optic cable."

After studying her target, Lilian closed her eyes and dreamed about meeting Poppy in another time.

"Blow me a kiss? Girl, you do not know what you just did."

Flight 575 on Delta Airlines departed Taipei–Taoyuan Airport for San Francisco. Poppy knew Cybercom Systems had created the backhaul QoS software. She knew Fiberex needed this software solution quickly to meet their investors' expectations and to serve the Operation Dragon Vault project.

Poppy's assignment at the newspaper as a freelance writer granted her access to several industry events and even interviews with industry CEOs. For this trip, her mission was very clear: steal the final cryptography key chain from the source code from her target, William Kendall.

"Thank you all for flying Delta Airlines. We will be landing in San Francisco shortly," the flight attendant said over the intercom.

Chapter 8
Lisbon

Delta Flight 2761 (Lisbon, Portugal)

As the aircraft descended, Jack woke up from the turbulence, jostled by the plane's approach to Lisbon International Airport.

"Nel, my love. It's time to wake up. We're landing," Jack said, gently squeezing Nella's shoulder.

What will I say to her father? Do I give her mother a hug? All these questions lingered in Jack's mind as Nella opened her eyes.

"Jack, you look a little pale. Are you okay?" Nella asked.

"I am fine," Jack replied.

As the plane continued to taxi to the gate after a smooth landing, Nella was already on the phone with her parents, speaking in Portuguese.

"Yes, Mama, Jack is here. We will be there shortly." Nella smiled, looking over at Jack. "Yes, you can hug my mother. She would love it!"

Jack smiled back and gave Nella a kiss on her lips. "I love you my Nel."

Nel felt tears spring to her eyes. She could not contain her love and emotion towards Jack.

"But Jack, please don't hug my father. A handshake will work," she said seriously. Jack appreciated how earnestly she also regarded his first meeting with her family.

After the plane docked at the gate, Jack and Nella walked off the plane with a carry-on bag. As Nella stepped off the plane, a man bumped into Jack, knocking him sideways so he fell into the final row of seats, and pushed past him.

"Hey!" Jack yelled.

The offender turned around and stared back at Jack.

"Qui, vous-etes merde!" The man swore in French.

"Merde?" Jack replied.

As the man approached Jack, Nella jumped between the two men and jokingly said, "Okay, guys, back off."

The Frenchman laughed as he turned around and walked off the plane.

"Nella, I had him, you know," Jack proclaimed.

"Of course you did, but I need you to meet my parents, please, not the police!" Nella hissed under her breath.

Jack nodded his head and grumbled, "Yeah, you are right. But you saw it. I had him!"

Nella shook her head and continued walking towards the gate. When Jack reached the end of the gate, he showed his passport to the immigration officials.

After a brief look, the officer stamped his passport and stated, "Proceed. Welcome to Portugal."

Nella and Jack headed to the international gallery to find Nella's parents, Jorge and Wei.

"Mama and Papa!" Nella cried out with joy.

Jorge saw his beautiful daughter coming toward them with an unfamiliar man and walked over slowly to greet them both.

"Hello sir, I am Jack. Very nice to meet you, Jorge."

Jorge was not impressed with Jack's greeting. "Nella, who is this?" he asked sternly in Portuguese.

"Papa, this is Jack, my boyfriend and my love," Nella replied.

Wei, Nella's mother, walked over to Jack and said, "Very nice to meet you, Jack. I am Wei. Welcome to our country."

Jack thanked her with a big smile and reached over to give Wei a hug, only to feel a punch in the arm from Jorge.

"You are here five minutes, and you think you are going to hug my wife!" Jorge bellowed.

"Sir, I apologize," Jack replied holding up his hands.

Wei didn't want Jack to feel embarrassed. She reached out to Jack and gave him a hug. Jack smiled back at Wei. He bent to pick up Nella's bags along with his luggage and followed Jorge to the car.

"I think your dad hates me," Jack said as he walked behind Nella.

She crinkled her nose. "Yea, well, my mother likes you."

When they reached the car, Jack dutifully handed Jorge each piece of luggage as he Tetris-ed them into the trunk of the small car.

"Jack, are you hungry?" Wei asked.

"I am. Nella, are you hungry?"

"Yes, I am hungry. Mama, could we stop at the Invicta?"

Invicta, Nella's favorite restaurant in all of Lisbon, was known for its oysters and lobster soup.

"Of course, dear. Jorge, let's go!" Wei said enthusiastically.

Jack could not believe how beautiful Lisbon was as they drove through the ancient streets. The city was full of Gothic, Baroque, and Manueline architecture that reminded Jack of Spain and Italy. Jorge drove by the Belem Castle and countless beautiful cathedrals on their way to the restaurant.

Jack was glued to the window. "Nella, is that the Portuguese version of the Golden Gate Bridge?"

Nella smiled. "Yes, that is the Ponte 25 de Abril, or April 25th bridge. It is constructed exactly like the Golden Gate."

Jack also noticed a colossal statue standing on the other side of the famous bridge lit up by the final rays of the setting sun.

"Is that statue from Rio, Brazil?" Jack asked.

"Yes, Jack, that is the Christ the King Statue," Nella replied.

"This is a beautiful city, Jorge. Thank you so much for having us," Jack said earnestly.

Jorge was still not sure what to think of Jack and only after an elbow from Wei did he grudgingly reply, "You are welcome."

Jorge parked the car a block away from the restaurant on a tight side street.

"Beautiful night for a walk," Wei stated.

Nella took Jack's hand and walked down the street. Jack could see the famous Jerónimos Monastery in the distance. For a moment, it made him think back to his adventures finding the Monastery in Vietnam many years ago. After a few moments of walking and taking in the sights, they arrived at Nella's favorite restaurant, Invicta. Nella spoke to the waiter in Portuguese. She asked for a table with a view of the water. The waiter gave Nella a look and slowly opened his hand behind a menu. Nella knew this routine and placed a twenty euro note in his palm.

"This way, please," the waiter said.

The table offered a perfect view of the water. Jack waited for Wei and Jorge to sit first.

"Sit," Jorge commanded.

Jack internally cringed at his future father-in-law's behavior towards him and questioned what he was doing there. *Do I need to do this at the age of fifty-six?* Lost in his thoughts, Jack drifted off not hearing the conversation continuing around him.

"Jack, hello!" Nella squeezed Jack's arm resting on the table.

"Sorry dear, I was having a jet lag moment."

"Jack," asked Wei, "do you love my daughter?"

Wei's directness startled Jack.

"I see where you get your directness from, Nel," Jack said, smiling. "Yes, Wei, I love your daughter very much."

Wei smiled back at her daughter, giving her a mother's look of approval.

"So, Jack. Nella tells me you are into technology troubleshooting," Jorge stated, cutting into the conversation.

"Yes, Jorge, I focus on global security communications."

Jorge was not impressed with Jack's occupation. "I was an architect. I built things that last a lifetime, like a good marriage!" Jorge proclaimed.

Jack sensed an excellent opportunity to engage in some verbal judo with Jorge. "Well, I am a digital architect, Jorge. I build global networks so billions of people can talk, exchange emails, and execute business commerce securely."

Wei smiled faintly at Jack's return comment. She reached down and pinched Jorge's leg, reminding him to behave.

"Nella, darling, how is the investment business in California?" Wei asked.

"Well, the economy and global conditions are forcing many commercial properties to go under. Residential holdings are in decline because of the lack of foreign capital. I am thinking of switching portfolios and focusing on capital improvement projects."

Wei was impressed with her daughter's knowledge and passion for work. "I have heard the states are finally going to fix roads and bridges by seeking outside investments to fund their projects," Wei replied.

Jack took a small, deep breath. He was impressed with Wei's knowledge of business issues in the United States. "Wei, I am very impressed by your knowledge of the happenings in America, especially when you're here in beautiful Lisbon."

Wei thanked the compliment from Jack. Jorge was becoming increasingly agitated as Jack continued to impress his wife. He directed his attention on Jack and asked, "Okay, American, how about you pick the wine tonight?"

Jack was always up for a challenge. "Jorge, absolutely. Wei, what do you plan to eat tonight?"

Jorge was clearly caught off-guard by Jack's question to his wife.

Wei answered, "Oh, I am going to have the beef in red wine sauté. Thank you for asking."

Jack turned to Nella and asked, "My love, what do you plan to have?"

Nella was happy that Jack knew to ask about the food choices before selecting the wine. "I am having the lobster soup and mussels."

Jack then turned to Jorge. "Sir, what are you planning to have?"

Jorge appreciated Jack for the first time since their meeting and answered, "Well, I am having the scallops and white wine."

After Jack looked over the menu, he stated, "And I am going to have the grouper fish in lemon sauce."

Nella smiled at Jack. She always knew Jack would shine in front of her parents.

After a few minutes of studying the wine and beverages menu, Jack announced, "After careful consideration, I recommend we drink some Sagres beer instead of wine."

Jorge looked amused at Jack's request. "Oh, why Jack?"

He took a quick drink of water and explained, "Well, each of you ordered a main course with wine. Any wine you order as your beverage will most likely affect your ability to enjoy your food. However, a beer, especially a local historical one like Sagres, will provide the needed refreshment while adding a new flavor to your dish."

Nella beamed with pride at Jack's answer and could not contain herself. "I love you, my Jack," Nella whispered.

Jorge felt somewhat defeated with all the attention on Jack and decided it was time to ask the real questions. "Okay American, what is your plan with my daughter?"

Knowing that this conversation was coming, Jack decided to sidestep the subject until everyone had a couple of drinks in them.

"Jorge, I plan to make your daughter even happier each day that we are together."

Wei smiled with joy that her daughter finally found an honorable man. "Jack, how do you plan to take care of my daughter?" Wei inquired.

Jack tried to find a way out of this conversation. He took a deep breath to explain to Jorge and Wei his plan just as the waiter delivered the beers.

"Ah, the beer has arrived. Waiter, could the grand lady of the table please be the taster?" Jack flattered Wei with his gesture.

Jack turned to Jorge and Wei and asked, "Let's chat later about my plans."

Jorge nodded and gave his daughter a long look of dissatisfaction. Nella smiled from within and admired Jack even more. He made the trip to meet her family and even ordered beer instead of wine in front of her father.

"Jack, you are one of a kind," Nella said.

Dinner became a series of quick conversations while the group enjoyed their various dishes. Jack, a huge fan of grouper, enjoyed the fish with vegetables. Nella and her mother shared a table-side lobster along with their soup. Jorge ordered additional mussels to be shared at the table.

"Jack, tomorrow we will head off on scooters to Cascais, one of the most beautiful seaside cities here in Portugal," Nella said.

Jack loved traveling globally and felt that Portugal would be a place he would be visiting again and again.

"Nella, that sounds great. I have not ridden a scooter since Vietnam," Jack said.

Jorge looked up from his food and asked, "You were in the war?"

"No sir, I was visiting as a tourist many years after the war was over," Jack replied.

Nella knew Jack owned a water company and had been in a relationship with a woman from Vietnam. "Jack also owned a water company in Vietnam. He used the funds to support the orphans in the city," Nella said.

This impressed Wei. She exclaimed, "I have never traveled to Vietnam; however, I've heard how beautiful the country is."

Jack explained, "Yes, in some places, the post-war recovery has gone well. However, there is still widespread poverty and corruption."

Jorge took an interest in Jack's background. "I also heard you were in the military. Is that true?" Jorge asked.

"Yes, I served in the United States Marine Corps for seven years," Jack replied.

Jorge took a moment to study Jack. He suddenly decided to just enjoy the dinner and not ask any more questions.

Once dinner was over, the waiter brought over the check.

"It's my honor to meet you and Wei. May I pick up the check?" Jack asked.

Jorge was insulted by this request. "You are in my land, American. I will pay for dinner."

Jack nodded with approval and respect for his future father-in-law.

Wei looked over at her daughter and quietly whispered, "I love him. I hope he stays around."

Nella beamed with pride that her mother appreciated Jack, and whispered, "Yes, I love him, too."

After Jorge paid the bill, Jack looked around the restaurant and admired the beautiful view of Lisbon. While he departed the restaurant, he noticed a smell coming from a booth near the door.

I know that smell from somewhere, Jack thought. He stopped for a moment to see where the smell came from.

"Jack, come on," Nella called.

Jack pondered the mysterious scent, and he remembered the French guy from the plane had a very similar smell.

"Okay, Nella, I am coming." Then Jack approached Nella and whispered into her ear, "Thank you, love, for bringing me here."

Nella reached over and kissed Jack on his lips. Jorge turned around and said with exasperation, "Do you mind?" Jack and Nella smiled playfully.

Back at the restaurant, an older French gentleman dining alone, ordered another glass of wine. "Merci," he said to the waiter.

The morning sunrises in Lisbon completely took Jack's breath away. He noticed the gaze of the yellow and orange morning lights over the water in Lisbon. The view filled him with a joyful energy that he hadn't felt in quite a while. He reflected on the last sunrise that had made him feel this way. *I thought the sunrise in Saigon was special,* Jack thought, realizing how important life was by living in the moment and not letting the past control him.

Jack took out his smartphone and photographed the sun rising. After he snapped a few pictures, Jack thought, *Jack, Lisbon is in your soul. Saigon will always be in your heart.*

Nella watched Jack taking pictures and walked over to him. "Darling, the scooters are ready."

After Jack and Nella kissed Wei goodbye and hugged Jorge, they headed down to the scooters.

"Okay, Jack, remember, take it slow, especially around the turns here in Portugal," Nella warned.

Jack acknowledged Nella's concern with a thumbs up. He placed the helmet on his head and started up his scooter.

"Good, let's go," Nella said excitedly.

"Good, let's go," Nella said excitedly.

Chapter 9
Covert

ADConnect Offices (101 Building, Taipei, Taiwan)

A little after 11:00 pm local time in Taipei, Lilian landed at the airport. She focused on her mission ahead. She cleared customs and passport control and headed to the taxi line. She hailed the first taxi. "Taipei Marriott."

While en route, Lilian checked her secured emails and chats from the Dragon Vault team. She received an urgent message from the general.

"Tang, do not fail. Do whatever it takes for you to get hired at ADConnect."

Lilian acknowledged the message and replied, "Yes, sir." She fully understood the importance of her mission.

The ride to the Taipei Marriott took less than thirty minutes. The driver opened Lilian's door and removed her bags. He was awestruck by her beauty. Lilian entered the hotel and headed to the front desk feeling the driver's eyes still glued to her.

"Passport, please, miss," the front desk manager requested.

Lilian handed over her passport and surveyed the hotel lobby for anyone who may have followed her.

The front desk manager handed Lilian's passport back to her and instructed, "Ms. Tang, you are on the top floor and have access to our executive lounge. Welcome to the Taipei Marriott. A bellboy will assist you with your baggage and escort you to your suite."

Lilian nodded while she collected her bag and passport. After heading up in the elevator to the top floor, Lilian was guided to her room by the bellboy. He opened the door and placed her luggage in the room. Lilian tipped the bellboy and closed the door.

She entered the living room when her phone rang.

"Tang, this is Bao. That dress on you looks amazing."

Lilian, annoyed with Bao's comment, said, "Look, you are blowing my cover. I am a proud mother of 2 looking for a new job!"

She hung up the phone and threw it down on the couch. Lilian set her alarm for 5:00 am. This would give her plenty of time to shower, enjoy breakfast, and check her emails.

After a restless night, Lilian turned off her alarm five minutes before it was supposed to go off. She checked her messages and noticed one from Bao.

"Tang, be mindful of the Taiwan Secret Service. They will have security men at ADConnect."

While enjoying her coffee, Lilian continued to read up on Sunny Ho, CEO of ADConnect. Reading his bio online, Lilian gained a slight element of respect for him.

"This guy's company is small, yet he controls ninety-five percent of all backhaul fiber in Taiwan, including TAINET. His company has shared crypto key management with the national government power and military systems. Impressive!" Lilian put away her documents and finished getting dressed. She headed out of the hotel feeling prepared to execute her mission.

Lilian walked over to the next available cab to head over to the ADConnect headquarters inside the Taiwan 101 building. Taiwan 101 was built in 2004 as one of the largest buildings in Asia. The 101 building is the center of trade and financial offices in Taiwan.

The cab driver looked at Lilian with awe. "Where to lady?"

Lilian replied, "The 101 building."

As they arrived, Lilian exited the cab. She was amazed at the height of the building.

"Wow, so this is the famous 101," Lilian whispered.

She headed over to the ADConnect offices within the 101 Tower for her interview with Sunny Ho. She walked through the door with her red Versace dress and black over-the-knee boots. She felt confident in her dress, which accentuated her curves in all the right places, yet still maintained an aura of professionalism.

She embodied her Vulturess mantra: "Make an appearance they will never forget."

Lilian approached the ADConnect front desk and asked, "Mr. Ho, please. I am Lilian Tang. We have an appointment."

The receptionist replied, "Yes, Ms. Tang, good morning. Please fill out these forms while I let Sunny know you've arrived."

The ADConnect offices were situated on the sixty-fifth floor. Lilian took the documents and sat in a chair overlooking Taipei.

Sunny appeared as she stared out at the view. "Quite a view, Lilian, I am Sunny. Thank you for coming to see me."

Lilian rose from the chair. "Sunny, great to meet you finally."

"Come this way. Let's chat." Sunny showed Lilian back to the board conference room. "Lilian, have a seat. Can I get you anything?"

"No, thank you."

Sunny cleared his throat, assuming his professional tone. "I asked you here to discuss a new business opportunity. We have an upcoming project and my contacts in the Information Technology field highly recommend you."

Lilian focused on the task at hand and remembered what the general told her. "Yes, let's get down to business. I am available for new projects," Lilian replied.

Sunny read the latest intelligence about Lilian's background from his tablet. He looked up at Lilian. "UCLA, Binarycore, Intel, internship at Qualcomm... excellent qualifications."

"Thank you, Sunny, not to mention I speak five languages," Lilian said proudly.

"Okay, Lilian, I'll run through the project details. Behind me is a fiber backhaul cabling scheme for an upcoming project," he said gesturing to a whiteboard on the wall. "All our best people have spent 500 hours or more to design this optical network. Our client wants this project operational in the next six months. How much do you know about the Internet of Things?" Sunny asked.

Lilian seized the opportunity to show off in front of Sunny and quickly replied, "Five hundred hours? Are you kidding me? What a waste of the time."

"Really? How so?" Sunny asked.

"Well, for starters, your design is bullshit," Lilian asserted. "Your architects are using a 1996 optical sonet-ring technology with a basic level of wave division multiplexing. The next generation networks as part of the new standard of 5G for wireless will require a density of bandwidth across all optical fiber color spectrums to meet the bandwidth and redundancy requirements. In your design, you need to move up to dense wave division multiplexing so you can allow for greater bandwidth per color and support for different frequency spectrums across each fiber link."

Sunny took in each data point Lilian made and asked, "So switching to the dense model we will meet our goal to deliver greater bandwidths over longer distances, using fewer fiber cables in the ground or in the water?"

Lilian knew she had already impressed Sunny with her knowledge. "Yes, if you are considering connecting to the Internet of Things devices across Taiwan including streetlights, hospital medical devices, military command center devices, and sensors, this is the only way to do so with proper encryption."

Sunny took a drink of his spring water over ice and replied to Lilian, "So, the cabling diagram is bullshit... you caught me. I will need you to advise me on the 5G networks technical requirements and cybersecurity framework that will be connecting to the Internet of Things devices and sensors. This project is a top priority for President Yu Chu Fong of Taiwan, and execution of this strategy is imperative to our president and our nation. Her administration is the driving force behind an accelerated advancement of Taiwan, striving for independence from China. At the core of her campaign lies the pledge to transform every township in Taiwan into a smart city, equipped with Internet of Things devices and sensors, along with the fastest internet access for all citizens. By having smart cities connected through TAINET, every citizen could work anywhere and gain access to more information and education than ever before via their mobile devices and computers. Once every city becomes a smart city, Taiwan could become the first smart country in the world. Our president envisions Taiwan as being a country seamlessly integrated through connectivity. With this capability, other nations could foster stronger connections with ours. Therefore, we require this new SONET-fiber network to propel our nation towards global leadership in connectivity."

Lilian listened to Sunny's passionate explanation of the project and replied, "Giving our people opportunities to access education, jobs, and resources remotely, without having to move to another city or commute to work would be an incredible advantage. Okay, Sunny, where do we go from here?"

Sunny beamed with pride and appreciated Lilian's determination and drive to enhance their nation's infrastructure. He leaned in towards Lilian,

"I know having someone like you on our team will increase our probability of success, however, I need to know one thing before we move forward."

Lilian held her breath. She wasn't sure what information Sunny may have about her. "Of course. What can I answer for you?"

Sunny cleared his throat and leaned back in his chair. "We know who you are, Tang. My friends informed me about you, Vulturess."

Lilian froze, unsure what this might mean for her role with ADConnect, let alone the Fong Gao Triads, and chose her next words carefully, "I am sorry, who is this... Vulturess?"

Sunny was amused by the apparent denial from Lillian. "Well, you are Vulturess. Do you deny this?"

Lilian calculated her options. If she confessed to being the hacker, Vulturess, she would not get hired and would likely be reported to Interpol by Sunny. If she denied it, they could see her as untrustworthy. Her identity as Vulturess was supposed to remain a secret as part of her exit package from Binarycore. She made up her mind looking at Sunny. "When I worked for Binarycore, I experienced things that made me very angry. Things I'm sure would never take place in a company like ADConnect. That chapter of my life closed when I left Binarycore. May I ask who disclosed this information to you? Part of my exit package included a gag order from both parties to never disclose my identity as Vulturess, so legally, I cannot confirm this information."

Sunny smiled. He finally confirmed who the famous hacker's identity was. He was more than satisfied with himself having discovered the famous Vulturess.

"We did Binarycore a favor here in Taiwan a few years ago. So, they dropped the dime on you as part of our agreement just in case you ever surfaced again."

Lilian could hear her racing heartbeat; she had said the wrong thing and did not know how to answer or even continue the conversation.

She confessed, "If I were this Vulturess, I confess I did some terrible things back then that I regret, however, I have been off the Darknet for several years now."

As Sunny listened to Lilian, he opened his tablet to an encrypted email. "I have a contact in the Taiwan Security Service and the national financial banking network that informed me Vulturess still is an active player in the Darknet."

Lilian wiped her sweating palms on her dress under the table and tried to keep her face blank. "Is that why you asked me to come here?"

Sunny was amused by how easily he had cracked the Vulturess. He redirected the discussion. "Yes and no. Let's discuss your future here at ADConnect."

Lilian was relieved, but suspicious, "Okay, where are we going?"

Sunny closed his tablet and answered, "Let's take a walk."

He rose from his seat and motioned Lilian to follow him. Sunny led Lilian to the elevator and stepped inside, taking them to the ground floor of the 101 building. After a few tense moments, the doors of the elevator opened, and Lilian and Sunny exited. Sunny proceeded to open the main door of the office building, leading out to the crowded street.

"Let's grab a coffee and chat," he said, holding the door open for her.

Lilian wasn't sure why, but she felt she could trust Sunny. He may have uncovered her greatest secret, but he still looked at her with a kindness she couldn't explain.

She followed him across the street into the busy Xinyi district. Xinyi was a famous district in Taipei known for its small coffee shops and street food.

As they walked to the coffee shop, Sunny stopped to say hello to people he knew. Many of the shopkeepers and food stand vendors all knew the famous Sunny Ho. He loved to chat with his fellow countrymen and discuss food and politics during his work breaks.

"Here, Lilian, let's stop in and say hello to some folks."

Lilian was not a sociable person; she could only manage a tight smile on her face.

"Cho, two triple espressos," Sunny ordered.

"Thank you, Sunny," Lilian acknowledged as she glanced around the small, cozy shop.

Sunny smiled back and said, "Look, let's get to the point. Lilian, you are what we need, and what your country needs to get this project off the ground. Our company will become a world player in the Internet of Things space, our stock price will undoubtedly skyrocket, making our employees all millionaires, and hopefully they will invest in their country. We have a future away from China, and this is it."

Lilian felt a surge of pride for her country. She knew, however, that her life was not that simple. She was the property of the Fong Gao Triads on loan to the Chinese PLA cyber forces and General Vo. No matter how much pride she had for her country, she had a mission that her life depended on. Sunny may have known one of her secrets but did not appear to know more than what he shared.

"I am Taiwanese, Sunny. I want to do everything I can to serve my country."

Sunny tasted his expresso and replied, "You must not act against your own country as Vulturess again. However, I will call on you to help in the fight against China, and Vulturess has the skills we need. We know that the PLA has spies all over this country. The Triads also are in bed with the Chinese PLA."

Lilian's palms began sweating again and she used every bit of self-control to contain her conflicting emotions. The phrase, "I am that spy," flashed across her subconscious.

"Sunny, I am not that hacker anymore, however, if my skills are necessary to serve our country and help keep this project safe, I will be at your disposal."

Sunny reached out a hand to Lilian. "Welcome aboard. Let's start tomorrow."

Lilian cringed internally as she shook Sunny's hand, pushing down the rising conflict between her mission and nation.

Chapter 10
Interception

Cybercom Technology Conference (San Francisco Taipei Marriott)

While checking into the San Francisco Marriott, Poppy noticed several messages on her phone. She moved to a quiet space in the hotel lobby and logged into a secured app, reading her urgent message from the general.

Poppy, your target will land in three hours. He will be staying at your hotel. It is critical that you secure the crypto keys from his software package. Use any means necessary to secure these items. Ensure you leave your target in as much despair as possible.

Signed,

General Vo

While the plane was landing at the San Francisco International Airport, William connected his phone to the Wi-Fi to check his messages. After scanning through the normal work emails, William noticed a message from his sister.

Bro, be safe in San Francisco. I started at the law firm! I am already working with a client in China. I guess they have some enormous projects in Vietnam and Taiwan. Hello to Tricia.

Love, Reg

William smiled to himself at Regina's success. He loved his sister very much and was very proud of her.

"Good evening. We will land shortly in San Francisco. Please return to your seats." The flight attendant announced over the airplane's loudspeaker. William thought more about his relationship with his father and decided to send him a message.

Dad, I hope you are well and enjoying Portugal. I just landed in San Francisco for the Cybercom Global Conference. I am the keynote speaker at the event. I am showing our new QoS package. Our investors are excited. Thank you for guiding me in life. I am here because of you.

Love,

William

As the plane arrived at the gate passengers began to stand and deplane. William grabbed his bags and headed off the flight, making his way through the airport to ground transport. As he stepped outside into the sun he thought, *Conference, here I come*, and flagged down a cab.

William arrived at the San Francisco Marriott just in time to check in and prepare for the evening's reception.

"Mr. Kendall, welcome to the San Francisco Marriott. You are all checked in. Your room is on the top floor with a beautiful view of the city."

William felt a rush of anticipation for the conference. He grabbed the keys from the front desk manager and smiled while heading to the elevator.

"I need a shower," William said as he entered his room. He headed into the shower to relax and practice his speech.

William spoke aloud to his invisible audience. "Thank you, everyone. My name is William Kendall, chief architect for Cybercom. My thanks to the committee for hosting me here today as your keynote speaker." He took a deep breath and exhaled to calm his nerves.

After the long shower, William unpacked and hung up his three suits choosing his jet-black Brioni suit for the evening's events. Walking out to the door, he reminded himself of how important this trip was to him. Tricia, the baby, and his company were his whole world. As he made his way towards the elevator, he remembered he'd left his laptop and tablet open on the bed. He was usually a stickler about locking his devices in the hotel safe typically provided in each room, but he was already just going to be on time if he caught the next elevator. *Those will be safe*, he thought to himself.

As he entered the elevator, he was so preoccupied with his impending speech that he failed to notice the beautiful woman standing against the wall. Poppy coughed quietly to get William's attention. He glanced her way and caught a glimpse of her slender figure wrapped in a shimmering blue, satin, floor-length dress. She gave William a coy smile before looking away as the elevator doors opened.

"Mr. Kendall? Ralph Oswald, conference CEO. Thank you for attending and being our keynote!"

William fingered his cufflinks, being sure everything was in place as he replied, "Thank you for inviting me, Mr. Oswald."

Ralph led William over to a group of conference attendees and introduced him. "Everyone, this is our keynote speaker, William Kendall."

Nathan Richardson, CEO of Fiberline UK jumped in. "Kendall, cheers. Nat Richardson from London. Very excited about your QoS capability."

William nodded at Nathan and the group from the UK reaching out to shake their hands before Ralph steered William over to the bar for a drink.

"So, William, what do you have in store for us tomorrow?" Ralph asked.

William cleared his throat, and replied, "That is a surprise, sir. However, your conference is the perfect venue for our big announcement."

Ralph smiled back at William. "Enjoy the food and drinks tonight. I know there are many people, including the press, that would like to meet you. Don't be shy!"

William smiled, feeling confident he'd make lasting impressions. He ordered a glass of sparkling water with lime and turned as another gentleman walked over to greet him.

"Kendall, Allan Willis Smith."

William recognized the name and took his drink from the counter as he addressed the gentleman. "Mr. Smith, a pleasure, sir. It's very nice to meet you, and an honor to meet our company's largest shareholder."

Allan was impressed that William knew his importance to Cybercom. "Thank you, William. I am looking forward to your demonstration tomorrow. We plan to announce our IPO next week. Let's have a great showing."

William nodded in reply to Allan. "Yes, sir, tomorrow is our day."

Allan patted William on the shoulder and headed off to mingle with the other attendees. William needed to catch his breath before diving back into the reception. He walked with his drink in hand over to the balcony to see the city lights of San Francisco.

While William made his way outside, Poppy entered the reception. As she made her way through the conference hall towards the bar, her dress catching the light of the chandeliers above, heads turned. Allan noticed Poppy and walked over to her.

"Good evening. I am Allan Willis Smith, CEO of Barnhall Capital. Who do I have the pleasure of meeting?"

Poppy saw the twinkle in Allan's eye and introduced herself. "Poppy Ledger, I am covering the keynote tomorrow for New China News Media."

Allan recognized the name of Poppy's news outlet; he knew that many people at the conference coming from China were most likely intelligence agents or assets of the PLA army.

"Oh yes, I have read your blogs. Very nice to meet you."

Poppy turned and leaned against the bar, giving Allan full view of her stunning ensemble. "Mr. Smith, I read somewhere that you are the largest shareholder in Cybercom. Have you by any chance seen William Kendall?"

Allan felt a twinge of disappointment at Poppy's question but answered, "Yes, he is outside on the balcony, I believe... taking in the city's view. Would you like me to make an introduction?"

Poppy seized on the opportunity to leverage Allan as a possible future asset. "Mr. Smith, I have met Mr. Kendall once before and I've been trying to score an interview with him for over a year. If you can re-introduce me to him, that would be wonderful." She smiled softly, practically batting her lashes.

Allan replied, "Let me lead the way."

William always enjoyed the peaceful view of city lights. Whether he was in London, New York, Taipei, or Vancouver, he enjoyed taking a moment away from the commotion to just listen to the sound of the cities at night.

"The view is lovely, isn't it?" Poppy asked William in a hushed tone.

"Yes, San Francisco always has a special place for me," William mused, lost in thought. As William finished his sentence, he spun around to see Allan and the woman in blue from the elevator standing before him.

"Kendall, it's my pleasure to introduce Ms. Ledger of the New China News Media," Allan said standing to the side.

"Hello, Ms. Ledger. I'm William Kendall," he said in a professional tone.

"Mr. Kendall, a pleasure. You can call me Poppy. I'm the technology editor for the New China News Media."

William smiled and shook Poppy's hand. He looked away towards the doors leading back into the reception. "Pleasure to meet you, Poppy. I am sorry, but I need to go and get ready for my presentation."

Poppy quickly replied, "Please, may I get fifteen minutes to ask you a few questions?"

William looked at Allan while he departed back towards the conference gathering. He then glanced at Poppy, weighing his options. He nodded and motioned her to follow him to the elevator.

"Let's stop in my room. I need to pick up my camera and recorder," Poppy said.

William agreed and inserted his key in the elevator to the top floor.

"Oh, this is my floor as well," Poppy stated.

William smiled at the coincidence, remembering the gleam of blue behind him in the elevator. They stopped by Poppy's room to pick up her camera and recorder and proceeded to go to William's room. Once they arrived, Poppy got busy and moving the chairs aroundsetting up her camera tripod and recorder in the seating area at the end of his bed.

"Could you take a seat so I can check my angles?" Poppy asked. As William sat, she rotated her camera to point at him, scanning his room in the process. She took in his open laptop and tablet lying on the bed. *His laptop will contain the QoS software*, she thought to herself. Once everything was set, she sat across from William, their knees only inches apart, and began her handheld recorder as her camera blinked red.

"Good evening, Mr. Kendall. This is a very exciting time for Cybercom. What's your plan for the keynote here at the conference?"

William talked about the new software package being displayed tomorrow and all the business applications and countries that could benefit from this innovation.

"Mr. Kendall, is your company planning an IPO because of this announcement?"

William was ready to wrap up the interview and get back to his preparations. He replied politely, "No comment. One more question, please."

Poppy smiled and replied, "No further questions."

William showed Poppy to the door.

On her way out, Poppy stopped and said, "Oh, I left my pen by the chair."

Poppy walked back to her seat and quickly placed a small USB drive into William's laptop. The USB carried a malicious program designed to give Poppy remote access to William's computer. She picked up her pen, walked back to William, and said graciously, "Thank you again for the interview." She departed down the hallway to her room whispering with a sinister smile, "Ah, William, I got you."

Chapter 11

Ascending

Ralph Oswald opened the conference by introducing William. "Everyone, please welcome Mr. William Kendall, Chief Architect, Cybercom."

William took the podium to polite applause, gazing out over the crowd. At the end of the first row, he noticed a woman in a red dress opening her laptop to take notes and realized it was Poppy.

As the applause faded William began his speech. "Thank you, everyone, for attending the conference. I am William Kendall. Today we are going to discuss the capability of QoS across backhaul fiber connections."

William showed the functionality of dense wave division multiplexing or DWDM and the ability of service carriers globally to transmit more data across single strains of fiber underwater.

"Our software platform will be released in beta testing tomorrow. This will give the service providers greater ability to set priority traffic patterns dynamically based on real-time data patterns across all color fiber channels."

The audience applauded with enthusiasm in response to William's announcement.

William continued, "Our software will also help countries receive priority level traffic based on their end-user's requests. If a country is hosting a college course online in Japan, students in Brazil can receive this class at a higher rate of speed and clarity compared to the normal internet speeds today."

William executed a demo program using his latest source code to show off this new capability. Poppy watched William log onto the platform. She activated her trace and recording program from the USB still connected to William's laptop. This enabled her to capture everything William was doing on his computer.

"As you can see from this working demo, our host country, the United States, has a special underwater cable connecting into a fiber vault across the Pacific to the Philippines. The Manila Department of Education links their internet access to an optical fiber connection within their closed vault. Once the connection is established, our software will begin regulating and prioritizing the data based on the demand of students, even down to the video pixel levels."

The audience applauded again at William's demo. Poppy captured everything, including the encrypted key exchange to the source code. She uploaded these files to the secured cloud within the Xiamen China PLA data center. Within ten minutes, William's entire crypto keys and source code were sent for analysis and shipped off to Fiberex. Fiberex started cloning Williams's work immediately.

Poppy waited for William to speak again before she packed up her laptop and purse. She rose elegantly from her chair, slinging her purse over her shoulder, and paused for a moment to get William's attention. Poppy gave William a wink and sly smile as she slowly turned and headed out the door. William watched Poppy depart and felt his throat go dry. He took a drink of water and refocused himself.

"In conclusion, the software will be available shortly in beta. Our company encourages you to reach out to us for more information. Thank you."

After a thunderous round of applause, William departed the stage and headed off to the bathroom fighting a wave of nausea. As he returned from the bathroom, William was stopped by Allan.

"Well done, son." Allan congratulated William. "Our technology is going to revolutionize the global optical networking space and deliver groundbreaking functionality to everyone on the planet."

William smiled at Allan and asked, "I guess we can go public now?"

Allan leaned over to William and whispered, "Patience."

William finished talking to Allan and noticed several reporters were lined up wanting an interview.

"Mr. Kendall, can I get five minutes? Janice Words, Electronic Today Magazine." William nodded and sat down for the interview.

Poppy grabbed her bags and called for a taxi to the airport. She stopped, looked back in the conference's direction, and offered a silent atonement. *William, I am sorry.*

Poppy entered her cab and proceeded to the airport. While en route, she changed her destination from Shanghai, China to Vancouver, Canada. Once the news leaked out about the stolen code from Cybercom, Poppy knew she would need to hide out for a while.

She opened her secured messaging applications to all Dragon Vault team members.

Code upload, full crypto hijacking completed, video uploaded to the news site in the next 24 hours. Standing by for Fiberex cloning and branding task.

Signed,

Poppy Ledger

Bao sat in Taipei reading the inbound communication from Poppy Ledger and thought to himself, *good girl, very impressive.*

Bao opened a separate email communicator to contact Noah.

In Boston, Noah noticed his secured phone notification with an incoming message. Noah opened his secured application and read the urgent message from Bao.

Noah, begin the lawsuit and court order to block Cybercom from releasing Backhaul QoS. Our friend in Xiamen will continue to clone and brand their version of the software. They will be done in the next 24 hours.

Signed,

Bao

Noah reached for his desk phone and contacted Regina. "Could you come to my office for a moment?"

Regina was working on several legal drafts for their client in China and rose from her desk heading to Noah's office. As she entered Noah's office, she said, "Yes, sir."

Noah waved Regina into his office and instructed, "Reg, please don't call me sir. My name is Noah."

Regina smiled realizing it was hard to break habits she formed while in the Coast Guard.

"Reg, our clients in China are Dragon Vault, LLC and Fiberex. We found out that an American company is attempting to come to market with a version of software that is far too close to the version Fiberex is about to release. I need you to file a court injunction preventing Cybercom from coming to market."

Regina was shocked when she heard Cybercom's name. "Noah, that's my brother's company!"

Noah smiled back at Regina and replied, "And? I bet your brother is a nice dude, but his company is copying, or rather stealing, code from China, and from our very profitable and highly billable client, Fiberex."

Regina, still in a state of shock, replied nervously, "Noah, I just can't sue my brother. He doesn't steal. How do we know if the Chinese company didn't steal the software from him?"

Noah rose from his chair and contended, "Okay, let's start with this. Dragon Vault and Fiberex pay our firm $3,000,000 a year in fees. Your brother pays us zero."

Regina felt trapped by the turn of events and offered, "Let me call my brother and ask him to clarify if his firm did steal the software from Fiberex."

Noah looked visibly upset. "Reg, we have a non-disclosure agreement with Fiberex. We can't just call your brother." Noah took a slow walk around his office. "Reg, this is how global stuff works. We file an injunction with our friendly federal judge, and he places a freeze on Cybercom, for let's say six months to sort this out in court. Meanwhile, we collect another mil in fees and make our client happy."

Regina felt cornered and said, "Okay, I will get the motion filed, then I can speak to my brother's lawyers and see if we can reach some sort of understanding."

Noah realized his protégé was more astute than he thought. "That's my Reg, make it happen."

Regina departed her boss's office in complete shock and disarray. She could not believe how her professional life was now affecting her family life.

Noah sat back down in his chair and lit a Cuban cigar. He basked in deep satisfaction with himself, throwing his legs onto his desk and reclining. He accessed his secured application to send Travis a message.

Message to Travis, protégé filing motion as we speak. Cybercom cannot release its code. Fiberex will release their version in the next 24 hours.
Signed,
Noah

Halfway around the world in Taipei, Travis opened his secured application and read the incoming message from Noah. He said under his breath, "Kendall, your world is ending, pal."

Travis reviewed his secured messages, pleased with the swift progress of the plan. He thought to himself, *the communications center in Vietnam is progressing thanks to those morons at the World Bank. Fiberex is cloning the code as we speak, and our law firm is about to shut down Cybercom.*

Travis felt immensely proud of his plan. He reached out to Bao to review the latest updates. "Bao, Travis here. I told you I could deliver!"

Bao knew Travis was fishing for compliments and wasn't interested in appeasing his ego. He answered in a sarcastic tone, "Jones, *very* impressive so far. This project could *never* succeed without the likes of you.

Travis, ignorant of Bao's sarcasm, felt touched by his response and replied sincerely, "Thanks, Bao."

Bao quickly grew tired of Travis' ignorance and arrogance. He began to consider options for what to do with Travis after the Dragon Vault project was completed.

"We may have something new for you, Travis. Hang tight in Taipei... more instructions to follow."

Travis thanked Bao and hung up the phone.

Chapter 12
Peril

Jack pressed the accelerator on the scooter as he powered past Nella while they headed out of Lisbon. He remembered his days in Vietnam using a scooter to visit clients. He loved the thrill of riding through busy streets up close and personal with all the sights and smells of the city.

"Jack, slow down on the turns!" Nella hollered.

"I got it," Jack yelled back to her.

As the couple bumped down the cobblestone streets of Lisbon, Jack couldn't recall a happier time in his life. Nella was back in Portugal, visiting her parents. Together they embarked on a day of exploration, indulging in food, sightseeing, and wine tasting in Cascais.

Cascais was known for having one of the most beautiful harbors in the world. The town was filled with the finest walk-up cafes, cozy coffee bars, and delectable seafood restaurants. Nella had high hopes for their evening together, as night fell and the harbor lights illuminated the still water, she hoped Jack would be proposing to her. As they enjoyed the beautiful mountain scenery, Jack looked in his rear-view mirror to discover someone in a black Audi A5 tailing them closely.

Concerned for their safety, Jack pulled over on his scooter and waved to Nella to do the same. When Nella came to a complete stop, Jack waved the car to go ahead. The car slowed down while approaching the couple. Nella looked over at the driver and waved. The driver seemed disinterested in the couple and sped ahead.

Jack had time to do a double-take of the driver. *That guy looks familiar,* thought Jack.

Nella moved her scooter alongside Jack and asked, "What is it, love?"

Jack stared at the black Audi as it sped away. He yelled, "I know that guy, Nella. It's that French asshole from the airport."

Nella looked at Jack with concern and said, "Darling, maybe he is on vacation like us?"

Jack noticed the sparkling harbor of Cascais from the top of the road. "Nella, is that the place?"

Nella smiled back at Jack while starting up her scooter. "I don't know. You might have to catch me to find out!"

Jack watched Nella take off on her scooter. A smile of immense joy spread across his face.

"Here we go!" Jack exclaimed as he revved his scooter and set off after Nella. Determined to catch up before she reached town, he accelerated, nearly veering off the road in his haste. With a few tense moments behind him, Jack regained control and eased down the hill into the picturesque town. Nella awaited him under a blue umbrella overlooking the historic harbor. Her smile widened as Jack approached.

"Well, if it isn't Mr. Kendall, global scooter master himself!" Nella giggled.

Jack was not in the mood to joke around. "I almost died lady. That last turn damn nearly killed me!"

Nella rose from her seat and put her arms around Jack's neck. "Oh, poor baby, I'm sorry. Let me buy you lunch!"

Jack's ego was still tender. "Lunch! I will need more than lunch to recover from this!"

Nella smiled and gave Jack a loving kiss and hug. "Come on honey. I will buy you your favorite—grouper fish."

Jack smiled and added, "And a local beer, please."

Nella smiled and waved the waiter over. The waiter delivered two pints of local Portuguese beer, Sagres, and two sparkling waters.

Nella raised her pint to Jack. "Saúde!" she cheered, clinking glasses. "Jack, I'm so glad I got to bring you here. This is my favorite city in the world. Someday, I would like to purchase one of those apartments overlooking the harbor."

Jack turned around to see the apartments. He noticed a huge Portuguese flag flying on top of the hill and asked, "Who lives up there?"

Nella turned around as well and answered, "Oh that. The King of Portugal lives there!"

Jack was impressed with the beautiful city of Cascais. He declared, "Well, if the king can live here, I guess we can, too!"

Nella realized Jack's choice of words. "We?" she asked, wide-eyed.

Jack looked into Nella's beautiful brown eyes. "Yes, we, Nella, if you will have me?"

Nella flushed. "Every day for the rest of my days, Jack."

Jack reached into his pocket, pulled out a box, and rose from his chair, dropping to one knee. "Nella, my love, I want you to be my wife. I want to spend the rest of my days with you as well! Will you take me as I am?"

Nella felt her throat tightening and exclaimed, "Of course, I will marry you, Jack!"

Remaining on one knee, Jack leaned in to kiss Nella passionately. "You have made me the happiest man," he murmured.

Tears of joy streamed down Nella's cheeks. "You make me so happy, Jack!"

While the two embraced, wrapped up in their moment of joy, a Frenchman sitting twenty-five meters away viewed the event between Jack and Nella. He secretly texted a message on his secured communications app.

Confirm, you want the female removed, not the male.
Signed,
Benoit

Bao was hustling between meetings with the Fong Gao Triads and some local law enforcement officials in Taipei when he stopped to check his messages.

"Ah, the Frenchman." Bao sat down in the hallway of the meeting center and typed back a response.

Confirmed.
Only the lady. Your money has been wired to your account in Vietnam.
Signed,
Bao

Benoit read the reply and he acknowledged it with a return character and closed his phone.

"Jack let's finish lunch and ride around the town. There is so much to see," Nella said.

Jack nodded in agreement. After finishing the wonderful grouper Nella ordered for him, he paid the check, swooped down, and picked Nella up from her chair.

"Let's go, Mrs. Kendall," Jack playfully teased.

Nella already liked her new name and playfully teased in return. "Not yet pal. You have not said I do, yet!"

Jack laughed placing Nella gently on the ground. He mounted his scooter waiting for Nella. Nella started up her scooter and began rumbling ahead of Jack. Jack turned his key over and over, but his scooter wouldn't start.

By then Nella had started up Avenue Marginal towards the center of town. She did not notice that Jack was having problems with his scooter and proceeded up the hill ahead, weaving through the heavy foot traffic. Jack kept his eye on her as Nella reached to the top of the hill and stopped her bike. She turned around and could not see Jack through the crowd. He shouted to no avail over the street noise.

Frustrated, Jack left his scooter near the tables and ran after Nella. As he approached the Avenue Marginal hill, Jack noticed Nella at the top of the hill waving at him. He climbed the cobblestone street. As he reached the top of the hill, he stopped for a moment to catch his breath. Nella was still mounted on her scooter as she watched Jack approach her, giggling as he fought to reach her. Jack looked up at Nella with a big smile and waved back at her. As Nella smiled back, she suddenly looked to the left as a car coming down the opposite hill sped up. Trying to avoid the speeding vehicle, Nella leaped off her scooter only to get hit directly by the on-coming car. Jack watched the horror in slow motion.

"Nella! No!" Jack screamed.

As the speeding car collided with Nella, her body was hurled against the stone wall of the building adjacent to the intersection. Jack sprinted forward, his voice echoing in frantic screams. "Someone stop that car!"

Nella lay on the ground with blood gushing out from a huge wound on her head. She could not speak.

"Nella, no, stay with me, my love," Jack cried. He ripped off his shirt and pressed it against Nella's head, trying to stop the bleeding.

Pleading desperately with the crowd, Jack asked the people surrounding the accident scene, "Please, call 2-1-1! Someone, help me! My fiancé needs an ambulance! Someone, please call 2-1-1!"

A shopkeeper who spoke English responded, "Yes sir, I called. Here, use these." The shopkeeper brought more towels to help staunch the bleeding.

"Jack, I can't see you. My love, it hurts," Nella whispered.

Jack cried out in anguish, "No, Nella, stay with me!"

Nella's breathing slowed as she closed her eyes for the last time.

Jack felt his heart tearing in two. He hugged Nella. "No! Please, Nella, stay with me," Jack cried.

A few bystanders also tried to help.

Jack asked the crowd, "Did anyone see the car?"

The bystanders shook their heads in response. Most couldn't understand English and were in shock at the unexpected tragedy.

The Audi driver, a Frenchman named Francois, realized his head had crashed into the windshield upon hitting the woman on the scooter. He steered the car into a nearby garage a block away from the scene. Stumbling and bleeding from his injuries, the French assassin grew dizzy from the impact. Francois doubled over, leaned against a building, and waved off the few people who had approached to see if they could help.

"No, I am fine, leave me!" Francois shouted.

Once he had regained some stability, he walked down the hill and made his way past the harbor to find the escape boat Bao had promised would be waiting for him. Scanning the waterfront for any sign of the boat, Francois finally spotted it, named "The Vault" in large print along the stern. He boarded the vessel, evading the police and rescue vehicles heading toward the crash site.

Muttering to himself, he declared, "You're finished, American."

The boat captain instructed Francois to sit in the boat's bow as they sped away from Cascais harbor. The captain received instructions to take his passenger past Sages towards North Africa. Francois used a towel and water from the captain to clean his head wounds. The boat captain checked his messages for any updated instructions.

Message to skipper.

Dump the cargo.

Signed,

Bao

The captain acknowledged the order and retrieved his pistol from a compartment in the hull of the boat. He quietly approached Francois, who was busy cleaning his wounds, and fired two shots into Francois's head. The captain then disposed of the body overboard into the Atlantic Ocean. As he watched the body sink, the captain messaged Bao.

Cargo dumped.

Send final payment.

The Skipper.

Bao received the message and replied.

Acknowledged.

Funds deposited in Macau.

Signed,

Bao

Jack tried to revive Nella, administering first aid, and signaling urgently for medical assistance amid the crowd that had gathered around them. Eventually, local police and rescue teams arrived on the scene. Emergency personnel immediately attended to Nella, while the police managed the growing crowd.

"Sir, please move away from the body," the medic ordered. Jack moved away while still holding Nella's hand.

"Sir, move away," the police ordered, attempting to secure the crime scene.

Jack complied, allowing the rescue teams to attend to Nella.

"Passport," the police officer demanded. Jack dug out his and Nella's passports from his bag and handed them to the officer. "What happened?" the officer inquired.

Jack recounted the scooter ride from Lisbon to Cascais and gave a description of the driver and the black Audi car that collided with Nella's scooter. He tried to explain to the officer that the driver could have been a Frenchman that came on the same flight as him.

"You mean you know him?" The officer inquired.

Jack replied, "No, I don't know him personally. I only saw him on the plane."

The officer looked frustrated with Jack. "Sir, did you see this man in the car that hit your girlfriend?"

Jack knew where this line of questioning was going. "No, I did not actually see the Frenchman drive his car that hit my fiancé."

The officer shook his head and approached Nella's body to check for signs of life. A rescue worker covered Nella's body with a white sheet gestured to Jack, indicating the unfortunate outcome. Jack fell to his knees. Overcome with grief, he struggled to comprehend the tragedy that had occurred before his eyes.

An officer approached Jack, extending his condolences. "I'm sorry for your loss. Do you happen to know where she lived in Lisbon?"

Knowing little about Nella's life in Portugal, he responded, "No, I don't. I only met her parents yesterday. Their names are Jorge and Wei Fiero."

The officer wrote down the names in his notebook and went over to his motorcycle to use the radio. The rest of the officers began taking statements from other witnesses. No one captured any evidence other than the color of the car and make. No one had seen the driver or where the car went after the collision. After an hour of processing the scene, the officer asked Jack to come with them to the police station. Before Jack got into the car, Jorge and Wei arrived on the scene, visibly shocked.

"Where is my daughter?" Jorge yelled in distress.

Wei trailed behind Jorge, tears streaming down her face, pleading to see her daughter. Jack hurried over to Jorge to explain what happened. "Jorge, she is here. I am sorry." Jack tried to comfort Jorge and Wei.

Jorge stopped near Jack and erupted, "You terrible American! You killed my daughter!"

Stunned, Jack stood frozen, tears still staining his cheeks. "I'm sorry. I do not understand how this could have happened."

Jorge lunged forward and punched Jack repeatedly in the face sending him tumbling to the ground. The police watched the fight unfold but opted not to intervene as Jorge continued his assault. After enduring several blows, Jack employed a karate move to push Jorge back.

"I didn't kill your daughter!" he shouted back at Jorge.

Wei walked over to uncover her daughter's face and wept as she gazed upon Nella's lifeless form.

"My daughter, be with God, my child." Wei mourned as she knelt beside her daughter's body.

A policewoman helped Wei to her feet while the other officers restrained Jorge. Bloodied from Jorge's punches, Jack rose from the ground and approached Wei. "I'm sorry. A car came from nowhere and struck her. The driver vanished, and no one saw who it was."

Wei smacked Jack's face and yelled, "How dare you! You ugly American!"

Jack met Wei's gaze with profound sorrow. "I loved Nella. I'm so sorry." His voice trembled with grief.

Wei boarded the ambulance transporting Nella's body, casting one last look at Jack. Jorge, still in anguish and threatening Jack through his tears, was being dragged away by the police. "I am going to kill you, American, one day!"

As the ambulance departed with Nella's body, Jack, still reeling from shock, complied with the officer's inquiries. "Mr. Kendall, I have some questions for you. Where are you staying?" the officer inquired.

Lost in turmoil, Jack responded, "I don't know. My belongings are at their place in Lisbon."

The officer nodded. "Alright, we will have a car take you to the hospital," he informed Jack.

Upon arrival at the hospital, Jorge arranged for Nella's body to be transported back to Lisbon. Wei, still in shock, sat in the waiting area staring at the wall.

Jack approached Jorge, his heart heavy with grief. "Jorge, I'm deeply sorry. I want to help in anyway I can." Jorge turned away from Jack and sat down next to Wei.

Undeterred, Jack followed Jorge to Wei. "Wei, I will do everything in my power to find out who is responsible," Jack vowed resolutely.

Wei shot Jack a look of disdain. "You are the reason my daughter is dead. I never want to see you again!" She hissed with contempt. Jack finally knew there was nothing he could say to Nella's parents when they were feeling such immense pain. He found a seat down at the end of the row from them and sat in grief-stricken silence, staring at the flickering fluorescent lights on the ceiling.

Within the hour, the hospital released Nella's body to the funeral home, commencing the journey back to Lisbon. The police recovered Jorge's car and delivered it outside the hospital. With nothing more to do, Jorge and Wei climbed into their car.

Before they drove off, Jorge rolled down his window and shouted at Jack, "American, your stuff will be out on the street!" With that, he drove off without another word to Jack.

A policeman from the scene noticed Jack being abandoned and approached him. "American, hop in." The police officer gave Jack a ride to Jorge's apartment.

As Jorge promised, Jack's clothes, luggage, and computer littered the street in front of their apartment. While gathering up his stuff, the officer offered to help. "American, do you have a place to stay?" he inquired.

Jack shook his head.

"Alright, let's get your things." The officer helped Jack load his gear into the car and drove him to a Marriott near the airport. After a brief twenty-minute drive, the officer recommended, "The Marriott always has rooms available."

Jack thanked the officer, collected his belongings, and entered the hotel lobby. He approached the front desk, handed over his passport, and requested a room for the evening.

The front desk manager greeted Jack. "Mr. Kendall, welcome to the Lisbon Marriott. How long will you be staying?"

Jack was still shaken by the day's events and replied, "Four days."

Recognizing Jack's rewards status, the hotel manager promptly upgraded his room to the master suite on the top floor. "Here you are, Mr. Kendall. Thank you for being a rewards member," the manager said as he handed Jack the keys.

Jack nodded, offering a weak smile. He accepted the keys from the manager and proceeded to the elevator with his bags. As he passed by the bar, Jack noticed a news broadcast on the TV screen with English captions: "A Black Audi A5 car hit a woman today in Cascais. The woman was pronounced dead on the scene. The victim was traveling in Cascais with her American fiancé. If anyone has any details, please contact Lisbon's Special Investigation Unit."

Reliving the tragic moment, Jack dropped his bags and tears welled up in his eyes. Sensing Jack's distress, the manager asked some hotel staff to assist Jack to the bar.

"Mr. Kendall, I am deeply sorry," the manager expressed sympathetically. "Is that you on TV?"

With a heavy heart, Jack nodded. The stunned manager guided Jack to a seat at the bar and requested that everyone leave the area.

"Mr. Kendall, please let me get you something to drink," the manager offered, returning with a cold Sagres beer. "Here sir, please."

Jack turned away slightly and replied, "I'm okay, thank you." After a few minutes, Jack slowly drank his beer, gathered his things, and made his way up his room.

Chapter 13
Intensify

"My fellow Taiwanese, as your president, I swore an oath to uphold the safety and security of our nation. Our country is not China, and China is not our country." The crowd gathered outside the Presidential Palace in Taipei roared.

"My countryman, today we stand stronger than ever before. Our children are growing up resilient, our parents are living longer, and our nation stands up for democracy," the president declared, pausing briefly to acknowledge the cheering crowd.

"Today, our country, through our innovation and home-grown technology, has become the world's first smart country!" The crowd cheered even louder. "We will make all our urban centers and townships smart cities. We will then connect our cities to other smart nations. Thanks to our friends at ADConnect here in Taipei, we will add more capacity towards TAINET. We now offer our partnering nations faster connections to our country." The president took a deep breath and continued, "Taiwan will open our digital technology to the world to revolutionize the Internet of Things, smart cities, and now, smart countries. Our global trading partners will gain access to a wealth of information for trade, education, and collaboration with our companies and universities. This enhanced connectivity with the world will help promote jobs here in Taiwan and drive a greater sense of innovative thinking and digital creativity."

The president looked out over the crowd and proclaimed, "Taiwan will embark on developing the next generation cyber security fortress to protect our data, our intellectual property, and our people from foreign and domestic terror. It is my mission as your president to see this transformation in our era. The outcomes will be self-evident. Thank you."

As the president departed the podium, she stopped to wave at the audience, thanking her countrymen for their support. Spotting Sunny Ho standing by the stage, she addressed him. "Sunny, our country thanks you for your unwavering contributions."

Sunny looked up to his president and replied, "Madame President, I thank you for your vision and leadership." Sunny shook the president's hand and bowed out of respect.

"Sunny, we need to deliver this promise on time for our people."

Sunny smiled. "Madame President, we will deliver earlier than expected."

The President smiled and waved as she walked away from Sunny.

"A free and democratic Taiwan?" General Vo swore vehemently while he sat in his office in Beijing. "Free my ass, we have you, Taiwan. You are a Chinese province, not a country."

Vo stood up and paced around his office when he noticed the Premier of China calling on the red phone. Vo answered, "Yes, Premier, I watched the press conference. Yes, sir, Operation Dragon Vault is ahead of schedule. We will have access to TAINET in a few weeks. Our operatives are on the ground as we speak. Yes, sir, I understand sir, I want to crush the president as much as you do." Vo continued to speak before noticing the premier had hung up.

Vo mumbled to himself, "Yes, Premier, we will crush them."

Vo opened the secured communications application to all Dragon Vault team members. *As you can see, the Taiwanese think they are going to break away and make their own country. Our premier, himself, ordered us to crush the Taiwanese now. Our mission is to control all Internet of Things, healthcare, and system controls. It is critical to bring them to their knees. Each of you need to execute your portion of the mission for the good of your family, for your own safety, and for China. No failures!*

Signed,

Vo

Within minutes, each member of the team received the general's message.

After receiving the flash message from the general, Abe, CEO of Fiberex, contacted his software engineering team for an update on the cloning process.

"Engineering, Abe here. I need a status on the cloning of the backhaul QoS code!"

Voung, young engineer, replied to his CEO, "Sir, the cloning process is complete. We are creating our branding and legal inserts to show this is our software. I will complete the cloning process in the next eight hours. Engineering testing is ready to verify code validation as well."

Abe was not satisfied with the current situation and demanded, "I want the branding and legal completed in the next hour and I want the operational verification done in the next three hours!"

"Yes sir," the junior engineer replied.

Abe reached for this phone to call Noah. "Noah, we will be ready for operational validation in three hours. Where is the legal injunction?"

Noah woke up after receiving the call from Abe. "Hey asshole, it is 4:00 am here in Boston."

Abe was not the least concerned about Noah getting a restful night's sleep. "Oh, what a pity. Should I find another firm that doesn't sleep?"

Noah, rubbing the sleep from his eyes, gathered himself. "Look, we have a hearing with the federal court in five hours. We will get the injunction."

Abe smiled for a moment and asked, "Good, send the court order to me. When do you plan to serve Cybercom?"

Noah looked at his calendar on his cellphone. "We will serve them at 2:00 p.m. Eastern Standard Time. William Kendall will be back from San Francisco by then."

Abe checked his calendar as well. "Good, we have a press conference tomorrow at 8:00 a.m. our time to announce the release of Dragon Vault Accelerator program 1.0."

Chapter 14

Propagation

A reporter from Wired Magazine asked, "Mr. Kendall, last question please. How secure is the software and do you expect this program to become operational globally?"

William, already exhausted from his big keynote speech and doing back-to-back interviews, responded warily, "Yes, our goal is for the secured package to be ready for global distribution within three months."

"Thank you, Mr. Kendall."

William rose from his seat in the press briefing, thanked the reporters seated in front of him, and grabbed his bags. He was ready to head out for the airport.

"Kendall," Allan called out. "How was your conversation with the lady in blue last night?"

William nervously turned to look at his largest investor. "It went well I believe. Hopefully, we get some good press in the New China Media from Ms. Ledger."

Allan thought that more may have occurred between William and Poppy and responded with a wink. "Oh, interview... got it. Safe travels, son," he said patting William on the shoulder.

William half smiled and shook his head as he walked out the front doors of the hotel. He lifted his hand when he reached the curb. "Taxi!"

As he entered the taxi, William noticed a message from Tricia. *My love, safe travels home,* it read with a bright red heart emoji at the end.

William messaged back. *I am on the way home, my love. Heading to the airport now.*

Tricia read the message from her husband and contemplated the life she envisioned, thinking to herself, *We will have a new baby, a new home, and with the IPO, we will be rich!* Tricia couldn't help but smile to herself, feeling grateful for everything life had in store for her and her growing family.

"Your honor, our emergency injunction on behalf of our client, Fiberex, is to prevent their valuable investment in their packet accelerator technology from being stolen by an American firm, Cybercom. Our research team in Xiamen, China, has determined that several lines of code that originated in our source code also showed up in their online documentation." Regina pulled up her PowerPoint slides in the federal courtroom to show Judge Wilson, the presiding federal judge, the evidence.

"Objection!" Louis Parr, legal counsel for Cybercom, interjected. "Your honor, this is a fake injunction, sir. Fiberex somehow got hold of our source code and crypto keys and they reverse engineered our software package."

Judge Wilson had been sitting as a federal judge for twenty-four years. "I admit, counsel, I am not very technology savvy. So, what you are saying is, you are the original owner of the code and Fiberex has stolen your code... stuff?"

Louis took a deep breath and replied, "Yes, your honor, we own the patent for this code. We have rights to the source code. No one else should have access."

Regina was ready with her counterattack. "Your honor, if I may, please notice the date and time stamps on the screen. Our code was originally created in 2014, six years ago. Cybercom was not even a company then."

Louis stared at the screen in disbelief and argued, "Your honor, that is impossible. It is a known fact, sir, that the Chinese government has been stealing American technology for years. The PLA leveraged a series of cloning technology to steal from American companies. This date time stamp means nothing."

Judge Wilson pushed his glasses up his long nose and read through the documents to be sure he had all the facts and asked, "Okay Mr. Parr, do you have any proof that someone has been stealing your code prior to seeing this today in my courtroom?"

Louis knew he needed to be cautious with his wording and responded, "Not sure, your honor. This is the first time we have seen our source code outside of our secured systems."

The Judge prodded and inquired, "So, how secure *are* your systems, Mr. Parr?"

Louis felt cornered by the judge's question and truthfully answered, "Very secure."

"So, if your system is that secure, then the code developed by Fiberex also is an original property?"

Louis was taken aback by the judge's line of thought and replied shakily, "Your honor, this is our code. If the court allows a brief recess, I will get hold of our chief architect and ask him to confirm a few details."

Judge Wilson looked down again at the documents before him, pondering Louis's request. He shook his head as he slowly answered, "Mr. Parr, I am going to approve the injunction by Fiberex and request that Cybercom delay their release of their software package for QoS until the court becomes satisfied that neither company has stolen the other's property. The court will adjourn for thirty days and then we will reconvene."

"Your honor!" Louis contended. "That is unacceptable! This is our software package! Cybercom should not be punished over a simple unproven accusation by a foreign power!"

Judge Wilson reddened as Louis challenged his judgment and straightened in his seat. He became flustered by the thick atmosphere of tension present in his courtroom,. "Mr. Parr, you raise your voice at me again *in my courtroom* and I will hold you in contempt. Hearing adjourned!"

Louis seethed as he gathered his documents and headed out of the courtroom. He walked to an isolated location to make a call. "Hello, this is Louis Parr. I need to speak to Allan Smith, urgently."

William woke up as his airplane touched down at Dulles International Airport. The past twenty-four hours had drained William, from finally executing his keynote speech that he'd been planning for months to his strange interactions with the journalist, Poppy Ledger. Nothing had happened explicitly, but he still had a pit in his stomach when he thought of that look Poppy gave him as she walked out during his speech. He closed his eyes and pictured Tricia, probably tidying the house, maybe even preparing his favorite dinner if he was lucky. God, he loved his wife and was so excited, if not a little nervous to welcome their new baby into his family. He was on the brink of being the founder of a company going public on the New

York Stock Exchange. It was going to be a new chapter full of excitement and new doors opening!

"Allan here."

Louis covered the phone's speaker and looked around to ensure no one could hear his call. "Mr. Smith, Louis Parr, General Counsel," Louis said, introducing himself.

Allan recalled encountering Louis multiple times during recent board member meetings focused on Cybercom's IPO. "Yes, Louis, what can I do for you?" Allan asked.

Louis composed himself before replying, "Sir, I just got out of a Federal Court hearing in Boston. A Chinese company, Fiberex, has filed an injunction claiming we stole their source code to their Dragon Vault Packet Accelerator software. The judge approved their request for a thirty-day injunction, blocking our ability to launch our product."

Allan froze as he took in the news, then replied sharply, "What? How the hell did they steal our code?"

Louis moved the phone away from his ear as Allan's loud voice pierced through the receiver. "Sir, I don't know. Only three people have access to the crypto code and keys."

Allan pinched the bridge of his nose and took a deep breath, trying to keep his temper in check. "Thirty-day injunction? Can you appeal this, Louis?" Allan said his name through clenched teeth.

Louis anticipated this question. "Yes, Sir, I am working on that. However, we need to ascertain how exactly Fiberex stole our code. Once we determine this, we will get back into court and show just cause."

Seething, Allan replied, "Alright, I'll be on the next plane to Boston. I want everyone in the conference room at 9:00 a.m. tomorrow!"

"Yes, sir," Louis acknowledged with grave concern.

William turned his phone on as he walked through the terminal, realizing that he had missed several messages from Louis Parr and Allan Smith. He rang Louis first.

"Louis, what's happened?"

Louis stepped into a quiet area whispering into his phone, "William, some Chinese firm stole our code and convinced a judge in Boston to grant a thirty-day injunction. Smith wants everyone in Boston in the morning for an emergency meeting."

William dropped his luggage in complete shock. "Oh, Shit! I'll grab the next flight to Boston," he said and hung up.

William called Tricia. "Honey, we have an emergency. I need to fly to Boston. I will call once I land. I'm so sorry, my love."

Tricia's heart sank as she sat down. She tried to hide her disappointment as she replied, "William, are you okay? What kind of emergency are we talking?"

William tried to remain calm as he walked towards the ticket counter and responded to his wife. "I am okay, babe, nothing life-threatening, but some things are going down with Cybercom. I will call you later when I know more and can talk." William hung up the phone, made eye contact with the gate agent, and asked, "Can you put me on the next available flight to Boston?"

Amidst the news of the pending injunction, the Boston office of Cybercom plunged into chaos. Phones were ringing off the hook, and reporters, investors, and employees alike sought to understand the situation. At 2:00 p.m. Eastern Standard Time, a courier bearing a yellow envelope arrived at the office.

"Hi there, is this Cybercom?" the man inquired as he approached the reception desk.

Janice, the nineteen-year-old intern receptionist, responded, "Yes, may I help you?"

The courier replied, "Yes! I represent Blake, Wilson, and Todd. You are officially served."

Janice, not fully grasping the situation, accepted the envelope and signed the court release form as if it was a package from the UPS. The court document server smiled as he walked out the lobby.

Janice got up from her desk and made her way back from the main lobby, through the turmoil of the office to the CEO. She knocked on the CEO's door and entered. "Mr. Kim, this came for you."

Roger Kim, acting CEO of Cybercom, who had spent the entire morning on phone calls with Louis Parr and Allan Smith, became very upset. "What the hell did you do?" he asked, his anger palpable.

Janice, bewildered by the CEO's reaction replied, "I am sorry, sir. I signed for this. It looked important."

"Get out, you're fired!" Roger spat. Janice just looked at back at him with wide eyes. "NOW!" he bellowed. Janice rushed out of the office, gathered her belongings, and left in tears. Roger picked up the phone and called William. "William! This is Roger, where are you?"

Noticing the anger simmering in Roger's tone, William nervously responded, "I Just landed in DC, waiting to board my flight to Boston now."

Roger erupted, his voice reverberating through the office and William's eardrum. "How the fuck did the Chinese get our code and keys?"

William rubbed his temples in despair. "I am assessing this now. I'll be landing shortly."

Roger slammed the phone down, taking a moment to collect himself. He reached again for his phone, contemplating his next move. "I need to call the Boston FBI office."

Within minutes of dialing the emergency number for the FBI office, he connected with the Special Agent in Charge on duty.

"Mr. Kim? Gerald Burns, Special Agent in Charge, FBI Boston Field Office, how can I assist you, sir?"

Roger took a deep breath. I need to report a cyberattack against our company."

Gerald Burns, a seasoned FBI veteran, responded, "Does this have to do with the injunction awarded this morning in Federal Court to a Chinese firm?"

Roger paused to gather his thoughts. "Yes. Would you be available to meet at Cybercom's office at 9:00 a.m. tomorrow? We're convening an emergency board meeting to determine how this happened."

Gerald consulted his calendar. "Yes, I can be there."

Roger hung up, pondering the implications for the company's IPO prospects. "We are so screwed. How did the Chinese manage to steal and clone our source code so quickly?"

Flying high above Seattle, Washington, Poppy connected her phone to the airplane's Wi-Fi. She opened her secured messaging app to check all messages while her plane headed for Vancouver, Canada. Now that the code and keys were safely transmitted to Fiberex, she had to disappear. She knew that William, his company, along with the FBI and Interpol, would soon be searching for her. She thought, *I am positive that the hotel cameras will show me and William heading into his room.* She knew she'd have to lay low for a while and change her look. She secretly loved this part of her job, changing her identity, getting to make up whatever life story popped into her head. She often pulled pieces of her identities from the people she wrote about for New China Media, little things like a hairstyle or a place they'd lived... all to keep herself alive for another day.

Chapter 15
Cataclysm

Cybercom Headquarters (Boston, MA)

"Alright people," Roger shouted. "What the hell happened here?"

It was 9 a.m. and the leadership, software development, and production teams for Cybercom did not know where to begin as they sat around the massive oak table in the conference room.

Roger continued, "Let me restate the question. What the hell happened to our source code and how the hell did a Chinese firm jack the code, clone it in mere hours, and get a U.S. Federal Judge to approve a thirty-day injunction against us?" No one could make eye contact with Roger as no one had any idea how any of this could have happened.

"Great. Well, I have asked Gerald Burns, Special Agent in Charge of the Boston FBI Office, to be here today to hopefully get us some answers." The group nodded and gave tight lipped smiles in Gerald's direction.

Allan rose from his seat to address the room. "Everyone, as your largest shareholder, I am extremely disturbed by the recent events. What exactly happened?" he asked, repeating Roger's question, his voice beginning to rise at the blank stares around table.

William, sensing the tension starting to rise, interjected, "Alright, I'm still not sure what could have happened. Today we will thoroughly investigate every system to check for any software that could have allowed the Chinese to gain access remotely."

Roger jumped to his feet, his voice rising. "What? Are you kidding me? How much did we invest in cybersecurity last quarter to prevent this kind of shit from happening?"

William waited for the CEO to calm down before responding. "Yes sir, we spent a ton of money on cyberattack prevention tools across all systems." William collected his thoughts and continued, "I believe they may have accessed our cloud storage repository directly. That's the only place we uploaded the finalized code version. The version they presented in court documents appears to be the one they cloned."

Roger was not happy with William's explanation and turned to the FBI SAC. "Gerald, what can the FBI do here?"

Gerald, experienced in many cyberattack investigations against American companies, responded calmly, "I've reviewed the court complaint filed by the law firm. Their lead counsel is Regina Kendall. Any relation?"

William was taken aback by this revelation and stammered, "Yes, she's... my sister. Are you telling me she is the one that filed this motion?"

Gerald maintained his composure. "Did you discuss any of your work here with her?"

With all eyes on William, he admitted, "Yes, we spoke about it. She knew we were going public. I didn't know which firm she joined."

Roger, in a fit of frustration, hurled his laptop against the whiteboard, causing everyone to recoil in shock.

Gerald directed his attention back on William. "William, your sister's firm, Blake, Wilson, and Todd, has longstanding ties and affiliations with China. For years, they have defended Chinese companies in U.S. courts against lawsuits for intellectual property theft."

William paled at the realization that his own sister was involved with the injunction to block his product release.

"Mr. Kendall, I have to ask. At the conference in San Francisco, Mr. Smith reported that you disappeared with a news reporter from New China Media, Ms. Poppy Ledger. Is that correct?"

Before William could answer, Allan Smith interjected," Yes, William, who is she?"

William, feeling uneasy, explained, "We left the reception to get her microphone and camera for an interview. After that, we conducted the interview in my room."

Gerald posed another question. "Were your laptop and devices secured in your room?"

William recalled that he had left his devices out on his bed. "No, I did not lock up my laptop." As a cold sweat formed on his brow, William recounted. "We entered my room, she set up her equipment, and we conducted a fifteen-minute interview."

Gerald glanced at Roger and Allan, continuing, "I have a few more questions to ask William, but I suggest we hold off until later today." Roger and Allan agreed.

Roger addressed the group. "Everyone, go back to your desk, check your security software updates and reboot all systems." Everyone stood up, acknowledged their CEO, and departed the conference room.

William spoke to Roger directly. "I need a minute to make a call."

Roger gestured to the door, granting William permission to step out.

"Reg, what the *hell* did you do to me?" William half shouted as he stood in the bathroom of Cybercom.

Regina was expecting this call from her brother. "Will, come on, I am only doing my job. The firm represents your biggest competitor, and they claimed your firm stole their software. I wanted to tell you, b—" Regina tried to explain as William cut her off.

"Reg, are you kidding me? I wrote that software and our company is about to be ruined because you are representing a Chinese Government front company!"

Regina knew how upset her brother was and tried to stay calm. "Will, I know this is a huge issue for you and your company. But please try to understand my position. Your firm has thirty days to prove us wrong, which gives you plenty of time to prove you're right. Have you heard from Dad?"

William, completely flustered by his sister, erupted. "Don't deflect! You need to shut this thing down or I am done."

Regina weighed out her options and proposed, "Alright, let me talk to the partners and see if we can do something here. I'll get back to you."

William seething with frustration, snapped at his sister, "Reg. you're dead to me," before abruptly ending the call. Returning to his office, he noticed Gerald, Roger, and Allan waiting for him.

"William, please take a seat," Roger sternly instructed. "We need more information about this reporter."

After landing in Vancouver, Canada, Poppy cleared customs using the diplomatic passport General Vo issued her. She climbed into the unmarked car arranged for her by the Chinese PLA team stationed in Canada and was brought to a safe house in the wealthy section of Vancouver. The neighborhood was made up of multi-million-dollar mansions predominantly owned by wealthy Chinese citizens. While enroute, Poppy discreetly checked her secured app for any urgent messages. a flash message from General Vo awaited her.

Poppy, release the video.

Signed,

Vo

As they drove, Poppy loaded her secure web browser to hide her IP address and location. With precision, she proceeded to upload the news clip video discussing the possible downfall of Cybercom and the crippling cyberattack. As the upload completed, she quietly murmured to herself, "Mission complete."

"William, we need to ask, did you know the reporter?" Gerald asked.

William was offended by the implication of his question. Trying to keep his voice level, he replied, "No!"

Allan, disgusted by the turn of events, locked eyes with Roger. "Roger, I am going to sue you and your firm over the breach of the morality clause in our contract. My investment? Ruined! There's no way we can go public with this out there!" Allan's gaze then shifted to William as he exclaimed, "You're finished! I am coming for you too!" With that, Allan stormed out of the office and slammed the door behind him.

Roger turned to William and sternly demanded, "William, you need to find out how she got the code and the keys immediately." William nodded and agreed.

After Gerald and Roger departed from his office, William grabbed the chair next to his desk and slammed it repeatedly against the wall. He threw it to the ground and headed out of his office to investigate what happened to the source code.

Chapter 16
Sanctioned

"Hello, this is Mr. Kendall in room 6024. Please let me know when the police show up."

The desk manager at the Lisbon Marriott replied, "Yes, Mr. Kendall, they just arrived."

Jack gathered his laptop, passport, and cell phone as he made his way to the lobby. Before he entered the elevator, he noticed he missed a call from his son, William. When he arrived in the lobby, he called his son before meeting with the police.

"Son, I got your call."

William noticed a troubling tone with his father. "Dad, are you alright?" he asked with a concerned tone.

Jack, unsure whether to share the bad news with his son or not, hesitantly replied, "William, it's not a great time. Nella was killed this morning while on a scooter. The National Police are here to speak to me. Let me get this sorted out and I will call you later."

William felt lightheaded and shakily replied, "What did you say? Nella was killed?"

"Yes, I think it was a hit. Some French guy. I am still trying to sort it. Let me call you later." Jack hung up the phone.

"Oh, my God, Nella." William felt his head spinning and without thinking, dialed his sister. "Reg, it's Will."

Regina replied harshly, still stinging from their conversation that day. "Will, don't call me. You guys are in real shit."

William, still reeling from the wild news, cut off his sister. "Sis, shut up for a moment. Someone killed Nella in Portugal this morning!"

Regina had been walking down the hallway to pick up some documents and halted in her tracks. She ran back to her office and shut her door sliding down to the floor. "What? How? Where?" she asked vehemently, her pitch rising with every word.

William took a deep breath. "I don't know. Dad hung up on me. He's with the police now. He thinks it was a hit by some French guy."

Regina rubbed her face looking up at the ceiling. "Hell, William, first the injunction, now Dad?"

William felt deflated. "Yeah, I'm in my office now trying to figure out how the source code was stolen."

Reg remembered then that she was responsible for protecting the Chinese company that was suing William. "You know I can't talk about this," she groaned.

"Affirmative, Reg," William replied. "Let me know if you hear from Dad and I'll do the same." They hung up, both feeling lost, unsure how life had taken such a dark turn for their family.

"Mr. Kendall, Investigator Rico Lopez. I am sorry for your loss," Rico, the Chief Investigator of the Portuguese National Police, said.

"Thanks. What do you know so far?" Jack asked.

The investigator opened his notebook. "Well, very little. Our cities do not have a ton of security cameras. We got a picture from a tourist cell phone showing the car racing away. Yes, the black Audi A5 was stolen in Lisbon yesterday. We also searched your flight, looking for a Frenchman. We found no one with a French passport on your plane."

The investigator stopped for a moment and asked Jack, "Mr. Kendall, how do you know he was French?"

Jack remembered the man's scent and foul attitude as they departed the airplane. "He pushed me when I got off the plane and said, '*merde,*' to me."

The investigator nodded. "The French are a rude people to be sure. Our airport cameras picked up this man. Is this him?" Rico asked while showing Jack a grainy black and white picture of a man walking through the airport.

Jack's eyes widened. "Yes, that is him! Who is he?"

Rico replied, "We don't know, at least not yet. However, we are checking with Interpol and other assets."

Jack looked greedily at the photo and requested, "Let me get a copy of that."

Rico declined. "Sorry, Mr. Kendall, that's evidence."

Jack asked again, pleading. "Look, I know someone who can help. Please."

Rico reluctantly gave Jack a copy of the photo. "By the way, Mr. Kendall, what was the purpose of your trip?"

Jack looked down at his hands. "To ask for her hand in marriage." He kept his jaw clenched as he said it. Rico put a hand on his arm, not knowing the right words to say.

Jack turned from him and opened his laptop that he'd brought down from his room. He uploaded the photo from Rico to his computer and sent it to Forest Adams, CIA Station Chief in Vietnam. Forest helped Jack years before when he was traveling in Vietnam.

Forest,

I need some intelligence on this Frenchman. He may be from your neck of the woods.

Signed,

Jack

Noah contemplated how he could make matters worse for the Kendall family as Regina entered his office. Regina was still feeling lightheaded from her short call with William that sent their already fractured family into a tailspin. "Your work today in court helped our client stop your brother's firm from launching their software. You've shut them down for now, at least. Our client has doubled our fees and wants us to file a full injunction in thirty days. Cybercom will have no choice but to close shop."

Regina was stunned by her boss's disclosure and felt her sadness quickly turn to rage. "A Chinese front company gets to release their code to the market? And you are happy?" Regina asked, incredulously.

Noah smiled ear to ear as he bragged, "All the way to the bank, baby!"

Regina stood; she could not believe what she was hearing from her boss. Was this his plan all along, to hire her just to ruin her brother? Her nostrils flared as she walked towards Noah and slammed her hands down on the desk in front of her. "I quit, Noah! I don't know what is going on here, but I *will* find out and you will be sorry you fucked with a Kendall," she said turning on her heel.

Noah smirked at the back of Regina's head and snickered, "Oh, you forgot about the non-disclosure you signed?"

Regina paused with her hand on the doorknob, casting a glance back at Noah. "What about it?" she asked, snorting at his feeble intimidation attempt.

Noah snapped arrogantly, "Well if you discuss anything with anyone about this, you will break the Attorney-Client Privilege."

Regina took a deep breath. She was fresh from law school. Of course, she knew this. How had she not seen this condescending fool for what he was in the beginning? "Noah, let's see where this goes, shall we?" she snapped as she stormed out of Noah's office.

As Regina headed to her office, Noah called the firm's security. "Security, detain Regina Kendall. She is to leave the building with her personal items only."

Upon entering her office, the building security officer entered abruptly. "Ms. Kendall, please step away from the computer and files. You may place only your personal items in this box, and we will escort you from the building."

Regina complied, gathering her personal belongings and placing them in the box. Once the security officer confirmed that she had taken nothing owned by the firm, Regina followed him to the exit. As she walked out, she heard Noah guffawing from his office.

Noah had celebrated his supposed victory by calling his dubious partner. "Travis! What a fucking beautiful day. Cybercom is toast thanks to the court injunction. Jack Kendall's girlfriend died in a scooter accident, and the fiber from Xiamen is about to go live! What a day, bro!"

Travis, on the other end of the call, echoed similar sentiments. "Noah, great job, man. Yes, we're set for life now. Once that fiber is hooked up and starts draining the Taiwanese data streams, we'll be swimming in riches; we'll practically own the country."

Noah took great pride in their despicable actions. He eagerly inquired, "Trav, what is next?"

Travis instructed his old college buddy, "Lay low for a while and get out of the country. Things are going to heat up. Head over to Okinawa, where we'll set up shop. Contact me once you're settled."

Noah was perplexed. "Okinawa?"

Travis boasted, "It's a new venture, bro." Noah hung up with a wide grin.

Regina felt sickened listening to Noah's exchange with someone on the phone. "*Fuck* him," she cursed under her breath. She couldn't make out the words he'd said, just the jubilance in his tone.

Regina was escorted to her car, where she placed her belongings in the trunk before dialing her brother. "Will, I am heading your way. Driving from Boston. I should be there in about nine hours. Keep the faith! We will sort this shit show out."

William had returned to Virginia earlier that day exhausted and feeling humiliated. He was grateful to know his sister was back on his side. He thanked her as they said their goodbyes and ended the call.

As she settled into her car, Regina reflected on the cascade of tragic events. Never in her life had she seen so much sadness all at once. Driving to Virginia seemed like the best therapy for her now.

Chapter 17
Detonation

Jack walked out of the lobby of the hotel to give William a call back. "Son, it's Dad. Is everything all right?"

William did not know where to start with this father. "Dad, I'm so sorry to hear about Nella. A lot has been happening here."

Jack, still grieving, wondered what fresh hell awaited him now. "Son, what happened?"

William grimaced as he spoke. "Dad, the Chinese stole my source code and cloned our package. Regina and her law firm managed to secure an injunction against us."

Jack was stunned. "What?" he exclaimed.

William continued, "Regina's firm is the one that represented the Chinese company. And there's more."

Jack steadied himself before asking, "Son, go on. What else happened?"

"When I was in San Francisco a few days ago, I was the keynote speaker for the fiber conference. I met a reporter from the New China Media, and she asked for an interview. We went to her room and grabbed her recording equipment and camera and then moved to my room for the actual interview. At some point she planted malware inside my laptop and stole my software. I'm not sure when it could've happened. I was so focused on getting it over with, and she was giving me these intense looks... I just wanted her out of my room."

Seated on a bench outside of the Lisbon Taipei Marriott, Jack inquired, "She took the QoS software?"

William, devastated, admitted, "Yes."

Jack sighed heavily. "Son, do you remember her name?"

Shaken, William replied, "Yes, it was Poppy Ledger."

Jack's expression turned grave. "I know that name," he muttered. "Son, I know her. She is a hacker out of Australia and often poses as a reporter. Last we knew, she was sitting in a prison somewhere in China. Interpol would love to get their hands on her."

William felt crushed by his father's revelation. "I'd like to catch her myself," he said bitterly.

"In due time, son. Right now, I need to get back inside with the Portuguese police," Jack replied. After promising to help if needed, William hung up, offering his condolences once again. Jack returned to Rico. "Anything else you need from me, Rico?"

Rico nodded. "Yes, Mr. Kendall we are returning to Cascais tomorrow. If you don't mind, we would appreciate it if you came along?"

Jack agreed to accompany Rico the following morning. After Rico left, Jack headed back up to his room. Before entering his room, he scanned the hallway for any suspicious activity. His call with William deepened his suspicion that Nella's murder was not a freak accident. Someone seemed to be after his family. Once inside, he sat down on the edge of the bed and prayed. "Dear God, please look after William and Regina. Please, God look after Nella and give her a hug for me. Amen." His throat felt tight with emotion, but he swallowed, forcing himself to exhale, refusing to succumb to the despair that was so eager to keep him in its clutches. He reached for his phone and dialed his boss. "Thomas, can I have five minutes, please?"

Thomas Wilson sensed Jack's distress and asked, "How is Portugal?" Jack's throat tightened again while he recounted the tragic events. "Damn it, I can't believe it!" Thomas exclaimed. Jack also briefed him on Regina's firm and the injunction against Cybercom. "Jack, I have a hunch. These things are way too connected. I will investigate it," Thomas stated.

Jack woke with a splitting headache but knew he had to leave with Rico to Cascais.

As they drove, Rico had questions about the case he wanted to ask Jack. "Mr. Kendall, tell me more about this Frenchman?" Rico inquired.

Jack closed his eyes, trying to recall what the Frenchman looked like. He began to describe the hitman to Rico. "Tall, fat, gray hair, and a strong build."

Rico asked Jack for more details. "Anything else you can remember?"

As wracked his brain for details, the scent of the man finally clicked. "Yes, he smelled like stale clove cigars."

Rico acknowledged Jack's details and asked, "Anything else?"

Jack thought for a moment. "No, he just seemed like a royal asshole."

Rico laughed and commented, "Aren't they all?"

Jack and the police arrived in Cascais as planned around 11:00 a.m. Rico requested, "Mr. Kendall, if you don't mind, could you walk the exact route you took on that day, please?"

Jack jumped out of the police car and started towards the blue umbrella and tables near the harbor. After he found the exact table where he had proposed to Nella that day, he sunk into the chair she'd been sitting in and became overwhelmed with grief and guilt. Jack stared off towards the horizon, thinking of Nella's laughter and tears of joy as they celebrated their love. The bustle of the town carried on, even though Nella did not.

The harbor water still shimmered under the Mediterranean sun. The shop owner kept serving beers, and people kept cherishing each other. After a few minutes, he rose from the chair and broke into a run as he made his way towards the Avenue Marginal. Jack reached the foot of the hill, stopped, and waved up at the crowd, just like he had on that tragic day. Jack climbed the hill and paused to catch his breath, his hands on his knees. Jack pressed forward until he reached the crash site where Nella had lain bleeding after the Frenchman's car struck her. He turned to Rico and pointed. "Here! This is the spot I found her after that fucking asshole hit her with his car."

The officers trailed Jack and marked the spot on the road. Rico instructed, "Proceed, Mr. Kendall."

Jack bent down like he was helping Nella again. Reenacting the day hit Jack with overwhelming grief and emotion. He collapsed on the hill and cried. The officers knew this could not be easy and let him be. Jack sucked and gulped down air like he'd been underwater and got to his feet on shaky legs. He walked over to the officers and explained, "After I bent down, I heard the car race away in that direction."

The officers' gaze followed Jack's outstretched arm, pointing down the hill towards Avenue Marginal South. They led the way down, Jack following closely, scouring the street for clues and the whereabouts of the black Audi A5. For nearly an hour, Jack wandered along the streets of Cascais, searching for any trace of the car. Pausing for a coffee break, he offered to buy a round for the police too.

"Café?" Jack queried.

The officers all responded, "Yes."

After handing out the fresh coffees, Jack leaned against the café wall, thoughts drifting to William and Regina. He had a sudden longing to be with his family; they were his entire world; all he had left. "I'll be home soon," Jack silently vowed to himself.

Finishing his coffee, he threw out his cup, noting the scarcity of cars parked along the streets in the small Portuguese town.

"Investigator, where do people park their cars?" Jack inquired.

The officers exchanged puzzled glances before replying, "Usually, people park in the underground garages of their apartment buildings."

Jack looked at one of the police officers, his eyes widening. "Which buildings have parking garages?"

One of the officers pointed to an older building fifty meters away. Jack sprinted towards the off-white building at the end of the street with the officers trailing behind, weapons drawn.

"Officer, how can we check this place out?" Jack impatiently asked.

The officers motioned for Jack to wait as they entered the building. Jack paced outside, anxiety gnawing at him. He noticed a large door on the side of the building, likely leading to the underground garage. He attempted to force it open but failed. He stumbled back as the door flung open towards him and the team of police officers emerged into the sunlight.

"We found the car, Mr. Kendall," they announced.

Jack felt a surge of relief, stepping away to give them space. "I will wait here," he said.

Additional units, including the crime scene technicians, were called to assist. Jack leaned against the building where the car was found, noticing a red spot on the wall. He beckoned for an officer to join him.

"Sir, could you take a look at this red spot? What do you think it is?" Jack asked.

The officer approached and looked closely at the red smear. "Ah, is that your blood, Mr. Kendall?"

Jack looked puzzled at the officer and replied, "No sir."

The officer called over the crime scene technician to take a sample of the blood. The technician processed the crime scene and collected a sample.

"Please send this to the lab immediately," the officer instructed. The technician nodded in acknowledgment.

"Mr. Kendall, please walk with me," Rico requested. The two gentlemen walked down the hill towards the tables and umbrellas next to the harbor. Rico turned towards a different restaurant along the water, thinking it would be best to steer clear of the restaurant Jack and Nella had dined at together.

"May I call you, Jack?" Rico asked.

"Of course. What should I call you?"

Investigator Lopez replied, "Rico."

Jack smiled as the two men approached the tables with red umbrellas this time. They took a seat at the first open table, and a waiter came over, "Gentleman, a couple of beers?"

Both men nodded yes to the waiter as Rico asked Jack, "Before I tell you what I think, I need to know if you are into something bigger than just visiting my country?"

Jack recognized the direction of Rico's questioning and responded, "Rico, I am not entirely sure. Yesterday, the Chinese stole some software from my son's company. My daughter's law firm in Boston somehow blocked my son's company from releasing their software package. The Chinese state-sponsored company that stole the software is attempting to release theirs first. And all of this happened on the same day my Nella was killed."

Rico turned concerned and replied, "Let's analyze the blood and find out who this French piece of shit is first, that will provide some answers for you."

Jack thanked Rico for his help.

"One more question," Rico asked as the beers arrived, "outside of the Chinese company, anything else you can think of that will link this murder to something else?"

Jack took a drink of his beer before he answered, "Well, yes, there was a deal in Vietnam that our company, Techline, was pursuing. The project got hijacked by some Limited Liability Corp in Xiamen, China. The World Bank sponsored the Vietnam project and at the last minute moved the deal to this shadow company, which didn't make any sense."

Rico regarded Jack with apprehension. "Jack, that's two shadow companies, both based in China. Plus, a questionable law firm recruited your daughter to sue your son's company?"

Jack glanced at Rico, realization dawning on him. "Shit, you are right. There must be a connection."

Rico finished his beer and said, "Follow me, Jack."

The two men strolled closer to the boats moored in the harbor. Rico spotted a boat with a familiar name, *The Vault*, and motioned for Jack to join him. He walked up the boat and waved at the captain.

"El Capitaine, may I have a moment, please?" Rico requested in Portuguese. The captain appeared guarded and reluctantly allowed the two men on board. "Captain, I'm Chief Investigator Lopez and this is my friend Jack Kendall. We'd like to charter your boat."

The captain was in the midst of cleaning up some red substance on the deck. "Boat busy, go away!" he said in broken English.

Sensing something was amiss, Rico drew his service pistol and commanded in Portuguese, "El Capitaine, hands up. Now!"

Jack stepped back giving Rico space. Rico repeated, "Captain, down on your hands and knees." Rico reached for his radio. "All units, converge on the harbor to the boat named *The Vault*, immediately."

In a split second, the captain leaped up, shoved Rico aside, and attempted to flee. Jack anticipated the captain's move, delivering a forceful punch to the side of his head.

"You just sit there, asshole!" Jack yelled.

Rico regained his balance, handcuffed the captain, and pressed his face against the deck. Within minutes, police units arrived and took the captain into custody.

"Lab team, get me a sample of this red matter!" Rico commanded. He turned to Jack. "Are you alright, Jack?"

Jack nodded, "Yes, I'm good. Haven't hit someone like that in years." Both men chuckled as they surveyed the boat.

Rico went below and started searching the cabin while Jack stayed topside. After a few minutes of searching, Jack found the captain's laptop and cell phone by the haul. Noticing the phone required a fingerprint to unlock, Jack dashed off the boat to the police car yelling, "Officer, I need his finger, please!"

The officer restrained the captain while Jack used his finger to unlock the phone. After a few attempts, and much cursing, Jack unlocked the device using the captain's newly broken finger. The captain strung together a sentence in Portuguese that sounded an awful lot like he was referencing Jack's mother. Staring at the captain, Jack landed another punch to his face. "I am not done with you yet, asshole."

Jack searched through the captain's messages and applications. He came across a mobile chat application he had never seen before. After using his finger again to unlock the secured application, Jack read through the messages.

"Rico, look at this," Jack called.

Rico came over to see what Jack was reading.

Message to Captain, throw the cargo overboard, funds sent to your account in Macau.

Signed,

Bao

Jack discovered for the first time a major link to the possibility of a much bigger connection to the murder of Nella. "This asshole probably dumped the Frenchman somewhere in the ocean yesterday. I bet that's his blood."

Rico nodded in agreement. "Jack, I will find out more about this Captain."

Jack looked at the phone. "I will find out who this Bao asshole is."

Jack headed back to the table and opened this secured communication application. *Message: Forest Adams: Encryption: Secured: My friend, I have not heard from you for quite some time. I need your help most urgently. A French hitman killed Nella here in Portugal. His getaway plan failed, and the captain of the boat received funds from some guy named Bao. Any help would be appreciated.*

Signed,

Jack

Jack sent the message to Forest Adams, feeling concerned about not hearing from his friend for a long time. He closed his phone and approached Rico, who had returned from his search of the cabin. "Rico, I need to go back to Lisbon."

Rico nodded, "Let me arrange a ride for you." He signaled to one of his officers to escort Jack back to his hotel. "Let's have a conversation before you leave the country. I need to get a sworn testimony from you," Rico said.

Jack nodded in agreement as he turned to follow the officer to his squad car.

Jack returned to the hotel exhausted after a long day in Cascais with Rico. While settling down for a nap in his room, he heard a knock on the door.

The front desk manager was waiting for him at his door. "Mr. Kendall, an urgent message for you, sir." Jack thanked him and opened the message.

Marine, sorry for the delay. Bui is terminally sick with breast cancer. Your request for a meeting within scope 4,9,10,12,22,15,8 at 10:00 a.m. GMT is confirmed.

Jack remembered the old United States Marine Corps code phrase Forest was using. He decoded the message Forest sent him.

No projects in the jungle location you requested information about. New apartments are opening in the same area with limited tenants.

Signed,

Forest

With new information to mull over, Jack decided to head down to the hotel bar for a beer. He took a seat at the bar, trying to understand Forest's message. *Apartments and tenants? Someone else is building something in Vietnam.* Jack thought to himself as he asked for a glass of cold local beer with lime from the bartender.

"Mr. Kendall, compliments of the house, sir."

Jack was thankful for the generosity and thanked the barman for the drink, opening his secured messenger on his phone again.

Message to Adams: I received your message. I will be ready for your call at 10:00 a.m. GMT.

Signed,

Jack

While Jack sat in reviewing his messages from Forest, he considered sending a message back to his contact at the World Bank to confirm if the actual Vietnam Jungle Project was happening. Jack grabbed his drink and headed up to this room to use his laptop in privacy.

Jack opened his laptop to access his Gmail account along with his notes about the project from a year ago.

Message to Pedro Gomez

World Bank Project Manager

Mr. Gomez, this is Jack Kendall, lead troubleshooter for Techline. Last year we bid on the Vietnam Jungle Project. Our company disclosed all the compliance documents required, including information about our investors in Japan. Yet, the World Bank awarded the project to a firm called Dragon Vault, LLC, out of Xiamen, China. We have no record of this organization in the United States. We also understand the World Bank distributed funding of over $90,000,000 two months ago to this firm. Yet, our people in Vietnam confirmed that the jungle restoration project is not underway. However, there is a construction project happening within 2 km of the proposed location. Our people believe this construction activity is not within the scope of the World Bank Project you are managing. Please confirm, sir, that the project as described is happening.

Thank you,

Jack Kendall

cc: Thomas Wilson

Jack sent the email to Pedro wondering if his suspicions were true.

Enjoying morning tea at his office in Washington, Pedro Gomez read the email that had just come in from Jack Kendall. *Oh my gosh, what a sore loser*, he thought to himself. As Pedro began reading more into the email, he suddenly realized what Kendall was referring to. "What? The project is not happening?" Pedro got up from his desk, walked down the hall to his director's office, and knocked on the door.

Fred Simon, Chief Managing Director of Global Projects for the World Bank, answered,

"Yes, Pedro, come in."

"Sir, I think we have a problem. The Techline leadership team has informed me, via email, that the Vietnam Forest Project is not happening as planned. We awarded the project to the Chinese firm, Dragon Vault, LLC. We have already fronted them the funds of $90,000,000, however, we received no status reports from them in months," Pedro stated.

Fred looked up, concerned, "Who is Dragon Vault, LLC? Never heard of them."

Pedro walked through the company's setup, their leadership structure, and the reasons for awarding them the project. "Dragon Vault, LLC, is managed by a Chinese PLA holding company. Their legal representation is from Blake, Wilson, and Todd out of Boston. General Vo, the Chinese PLA Chief, funded a portion of the Vietnam project."

Fred stared at Pedro, his voice tinged with disbelief, "What? We gave a project in Vietnam to a front company of the PLA?"

Pedro felt a wave of tension as he recognized the harsh tone of his director, prompting him to reply anxiously, "Yes sir, General Vo has many connections in Vietnam. He wanted to oversee this himself and offered additional support if our funding came up short. Techline did not have any external funding except from a Japanese holding company."

Fred scowled at Pedro, "Wait, did you inform the Vietnamese government about this decision?"

Pedro looked bewildered and nervously asked, "Why would they care, Mr. Simon?"

Fred spun around in his chair and bellowed, "Why would they care? Are you out of your mind? The Vietnamese do not trust the Chinese! What alternate universe are you living in?"

Pedro realized his error and replied, "I didn't know, sir." Pedro began to feel trapped and overwhelmed with anguish.

Fred grabbed his phone and shouted for his executive administrator, "Maggie, get me the American Embassy for Vietnam on the phone, now!"

With disdain in his eyes, Fred ordered his program manager, "Get me everything on this Dragon Vault, LLC, immediately! Get it on my desk, NOW!"

Pedro hurried out of Fred's office and headed back to his desk. On the way, he made a quick stop at the men's room. Once inside a stall, he sat down, opened his cell phone, and accessed a secured application loaded last year by his overseas contact.

Message to T. Jones, project redirection discovered, going dark.
Signed,
P

After Pedro sent the message, he removed the SIM card and threw it in the toilet, flushing the incriminating evidence. Nervously, he left the bathroom and returned to his desk, packing his personal items before heading to the elevator, the color drained from his face. He was careful not to make eye contact with anyone as he waited for the doors to open.

Impatiently, Fred stormed out of his office to find Pedro. "Has anyone seen Pedro?" He demanded to the office.

The team members at the World Bank hastily replied, "No, sir!"

Team Leader, Alice added, "Sir, I saw him leave in a hurry."

Fred reached for his phone, "Security, stop and detain Pedro Gomez."

As Pedro exited through the main doors, several security guards drew their weapons, "Freeze, Mr. Gomez." Instead of heeding the warning, Pedro ran towards Dupont Circle in Northwest Washington, DC.

The security guards also chased Pedro, yelling, "Stop, or we will shoot!"

Closing in on Pedro, the guards perused him. Oblivious to his surroundings, Pedro continued running as he reached the street. Suddenly, a Federal Express truck collided with him, sending his body flying onto the sidewalk. As the security guards approached Pedro's lifeless body, they realized he had died on impact.

Unaware of the chase's end at Dupont Circle, Fred remained focused. "Everyone! Lock all down systems now. Foreign hackers have compromised our systems. Change all passwords now!" Fred ordered urgently.

Within ten minutes, the World Bank entered total cybersecurity lockdown. All systems globally went offline, and all remote access was cut off. These emergency measures were immediately noticed by several global hacking groups.

While enjoying her time in the Vancouver safe house in secrecy, Poppy noticed her remote secured link to the World Bank going down. "What?" she screeched. She attempted several backdoor connections to establish her remote data mining tools. Her access to the World Bank granted her entry to all system files and financial transactions. Poppy had used this connection to give General Vo access to a rival's bid for the Vietnam project last year.

"Uh-oh! I need that access," Poppy muttered, "this is bad." She opened her secured communication app and sent a message to the General.

Message to Vo, secured access to the World Bank down. No connections possible.

Signed,

Poppy

General Vo was sitting in his office in Beijing when he received the flash message from Poppy Ledger. "What!" The General yelled.

Vo replied to Poppy.

Poppy, we need to connect back online. Without that connection into the World Bank, our Vietnam project is compromised.

Signed,

General Vo

Poppy received the message from the General and replied,

Affirmative, General.

Signed,

Poppy

Poppy started booting up several computers inside her safe house in Vancouver, attempting to reconnect to the World Bank.

Fred picked up his phone again to speak to his admin, "Get the FBI now, Maggie."

As Fred's executive assistant was attempting to place a call to FBI head-quarters, the World Bank security team and D.C. Police were securing the crime scene in Dupont Circle. Security Guard Staff Sergeant Harmon dispatched a call to Maggie. He gave her an update on Pedro Gomez, requesting to speak with Mr. Simon.

Maggie rang her boss, "Sir, I have Security guard Harmon on line 4."

Fred reached for his phone and inquired, "Harmon, did you catch him?"

Harmon moved discreetly away from the police cars that were surrounding the crime scene and spoke, "Sir, we didn't catch him in time. He jumped in front of a truck, killing himself."

"Where the hell are you?" Fred asked impatiently.

"Dupont Circle, sir." Harmon replied.

"Okay, I am on my way." Fred said hurriedly as rushed past Maggie. He instructed, "Maggie, get the FBI to Dupont Circle immediately!"

Maggie finally reached someone at the FBI Office, "This is Maggie at the World Bank, Fred Simon's office. We need the FBI to meet Mr. Simon at Dupont Circle ASAP."

The FBI agent on the other line replied, "Maggie, this is FBI Special Agent, Bill Parker. DC police are heading there now. Is this request related?"

Maggie, not knowing the full story, said, "Yes sir, Mr. Simon is en route."

Bill replied, "Okay, we will send a team." He contacted the FBI Escalation Team. "I need the React 5 Team deployed to Dupont Circle. The World Bank is experiencing a cyberattack against all its systems. Someone jacked their files and attempted to run off with them!"

The React 5 Team Leader replied, "Deploying now, sir."

I should check this out, Bill thought to himself.

Within 15 minutes, Fred Simon arrived at Dupont Circle. "Harmon! Where is he?"

"Over here!" Harmon shouted.

Fred and Harmon walked over to the yellow police tape. "Sir, you can't cross here," said the DC police officer.

Fred interjected and flashed his World Bank badge, "Officer, I am Fred Simon, The World Bank CMD. This deceased person may have compromised our cyber systems and stolen some very sensitive World Bank files. He may have a classified computer chip or USB drive on him."

The officer waved them through to the body. The crime scene technicians were already collecting Pedro's belongings.

"Excuse me, have you found a chip or USB drive on the victim?" Simon asked.

The technician replied, "Yes, we have found four USB drives on the victim."

The lab tech handed over the USBs in a plastic bag to Fred. A police officer stopped the exchange stating the drives were evidence and could not be removed.

"Damn it," said Fred as he handed the bag of USBs back to the tech. "I will need to get copies of those."

The officer replied, "Yes, sir, we need to protect any evidence, but we will make sure you get copies."

Fred and Harmon moved back further down the sidewalk. After a few minutes, someone shouted out, "Who is Simon, World Bank?"

Fred raised his hand, "Here!"

"Bill Parker, Special Agent, FBI. I spoke to your admin. You want to tell me how your guy ended up here?"

Fred recounted the meeting he had with Pedro an hour ago.

Bill commented, "Let me get this straight. After you questioned him about some project that he funded for a Chinese PLA holding company, doing business in Vietnam, he took off with a bunch of USB drives and got hit by a FedEx truck?"

Fred was exasperated, "Yes, he approved a project that should have gone to an American firm; instead, it went to a company in Xiamen, China."

The FBI Special Agent took a deep breath and sighed, "Okay, that is a problem."

Chapter 18
Connection

Jack Kendall's Hotel Room (Video Call with Forest Adams, Lisbon Portugal)

Jack checked his watch in Lisbon as the time approached 10:00 a.m. GMT. It was almost time to meet with Forest. Jack loaded his secured browser application on his MacBook Air and waited for Forest to connect. Within minutes, the video app began to ring.

"Jack?" Forest asked.

"Here Forest," said Jack, turning on his camera.

"Good to see you again, Marine. I am sorry about Nella, you have my deepest condolences."

Jack thanked him as he asked, "How is Ms. Bui? I am sorry to hear about her breast cancer."

Forest looked exhausted and much older than Jack remembered from their time in Vietnam together. The lines on his face became more pronounced as he said, "Stage 4, the doctor says she only has a few days left."

Jack felt a great deal of empathy for his friend. "Please give her my love, always."

Forest nodded. Both men sat quietly, reflecting for a few moments.

"Okay, I got your message, Marine. Here is what I know so far." Forest took out his notepad. "The Vietnam Jungle Restoration Project, you guys were supposed to win? Someone at the World Bank diverted that project to Dragon Vault, LLC. Your contact, Pedro Gomez, allegedly killed himself yesterday while attempting to escape from the World Bank security team."

inhale, "What! Do we know for certain it was suicide?"

Forest replied, "Not sure. FBI React 5 Team is looking into it. I guess they found a bunch of USB drives on him. His boss, Fred Simon, Chief Managing Director of World Bank, questioned Pedro about this Chinese front company. Somehow, Dragon Vault, LLC, won this contract, yet based on the project location coordinates, they are building something else. Whoever is there, they are not building anything close to what World Bank awarded."

"What do you know about this guy, Bao?" Jack asked.

Forest took a sip of his scotch and explained, "Well, that is where this gets very complicated. Bao is Bao Xu, global lawyer, with connections all the way up to the Fong Gao Triads. He is the outside counsel for all their activities including extortion, money laundering, human trafficking, and cyberattacks. Based on my digging, he also interfaces frequently with a Chinese PLA cyber group. According to my intel, he deals directly with General Vo, himself."

Jack contemplated the details Forest had shared. "Let's think about this, we have a scumbag lawyer playing middleman between the PLA and the Triads. For what purpose?"

"I don't know Jack. Why would they order a hit on Nella? It makes no sense. The only person who benefited from you staying in Portugal and out of the picture is that asshole, Travis Jones."

Jack suddenly slammed his fist into the wall of his hotel room. "Damn it! I knew that bastard was somewhere in this shitstorm. That explains Regina's recruitment and the hack against William's company!"

Forest was taken aback by Jack's outburst, "What are you talking about? What does this have to do with Regina and William?"

Jack proceeded to fill Forest in on Regina's recruitment by the Boston law firm and her representation of the Chinese company that filed an injunction against William's company.

"Oh, Jack, this is way too connected to be a coincidence. I'm willing to be bet Jones has a mole in the law firm that somehow needed to get William's software to the Chinese. The Chinese now have the software. An American law firm has your daughter under NDA. Now she can't talk to the FBI without risking disbarment. They have you tied up in Portugal chasing a dead Frenchman." Forest summarized.

Jack saw the pieces falling into place. "You're right, Forest."

"Jack, you need to wrap up things in Portugal. I would suggest you hold off coming back to America. Stay put in Lisbon for now. Let me dig some more."

Jack replied, "I need to get home and be there for the birth of my grandchild."

Forest understood Jack's dilemma and jumped into action, "Jack, let me make some calls. Stay put, Marine."

The video connection between Jack and Forest went dead. Jack sat motionless in his hotel room. He promised himself, *I am going to kill Travis Jones.*

Jack gulped down a cold beer from the mini bar in his room. He then phoned Rico Lopez, "Rico, are you near my hotel?"

Rico was at home with his wife and children. "No, I am at home, Jack. What's on your mind?"

Jack chose his words carefully. "I have some information from my source. Can we meet?"

Rico looked at his watch and answered, "Yes, give me one hour."

Jack hung up and sat on his bed exhausted. He thought about what he should share with Rico.

An hour later, Rico entered the Lisbon Taipei Marriott and saw Jack sitting at the bar. "Olá, Jack."

Jack nodded at Rico, "Thanks for coming."

Rico smiled taking a seat at the bar, "What's up that can't wait until morning?"

Jack ordered his friend a beer. "I spoke to my contact in Singapore. Our guy Bao, his full name is Bao Xu, he is a lawyer for the Fong Gao Triads."

Rico's face paled, "Triads?"

Jack nodded. "That's not all. Do you remember when you asked me if I was into something bigger than coming here?"

Rico took a drink and replied, "Yes."

"Well, I found out my contact at the World Bank gave the project award to some shadow Chinese company. After he was discovered, he allegedly committed suicide by jumping in front of a truck."

Rico was shocked and asked, "What? Why?"

Jack was still stumped by this part of the story and shook his head in despair replying, "Not sure. The FBI is looking into it."

Rico was stunned by Jack's revelations, "I guess this could not wait."

Jack continued recount the detail he'd learned from Forest. "Well, to make matters worse, my contact in Singapore confirmed the World Bank project for Vietnam hasn't been worked on in three months. Yet, the firm in Xiamen, China already received $90,000,000 upfront from Gomez."

Rico scratched his chin, "Wait, you said Vietnam?"

Jack looked up at his friend, "Yes. Why?"

Rico jumped up from his seat and signaled that he was about to make a phone call, "Back in a moment."

As Rico stepped away, Jack called William to check in, "Son, is everything okay?"

William swallowed hard, "Yes, Dad, Regina is here, she is safe, and Tricia is doing well."

"Will, I am going to be here in Portugal a little longer. I am still working on finding Nella's killer. We found out that the cyberattack, Regina's recruitment into the law firm, and Nella's murder are all connected."

William was shocked. "How, Dad?"

Jack decided that now was not the time to disclose too much to his son and said, "I will provide some details later when I know more, Will. Please, take care of your sister and Tricia. I will be in touch."

William was left stunned and confused but thanked his father as he hung up.

Rico returned to the hotel bar to find Jack. "Please confirm you said Vietnam?'

Jack looked at Rico and said, "Yes, why?"

Rico took another sip of his beer before replying, "We have identified the Frenchman from the blood in the car and on the boat."

Jack felt a wave of relief mixed with apprehension to learn how this could connect some of the dots, "Who the hell is he?"

"Francois Benoit, a known hitman for hire."

Jack was not surprised by this news. "That figures. So this Bao character hires him to take out Nella to keep me here in Europe. While the Dragon Vault, LLC, hijacks the Techline project in Vietnam and steals Will's source code."

Rico looked at his friend as he replied, "Jack, that is not all. Benoit traveled on a Vietnamese passport."

"Special Agent in Charge Gerald Burns?" Bill Parker asked.

"Yes, who is asking?" Gerald replied.

"Bill Parker, Special Agent FBI React 5 Team in DC. Do you have a moment, sir?"

Gerald checked his calendar, "Yes, I have ten minutes. What's going on, Special Agent Parker?"

Bill gathered his notes as he replied, "Sir, I understand you are investigating a possible cyberattack of a specific source code from Cybercom by the Chinese PLA?"

Gerald didn't want to give up his information and replied cautiously, "Go on Parker."

"Sir, I am investigating the apparent suicide yesterday by a World Bank employee at Dupont Circle. I think our cases are linked."

"You think they are linked? How?"

"Sir, the World Bank diverted a project slated for an American firm to a Chinese front company based in Xiamen, China. The employee fronted the company $90,000,000 three months ago. Yet, sources in Vietnam have reported that nothing has been done."

Gerald was still unsure how much to share with Bill, "You're saying the World Bank gave a project in Vietnam to a front company of the Chinese PLA and those funds have gone missing?"

"Yes, sir," Bill replied.

Gerald knew he needed a moment to connect with his colleagues, "Okay Special Agent Parker, let me get back to you."

Bill thanked Gerald and hung up the phone.

Gerald immediately dialed Roger Kim at Cybercom. "Roger? SAC Gerald Burns, FBI, do you have a moment, sir?"

Roger was stressed over the lawsuits and financial investors withdrawing from the company, "Yes, what can I do for the FBI?"

"Mr. Kim, where is William Kendall now?"

"He is in Virginia with his very pregnant wife."

Chapter 19
Intrusion

"Mr. Ho?" Lilian asked.

"Call me Sunny, please."

"Sorry, Sunny. Thank you for the opportunity to join your company," Lilian said, beaming.

Sunny smiled at his new Chief Architect for fiber optical connections. "Yes, let's get started. Did you see the President's speech last night?"

Lilian smiled back at Sunny. She knew that the Taiwanese president's speech must have made General Vo and others in Beijing very upset. "Yes, I loved it. I could not be prouder to be Taiwanese."

Sunny smiled at his newest recruit. "Okay, first, we need you to design and execute the new Wave Division Optical connections from our fiber backbone network into TAINET. The TAINET engineers have already started interlocking the first 10,000 Internet of Things sensors into the 5G radio networks. We will connect those TAINET sensor devices to our fiber network to set up the first city-to-city smart connection."

Lilian seized the opportunity to get more information. "Sunny, what will be the first two cities?"

"Kaohsiung and Tamsui," Sunny responded.

Lilian simmered with elation. She needed access to the secret fiber vault owned by World Global and Travis Jones located outside of Kaohsiung along with access to the fiber cross-connections for her secret back-door maintenance nodes. These secret nodes would provide the needed connection for the Dragon Vault Fiber connector coming from Xiamen, China.

"Excellent. I have family in that city and would love to visit with them while working on those nodes," she said, grinning.

"Perfect, please head down to Kaohsiung tomorrow. Send back your design guides for approval and create the needed change control orders for my approval."

Lilian rose to shake her boss's hand. "Thank you, sir."

Lilian went back to her office to send a secured communication.

Message: CEO Abe Yung: Encryption: I will have access to the secret fiber vault in 3 days. Update me on the status of the underwater cable's location. I will create the maintenance node in parallel to live optical cross-connections into TAINET the same day.

Signed,

Tang

Abe sat in his office in Xiamen, China as he reviewed the court order injunction against Cybercom.

Message to Tang. Ocean fiber optic cabling is terminated 5 meters offshore from the secret vault. The scuba divers and cable teams will have fiber cross-connection done for Dragon Vault in 24 hours. Confirm maintenance node up and operational so we can test packet acceleration.

Signed,

Abe Yung

Lilian received the message back from Abe and sent a secured communication to Poppy.

Well done on the code snag, sweetie. Promise, champagne on me for our next meeting. ;)

After the morning briefing with Chinese leadership, General Vo returned to his office to check on the progress of Operation Dragon Vault and called Bao.

General Vo asked, "Bao? What is the latest?"

Bao walked away from his meeting with local officials in Taipei so he could speak privately with General Vo. "Good morning, General. With the injunction in place, the fiber optic cable has arrived in Kaohsiung. The crypto code and keys passed the initial testing. Our assets on the ground will have a cross connection in TAINET in the next three days."

General Vo smiled at the report. The plan was falling into place.

Chapter 20
Confluence

"ADConnect operations? This is Lilian Tang. Standby to cutover MDF 124." The fiber optical team turned down the fiber circuit. "Operations, standby," Lilian ordered.

As part of the cross-connection for the new fiber network into TAINET, Lilian began connecting the new fiber hub systems together for the new Internet of Things sensors so it could become operational with the various communication networks across Taiwan. These cross-connections are critical for ADConnect to meet the president's mandate for all Taiwanese smart cities to share data faster with each other.

"Operations, what the hell are you doing? Node 124 is still up!" Lilian yelled.

"Ms. Tang, this is Operational Officer Yu. We are not allowed to bring down 124!"

Lilian was furious at the reply from operations. "Look, you ass, turn down the node, or else I will personally rip your nuts off your body!"

Sunny, who was also on the live line, interjected, "Lilian, calm down. This is Sunny on the line."

Lilian maintained her stance. "Sunny, I need the node down to finish the cross-connections."

Sunny put Lilian on hold. He called the operations center on a separate line. "Yu, I am allowing the node to shut down."

Yu hearing the order directly from his CEO, replied angrily, "Yes, sir," as he shut down the node.

Lilian watched the circuit go down. She smiled in satisfaction and thought to herself, *I am still going to rip that guy's balls off!*

While the node circuit came down, Lilian completed the cross-connection to the new node. At the same time, Lilian added a second connection to a maintenance network she constructed to connect into the fiber vault in Kaohsiung. By creating her secret network, Lilian could siphon data from the TAINET network and feed the information directly through the Dragon Vault fiber link back to Xiamen, China.

No one knows that a simple maintenance network will have global access to all data flows back to China. I am brilliant, proclaimed Lilian to herself. After a few minutes of finishing code and configuration checking, she called the operations team. "Okay operator dickless, reactivate node 124."

Yu, not happy with the tone from Lilian, reactivated the node and placed the circuit back online. Sunny, seeing the circuit reenergize, felt a ping of pride for his country. He grabbed the headset and congratulated everyone. "Great work everyone! I want Internet of Things sensor testing and 5G connector testing in the next thirty minutes."

Everyone on the line acknowledged except for Lilian. "I am done here," Lilian proclaimed after she hung up.

While shutting down her systems, Lilian launched her secured application to send an update.

Message: Dragon Vault: Encryption: To all Dragon Vault teammates, all cross-connections completed, heading to underwater Vault now to finalize connection uplink. ETA 48 hours.

Signed,

Tang

After sending the message, Lilian packed up and headed to her car. Once in the car, she checked her messages to see if she received any replies.

Message to Tang, interface with the local Fong Gao guards for protection, proceed with caution.

Signed,

Bao

Lilian knew the Fong Gao Triads provided the security and the muscle if needed in Taiwan. The organization stood to gain millions from the Chinese PLA just to protect the Vault from the Taiwanese government.

Message to Bao, Affirmative.

Signed,

Tang

Lilian put her car in gear and headed south to Kaohsiung.

Poppy spotted the incoming message from Lilian. The possibility of trying out the backhaul code she stole from William's company thrilled her.

Message to CEO Yung. Please confirm code availability once the fiber vault in Taiwan becomes connected. I am ready at the safe house to start alpha testing.

Acknowledge,

Poppy

After Poppy sent the message to the CEO of Fiberex, she also drafted a message to the general.

Message to General Vo, please confirm that the target in Lisbon has been eliminated. Confirm target ID.

Signed,

Poppy

General Vo, while in the meetings with the Communist Party officials in Beijing, noticed the incoming message from Poppy.

Poppy, you are not cleared to view this information.

Signed,

General Vo

Poppy read the response from the general. She began her own research to find out who the target was in Portugal. She scanned the Binarycore News feeds, Fox News, and the Guardian News line. Poppy connected into the Darknet under her hacking tag of *Yellowslayer*. Darknet is known globally as the computer hacker underground network.

The Darknet surfaced years ago as a place for global hackers to converse and auction off stolen goods, including credit card numbers, social security numbers, and passwords to various banking sites, including Wells Fargo. Poppy searched for recent unsolved murder cases in Portugal and Spain.

Several chat windows appeared with questions. "Hey, why do you want to know?"

Poppy knew that some hacker groups were being paid to monitor the Darknet for additional queries into this event.

She answered the various chat windows. "Seeking similar talent to assist with another target. Bitcoin available for payment."

A Darknet hacker recorded the message. Once the message from Yellowslayer to Darknet was recorded by the hacker, the site controller killed the connection from Poppy's computer.

"What the hell?" Poppy fumed as she frantically tried to open another line of communication.

Within seconds of the conversation ending, the site hacker issued a warning to all within the secured portal. "Be mindful, intruder on Darknet, query Portugal."

Within a matter of seconds, the core hacker group within Darknet noted the connection from Yellowslayer. Poppy, unaware that her tag name had been compromised, continued to send queries. After several minutes, Poppy picked up a stolen message from Interpol's email system that was posted thirty minutes ago.

Notice: Portugal Station: Interpol. Local police in Lisbon reporting a French hitman, Francois Benoit, traveling under a Vietnamese passport is under investigation for killing an American tourist in Cascais three days ago. Local investigators found Benoit's blood in the car that was used to murder the American. The American, traveling home to Portugal, was identified as Nella Liu Fiero of Irvine, California. Her companion, Jack Kendall, also from Irvine, California, is assisting in the investigation.

Poppy's eyes widened and suddenly became lightheaded. She dropped her laptop on the floor of her safe house in Vancouver. She made the connection between her target, William, and the victims in Portugal. "Oh, shit!" she cursed under her breath.

Lilian, under the direction of General Vo and the Fong Gao Triads, headed to Kaohsiung to secretly hook up the underwater cable from Xiamen, China.

After driving for nearly seven hours, Lilian arrived at the abandoned seaside warehouse in the port city of Kaohsiung. She noticed several guards protecting the building and knew they were the local Fong Gao Triad soldiers. She approached the main gate of the warehouse. "Tang, codesign 41383alpha."

The lead security team member walked over and said, "You have two hours."

Lilian nodded. She entered the abandoned building and walked over to the digital data equipment rack. Lilian noticed the underwater cable fiber optical connectors were already terminated in the correct wiring closet. She extended the fiber termination point into the data equipment using a series of patch cables and fiber extensions. After the initial plug-in, Lilian connected her laptop to the secured TAINET network. Executing this critical fiber cross-connection was her core mission.

Lilian hooked the underwater connection into her encrypted maintenance subnet network without Sunny Ho and the rest of ADConnect operation teams becoming aware of her rogue connections. While Lilian continued her connections into the TAINET, Sunny suddenly became worried about where she had headed off to.

Message to Lilian, what is your ETA at the node 229? We need the final cross-connection completed in the next four hours. Confirm your location.

Signed,

Sunny

Lilian checked her secured communicator and noticed the urgent message from Sunny. She knew that her time was running out. Lilian needed to finish her covert connection to the fiber network and head up to Taichung quickly to finish the patch work for Sunny.

Message to Ho, still enroute. ETA 2 hours.

Signed,

Tang

Sunny knew the route that she should have taken and that she should have been arriving any minute. He started to feel apprehensive about Lilian and whispered to himself, "Where is she?"

"ADConnect operations? Sunny here. Run diagnostics on all backhaul fiber nodes. Something is wrong here!" The operations team in Yilan, Taiwan acknowledged the order.

"Yes sir, running test mapping now. ETA for completion, four hours." Sunny began to sweat.

"Fiber activation team, stand by. Underwater cable activation testing in ten minutes," Abe said. Being CEO of China's largest fiber optic carrier, his company's future, and probably his own life, depended on the success of Operation Dragon Vault. He needed Lilian to finish the cross-connection to the TAINET network before he could activate the packet accelerator program.

"Mr. Yung, the press conference is in thirty minutes," Yuan, the marketing and press secretary for Fiberex, said.

"On my way," Abe replied.

While reviewing his speech, Abe noticed a flash message came over his secured communicator.

Message to Yung, fiber cross-connection completed at Dragon Vault, activate now.

Signed,

Tang

Abe's heart pounded faster. His palms began to sweat as he made his way to the press conference. He called to his fiber optic engineering team urgently and screamed, "Fiber team, activate!"

Within a few moments, the underwater long-haul fiber activated the connection from Xiamen, China to Kaohsiung, Taiwan. With the first successfully connected cable directly into the heart of the entire Taiwanese communications backbone network, Abe felt relief wash over him. He could not be more pleased with himself and his team as he entered the press conference.

"Ladies and gentlemen of the press, please welcome Mr. Abe Yung, CEO of Fiberex."

Abe approached the podium and was overcome with deep emotion. The successful launch of this project would have a historical impact on his company. This moment would create a huge ripple of success for him, his company, and his country.

Abe began his speech with great enthusiasm. "Good morning, good afternoon, and good evening to the members of the press around the world. Thank you for joining me today. Today marks a new day for China and innovative companies like Fiberex. Today, we mark a monumental accomplishment. Our company, after spending years of research and development, created a new compelling technology in high-speed optical networking. We are pleased to announce the release of Dragon Vault Packet Accelerator 1.0."

The press corps assembled in the corporate headquarters of Fiberex, located just outside of Xiamen, China, applauded.

"Thank you," Abe said, beaming at the crowd before him.

The proud CEO continued. "Dragon Vault Packet Accelerator 1.0 will deliver to the world market a faster and simpler way to push data through underwater cables. Our software will allow for greater amounts of data access to countries that have embarked on the decision to embrace The Internet of Things and Smart Cities. With our software, we can pass large amounts of data across the length of oceans to make e-learning accessible to developing nations. We can create faster e-commerce connectivity for small businesses in Africa selling to their customers in China faster than ever before. We can help reduce the cost of true video-to-video chat communications between mobile and portable communications systems. A doctor sitting in Beijing can now video chat with a patient quickly and securely anywhere in the world with no latency or data packet loss. Today, we bring to the world an ability for the good of all mankind. Thank you."

The press continued to applaud.

"Thank you. Mr. Yung will take a few questions," Yuan said.

"Mr. Yung, Jones Wilson, Guardian Newspapers UK. This technology looks very similar to Cybercom's recent product announcement at the fiber convention a few days ago. Are you in competition with them, sir?"

Abe cleared his throat before answering. "Sir, we are not competing at all. We are the only solution in the marketplace that can deliver this. The American company is currently under an injunction from releasing its software. Next question!"

"Mr. Yung, Li Tai, New China News. How many jobs will Fiberex create for China in the next year because of this new product offering?"

Abe smiled. "Excellent question. Globally, we can expect 15,000 new jobs to be created for our country." With that question, Abe descended from the podium waving at the reporters and thanking them.

"Fifteen thousand Chinese employees globally? Yung, that is 15,000 new cyber security assets for me!" General Vo declared. He foresaw that with the success of Fiberex, their global employees would secretly become his cyber assets. The general knew this new platform would provide easier access to Western Government's critical systems in countries like Germany, Italy, Spain, and Portugal. "Yes, your employees will become my cyber spies!" Vo proclaimed.

Abe made his way back to the operations center to confirm the fiber link to Taiwan was operational. He read a critical message from Lilian and replied.

Message to Tang, please confirm final cross-connection to TAINET, standing by to activate packet accelerator stage 2.

Signed,

Abe

Lilian scrambled to complete the final covert cross-connection then replied to Abe. *Underwater fiber activation complete, confirmed connection to TAINET.*

Signed,

Lilian

Lilian packed up her equipment and left the warehouse, heading to her car.

"Hey, Vulturess," one of the Triad soldiers called out. "Ready to party?"

The Triad guard lunged, his knife drawn, aiming directly at Lilian. Lilian anticipated the soldier's attack and swiftly stepped back, dropped to the ground, and pulled her pistol from her pant leg. She shot the soldier twice in the abdomen.

"Ah, you fucking bitch!" The wounded Triad soldier screamed, falling to the ground. Other guards ran over to assist their fellow soldier, circling Lilian.

Lilian glanced around the growing circle of soldiers as the wounded guard took his last breath. "Which one of you assholes wants two in the balls!" Lilian hollered, whipping around, frantically trying to be aware of any sudden movements. The guards drew their weapons, stepping in closer.

The soldiers suddenly stiffened to attention. An order was coming in over their earpieces. "This is Bao. Stand down. Let her go!"

The guards slowly began to lower their weapons. Within a matter of seconds, Lilian was sprinting to her car, not waiting to see if the soldiers were truly standing down. She threw her pack and pistol on the passenger seat and took off, speeding north to her next target, Taichung. It was urgent that Lilian be near node 86 and 229 to complete the cross-connections to TAINET for ADConnect to finish with the first city-to-city smart connectivity.

She realized she was gripping the steering wheel so hard that her knuckles were white when she heard her phone ringing. She took a couple of deep breaths trying to calm her racing heat. She kept her eyes on the road, groping in her pack for her phone.

"Lilian, where are you?" Sunny Ho sounded worried, with a note of accusation over the line.

Lilian realized her phone was being tracked by ADConnect. Out of breath, she replied, "Just north of Kaohsiung, boarding the HRT train to Taichung. I should reach Node 229 and 86 in 1 hour."

"Lilian, why did you stop in Kaohsiung?" Sunny demanded.

Lilian's heart was pounding in her ears, but she stuck to her back story, calmly replying, "To see a friend. She is visiting here from Hong Kong."

Sunny remained suspicious but didn't want to spook Lilian into disappearing. "Alright, make sure to check in once you reach both nodes." Lilian acknowledged the instructions and ended the call.

"ADConnect operations. Confirm all fiber connectors to and from Kaohsiung. Please tell me if you see any new rogue connections," Sunny instructed his team.

"Operations confirmed," the lead engineer replied.

Sunny thought about Lilian. He was beginning to regret his decision to bring on such a loose cannon—brilliant but not necessarily trustworthy. He thought to himself *If she chooses to act as Vulturess again, our whole project will be screwed*!

Poppy was ready to test the packet software stolen from William's company. She carefully ran through her checklist so nothing would be left undone. "Once Lilian connects Node 86 and 229 to the Internet of Things Network within TAINET, and she completes the cross-connections to her secret maintenance network, I will activate the packet accelerator software and send data back to China." Poppy quietly began to celebrate all the possibilities of this moment. "I will be the world's greatest hacker!"

Chapter 21

Burnt

"You've got to be kidding me!" Roger Kim roared as he watched the live press conference from Xiamen, China. His rival, Abe Yung, CEO of Fiberex, had just announced the planned product release that should have been Cybercom's. "You stole our code!" Roger reached for his coffee mug and hurdled it against the glass wall in his office. With investors threatening lawsuits and employees resigning, Roger knew he faced the real possibility of Cybercom shuttering in the next few weeks.

"You just wait, Abe. Once the thirty-day injunction is up, we'll come for you!" Roger angrily shouted at the TV.

As the press conference continued in the background, Roger answered his phone, "Roger Kim, here."

Allan Smith, Cybercom's primary investor, felt no pity for the struggling CEO, replying, "Roger, I am watching my investment getting flushed down the toilet, thanks to you and your team. The Chinese clearly know how to play hardball while you, the acting CEO, played tennis and drank your fucking espressos!"

Roger had no fight left in him. "Yes, sir, we were clearly asleep at the wheel. We have our lawyers filing for a removal of the injunction now so we can at least bring our product to market."

Allan frowned, clearly unimpressed with Roger's strategy. He responded harshly, "Roger, pack your shit. I want you out of that office by 5:00 p.m. today. I am calling an emergency board meeting. You'll be relieved of your duties as acting CEO, effective immediately." Before Roger could utter a word, Allan abruptly ended the call.

William was holding Tricia's hand as she lay snoozing in the hospital bed when he felt his phone vibrate. "This is William."

"Will? Roger. How is Tricia?"

William spoke quietly into his phone. "She is resting."

Roger asked, "Did you see the press conference from that asshole at Fiberex?"

William had been speeding down the highway, all consumed with making it to Tricia's side before the birth of their baby, to watch the news conference. He took a deep breath as he replied, "No, I missed it. Anything good?"

Roger shared the details with William about Fiberex CEO's announcement regarding their new product, Dragon Vault Packet Accelerator 1.0.

William pinched the bridge of his nose. "Well, that was fast. They stole the software and in a matter of a few days, they have a court injunction and a product ready to ship."

Roger could only think of Fiberex and Cybercom and said, "Allan Smith called today. He is calling for an emergency board meeting. I am being removed as acting CEO." William was not shocked to hear that Roger was being removed, but still felt for his CEO. "Anyway, I just wanted to call. Let's stay in touch."

Will jumped in before Roger could hang up. "Roger, I know this isn't going to be easy for anyone, but it's been great working with you."

Roger thanked him and they ended the call. William turned to look back at Tricia as his phone vibrated again.

"Hello?"

"William? This is Thomas Wilson, CEO of Techline. Your dad works for me."

William replied, "Ah yes, Mr. Wilson, I know who you are. Have you heard from my father?"

"Yes, he is still working with the National Police in Lisbon to solve Nella's murder. How is the baby coming along?"

William looked back at his wife. "No baby yet."

Thomas changed the subject. "Someone I trust very much just informed me that your CEO is about to be ousted."

William paused before responding. "Yes, that's correct. Roger is being fired today by Allan Willis Smith. I can imagine Allan isn't thrilled about losing millions of dollars either. How do you know Mr. Smith, Thomas?"

Thomas smiled as he explained, "That son of a bitch and I go all the way back to the Vietnam War. We served together in the 25th infantry from 1966 to 1968."

William was surprised to learn about Thomas's military service. "Thank you, for your service," William said sincerely.

Thomas appreciated William's acknowledgment.

William then inquired, "Thomas, what do you make of the whole injunction and someone stealing my code?"

Thomas shared the details that William's father had omitted in their conversation. "China has been stealing from us for years, using our laws to get away with billions of dollars of stolen technology. You were brought in for a reason. The real mastermind behind this is Travis Jones. He is a global scumbag and likely the one that ordered someone to steal your code." Thomas paused, allowing his words to sink in before he continued.

"Now, Nella's assassination is a whole different ball game. Your father is going to find out why, and if I know Jack, and I do, he is certainly going to do something about it."

William listened to Thomas's words and agreed.

Thomas went on. "William, I am going to help here with Cybercom's problem. Please bear with me while I make a few calls." William greatly appreciated Thomas' willingness to help Cybercom. "William, we need to get everyone on a video call—the FBI, Portuguese police, and your father. I need to get a hold of someone."

Thomas stood from his desk as he dialed Sunny Ho in Taiwan. "Sunny, Tom Wilson. Got a minute?"

Sunny Ho, CEO of ADConnect in Taiwan, was thrilled to hear his dear old friend and comrade. "Thomas, you old sea dog. How long has it been?"

Thomas smiled and was pleased that his old pal remembered him. "Years, my friend, not since the technology summit in Saipan in 2001."

Sunny laughed with joy as he remembered the last time they had been in the same room. He asked his old friend, "What's the call for, Thomas? Everything okay?"

Thomas answered with a question. "Did you happen to catch the Fiberex press conference?"

Sunny looked at his door to make sure it was fully closed. "Yes, and I heard about the injunction on Cybercom. I bet you are about to tell me that my cousins in Xiamen, China jacked the code and came to market today with it?"

Thomas appreciated his friend's quick wit and replied, "Yep, they made their big announcement today. I am not sure why they suddenly needed a backhaul packet generator unless they plan to do something with it."

Sunny pondered Thomas's words and thought, "Oh, shit! We are just about to connect our Internet of Things and 5G networks into TAINET so our cities can become connected to other smart cities. Did you catch our president's speech two weeks ago?"

Thomas didn't think he'd seen it. "What speech?"

Sunny scrambled to find the speech on YouTube. "Sending the link now."

Thomas clicked the link and watched the president of Taiwan's speech, his eyes widening. "Oh no!" Thomas took a deep breath before he replied to Sunny, "Let me get back to you, Sunny." He hung up quickly and called William back.

"Son, I need to ask you a question. What is the maximum distance that your software can send data with a high quality of assurance?"

William heard the urgency in Thomas's voice and listened with concern. "Nine hundred fifty six kilometers. Why?"

Thomas opened his Binarycore map and typed in Xiamen, China to Kaohsiung Taiwan. Dread washed over Thomas as he read the number aloud. "Three hundred fifty three kilometers."

Thomas conferenced Sunny into the same call with William.

"Sunny, I am here with William Kendall, Chief Architect for Cybercom. He just confirmed his software could send high-speed packets across underwater dark fiber with a range of 956 kilometers. The distance from Xiamen, China to Kaohsiung, Taiwan is 353 kilometers."

Sunny felt the pieces of a nefarious plan falling into place. He anxiously replied, "Thomas, let me call you back."

Sunny called his system and network operations center in Yilan. "Operations Team, is that fiber network validation done yet?"

The lead engineer nervously replied, "Sir, it will be done in the next hour."

Sunny grew impatient and demanded, "I need to know if you have detected any rogue or orphaned fiber hubs or maintenance routes?"

The operations team acknowledged Sunny's order. "Sir, we do not see any of these hubs or rogue maintenance routes."

Not convinced, Sunny replied abruptly, "Look again!"

Sunny picked up his phone to call his admin. "Yuli, please get the president of Taiwan on the phone!"

Sunny tried to find where Lilian Tang was and dialed her number. "Lilian, where are you?" Sunny asked with great agitation.

Lilian arrogantly replied, "Chill boss! I am here at node 229 and I just finished the cross-connection. I am ready to activate the node into TAINET."

A chill ran down Sunny's spine as he asked, "Lilian, please, undo your connections. We need to consider another city."

Sensing something was amiss, Lilian exclaimed, "That could take hours!"

Suddenly realizing Lilian's betrayal, Sunny instructed, "Lilian, stay where you are. I am sending an operations team to help."

Lilian knew her cover was blown and replied cautiously, "Yes, sir."

Sunny called his operations team. "Operations! Shutdown all access for Lilian Tang, ASAP; all accounts and system access. Everything!"

The operations team in the Yilan facility immediately began shutting down all access to accounts and passwords assigned to Lilian. However, she had already completed her rogue fiber optic connections and smirked to herself, "Losers, I am out of here!"

Chapter 22
CONFAB

Video Conference (Fairfax Hospital, Fairfax, VA)

William followed the advice from Thomas and arranged for a video call via the Cisco WebEx Video Conferencing System with the FBI, Regina, Jack, Thomas, Allan Smith, and Sunny Ho. He dialed Thomas. "Everyone has accepted the meeting invite. We will be on in the next hour," William confirmed.

William set up his laptop in Tricia's hospital room to connect to the video conference. The hospital wheeled in a large monitor with a camera. He connected his laptop to the monitor and joined the Cisco WebEx video system. Noticing his father was already online, Willam started the meeting.

"Hey Dad!" William exclaimed. He felt a great sense of relief finally seeing his father after so much had happened in the last week.

More people began connecting into the video conference call including Sunny from his office in Taipei, SAC Gerald Burns from the FBI Boston office, SA Bill Parker with React 5 from the FBI Washington office, Allan Willis Smith, and finally, Thomas Wilson.

Thomas addressed the group on the video call. "Now, for those who don't know me, I am Thomas Wilson, CEO of Techline. I have asked my dear friend and business partner, Sunny Ho, CEO of ADConnect in Taiwan, to join the call." The group greeted Sunny. Thomas continued. "I have also asked the lead FBI Special Agents in Charge to attend—SA Bill Parker and SAC Gerald Burns."

William smiled at Gerald through his screen, grateful for his presence.

"Jack, how about you kick this party off?" Thomas suggested.

Jack cleared his throat, looking out at the city lights from his hotel room and addressed the meeting attendees. "I am here in Lisbon, Portugal, with Special Investigator Rico Lopez of the Portuguese National Police."

Rico greeted everyone in excellent English. "Olá, Special Agent in Charge Burns, it's been a long time. We worked on an Interpol drug case a few years back."

Gerald smiled and replied, "Rico, great to see you again."

Jack methodically walked through the tragic events that occurred in Portuga., "A French hitman killed Nella last week here in Portugal. What we have discovered is that Frenchman traveled under a Vietnamese passport." Before Jack could continue, another person joined the video conference.

"Sorry, I am late," Forest Adams said. "It's 4:00 a.m. here in Singapore."

Jack instinctively swallowed the lump in his throat; he became overwhelmed with emotion that his dear friend, Forest, took the time to make the call.

"Wait! THE Forest Adams?" Gerald proclaimed.

Forest paused for a moment, smiling at the recognition, and humbly said, "Yes, Special Agent in Charge Burns, it is I."

Gerald could not believe Forest was on the call. "Mr. Adams, it's an honor, sir."

Forest waved off the compliment and nonchalantly requested, "You as well, SAC. Jack, continue, please."

Jack continued his narrative. "Benoit traveled on the same flight with Nella and me. He tracked us to Cascias, using a stolen car to run down Nella, who was on a scooter. The assassin injured himself in the crash and his blood was found on a wall near where the stolen car was discovered. Benoit made his way down to the harbor and boarded a boat. We later found the boat with his blood. Once Rico took the captain of the boat into custody, we found his cell phone. We retrieved a message sent to the captain by some guy named Bao Xu. Bao paid the captain to dump Benoit's body overboard."

Jack took to a drink of water, the impact of the events still fresh, and continued, "I forwarded the photo of the Frenchmen and the messages from the captain's cell phone to Forest."

Forest instructed, "Everyone! I am not here. I was never here. Clear?"

After everyone nodded in agreement, Forest continued. "Okay, this Bao character who paid off the captain and hired the hitman, is Bao Xu. He is a high-powered lawyer and the broker between the Fong Gao Triads and the Chinese PLA Army. He is also a middleman and a major player in whatever the PLA is up to."

Gerald raised his hand and questioned, "Ah, did you say Fong Gao Triads?" Forest nodded yes. "Oh, shit! Not those guys," Gerald said.

Forest checked his notes before he continued. "We tracked Benoit's passport back to Vietnam. He was a resident of Da Nang for several years. He primarily only worked for the heroin monkeys inside the Golden Triangle."

Jack picked up from where Forest left off. "So, we know the Triads ordered the hit on Nella to keep me in Portugal. However, I believe there is one more player out there, Travis Jones."

Regina appeared bewildered, shock evident on her face, as she stated, "Dad, my boss, Noah Blake, spoke to him the day I left the firm." Both FBI agents took note of Regina's comment.

Jack appeared surprised by Regina's revelation. "Reg, are you sure he was speaking to Travis Jones?" Regina nodded.

"Thomas! That's it! That's the connection! All of his has to be about getting revenge from the Vietnam World Bank deal," Jack exclaimed excitedly.

Bill Parker, upon hearing the mention of the World Bank, asked cautiously, "Wait. Hold on. What World Bank project?"

Thomas provided a detailed explanation. "Last year, Jack and I bid on a project in Vietnam with the support of a Japanese investor and the World Bank to fund the rebuilding of several miles of jungle that was destroyed by war and nature. Our company was supposed to win the project. However, Jones' firm, World Global Transformation, LLC, placed a low-ball bid for the deal. Jack flew to Detroit to meet with Jones personally to convince him to withdraw his bid for the project."

Everyone in the room listened more intently as Thomas continued. "Jack confronted this guy with some intelligence data from Forest. In a rage, Travis kicked Jack out of his office. A week later, after Jack headed to Portugal, the World Bank awarded the deal to Dragon Vault, LLC, out of Xiamen, China."

The color drained from Regina's face as she said, "I can't believe I represented them in the lawsuit against Cybercom."

Allan Smith spoke up angrily. "You are the one! When we are done here—"

"Allan, not here, not now!" Thomas interrupted Allan. He stared Allan down, pausing for a moment, then continued his narrative. "Then, this guy Pedro Gomez, the project manager at the World Bank, informed me that the deal went to Dragon Vault."

Bill interrupted. "Wait! Is this the same guy who committed suicide at Dupont Circle while running away with a bunch of USB drives?"

Gerald, listening to his FBI counterpart, inquired, "He committed suicide?"

Bill nodded. Gerald gathered his thoughts before he spoke. "FBI Boston is investigating a data and source code theft of the backhaul QoS package being developed by Cybercom. Will, I know you are a little preoccupied right now, but could you provide some insight?"

William carefully explained, "A week ago, I keynoted at an event in San Francisco and met with a reporter representing the New China News Agency. She must have had access to the source code before. However, she needed to gain access to a cell phone or laptop to steal the crypto keys. We went to my room to conduct the interview. She must have placed something on my laptop to clone everything, including the crypto keys." He paused to see if anyone wanted to add anything. "So, in a matter of a few days, Fiberex stole the code, cloned the package, changed the legal terms, filed an injunction against my firm, and released their product."

Allan Smith was still fuming from being cut off and interjected, yelling, "Kendall, you are done!"

William stared at Allan and replied forcefully, "Not yet, Allan!"

Thomas summarized the situation. "Okay, let's recap. We have a front company for the Chinese PLA based in Xiamen, China. Not only have they stolen the software to transport data underwater faster, they also stole a World Bank project for reasons we don't know yet. Let's not forget that the Fong Gao Triads killed Nella in Portugal. Everyone clear so far?"

Everyone on the call nodded in agreement.

Jack added more context, "We can't forget this Bao character. We also know that Travis must be running this operation for someone else."

Forest clarified, "Jack, this goes all the way to the top. If PLA Cyber is involved, that means General Vo."

Sunny reacted immediately upon hearing Vo's name, "Excuse me! People, if General Vo is involved, that means the target is definitely Taiwan. He has been ordering cyberattacks against my country for years."

Thomas remembered the president of Taiwan's speech and exclaimed, "Hold on, Sunny! Didn't the president mention something about smart cities connecting to each other?"

Sunny hesitantly answered, "Yes, we just finished the fiber cross-connections between two cities into the TAINET network. Now these cities can access several Internet of Things devices and exchange high rates of data for video, education, and data mining."

Jack interjected, "Wait, why would Fiberex need Will's code?"

Thomas looked at William for clarification. "William, is the software only needed if someone is accessing the data from long distances?"

William looked confused as he replied, "Yes. Our QoS software is only relevant for long distances specifically for underwater fiber connections."

Gerald thought about the origins of Dragon Vault, LLC, and asked, "Regina, is Dragon Vault, LLC, registered anywhere?"

Regina knew if she disclosed that information, she would be compromising the Attorney-Client Privilege and she said so. "SAC Burns, I would be disbarred if I divulged that information." Regina, the youngest member of the meeting by far, felt everyone's eye on her.

"Regina, I understand that, however, I can get a warrant," Gerald advised.

Jack interjected, speaking directly to his daughter. "Reg, please, we are well past that at this point."

Regina thought about her options. She knew that she wanted to see Noah and this Travis character go down. She made up her mind. "Off the record, SAC, Dragon Vault, LLC registered in Vietnam."

Gerald suddenly rose from his desk and disappeared from sight.

"Regina, what did Dragon Vault, LLC, do with the $90,000,000 the World Bank gave them for the Vietnam project?" Bill Parker asked.

Regina felt uncomfortable but continued to divulge the client's information. "$70,000,000 went into a secret fund to pay for underwater cable repairs."

Gerald returned to his computer screen and interrupted, "One moment, Regina. Can you repeat your statement again, please?"

Regina repeated her statement. Thomas leaned back in his chair. "So, they muscled us out of the project in Vietnam and then utilized the funds to activate some underwater cable? To where?"

Sunny exclaimed, "Oh, shit!" Everyone was startled. Sunny explained his outburst. "I know where." Sunny detailed the cross-connections his company was working on. "My engineer, Lilian Tang, recently employed by us as an expert in fiber optic network and Dense Wave Multiplexing, handled the complex cross connections between our ADConnect nodes and TAINET."

William immediately recognized the hacker. "Wait! You hired Lilian Tang?"

Sunny cringed. "You know her?"

William gave a sharp look into the camera directly at Sunny. "You stupid asshole, you hired Vulturess!"

Sunny looked away from the camera in shame. "Yes, we did. However, she has not been involved with that stuff for years."

William addressed his father. "If Vulturess was on the ground in Taiwan, she could have hooked up the underwater cable and planned to use my code to copy the data back to Xiamen, China."

Sunny felt a deep sense of responsibility for his country and the dire situation. "Our operations teams are scanning the entire network for any new fiber nodes or connectors."

William turned his attention to Thomas. "Is that why you needed to know the distance?"

"Yes, son, that is exactly why I asked," Thomas replied.

Gerald jumped in. "Okay, we have a ton of intelligence on Lilian Tang. UCLA, Binarycore, Apple, and Qualcomm were her stomping grounds. She left Binarycore after she released footage of someone in the parking lot pleasuring her boss. Binarycore settled with Vulturess by sending her off with a huge separation package. We tracked her online movements under the tag of Vulturess for the last three years and then she went dark."

"Yes, that is about the time she started working within the Darknet," William stated.

William was met with confused faces. "What is the Darknet?"

William explained that most hackers, white hat or black hat, operated inside of a private cyber universe known as Darknet. "Vulturess has been very active on the Darknet over the last year. It is rumored on the Net that she is the central hacker for the Fong Gao Triads and is frequently on loan to the Chinese PLA Cyber Force under the command of General Vo. Last year, she jacked $100,000,000 in Bitcoin, rumored to be owned by the San-Hamada of the Yakuza, based in Tokyo. After the theft, she went radio silent."

As William finished, the room fell silent, deep in thought.

After a few moments, Gerald spoke up. "Will, thank you. We didn't have that in our files. What do you know about Poppy Ledger?"

William answered in frustration. "Regretfully, not enough."

Gerald continued, "Well, Poppy Ledger is a known global hacker and often works for the PLA cyber division, reporting directly to General Vo, himself." William became extremely despondent after hearing this revelation. Gerald added, "Poppy was last seen leaving the San Francisco airport under a diplomatic passport heading to Canada. We think she is hiding out in Vancouver."

William was disgusted with himself. He knew he had compromised his software by being ignorant of Poppy's true identity and intentions.

"We will contact the Canadian authorities and see if they can locate her," Gerald offered.

Thomas composed himself and then calmly replied, "Okay, so where do we go from here?"

Jack stretched for a moment, considered all options, and then replied, "Forest, what do you think?"

Forest answered, "Well, whatever is going to happen will definitely go down in Taiwan."

Everyone agreed, thinking of the role they had unknowingly played in this scheme.

Chapter 23

Masquerade

Forest directly addressed Jack. "Marine, I would suggest you get on the ground in Taiwan."

Jack carefully listened to his friend and firmly responded. "Forest, I need to be home with my family. Tricia is about to give birth to my first grandchild."

Tricia interjected. "Jack, go get them! William and Regina are here."

Jack smiled back at his daughter-in-law. "Thank you, Tricia."

"Sunny, you need to find those nodes and shut them off ASAP," Thomas interjected.

Gerald strongly urged, "Regina, we need to have a long talk. We will need your help to take down this law firm of yours."

Jack interrupted everyone and spoke authoritatively, "Hold up! Everyone, stop for a moment." Everyone froze to listen to Jack. He continued, "We need to do nothing. We need to play this out. If we go on offense, they will go underground, and we will lose access to them."

Gerald disagreed with Jack and interrupted, "Mr. Kendall, we have a foreign government about to execute the hack of the century against an American ally."

Jack asserted, "That's true, but if we stir up the world around them, we won't catch the main players."

Bill Parker spoke up. "SAC, I agree with Kendall. Let's line up the resources but keep this on the down low."

Gerald reluctantly agreed and turned his attention to Regina. "Regina, we will need to take you into protective custody."

Regina retorted firmly, "No way! I am staying!"

Thomas calmly suggested, "SAC Burns, I will take custody of her."

Jack smiled at Thomas in relief through the camera and said, "Thanks, Thomas."

Returning the smile, Thomas nodded in acknowledgment.

"Thomas, please send someone to my condo in Pasadena. Ask them to send my bike and equipment to Velo Bike Shop in Pasadena on Colorado Blvd. Please ask them to pack and ship my bike to the Taipei Marriott."

Curious, Thomas inquired, "Going somewhere, Jack?"

With a grin, Jack replied, "Oh yes, I always wanted to cycle Taiwan."

Thomas smiled and affirmed, "On it."

"Will, a moment please," Thomas requested.

"Yes?"

"Look, son, I am going to handle Smith for you. I need you to focus on finding out what's going on with this Dragon Vault project in Vietnam and Taiwan. Check the Darknet and your hacker connections." William felt invigorated by his new assignment.

Thomas walked down the hallway to call to Allan Smith. "Allan, Thomas."

Allan did not respond immediately; he was still upset from the video call, but replied, "Thomas, you have some nerve." Thomas let Allan vent for a bit.

"Look, Allan, I need you to keep your money where it is and drop any legal action against Cybercom."

Allan was shocked by Thomas' requests. "Why would I do that?" Allan exclaimed.

Thomas replied patiently, "Because, I am going to acquire Cybercom and become the CEO."

Allan was surprised by Thomas's sudden decision. "What? When? How?" he asked in quick succession.

Thomas sternly requested, "I need your support, Allan. I will buy up all outstanding shares. That will still leave you as the majority shareholder and chairman. I will take over as CEO."

Allan was flabbergasted by Thomas's plan and asked, "Can you pull this off?"

Thomas, being an old-school businessman, said, "Allan, we will make Fiberex and the Chinese PLA pay for what they did."

Allan agreed. "I will drop the lawsuit and keep my money in play. What else do you need?"

"I need you to schedule another board meeting and announce the plan for the acquisition. I will get my lawyers working on the drafts."

"On it," Allan said and hung up the phone. He could not have asked for a better outcome to save his investment in Cybercom.

Thomas reached out to Regina. "Reg, I need your legal expertise, please."

Regina responded to Thomas in complete surprise. "Of course. How can I be of service to you before I get disbarred?"

After disconnecting from the video conference call, Sunny Ho checked in with his operations team. "Well?" Sunny snapped at his team vehemently.

"Sir, this is Lau in Operations. We have found no new nodes active. We have seen the activation of the new node cross-connections into TAINET. However, unauthorized fiber connections have been discovered."

Sunny was shocked and alarmed by the report from his team. "Look again! Check any new nodes or fiber vaults in Kaohsiung that are now live."

Lau agreed and hung up. Sunny called his communications officer next. "Yuli, keep trying to get the president on the phone."

"Sunny, President on line four," Yuli replied quickly.

"Madame President, thank you for your time," Sunny said.

President Fong, exhausted, took a break from her long day of meetings and replied, "This better be good, Sunny!"

Sunny detected from President Fong's tone how stressed she really was. He spoke confidently, "Madame President, I will cut to the chase. We believe the TAINET network was hacked."

The president of Taiwan, hearing for the first time about the cyberattack inquired, "What? By whom? Dammit!"

Sunny chose his words carefully and explained, "We are still investigating. We suspect the Chinese PLA Cyber Group and the Fong Gao Triads are in conjunction with some rogue elements out of Xiamen, China, are behind this fiasco."

The president took her glasses off and rubbed her eyes as she spoke. "Okay, small words here, Sunny. How did this happen?"

Sunny broke out his notes and patiently replied to his president. "We hired a highly qualified fiber optic consultant to help with the vital cross-connections. She secretly hooked up an old underwater cable into a fiber vault somewhere in Kaohsiung. The fiber leads back to Xiamen,

China. We believe the PLA planned to pull off a massive data heist off the TAINET network to include important data from the Smart City Network Project."

Sunny composed himself before he continued. "The Chinese stole a piece of software from an American company and rebranded it into their own software."

The president processed the bad news from Sunny and began to consider all her options. She spoke authoritatively, "Okay, can we just shut down the network and look for these cross-connections?"

Sunny used small words to explain to the president the available options. "Yes, however, this will disrupt our data exchanges that we have set up already between the two host cities."

The president shook her head in disgust. "Sunny, thank you for screwing up my day. What is the plan here?" President Fong asked impatiently.

Sunny considered the plan with the Americans by placing an asset in Taiwan within forty-eight hours to help shut down the fiber nodes. However, he decided not to brief the president on Jack's mission and replied reluctantly, "We are looking at all options, Madame President."

The president clenched her hand into a fist and pounded her desk. She considered how she wanted to handle this situation and stated, "Sunny, I want all options on my desk in twenty-four hours." The President slammed the phone down before Sunny could answer.

Sunny felt the pressure to come up with a plan to save TAINET. Simultaneously, he also needed to shut off the possible data leak back to China. "I need a miracle," Sunny muttered.

Thomas called Regina to discuss the merger between Cybercom and Techline. Thomas opened the conversation. "Okay counselor, I am planning to take over Cybercom. Allan Smith will stay on as the chairman, and I will become the CEO. The company will stay privately held, with a value share of $37.50 per preferred stock. I need you to create a tender offer to all outstanding shares at $45.00 per unit so I can acquire what Allan doesn't already own. Can you draft something like this, please, so we can send the stock offer via secured email to all minority shareholders?"

Regina opened her laptop and began creating the legal draft stock offer. She created all the legal offerings including the stock share acquisition contract. "Thomas, give me an hour," Regina requested.

William went to the car outside the hospital to get his secured crypto laptop specifically designed to surf the Darknet. The laptop codename, *Lerch,* was specifically designed by William to include the latest cryptography for data at rest, data in transit, endpoint security software, and three layers of personal firewall.

William also created a custom web browser with integrated Docker Sandbox Container software. He signed into the hospital's wireless network and logged into the Darknet realm as Knight2Rouk7. William used his tag name while moving between the various chat rooms and secured vaults within Darknet. He spent over 30 minutes dropping multiple time-bomb messages within the various message boards seeking talent around backhaul data exfiltration hacking.

William left messages with five-minute timeouts, but did not receive a single inquiry back. He became more aggressive with his communication to see if anyone would respond to his message.

Knight2Rouk7 to all in Darknet members. Suspect an island hack going down. Looking for currency backing, asking for $50,000,000 in crypto. Deposit funds into a Danang crypto account. Reference: Dragon Vault.

William set the message time-bomb to expire in sixty minutes.

Poppy checked her latest messages in Darknet, looking for anyone querying her tag, *Yellowslayer*. After she dropped messages into her normal chat boards and secured vaults, she noticed an all-hail message coming from a new player in the realm: Knight2Rouk7.

After she read the message about some island hack going down and a need for some crypto-currency, Poppy became concerned that the Dragon Vault attack was discovered by some government agency. She went fishing for more information inside the Darknet to find out.

"Hmm, that is strange. I need to let everyone know." Poppy disconnected from Darknet and opened her secured communications application.

Message to Dragon Vault team.

Darknet shows a new player seeking resources including crypto-currency for an upcoming island hack. Dragon Vault attack possibly compromised, holding for instructions.

Signed,

Poppy

Within minutes of the message flash from Poppy, General Vo called Bao on a secured line. "Bao, did you see the flash message? I want Lilian Tang dead now. No loose ends."

Bao considered the best way to respond to General Vo. "General, I am taking care of it."

The general was not satisfied with Bao's response and called Abe at Fiberex directly. "Yung, General Vo. When is the data extraction going to be operational? We need to move up our timetable!"

Abe felt the pressure to finish the beta testing for the stolen QoS source code. He replied aggressively, "General, we will be ready for full operation in seven days."

"I want it down to four days!" The general slammed down the phone in anger.

Abe sweated profusely, collapsed in his chair, and complained to himself, "We will not make it in four days."

Jack connected to the Wi-Fi on his flight to Taipei on Turkish Airlines to check his messages. He noticed an email from the Velo Bike Shop in Pasadena with the shipping information for his bike due to arrive in Taipei in the next seventy-two hours. Jack read the message that William sent into the Darknet. He hoped to get someone to respond before the message time bomb expired. He then read about Thomas's plan to acquire and merge Cybercom into Techline.

"Brilliant move, Thomas," Jack whispered. He also noticed that Regina was handling all the legal work on the stock purchasing.

"Reg!" Jack exclaimed with pride. He closed his laptop and began to brainstorm about all the things he needed to accomplish while on the ground in Taiwan. He began a list based on what he knew.

Jack researched how to catch the train from Taipei to Hualien. Once he arrived in Hualien, he would need to make it to Yilan. In Yilan he would be able to check the nodes in the area for any new equipment installations.

He thought to himself, "If everything checks out okay, I will take the train into Kaohsiung and cycle the coast route to see if any dock-based telecommunications hubs have become operational."

Jack was typing his notes when he noticed a message from Forest.

Marine, when you are on the ground, I hired you a cycling guide to help you navigate around the island. I got your back, Marine! Her name is Li Cao. She is a retired teacher and a mother of two. She will contact you at the hotel when you arrive.

Signed,

Forest

Jack greatly appreciated Forest for looking out for him and sent him a message.

Forest, thank you. That will help.

Signed,

Jack

Jack also sent a message to Sunny Ho.

Sunny, please keep my mission secret. I will navigate as needed to the various nodes. Please upload node and fiber plant maps.

Signed,

Jack

Sunny was under a strict deadline to get back to President Fong within twenty-four hours. He made an emergency video call to his operations and security staff. "Team, we suspect now that TAINET has been attacked. I informed the president this morning as well. We need every preventable option available to stop our country's data from being stolen and our networks from becoming compromised. We can't shut off TAINET because the critical Smart City data streams are now active."

Sunny's security analyst, Joon Lee, spoke. "Chief, I will run a skip trace program based on the two nodes that Tang had access to. That will help tell us to determine if her rogue cross-connections went active."

Sunny agreed and replied, "Make it happen! Anyone else have any other ideas?" Everyone was in a state of shock and had nothing else to add.

"Okay. Meeting adjourned. Be back here in two hours. I want options and results," Sunny commanded.

Bao departed from a secret meeting with the Fong Gao Triads in western Taiwan. He checked his messages for any update from the Dragon Vault team. He spent the better part of the day with the mid-level Triad leadership to discuss the fate of Lilian Tang. After several hours, the Triad leadership ordered Bao to keep Lilian alive at all costs. He knew that General Vo would not sit idle. He would attempt to kill Lilian himself. Bao focused his attention on gaining access to resources for Lilian to get out of Taiwan.

Bao opened his secured communicator application to send a message to Lilian with instructions.

Message to Tang, head to back up jump point. Destroy all communications.

Signed,

Bao

Lilian hid out in an apartment in Taichung, Taiwan. She reached for her communicator to see who messaged her. "Oh, shit." Lilian cussed. She followed Bao's instructions, smashed her communicator into pieces, gathered her stuff, and quickly headed out of the apartment. She needed to get to the backup jump point south of Taipei within two hours.

"This is going to be close," Lilian whispered.

Bao received the message from Lilian and immediately contacted the local leadership for the Triads in Taipei.

Chu, package arriving at your location, ship out asap to Naha, Okinawa.

Signed,

Bao

Chu was the local shot caller for the Triads. He was a very important soldier who handled all the human trafficking, weapons, and drug smuggling, and arranged for all the covert traveling for Triad leaders in and out of Taiwan.

Chu answered, "We have a team ready to ship via a cargo plane to Naha. The team in Okinawa is ready to receive your package."

Bao sent an update to General Vo.

Message to General Vo, Tang has been eliminated. Her body was dumped in the ocean en route to Naha.

Signed,

Bao

General Vo received the flash message from Bao. He smiled with great satisfaction that Lilian was allegedly killed. He sent a secure and secret message to Poppy.

Message to Poppy. You are now the team leader. You are responsible for all software and platforms for the Dragon Vault attack. Tang has been eliminated.

Signed,

General Vo

Poppy read the message from General Vo and became very concerned for her own safety. "Oh my! Lilian! I could be next!" She paced around in her safe house in Vancouver pondering her fate. "What if the general comes after me?" Poppy sat down, stared at the sunset over Canada, and planned her next move.

Chapter 24
G-Men

Immediately following the video conference, SAC Gerald Burns called SA Bill Parker to discuss the direction of the investigation. "Bill, this is Gerald. Do you have a moment?"

"Yes," Bill said.

Once he was settled in his office chair, Gerald began to strategize with his FBI counterpart. "Bill, this whole Dragon Vault mess is a lot more than the Chinese stealing software. Your guy at the World Bank jumped in front of the FedEx truck and killed himself. General Vo, head of all PLA Cyber, is personally hand-holding this project. Then there's the law firm, up here, in Boston, who suddenly isn't taking any external calls. What is your take on all of this?"

Bill followed Gerald's train of thought and replied, "We need to have a conversation with Fred Simon at the World Bank. We need to get Vo on the phone to admit to the redirection of the World Bank funds. If we can shake up Vo's world, he may panic and make more mistakes."

Gerald liked Bill's suggestion and commented, "Bill, I am going to speak to the director later today. I am going to recommend we merge our cases. I really appreciate how you operate."

Bill appreciated Gerald's compliment and replied, "Thank you, SAC, I will update you once I speak to Simon."

Gerald contacted the executive administrator for the FBI Director, Alvin Ramsey. "Lynn, this is SAC Burns. Please let me know if the director has fifteen minutes this afternoon for a meeting. We have a pressing case involving the Chinese PLA and the Triads in Taiwan."

Lynn looked at the director's calendar and answered, "Yes, SAC, you can have fifteen minutes at 4:00 p.m. in the director's office."

Gerald thanked Lynn and hung up.

Regina completed all the legal filings for the shareholder buyout. She worked on the counter-injunction against Fiberex and her old firm, Blake, Wilson, and Todd. As Regina reviewed the initial injunction, she discovered that her name was listed as the lead counsel for Fiberex. She realized that she would be disbarred for her past legal actions against Cybercom.

Regina decided to call Thomas for guidance. "Thomas, do you have a moment?"

Thomas attended a meeting with the new board of directors of the new company. He answered Regina's call. "Yes, Regina?"

Regina spoke cautiously. "I am listed as the lead counsel for Fiberex in the injunction. If I am to state now that I am the legal counsel for Cybercom / Techline I will be disbarred."

Thomas was already aware of this fact and carefully advised Regina. "Reg, please focus on the stockholder transfer. I will handle the injunction. At some point, the G-men, aka the FBI, will be here to question you about your old firm. All roads could lead to the disbarment of your legal license. However, I have other things I need you to work on after the merger is complete."

Regina was moved to tears by Thomas's support. She smiled to herself and she emotionally replied, "Thank you, Thomas."

Travis Jones enjoyed an early morning orange juice in his hotel room in Naha, Okinawa. He scanned his sources to better understand the pending merger between Cybercom and Techline. "Those bastards think that Thomas Wilson will save the day. Jack Kendall, I got you. Good luck leaving Portugal."

As Travis read the official statement to the press and shareholders of Cybercom and Techline, he carefully reviewed the thirty-day legal injunction between Fiberex and Cybercom. Travis's confidence and arrogance grew. "Cybercom is done. Without their product coming to market, they are finished. Fiberex will dominate the market and I will be fucking rich."

Travis reached for this phone to call Noah. "Noah, have you landed yet here in paradise?"

Noah had just arrived in Okinawa after a twenty-hour flight. He was jetlagged and answered slowly. "Fuck you! Yes, I will be at the hotel in an hour."

Travis was pleased and smiled from ear to ear when he heard his old buddy's voice again.

At 4:00 p.m., Gerald arrived at the Office of the Director of the FBI. Alvin Ramsey was sitting at his desk when Gerald knocked. He called out, "Come in."

Gerald entered Alvin's office and greeted his boss. "Director, thank you for seeing me on short notice," he said respectfully.

The director looked up with disdain. "Well?" Alvin asked.

Gerald cleared his throat before answering, "Sir, I need to brief you on a series of events that are currently unfolding between China, Vietnam, and Taiwan."

Alvin took his glasses off and said, "Proceed."

Gerald presented the narrative about the source code hack against Cybercom by the Chinese PLA Cyber Group and a front company in Xiamen, China. He also detailed Techline's fight with World Global and the funds from the World Bank that were diverted to some projects in Vietnam.

Alvin interjected. "SAC, can you get to the point, please?"

Gerald continued, "Sir, we believe the Chinese are behind Operation Dragon Vault. This cyberattack will siphon mass amounts of data out of Taiwan with Remote Access Trojan. These malicious programs would be embedded into thousands of devices throughout the island. This would allow the Chinese to control several financial systems, military infrastructure, and civil defense networks."

The director looked outside his window, admiring the view of Washington, D.C, and asked, "Has President Fong been apprised of the impending attack?"

"Yes, Sir." Gerald was confident in his reply to the director.

"SAC, am I to understand that this General Vo is operating autonomously? Is he creating this attack by leveraging Beijing's direct marching orders to reign in Taiwan once and for all? It appears he is doing all this without having to fire a single bullet."

Gerald appreciated the director's insightful analysis, "Yes, Sir. We believe he is operating on his own and with very little interference from the Central Committee or other members of the China military leadership. We confirmed that he is using the general narrative to fulfill China's goal by making Taiwan a province and crushing their dream to be an independent country. Sir, I request that SA Bill Parker and his React Five Team be placed under my authority."

The director looked perplexed at Gerald and asked, "Do you want to merge your cases?" After Gerald confirmed his request, Alvin approved the request. "Granted."

"Look, Gerald, this thing of yours is going to get very ugly very quickly. I will speak to the Attorney General and get her take on this before we approach the president of the United States," Alvin stated with conviction.

Gerald thanked the FBI director for his time. He returned to his office to call Bill.

"Bill, Gerald here. The director has approved our request to merge our cases. He is meeting with the AG today to discuss how we can assist the Taiwanese government and update President Taylor."

Bill was elated that he would be reporting to Gerald. "Thank you, SAC."

Alvin dialed up his boss, Marcia Robertson, the attorney general of the United States. "Madame AG, may I have ten minutes on your calendar?"

The attorney general of the United States, Marcia Robertson, carried a long history of being a federal judge and US attorney for San Diego. Alvin had always held Marcia in the highest regard and respect.

"Alvin, you get ten minutes," Marcia said.

"Ma'am, we have a tiered threat unfolding between the Triads, Yakuza, PLA, and Taiwan," Alvin quickly replied.

Marcia stared back at Alvin before sarcastically replying, "I guess you need more than ten minutes, then?" Marcia looked at her schedule and reluctantly agreed. "You have twenty minutes."

Alvin walked Marcia through the merging of the cases and the pending cyberattack against Taiwan with the hackers using stolen American software. He also discussed the concern that General Vo may have gone rogue, and the rest of the Chinese government may be in the dark about his plan to hack Taiwan.

"AG, we confirmed that General Vo is using the anti-Taiwan narrative. We don't believe that anyone outside of the general's inner circle are aware of his plan."

Marcia listened with full attention and sharply replied, "Okay, you think he is hiding behind the *crush Taiwan* at all costs banner, yet the rest of the Chinese leadership either doesn't know or they don't care as long as this is against Taiwan?" Alvin agreed with Marcia's understanding of the situation. Marcia replied, "I know a way we could find out."

Alvin looked at his boss with curiosity and asked, "Oh, how?"

The AG got up from her seat and motioned Alvin to follow her. Within the Justice Department building, there were several soundproof rooms. Being the attorney general of the United States, Marcia had access to her own special conference room. "This way, Director," Marcia instructed. The AG inserted her coded pass into a wall holder, and the door to the secured conference room opened. The AG and Alvin entered the sound-proof room.

"Okay, Alvin, this is top secret. We will not discuss this outside this room. Agree?"

Alvin focused on the AG's instructions and replied, "Agreed."

Marcia informed Alvin, "I went to school with Hai Ming, the Minister of Finance and Economic Reform for the People's Republic of China."

Alvin looked completely shocked by Marcia's revelation. "That guy is a butcher."

Marcia stared back at her FBI director and sternly replied, "Alvin, most people, in some form, have made terrible mistakes in their lives and committed unconscionable acts at the worst of times. I was the inspector general in Iraq in 2004. Our government made choices that destroyed human lives and cost our taxpayers over one hundred billion dollars."

Alvin understood Marcia's logic. However, he still was not a fan of Hai Ming.

"Alvin, I have a back channel to Ming. I will reach out to him personally and ask him to confirm if any attack against Taiwan is coming."

Alvin looked at Marcia and replied, "Ma'am, I don't know what to say, but thank you."

Marcia waved him off and said, "Alvin, get to the bottom of this Taiwan hack. Find me this asshole, Travis Jones, and put the squeeze on the law firm in Boston. Also, keep tabs on Jack Kendall while he is riding around Taiwan on his bike."

Alvin acknowledged the orders from Marcia.

"Alvin, we need to shake some trees first. Get this Simon guy in here. Have him contact the general directly and launch an investigation into the redirection of funds to Vietnam. That should make a few people nervous," Marcia recommended.

Alvin smiled at his boss's recommendations. "Thank you, AG." Alvin left the room and headed to his office to brief Gerald.

Marcia stayed behind and sat down in a chair to think. She whispered under her breath, "I am screwed if this gets out."

Alvin arrived back in his office and phoned Bill and Gerald. He spoke on the phone to both special agents. "Bill, bring in Fred Simon from the World Bank. We need to get the general on the phone and confirm that he ordered the funds to be sent to Vietnam." Alvin then instructed Gerald, "SAC, keep tabs on Kendall while he is cycling around the island."

Gerald laughed for a moment and replied, "Huh, yes, sir."

Bill departed the director's office and headed into the hallway to make a call. "Fred? This is SA Bill Parker, FBI React Five. I need you to come to the FBI HQ."

Fred Simon sat behind his desk at the World Bank and replied, "Yes, Bill, I am on my way." Fred grabbed his laptop bag, put on his jacket, and headed to the FBI office.

Noah arrived at the Okinawa Harborview Hotel in Naha, the capital city of Okinawa. He thought about what he would do with all the money he made from the Dragon Vault deal with the PLA and the Triads. "Holy shit," Noah whispered to himself, "I can buy an island and a dozen girls to serve me around the clock!" He smiled as he daydreamed about all the possibilities.

As the taxi pulled up, Noah noticed his old roommate and college buddy, Travis Jones, stood waiting for him.

Travis was elated to see Noah. "Loser! Get over here and give me some love!"

Noah grinned as he ran over and gave his pal a big hug. "Trav, you suck, seriously!" Both men laughed and headed to the bar overlooking the Naha Harbor.

Travis looked around before he spoke. "Noah, I need to ask, man, were you followed?"

It did not occur to Noah that there was a need to be cautious. "Except for the stewardess I banged on the flight, I spoke to no one."

Travis gave Noah an intense stare and replied in a serious tone, "I just needed to check. Man, we are in some serious shit and it is going to be more intense."

Noah ordered a couple of beers for him and his pal. He casually replied, "So, Travis, how is it coming together?"

Travis looked around again before he quietly responded, "Everything is going according to plan. Your protégé, Regina Kendall, won't be practicing law anymore. Jack Kendall isn't leaving Portugal anytime soon."

Noah grinned back at Travis and joked, "Outstanding! Now, when do I get paid?"

Travis became concerned about Noah's nonchalant attitude. "What? You got paid! I deposited $1,000,000 in Bitcoin into your exchange account in Vietnam. What the fuck are you talking about?"

Noah smirked and playfully asked, "Yes. Thanks for that. How about the balance?"

Travis leaned over to this friend and whispered in his ear, "When the data flows back to Xiamen, China, we will all get paid."

Noah slowly came to the realization of what the bigger picture really looked like. "Got it, thanks!" Travis tried not to show his growing impatience with Noah.

Noah asked, "So, why am I here, man? Okinawa? I am sure it is a great place, but I don't get it."

Travis took a drink of his beer and ordered Noah, "We have something developing here. I need you to sit tight and out of sight for a while. Once the data hack in Taiwan goes down, we will need to establish a new base of operations here in Okinawa. Just lie low, see the sights, and most of all, behave yourself."

Travis and Noah were completely unaware that their plan was already unraveling.

Chapter 25
Evergreen

Taipei Marriott (Taipei, Taiwan)

Jack arrived in Taipei after initially landing in Mumbai, India. The air was thick and muggy, causing Jack to feel very groggy. As he departed the plane to the main terminal, Jack stopped and looked around to see if he was being followed, especially after what happened to him in Portugal. Standing in a corner for a few minutes, he adjusted his glasses and continued to look around for anyone who looked suspicious. Jack proceeded through the health screener station and then to passport control.

While in line, Jack noticed three Chinese men, all with short hair, moving ahead to the front of the line. "I bet they are Chinese diplomats," Jack whispered to himself.

Jack surrendered his passport and after a few questions, the customs officer stamped his book with an entry to Taiwan. He went into the bathroom and noticed two of the three Chinese diplomats made the same stop. Jack stayed guarded while using the restroom and then departed without making any eye contact. He proceeded to baggage claim to collect this luggage. Jack could not see any of the Chinese diplomats. They were nowhere to be seen.

Jack concentrated on gathering his bags. After he picked his bags off the luggage carousel, he headed to the International Gallery. This place reminded him of Vietnam; a long line of taxi drivers honking and shouting, "Need a ride? Taipei Marriott? Hilton?" After getting in line for a taxi, he checked his messages. He received a new message from his bike tour guide that Forest hired.

Jack Kendall, this is Li Cao, your cycling guide. I am here at the Taipei Marriott. Please text me when you arrive.

Signed,

Li

Jack appreciated the message and responded back to Li while getting into a taxi.

Thank you, Ms. Cao. I should arrive at the hotel within the hour.

Signed,

Jack

Jack watched the taxi weave in and out of traffic at high speed heading into Taipei. He focused out the window to avoid getting sick. "This place is so beautiful, very green." He noticed the beautiful mountains of Taiwan covered in miles of trees. "I see why this place is famously known as evergreen," Jack whispered to himself.

As the taxi approached Taipei, the capital of Taiwan, he noticed the vast building called the 101. One of the tallest buildings in the world, the 101, became the financial and technology center of business for all of Taiwan and its business partners. Within a few minutes, Jack arrived at the Taipei Marriott. The bellhop helped Jack with his bags.

Jack approached the front desk and introduced himself.

The front desk manager replied, "Mr. Kendall, thank you for being a platinum reward member of Taipei Marriott. We have reserved a suite for you on the top floor next to the pool."

Jack smiled and thanked the manager for the upgrade.

"We will send your bags up to your room. I believe you have a guest waiting for you in the lounge," the hotel manager informed.

Jack remembered that his cycling guide would be waiting for him. He thanked the manager again and headed over to the lounge. Jack looked around the room for Li and realized that he had no idea what she looked like.

Li saw a tall American that matched Jack's description and called out, "Mr. Kendall? I am Li Cao, your guide. Thank you for coming to Taiwan. Your bike will arrive tomorrow. Would you like to join me for tea?"

Jack greeted and shook Li's hand. "Thank you, please, call me Jack." He liked Li's kind face and strong presence.

"Jack, thank you for hiring me. I am a retired schoolteacher and I have been hosting bike tours now for two years. Based on what Mr. Adams requested, you want to start here and cycle to Jiufen Street first, correct?"

Jack was still jet lagged from his twenty-six-hour flight from Portugal. With a tired voice, he answered, "Yes, I would like to stop in Yilan, Hualien, Taitung, and end up at Kaohsiung in five days. Li, if you don't mind, I am going to crash. After being on such a long flight, I am wiped out."

Li stood up from her chair and shook Jack's hand before departing for her room. Jack finished his tea before heading over to the elevators.

As he entered his room, Jack considered sending a message to Forest but held back because of Ms. Bui's medical condition. Jack proceeded to say a prayer instead.

Dear Lord, please take care of my dear friend Ms. Bui. She will be joining you soon. With her help, I found those nuns in Saigon. She also looked after me in my time of need. Please take care of Forest as well. Amen.

After drifting off to sleep for a few hours, Jack woke up from a terrible nightmare. "Nella!" Jack screamed. Now fully awake, he sat up in his bed in Taipei, drenched in sweat. Jack experienced PTSD or Post Traumatic Stress Disorder flashbacks. He relived the day the Frenchman killed Nella. He had trouble sleeping because he carried the guilt of not protecting Nella.

"If I was in better shape, I could have run to the top of that hill in time to save her!" Jack continued to punish himself. He mumbled in anguish, "Oh God, please look after her." Jack tried to fall back asleep.

Jack got dressed in the morning and headed down to the breakfast buffet. After finding the restaurant on the first floor of the Taipei Marriott, Jack noticed Li sitting alone by the window.

"May I?" Jack asked.

Li answered, "Please."

Jack ordered a triple espresso and headed to the buffet for breakfast. When Jack returned to the table, Li had a very concerned look on her face. "What is wrong, Li?"

Li sadly replied, "Two people were murdered yesterday in Taichung. Their throats were slashed. The police believe the Triads were involved."

Jack froze after Li mentioned the Triads. "Are they a problem here on the island?"

Li lived in Taiwan her whole life. She was well acquainted with the Triads. "Yes, since I was a little girl, they have been part of the island's culture. They deal in drugs, human trafficking, and murder."

Jack asked, "Do they have a rival?"

Li was confused by Jack's question, however, she answered, "Well, on the east end of the island, there is a long history of Japanese influence dating back to World War II. Many Taiwanese living in the east end have Japanese roots. My grandfather was Japanese. He married my grandmother after the war. Wherever there is Japanese, there is Yakuza."

Jack turned pale and looked at Li. "Yakuza? Here in Taiwan?"

Li tried to change the subject and replied, "So, your bike will arrive today. Let's discuss our plan."

Jack was ready to get down to business with Li and said, "Yes, please. How far is it to cycle to Jiufen Street?"

Li responded, "Forty-four kilometers from the train station in Yilan."

Jack planned the next stop to be Yilan and asked, "And how far is Yilan?"

Li replied, "We will need to catch the 8:00 a.m. train to Yilan."

Jack and Li departed the hotel after assembling his Cevelo S5. Li grabbed the helmets, the cycling safety gear, and carried them out to the front of the hotel. "Jack, follow me. This way to the train station," Li said.

Jack cycled behind Li while they swerved around the traffic in downtown Taipei. "Li, watch ahead of you!" Jack hollered.

Li slowed down and yelled, "Thanks, Jack."

Jack felt dizzy so he decided to pull over on his bike. He collapsed on the road and screamed, "Nella!" Li noticed Jack had stopped and heard him scream in panic. She turned her bike around and headed back to check on him.

"Jack, what happened? Are you okay?" Li asked with great concern in her voice.

"I am good, Li, thanks," Jack said.

Li looked at Jack and noticed his hands were shaking. "Jack, take a deep breath for me, please." She tried to calm him down.

Jack listened to Li and took a few deep breaths. "I am good." Jack collected himself, rose to his feet, and mounted his bike. "Thank you, Li," Jack replied gratefully.

Li walked back to her bike and rode off. After ten minutes, they arrived at the train station.

"Jack, we will need to check in our bikes at the security booth before we can board the train," Li instructed.

Jack followed Li down the stairs. After a check by the train station security, Li and Jack were allowed to proceed to the platform. Li booked two tickets to Yilan on the cycle boarding section of the train.

"Here, Jack, strap your bike there and have a seat." Li pointed to the back of the train.

"Thank you for having my back, Li." She smiled as Jack strapped his bike to the inside of the train.

Li sat back in her seat to rest while looking over at Jack with a peaceful smile.

Chapter 26
EverAfter

Hospice Room (Saigon/HCMC, Vietnam)

Ms. Bui spoke to her darling husband, Forest Adams, "My love, thank you for saving me all those years ago at the embassy gate in Saigon."

Forest remembered himself as a young U.S. Marine embassy guard during the fall of Saigon, on April 30th, 1975. "My Bui, I tried to lift you to safety," Forest reminisced.

Bui remembered the fateful date very well and whispered, "I know, my love; you came back for me. I will love you forever."

Ms. Bui, suffering from breast cancer, knew these were her last hours. "Forest, do you have any family left in America?"

Forest shook his head. "No, my parents died years ago, and I have no family. Only you, my Bui."

Bui cried and begged Forest, "Promise me you will find Jack. Be with him and look after him, please."

Forest teared up at the words from his wife. "I will, my darling. I promise."

As Forest held Bui's hand, he felt her grip loosen up. Heartbroken, he cried, "Bui, please stay with me!"

Bui, tilting her head to Forest, declared, "I love you, my Forest, always." With these words, Bui drew her last breath and went to her place in heaven.

Forest felt a complete sense of loss surging through him. He cried and held Bui's hand for several minutes. He reached up and closed her eyes. One last time, he kissed her on her forehead. The rest home assistants came over to comfort Forest as they moved Ms. Bui to the burial preparation room.

"Mr. Adams, we are very sorry for your loss. Please, come with us," the burial coordinator requested.

Forest walked down the hall of the rest home in Singapore. He noticed a message from Jack. Not having the strength now to answer, Forest put the device away in his pocket. After he spent an hour with the burial coordinator, Forest asked the rest home to cremate the body and place Ms. Bui's ashes in a gold urn for him to take back to Vietnam. She hoped to be buried in her home country of Vietnam.

"Please, let me know once the urn is ready?" Forest was barely able to speak through his grief.

Forest stepped outside into the courtyard of the rest home. He broke out his communicator to answer Jack.

Message to Jack: Bui has passed today. I will bring her back to Vietnam in a few days. She asked me to look after you, Marine.

Signed,

Forest

Jack received the message from his old friend and wept silently. He loved Ms. Bui very much. Ms. Bui was a tremendous help to him on his journey to find the Catholic nuns from Operation Babylift. It was Ms. Bui who helped find the location of the nuns and helped Jack complete a life journey to meet them.

Message to Forest, I am deeply sorry, my dear friend. I loved her too.

Signed,

Jack

Forest received the message and was grateful for Jack's quick reply. Ms. Bui's death was too fresh for Forest to receive any comfort.

Message to Jack. Marine, let me know whatever you need. I am here for you. I made a promise to Bui to look after you.

Signed,

Forest

Jack received the second message. He felt a tight bond with Forest because of Ms. Bui. Forest helped Jack in Saigon (HCMC) every time he ran into problems with the local authorities.

Message to Forest: Yes, Sir, when you're on the ground in Vietnam, please check on a bank in Danang.

Signed,

Jack

Forest wiped away his tears.

Message to Jack, Roger that Marine.

Signed,

Forest

Chapter 27
Ascension
Notre Dame Cathedral (Saigon/HCMC, Vietnam)

"We are gathered here today to say goodbye to Bui Liu Nguyen Adams," Father Flanagan chanted. He was the Catholic priest who served in Vietnam before the end of the war in 1975. He knew Ms. Bui and Forest Adams very well. The priest had been a part of the Notre Dame Cathedral in Saigon for forty three years. Father Flanagan had not only witnessed many people perish, he had buried many of them as well. Today, the funeral service for Bui was especially heartbreaking for the priest.

"I knew this lovely woman since she was seventeen years old. At the end of the war, she tried to climb the fence at the US Embassy, only to be pulled back into the crowd. A young American Marine desperately tried to lift her to safety, however, he was pulled away. It was a horrific day," Father Flanagan whispered solemnly.

Forest sat alone in the church. He was the only person attending the service for his beloved wife.

Father Flanagan continued, "On that terrible day, April 30th, 1975, a new life was born in the eyes of God. I picked up Ms. Bui and instructed her to come with me to this church. I also thanked the young Marine for trying to save her."

Forest bowed his head. "I remember that day very well, Father. I cannot thank you enough for saving her."

The priest's eyes watered, "Forest, thank you for coming to Vietnam years later to find her." The priest began to pray. "Father, we ask, that you receive your child, Bui, into the place where tears are no more. We ask that you grant remittance of her sins. We plead that she will be allowed to enter your Heaven. In the Name of the Father, and of the Son, and the Holy Spirit, Amen."

Forest repeated, "Amen."

"This concludes the celebration of life for our beloved Bui. Go in Peace," Father Flanagan said. Forest rose from the church pew and gave the priest a hug. "Forest, I will place her ashes here in the parish mausoleum, where she can reside forever. I will set aside a spot for your ashes right next to her, my son, when it is your time." Forest thanked the priest. Father Flanagan asked Forest to sit down. He motioned towards a pew in the back row of the church. "My son, how are you holding up?" The priest asked with great compassion.

"Bui was my life," Forest said.

The priest knew this to be true and asked, "Whatever happened to that American who came here to buy a water company so many years ago?"

Forest gave a small smile and replied, "Oh, you mean Jack Kendall. Yes, he is knee-deep in blood and guts again. Some Marines never change."

The priest smiled back at Forest. "You never did either, Forest. There you were on that terrible day in 1975, trying to save an orphaned girl."

Forest looked at the priest and asked, "Father, did you know her dying wish?"

The priest shook his head no. "What was her dying wish?"

Forest answered, "Bui asked me to look after Jack."

Father Flanagan took a moment and looked away. "That woman, she will be a saint someday," the priest said.

Forest sat in the cathedral in Saigon recalling the past. He had returned in 2004 after the U.S. built a new consulate in Vietnam. He remembered seeing Bui for the first time after thirty years. He recalled how they both cried and promised never to leave each other's side. The priest was overcome with emotions.

"Father? Are you going to be, okay?" Forest asked Father Flannagan as he handed an envelope. "Thank you, Father, for all you have done for Bui and me. Please let me know if you and your parish need any assistance. God bless you, Father." Forest was filled with gratitude and sadness at the same time.

"Son, I am in God's hands. Go. Take care of Jack," Father Flanagan lovingly admonished Forest.

Forest got up and gave the priest one last hug and headed for the door. Both men were fully aware they would not see each other again.

"Goodbye, my son." The priest made the sign of the cross as he blessed Forest.

Chapter 28
Take Down

Saigon Commercial Bank (Saigon Commercial Bank, Danang, Vietnam)

"Good afternoon, Mr. Adams, welcome to our bank," Thi Ngoc, the administrator for the CEO of Saigon Commercial Bank, said.

"Good afternoon. I'm here to meet with your chairman. Please, let him know that Forest Adams is here."

Thi reached for her phone to ring the chairman's executive assistant. "Mr. Adams is here to see Mr. Hyunn."

"Mr. Adams, please proceed to the elevator. Select the tenth floor."

Forest thanked Thi and headed off to meet with the chairman of Saigon Commercial Bank Danang Vietnam branch.

"Mr. Adams, what a great honor, sir," said Jun Hyunn, Chairman of Saigon Commercial Bank.

Forest was amused by his host and replied, "Well, I am glad you remember me, Jun. I came here because I need your help and time is not on my side."

Jun motioned to the couch. "Sit. Coffee?"

Forest said yes to the coffee and continued, "I am retired now from the CIA. I just buried my wife here in Saigon. I am doing this to help my friend and my country. Something bad is going on in Taiwan."

Jun listened to his old friend. "Go on."

"We believe the Chinese PLA Cyber has a backdoor into the entire TAINET network in Taiwan through a rogue fiber connection.

$20,000,000 in funds was diverted to a bank here in Danang from the World Bank account under the name of Dragon Vault, LLC."

Jun heard the name and instantly turned pale. He turned away from Forest and said, "Forest, I owe you so much for the years you helped my family. Please be careful about what you are getting ready to ask me."

Forest knew Jun had some knowledge about the funds. "Jun, we are on the clock. I need to know what happened to the money."

Jun walked towards the door and said, "Forest, please, leave. I have nothing to say."

Forest stood up from the couch and said, "Jun, let me put this in a different light. If the president of the United States catches wind that Vietnam had something to do with this data theft, you will move from the most favored nation status with him to a pile of shit next to Iran and North Korea." Forest was stern in his warning.

Jun closed the door and walked back to his desk. "After this we are even, Forest," Jun cautioned.

Forest understood.

Jun informed Forest, "The funds were deposited into the Dragon Vault, LLC, account three months ago. The law firm in the US allowed a Treksussia construction company with access to the funds to build a science communications center sixty-five kilometers east of here, somewhere deep in the jungle near the Laos and Thailand border. They leveraged the bank to make payments to several suppliers from Russia and Iran."

Forest took notes and encouraged him. "Go on, Jun."

"A lawyer named Travis Jones ordered the fund transfers to a group calling themselves, Emerald Forest. We do not know who they are or what they are. The rest of the funds were wired to a Russian construction company. I sent a surveyor out there last week to take pictures for insurance records."

Jun reached into his drawer and pulled out a folder. "Here." He handed the folder to Forest. Jun got up from his desk and finished their meeting. "I am going to the bathroom; I should be back in fifteen minutes." He left Forest in his office with the folder.

After Jun's departure, Forest went through the files and took pictures with his camera phone of the contracts and site itself. Forest took note of several microwave communications dish antennas pointing at a ninety-degree angle, facing east.

"That's strange. I need to upload these to William." After copying everything, Forest placed the file back in Jun's drawer and headed out.

Forest headed into the bathroom to find Jun. While washing his hands, Forest whispered under his breath, "Jun, thank you." Without saying a word, Jun headed back to his office. Forest rushed to get out of the bank. He headed back to his hotel room. He pulled out his encoded communicator and sent a message to Jack.

Message to Jack: A site in Vietnam is a communications center built by a Russian company. Call me.

Signed,

Forest

After arriving in Yilan near Jiufen Street, Jack heard his communicator ring with a new message. "Li, I need to get this," Jack said urgently. Li nodded and dismounted her bike. "Li, we need to get to a coffee or tea shop so we can access the Internet."

Li acknowledged and pointed to a tall building fifty meters ahead. "There!"

Jack and Li quickly remounted and pedaled their bikes to the coffee shop and quickly jumped off.

"Li, I need to get online. Could you order me an espresso, please?" Jack asked hurriedly.

Li answered, "Of course. I will be upstairs. I will get us a table."

Jack answered his phone. "Forest, when did you arrive in Vietnam?"

Forest had just arrived at this hotel in Danang and said, "I came to Vietnam to bury Bui."

Jack remembered Bui's passing with great sympathy. "I am sorry. May your beloved Bui rest in peace, forever."

Forest stayed silent for a moment and then spoke. "Jack, I am here chasing the missing $20,000,000. I found the bank in Danang and met with Chairman Jun. Long story short, your boy, Travis Jones, hired a Russian construction company to build a communications center near the Laos border. The bank also sent funds to an organization called Emerald Forest. I will upload these pictures for you now. Check out the microwave dishes."

Jack walked up to the top floor of the tea shop in Yilan, Taiwan. He replied to Forest, "Okay, let me get settled first. I need to get those pictures sent to William. Let me call you back." Forest acknowledged and hung up.

Jack dialed William and sent the photos. "Will, it's Dad. The $20,000,000 went to a Russian construction company and some outfit called Emerald Forest. Does any of this make sense to you?" Jack asked.

William answered, "I have been on the Darknet chatting with Sword-Bitch. He is the lead hacker from the San-Hamada Yakuza group. Let me send this to him and I will let you know."

Jack heard the word, Yakuza, and answered cautiously, "William, are you speaking to the Yakuza? Those guys are animals."

William heard the concern in his father's voice. He continued, "Dad, SwordBitch is the leader behind Rising Sun. This global hacker group runs all cyber for the Yakuza. Their arch enemy is the Fong Gao Triads."

Jack knew where William's plan was going. He cautioned, "Be careful, son. Li and I are here in eastern Taiwan. We are heading to Jiufen Street."

William thought for a moment. "Dad, we need to interface with the San-Hamada himself. He may be in your neck of the woods. Sit tight." William disconnected from his dad.

William received the datafiles, including the pictures of the communications building in Vietnam. "Why the hell are those microwave dishes pointing east?" William brought up a map of Vietnam. He started to geo-locate the position of the communications center... sixty-five kilometers from Danang. "If these microwave dishes are pointing east and they are attempting a line-of-sight communications connection, what are they trying to connect to?"

William searched Binarycore for information on these communications devices. "Russian made, maximum range of line of sight, two hundred kilometers. Holy shit." He drew a digital line on his map two hundred kilometers from the location of the communications center.

"That would put it here, one-hundred-forty kilometers in the middle of the South China Sea." William looked again at the pictures then messaged SwordBitch.

Message to SwordBitch: a hacker site in Vietnam recently built a communications depot, using line-of-sight microwave to the South China Sea. Some outfit called Emerald Forest received rogue funding from the PLA. We have an asset on the ground near Jiufen Street in Yilan.

Signed,

Knight2Rouk7

Asleep in his car in Tokyo after a long night of partying, Sword-Bitch checked his communicator device. While reading the message from William Kendall, he noticed the name, Emerald Forest. "Shit! You've got to be kidding me. Those guys surfaced?" He wiped the sand from his eyes and sent a reply message.

Encoded message to Knight2Rouk7: Darknet 24. Emerald Forest, rival hacking group out of Laos. Triads control them. We want them dead. Tell your asset to head to Jiufen Street, climb the steps to the top, tea house on the right, center table with the view. Look for the San-Hamada.

Signed,

SwordBitch

William read the message from SwordBitch and yelled, "Hell yes!" He reached for his phone to send a message to his dad.

SwordBitch confirmed. Emerald Forest is a rogue hacking group out of Laos. The Fong Gao Triad controls them. He got you a meeting with a Yakuza boss; you need to get to Jiufen Street quickly. Here are the instructions. Climb the steps to the top of the street, enter the last tea house on the right, center table overlooking the view, got it?

Signed,

William

Jack read the message from William and said to himself with pride, "Got it Will, well done!" He redirected his attention back to Li. "Li, we've got to go. I need to meet someone!"

Jack and Li got on their bikes and headed off to the meeting location. Arriving within minutes, Jack instructed Li to stay with the bikes.

Li said, "I understand. I will go do some shopping."

Jack climbed the steps up an alley near Jiufen Street. He had to stop several times to catch his breath before he reached the top. He entered the last tea house and walked to the tables with the view of the sea. Jack noticed a couple sitting at one table and a man sitting by himself at another table. He walked cautiously towards the man sitting alone. Jack took note of two enormous men sitting at a table behind the gentleman.

"Bodyguards. That must be him," Jack thought to himself. He walked up to the table and noticed the man had two sections of his pinky and ring finger missing from both hands. Seeing the missing fingers, Jack knew it was the Yakuza leader.

"Sit down, Mr. Kendall," the Yakuza leader ordered. Jack sat down and the man poured him a cup of tea. "I am San-Hamada. So, you want access to Rising Sun?"

Jack, not knowing much about the hacker group, Rising Sun, answered, "Yes, my son is having conversations with their leader."

The man snapped back at Jack. "I am the leader! They work for me."

Jack stared back at the man and said, "I respect that, sir."

The man took a sip of his tea before responding. "So, our Triad colleagues are planning to hack TAINET. Why is this a concern for my organization, Mr. Kendall?"

Jack gazed over at the men protecting San-Hamada and said, "If they steal the data, they can access your information and turn it over to the Chinese PLA Cyber."

San-Hamada stared back at Jack and snarled, "Kendall, nice try. The Triads will never touch our data, plus our data is fully encrypted and protected by Rising Sun."

Jack considered his next choice of words carefully, then spoke. "The Triads have activated Emerald Forest. They are operational and running out of secret locations in Vietnam."

San-Hamada put his tea down and gruffly stated, "Those Laotians are trash, Mr. Kendall. They are no match for my hackers."

Jack replied, "We believe they are being controlled by the PLA Cyber, under the command of General Vo."

San-Hamada smirked at Jack and chuckled. "Vo, huh? He has been chasing us for years."

Jack thought he was making some progress with San-Hamada. He continued, "Sir, we need access to Rising Sun to stop this hack from happening."

San-Hamada indulged in some more tea and then continued, "Mr. Kendall, what you are asking from us is impossible. Rising Sun only serves me and my organization; we are not guns for hire."

Jack sat back in his chair and respectfully asked, "Sir, without your team, we will not stop this from happening. After Taiwan, will they attack Okinawa and mainland Japan next?"

San-Hamada laughed back at Jack and said, "Mr. Kendall, the Chinese PLA Cyber and Triads would not dare."

After a few minutes, San-Hamada motioned to his protection team to let them know that he was ready to leave. "I need to go, Mr. Kendall. I regret that this beautiful country is about to lose a vast amount of data. However, this is not my problem."

Jack was determined to change San-Hamada's mind and implored, "Sir, there must be something I or the U.S. Government could provide as a token of our appreciation for your help?"

San-Hamada laughed again. "You and your government have nothing to offer me to give you access to Rising Sun!"

Jack thought about everything that had transpired so far. He watched San-Hamada walk toward the exit of the tea shop. Jack stopped San-Hamada with a bold statement. "We know where Vulturess is!"

San-Hamada stopped and glared back at Jack. Hearing the name Vulturess got San-Hamada's attention. He cautioned Jack. "Mr. Kendall, be very careful with what you are saying."

Jack stood up at the tea table and spoke with defiance. "We know where she is, San-Hamada."

San-Hamada turned around, walked back to Jack, stared into Jack's eyes, and demanded, "Go on!"

"Give us access to Rising Sun immediately and we will give you Vulturess!" Jack insisted.

San-Hamada waved his protection detail away and asked, "Anything else, Mr. Kendall?"

Jack took a sip of his tea and replied, "Yes, I need one heart attack, two drownings, and one poisoning."

San-Hamada narrowed his eyes at Jack and said, "Interesting." San-Hamada went back to the tea table and grabbed his secured communicator. "Mr. Kendall, give me a moment." Jack backed away from the table and went to the balcony for some fresh air.

Secured node request: Rising Sun: encryption: message to SwordBitch, Americans have located Vulturess. Fresh intel being sent. Proceed with providing assets for Taiwan counter-hack.

Signed,

San-Hamada

SwordBitch checked all his messages. His heart rate went up as he read the message from his boss. "Oh shit! They know who Vulturess is!"

SwordBitch switched his communicator to send William a message.

Secured Encoded message: Darknet24: message to Knight2Rouk7, permission granted, Rising Sun at your disposal. Send ID and location of Vulturess asap.

Signed,

SwordBitch

"Mr. Kendall, there is another matter. Vulturess made off with a $100,000,000 in crypto currency last year. We want it back," San-Hamada growled.

Jack looked at San-Hamada and assured him. "I will see what I can do."

San-Hamada headed for the door and saluted Jack. "Goodbye, Mr. Kendall."

Jack headed downstairs to find Li. He found the bikes chained up to a post. While looking around, Jack was not aware that Li was watching him from a distance.

After a few minutes, Li's phone rang. "Li, this is Forest Adams. Is Jack with you?"

Li remembered that Mr. Adams had hired her to take care of Jack and answered, "Yes Mr. Adams, he is about ten meters from me."

Forest once again implored Li, "Thank you, Li. That is good. Continue to look after him, please."

Li acknowledged and hung up. "Jack," Li called.

Jack looked over and waved at Li. "We need to go," Jack called.

Li ran over to the bikes and asked, "Where to?"

Jack pulled out his phone and showed Li a map Sunny Ho had sent him. He told Li, "We need to get this node; this is a possible hacked connection into TAINET."

Li did not understand anything Jack said. She advised Jack, "That location is fifteen kilometers south of here. We can get there in an hour if we hurry."

Jack and Li headed off on their bikes. Jack called Sunny while navigating on his bike. "Sunny, this is Jack. We are one hour away from node seventy-six."

Sunny checked his fiber map and reported, "Jack, that node has not been touched in years."

Jack acknowledged Sunny and replied, "Yes, but did Tang go near this location recently?"

Sunny checked Lilian Tang's phone records and GPS. "Oh shit, she was there two days ago."

Jack replied, "I will call you once I am there."

After spending nearly 12 hours in the air cargo container, Lilian arrived in Naha, Okinawa. She could finally hear and feel the cargo container being opened and yelled, "About time!"

Several armed men surrounded the container. "Tang, come with us," the Triad leader ordered. Lilian was escorted by the armed men towards the door leading to the airport hangar.

"Go!" The Triad leader signaled to Lilian.

Lilian looked at the man with confusion and questioned, "What, I am free to leave?"

The Triad leader handed a phone to Lilian.

"Tang, this is Bao. Go and hide out somewhere in Okinawa. Your funds are available. General Vo wanted you dead," Bao said.

Lilian heard the chilling orders from Bao and replied, "Right." She headed out the door and ran towards an opening in the fence at the Naha airport. After spending several hours in the container, she was sweaty, dirty, and hungry. She entered a restaurant and requested, "One for lunch and where is the bathroom?"

The waitress motioned to the back of the restaurant. Lilian headed to the bathroom. After taking a restroom break and cleaning herself up as best as she could, she walked to her table for some food. Due to exhaustion and hunger, Lilian failed to notice the video camera recording everyone in the diner.

SwordBitch acknowledged the orders from San-Hamada and messaged William.

Encoded message: Darknet 24: encryption: Message to Knight2Rouk7, orders received. Rising Sun at your service. Execution of Phase 1 attack imminent. We will try to block external access to the TAINET firewalls. We suspect the hacker group in Vietnam will attempt to hack The Internet of Things network.

Signed,

SwordBitch.

"Oh, shit!" William thought to himself.

Chapter 29
Devastation

General Vo was prepared for his plan to unfold. He moved up the timetable for the execution of Operation Dragon Vault.

Message to Dragon Vault: Move timetable to zero hour, execute underwater connection. Activate Emerald Forest. Begin data exfiltration.

Signed,

Vo

Abe, CEO of Fiberex, read the general's flash message and panicked. "We are not ready!"

Travis Jones was still hiding out in Okinawa. He read the message and exclaimed, "Oh shit, are you kidding me!" Travis moved to a separate communicator to send a message.

Message: encode encryption: Message to Emerald Forest, activate connection to TAINET when ready. Commence application bots deployment on all Internet of Things sensors.

Signed,

Jones

Yu Wong was the lead hacker for Emerald Forest. He messaged back to Travis.

Message: encode encryption: message to Jones. Threat vector attack sequence activated.

Signed,

Wong

Sunny Ho, CEO of ADConnect, reviewed his fiber mapping again to help Jack find the rogue connection when he received a flash message alert.

Sir, this is Yilan security operations, we are now seeing possible cyberattack across all TAINET nodes. The hackers are attempting to load up remote access tools inside the Internet of Things network.

Sunny ran out of his office and down the hall to his secured network center in Taipei. "Show me where the data is flowing! Lock down the firewalls. Block all external data traffic from leaving the island!" Sunny demanded.

The security operations team became quickly overwhelmed with the volume of attacks hitting the TAINET network. They attempted to login to the firewalls. The system operator yelled, "Chief, we are being blocked from accessing the firewalls!"

Seeing the attack unfold, Poppy performed her part of the plan by hacking into the ADConnect firewall systems by changing the passwords. This immediately prevented ADConnect from logging in.

"Right, asshole! I got your passwords!" Poppy was pleased with herself.

Poppy continued to monitor the Darknet for any messages from Rising Sun or Knight2Rouk7. By successfully blocking access to the firewalls, she ensured that all the data from the TAINET network passed through the

Dragon Vault Fiber connection back to Xiamen. "The hack of the century is on!" Poppy laughed in satisfaction.

Sunny reached for his phone and spoke frantically, "William? Sunny Ho, here. The attack is on. The hackers jacked our firewalls. We can't stop the data from leaving Taiwan."

William heard the panic in Sunny's voice and tried to remain calm. He replied, "Sunny, let me get on with Rising Sun." William moved to his secured laptop that was specifically built for access to the Darknet.

Message: encode encryption: Darknet24: SwordBitch. Attack on TAINET has started. ADConnect has lost all control for external firewalls. They can't stop the data from leaving. Need assistance, ASAP.

Signed,

Knight2Rouk7

SwordBitch had already sent the attack order for all the Rising Sun resources to begin their attack on Fiberex and Emerald Forest. "Shit!" SwordBitch yelled.

Message: encode encryption: Darknet 24: Knight2Rouk7, attack from Rising Sun activated already. Send location and ID now for Vulturess as part of the deal.

Signed,

SwordBitch

William uploaded into the Darknet24 chat room the complete biography of Lilian Tang, aka Vulturess. SwordBitch was still monitoring his hacking teams' progress when he saw the upload from William.

"Well, Lilian Tang," SwordBitch said.

SwordBitch downloaded the encrypted file and forwarded the contents to San-Hamada. *Message: Darknet24: SwordBitch to San-Hamada: Boss, file download from US source, target ID complete.*

San-Hamada sat in a private tea shop in Taitung, Taiwan, reading the incoming message from his hacker leader. "Vulturess! Finally! I got you!" He relished in getting his revenge on Lilian Tang.

SwordBitch turned his attention to the attack on TAINET. He messaged his hackers. *Message to all groups: focus on blocking data from leaving Taiwan, signed SwordBitch.*

The Rising Sun Hacker Team Four was feverishly working on hacking Fiberex. They traced all external network connections into the Chinese city of Xiamen. The team discovered several external connections coming into Fiberex's primary data center.

Message: Encode: Encryption: message to SwordBitch, executing a denial-of-service attack against all external connections into Xiamen.

SwordBitch read the message and screamed, "Rising Sun!"

Abe, CEO of Fiberex, while inside the secured center, saw first-hand the data flow, starting from within Taiwan after this team activated the packet accelerator tool. The applications team activated the stolen software from Cybercom. "Sir, the application is activated. We should see data flow extraction begin at any time."

Sunny Ho observed the data traffic from within the ADConnect network become powerless to stop the data exfiltration from TAINET through the rogue connections. He shouted, "Yuli, get me the president!"

Abe watched his rogue connection and his software suddenly stop work-ing. He noticed the data flow map from his data center in Xiamen, China back to Taiwan through the underwater cable turn red.

"What the hell is that!" Abe shouted.

The Fiberex network engineer realized what was happening. "Sir, the fiber connection is going down. We are under attack! All internet and fiber connections coming into and out of Xiamen have gone down!"

Poppy sat in her safe house and also noticed the data flowing into the TAINET firewalls had stopped. "What the hell is happening?" she won-dered.

Message to Dragon Vault: Encode: encryption: External firewalls showing data is dropping off. Massive connection failure out of the fiber vault, ac-knowledge!

Signed,

Poppy

Abe read Poppy's message and became enraged. "No shit lady! The entire city's connections are down!" Abe muttered to himself.

"Sunny, it's William. Rising Sun is running a denial-of-service attack against the entire city of Xiamen!"

Sunny watched the event unfold and yelled, "Shit! You should know this, William! The whole damn network in Xiamen is down. Those crazy bastards at Rising Sun killed every connection in and out of the city!"

Monitoring his global hacker team's progress, SwordBitch sent an encoded message to team three.

Message: Encode: encryption: Sword to Rising Sun three: confirm submarine IP routing is offline. We need to kill the connection to Emerald Forest.

Rising Sun hacker team three leader Kashi replied,

Message to Sword: still tracking submarine network connections, stand by.

SwordBitch messaged William to give him an updated status.

Message: Encode: Encryption: Darknet24: message to Knight2Rouk7. Denial of service attack working. The stolen data dropped at the external firewalls. Rogue hacker in control now of the ADConnect firewalls. Team 3 is locating an IP relay submarine, attempting to kill connection to Emerald Forest.

Signed,

Sword

William read the encrypted message from SwordBitch and immediately messaged him back.

Message: encode encryption: Darknet24: message to sword, great work. Target rogue hacker: Yellowslayer, aka, Poppy Ledger. PLA Cyber. Location; Vancouver safe house. Request all methods to stop her.

Signed,

Knight2Rouk7

SwordBitch read the updated intelligence from William. "Holy shit! An Australian hacker working for the PLA jacked the firewalls inside of Taiwan. Oh, that is going to be world news for sure!" SwordBitch laughed.

"Hai?" Marcia said.

Hai Ming, Minister of Finance for all of China, sounded shocked to hear from his old schoolmate. "Wow, Marcia, it's been a long time. When was the last time we spoke? Dinner in Boston? Or maybe the surfing lessons in Fiji?"

Marcia tried to keep her wits about her. She replied, "Ah, yes, splendid memories, Hai. I heard you remarried some rich and powerful lady who is only thirty years old?"

Hai made a small cough. "Humm, well, yes. Life moves on, right?"

Marica felt a break in the conversation. "Hai, I need a few minutes on the official business side of things."

Hai was not in the best of moods, especially with the latest trade war between the US and China. The trade war created a negative impact on his country's economy. "Marcia, I have a few minutes. What is on your mind?"

"Hai, we have good intel that your General Vo is up to something. It is highly possibly he is stealing data from Taiwan using stolen American software."

Hai smiled and replied, "The government of China never hacked the Island of Taiwan. Marcia, we don't hack our own people!"

Marcia realized Hai was part of the One China Policy, viewing Taiwan as a province and not a separate state. "Hai, we also believe that your general is leveraging the Fong Gao Triads in Taiwan to pull this operation off."

Hai froze. He had to think for a moment before he replied, "Marcia, if you are bullshitting me, I swear you and I are done!"

Marcia realized that she hit a nerve with her old friend. "Hai, I would not have gone there unless we knew for sure. We also know that the World Bank and some sleazy big law firm in Boston worked together on a project slated for Vietnam. The diverted funds ended up with some underwater cable repair project. The World Bank plans to freeze your deposits until they complete a criminal investigation against Dragon Vault, LLC, and Fiberex."

Hai became completely unhinged by this news. "What? The World Bank wouldn't dare!" Hai protested.

Marcia interrupted, "Hai, calm down for a moment. We also know who the middleman is between Vo and the Triads."

Hai was aware of how important this detail was and commented, "So, Marcia, that information would be useful to me."

Marcia discovered a way to move forward with her friend and diplomatically suggested, "Hai, we would greatly appreciate it if you would investigate this matter on your end. Fiberex stole the code from Cybercom while using PLA cyber assets. We, in America, call this action, state-sponsored espionage."

Hai did not like the direction Marcia was taking. He interrupted, "Hold on, Marcia. Fiberex is a very proud and honorable company. The pride of China!"

Marcia laughed quietly. She retorted, "Yes, I am sure they are Hai, so where do we go from here?"

Hai considered his options before answering, "Marcia, let me check a few things at my end and let me get back to you." Hai hung up the phone.

Marcia sensed anger in her old friend. "Yes, get back to me, asshole!" Marcia fumed at Hai. "Alvin, I need you, SAC Burns, and SA Parker in my office," Marcia ordered.

The FBI director, Alvin Ramsey, heard the order loud and clear and answered, "Yes ma'am, we are on the way." He texted Gerald and Bill to meet immediately in the attorney general's office.

"Ma'am," Alvin respectfully greeted Marcia as he entered her office.

"Sit down, Alvin. I just finished with Ming. Let's move to the secured conference room." Marcia led Alvin to the secured room.

"Alvin, I know what Hai Ming wants. He wants us to drop the dime on Bao Xu. What do we want in return?" Marcia asked.

Alvin replied, "We want General Vo!"

Marcia's eyes narrowed as she spoke. "Alright, what you are saying is we want the head of all PLA cyber security for China in exchange for a middleman to the Triads?"

Alvin nodded. Marcia considered for a moment the option of asking Hai Ming for General Vo. "I don't believe that will happen. Who else?" Marcia asked.

Alvin considered all the players involved with this hacking attack against Taiwan and came up with a name Travis Jones.

"We need Travis Jones. He is the key to the entire plan and possibly all future considerations. We do not know where he is or what he is up to." Alvin explained.

Marcia considered that to be a more acceptable request than General Vo. Just as Marcia was ready to respond, her phone rang.

Marcia answered her phone. "Minister Ming, what a pleasant surprise. We were just discussing you."

Hai was not amused by Marcia's tone. He remarked, "I bet. Look, we want this middleman. There must be someone you want to trade for."

Marcia seized on the opportunity. "Well, yes, Hai, we want Travis Jones."

Hai was confused by the request and asked, "Ah, who the hell is he?"

Marcia replied, "Oh, you don't know him? We believe he is the brains behind this whole Taiwan hack mess!"

Hai became more confused and muttered, "Marcia, I do not know who he is. However, let me check something and get back to you!" Hai hung up the phone.

"Well, that made him crap his pants. I bet he is calling Vo now!" Marcia exclaimed.

Hai entered the name *Travis Jones* into the Chinese secure PLA portal. "Let's see who you are," Hai whispered under his breath. After the system processed the request, a photo and biography appeared on Hai's computer screen. An *access denied* warning appeared on his computer monitor.

Hai slammed his fist down on his desk and reached for his phone. "General Vo, this is Minister Hai!"

Vo was monitoring the cyberattack against Taiwan. He bellowed, "Hai, what do you want? I am busy!"

"I need to know who Travis Jones is!" Hai shouted back.

The mention of Travis's name made the general freeze and ask, "Hai, how did you come by this information?"

Hai sensed he had hit a nerve with the general. He answered, "The American attorney general."

Vo became paralyzed and could not speak a word.

When the General finished his call with Minister Hai, his attack screen data from Operation Dragon Vault turned red. "What the hell is that?" Vo shouted.

The general picked up the phone and yelled, "Poppy, what the hell is going on?"

Poppy monitored the events of the attack. She replied quickly, "General, it looks like someone executed a denial-of-service attack against all external connections coming into Xiamen. The data exfiltration has stopped. We still control the firewalls, but the data is dropping!"

Vo, hearing this, slapped his hand against his computer screen in frustration and bellowed, "Poppy, listen carefully. Fix this!"

"Yes, sir," Poppy answered.

Poppy logged into the Darknet as Yellowslayer on her secondary computer. She sent a message to Rising Sun.

Message: Encode: Encryption: Message to SwordBitch, if you are behind the attack against Xiamen, you are dead! Disconnect now!

Signed,

Yellowslayer

SwordBitch read the encoded message from Yellowslayer and responded.

Message: Encode: Encryption: Dual send message: Yellowslayer and Knight2Rouk7: message: Yellowslayer, don't threaten me, Poppy Ledger, we are Rising Sun! We can get to you!

Signed,

SwordBitch

Poppy read the encoded message. "Damn! How did he know it was me?" Poppy realized SwordBitch also copied Knight2Rouk7.

"William," Poppy whispered.

William caught the message from SwordBitch. He said to himself quietly, "Shit, Poppy." William moved back to his computer to send a secured message to his father.

Message to task force: Global hacker, Poppy Ledger, identified in Darknet as Yellowslayer; is the rogue hacker controlling the TAINET firewalls. Recommend a complete remote serial connection reboot to kill her connection.

Signed,

William

Sunny read the flash message from William. "What? A freelance hacker for the PLA has control over my firewalls?" He contacted the security operations team in Yilan and ordered, "Operations, execute a full reboot of all external firewalls and reset the password to manual override."

The operations team rebooted all 350 external firewall clusters designed to protect all the data in Taiwan.

Lead engineer Voung replied, "Sir, we will have systems up within the hour. All traffic leaving the island is now safely blocked."

Poppy realized that she lost her remote access connection into TAINET. "What the hell?" Poppy shouted in frustration and sent a message.

Message to Dragon Vault: firewall access lost. The ADConnect team is rebooting all firewalls. All data leaving the island has stopped. Advise on next course of action.

Signed,

Poppy

After reading the message from Poppy, he messaged her back.

Poppy, you are dead if you don't get back online!

Poppy realized that the entire operation depended on getting all the data off the island. Without firewall access, the general would eliminate her. She thought about how to escape the safe house.

Sunny watched on his secured monitoring system. The entire TAINET network went off offline.

The president called Sunny. "Sunny, tell me you did this?"

"Madame President, yes, I gave the order to reboot all external connections off the island. We, thanks to some help, blocked the data from leaving the island. However, a rogue hacker somewhere in Vancouver controlled our external firewalls. This reboot will kick her off and allow us back in control again."

The president did not approve of the entire Internet network in Taiwan going down. However, she realized it prevented a devastating cyberattack from happening. "Sunny, get this network back online!"

Jack was en route to Kaohsiung with Li when he checked his encrypted message. "Oh, shit!" Jack cursed.

Li was asleep next to Jack on the train. She woke up and asked, "What happened, Jack?"

Jack looked over at Li and explained, "The attack has started."

Chapter 30
Return

Train to Kaohsiung (Taiwan)

Jack tried to read all the messages and realized that the entire Internet in Taiwan had gone offline. "What happened? I can't get to my messages." Jack woke Li up and asked, "Please check your phone."

Li sat up and checked her phone. "Mine is not working."

General Vo was scared that the attack had failed and unsuccessfully tried to call Poppy. "Why is she not picking up?" Vo wondered why as he tried to not panic.

Poppy noticed her phone was ringing. She became filled with fear when she saw that it was the general trying to reach her. She paced inside the safe house and began talking to herself. "I can't do this. I am dead. I got to get out of here." She gathered up her passport, money, laptops, a few items of clothing, and headed out the door.

The Chinese PLA security forces protecting the house did not know what was happening. "Poppy, why are you leaving?"

Poppy knew that if she did not leave immediately, the guards would kill her. She told the guard, "I am heading off for dinner. I will be back shortly." She jumped in the car and started the engine. Poppy headed to the protective gate where the guard motioned her to stop.

"Stop, by order of the general!" he yelled.

Poppy ignored the guard and rammed the car through the gate. After an enormous crash, she raced away to escape the PLA guards.

Travis Jones sat in his hotel room in Naha, Okinawa, closely monitoring portions of the attack on Taiwan. He checked with his chief hacker, Yu, at the top of each hour.

"Yu, talk to me!" Travis yelled.

Yu knew the attack was failing. He replied to Travis, "Sir, all connections through the fiber vault are down. We still have a connection to the submarine relay, however, our connection to the Internet of Things network on Taiwan went down."

Travis realized that something had happened to the overall operation and ordered, "Yu, shut down the hacker site and get everyone back across to Laos."

Yu heard the order directly from Travis and shouted to his team of hackers, "Everyone, code blue start, shutdown and fall back to Laos!"

Within minutes, the Emerald Forest connections went dead. The hacker team quickly assembled into jeeps and raced across the Vietnam jungle back to Laos.

Message: Encode: Encryption: Rising Sun Team Three: message to Sword-Bitch: IP submarine relay off the network. No sign of their IP address or any packets.

Signed,

Rising Sun 3

SwordBitch read the message from Rising Sun 3. "Off the grid? Great!" SwordBitch drafted a new message to William.

Message: Encode: Encryption: Knight2Rouk7: IP relay submarine went deep, off the network, no sign of her IP addresses.

Signed,

SwordBitch

William read the update from SwordBitch. "Well, that is a good thing. Now Emerald Forest is offline as well." William related the same message to the task force team.

Message to task force: Encryption: Rising Sun reports IP relay submarine went deep. Emerald Forest offline, no sign of any IP addresses.

Signed,

William

Jack read the message from William and felt a little relief. "Well, that is good news."

Li looked over at Jack and asked, "What happened?"

Jack replied to Li, "The hacker group in Vietnam is offline now, most likely they are hightailing it back to Laos."

Li didn't fully understand the crisis that Jack was dealing with but she genuinely cared.

Hai Ming pondered his next move against General Vo. He made a quick decision to go to Beijing and ordered, "Get my jet ready. I need to fly to Beijing."

Wie, Hai Ming's administrative assistant, responded, "Yes, sir."

Hai knew he needed to detain General Vo. He placed a call to General Wong. "Internal Security, this is Finance Minister Ming. This is a red envelope level eight secured order. Detain General Vo immediately. Move him to the internal security holding area quickly."

The head of China Internal Security Forces, General Wong, acknowledged the order. "Yes, Minister."

Sunny grabbed his phone and called his assistant. "Yuli, please get me President Fong."

While holding for the president of Taiwan, Sunny checked in with the system operation manager, and requested, "Xia, give me the latest."

"Sir, all external firewalls are back online. We have regained control. We are uploading all system logs so we can locate where the rogue hacking originated from. All Internet of Things sensors have been rebooted and are now functional. All the Internet connections are restored."

Sunny was very pleased with this team. Yuli connected Sunny with the president on the phone. Sunny spoke, "Madame President."

"Sunny, you have ten seconds to tell me we are all good or you're fired!" the president threatened.

Sunny anxiously replied, "We are green and operational, Madame President. All systems and external traffic off the island are operational."

The president felt relieved and grateful. "Sunny, is there a chance the PLA can reconnect back in and do this whole crazy stuff over again?"

Sunny calmed himself down before answering the president. "Yes, we have an asset heading into Kaohsiung to confirm. We know that the Fong Gao Triads have security personnel protecting a building near the harbor. Our asset will be there within the hour."

The president thanked Sunny and hung up. Hearing about the Triads alarmed her greatly. She ordered her assistant, "Hong, get me General Tang of the Taiwan National Police Force on the phone."

As the train to Kaohsiung came to a stop, Li informed Jack that they had reached their destination. "Jack, this is our stop. Let's go."

Jack grabbed their backpacks and bikes and then headed off the train. "Li, we are here at the train depot. We need to get to the warehouse building near the harbor. This looks like a ten kilometer distance by cycle."

Li nodded her head and said, "Okay, let me lead the way."

Jack fixed his bike with the camera so Sunny Ho could monitor their progress.

Jack called Sunny. "Sunny, it's Jack. We are at the station and heading to the warehouse. Please confirm you can view the camera."

Sunny saw the image on the camera and asked curiously, "Jack, who is the lady?"

Jack replied, "My guide."

As Jack and Li headed off on the road leading to the warehouse, Sunny sent a flash message to the task force.

Message: Encode: Flash Traffic :Encryption: message to task force: Asset on the ground in Kaohsiung, 10 km from suspected vault.

Signed

Sunny

Forest read the flash message from Sunny and responded with a quick message.

Good man, Jack, get those guys, Marine.

William also read the message and thought to himself, "Dad, you are truly living the dream again."

Alvin messaged the attorney general.

Ma'am, the cyberattack on Taiwan data stopped before the data could leave the island. An external resource played a big role. The asset on the ground in Taiwan is 10 km from the suspected fiber vault.

Signed,

Alvin

Reading the encoded message from her FBI director, Marcia sighed and snickered to herself. "Asset? Jesus."

Marcia contacted Thomas Wilson personally to let him know Jack was safe.

"Thank you, Madam Attorney General," Thomas Wilson said.

Thomas felt great relief from the news and replied to Marcia, "Thank you for looking after him. He lost his fiancé to these Triads in Portugal a few weeks ago. I hope we can get the guy who ordered the hit. I think his name is Bao."

Marcia was stunned by the revelation from Thomas and said, "Excuse me. You are saying General Vo and Bao Xu ordered the hit on Jack Kendall's fiancé in Portugal?"

Thomas shared a tense moment with Marcia. "I thought you knew."

Marcia became very upset. "Thomas, let me get back to you." Marcia picked up her phone. "Alvin, bring yourself and SIC Burns to my office. ASAP."

Chapter 31
Contender

SAC Gerald Burns, SA Bill Parker, and FBI director Alvin Ramsey headed back to the attorney general's office. "Ma'am, reporting as ordered."

Marcia Robertson looked deeply stressed about the chain of events unfolding over the cyberattack.

Alvin took a seat across from Marcia. She asked Alvin for a status report surrounding the Dragon Vault attack. Alvin reported, "We have the warrants ready to serve the law firm in Boston. The World Bank will freeze all Chinese deposits for the next ten days while they conduct the criminal audit."

Marcia was pleased with the progress. She inquired, "Something has happened to your civilian asset on the ground in Taiwan?"

Gerald answered, "Yes, ma'am. We need to bring him up on the video."

Marcia motioned the team to move into the next room. Her office had access to a twenty-four-hour-a-day WebEx session by Cisco Systems. "Okay, bring up the video."

Gerald connected the various team members to the video call.

"Madame Attorney General, this is Thomas Wilson, CEO of Techline/Globalcom."

Marcia looked up at the screen. "Good to see you again, Mr. Wilson."

Thomas nodded his head in acknowledgment. He introduced William. "This is William Kendall, Chief Architect for Cybercom. He wrote the software that was stolen."

Marcia chose not to acknowledge William and reacted directly to Thomas. "Thomas, would you mind giving us an update on Mr. Kendall?"

Thomas cleared his throat. "Jack made it to Jiufen Street in Eastern Taiwan. He and a cycling guide are heading to Node seventy-six. This node was one of many hacked by the Triads."

Marcia grew impatient and screamed, "People, why do I care?"

Thomas calmly suggested, "Madam AG, let me get Jack on the line."

Thomas texted Jack.

Pull over. I need you on video with the attorney general.

Jack read the incoming message and motioned to Li to pull over. "I got to take this!" Jack called out to Li. After he connected to the WebEx video session, he introduced himself. "Jack, here."

Gerald spoke, "Mr. Kendall, SAC Burns, here. We met at the last video conference. What is your situation on the ground?"

Jack looked at the screen and immediately saw the attorney general of the United States in the room. "Madam Robertson, here is the latest news." Jack took a breath and continued, "We have found the missing $20,000,000. A source in Danang traced the money to a Russian contractor that built a secured communication hacking center. Part of the funds went to a Laotian hacker outfit called Emerald Forest. This hacker group was hired by the Chinese PLA to hack into TAINET. The PLA hired them to prevent the cyberattack from being traced back to Xiamen. William and I have been in contact with San-Hamada. He is the leader of the Yakuza here in Taiwan and in Tokyo. We have recruited San-Hamada's hacker outfit, Rising Sun. This global hacker unit helped block the data theft from happening in Taiwan."

Marcia jumped out of her seat. "You did what? You interfaced with the Yakuza to help stop the Fong Gao Triads?" Marcia stared at Alvin. "Alvin, did you approve of this?"

Jack replied, "The director, Gerald, and Bill have nothing to do with this. We needed to act fast, AG. The Rising Sun hacker unit needed to get activated to stop the data from leaving Taiwan. Our source in Vietnam is—"

Marcia raised her hand and ordered, "Stop! Kendall, who is the source?"

Jack took a moment and replied, "Let me get him on the line."

Jack paused the video and called Forest. "Forest, I need you on the video call with the attorney general."

Forest was lying down in his room in his hotel in Danang when he answered Jack's call. "Alright Marine, patch me in."

Within minutes, Forrest sat in a chair and appeared on the video screen.

"And who are you, sir?" SA Bill Parker of the FBI asked.

Before Forest could answer, Marcia spoke calmly, "Forest Adams."

Forest looked into the camera and said, "Hello, Marcia. It has been a long time."

Marcia walked towards the large screen in the conference room and asked, "Where do you come from? How the hell did you get involved in this?"

Bill was surprised by the exchange between the AG and the unknown gentleman. He reached over to Gerald and whispered, "Who is he?"

Gerald looked back at Bill and answered, "A living legend."

"Marcia," Forest explained, "I am here to help my friend Jack. I confirmed with the chairman of the bank that the $20,0000,000 in stolen funds were used to build a hacker site in the jungle. I uploaded the pictures of the rogue Vietnamese hacker site already to William."

Marcia was still stunned to see Forest Adams again. "Forest, it has been years and not a word."

Forest nodded back to Marcia. "Another time, Marcia. We are on the clock here. Please listen to what Jack has to say."

Marcia drifted back to her chair and stated, "Mr. Kendall, proceed."

Jack cleared his throat and continued, "William is coordinating all cyber assets with the Rising Sun hacker group. I met with San-Hamada an hour ago. He agreed to grant William access to the Rising Sun team in exchange for the identity of the terrorist hacker, Vulturess."

Marcia had no knowledge of who Vulturess was. She asked, "And who is this Vulturess?"

William explained, "A Sea Turtle. A notorious hacker. She bounced from Binarycore years ago for posting a video online. She is the top cyber hacking asset for the Fong Gao Triads and was on loan to General Vo and the PLA."

Marcia heard Vo's name again. "Let me guess, Bao Xu coordinated all of this?"

William looked surprised by her statement and answered, "Yes, ma'am."

Marcia replied, "Okay, do we now have access to the Yakuza hacker squad to take on the Triad's gun for hire in Vietnam, who tried to steal a ton of data from the TAINET network in Taiwan?"

Jack spoke up, "Well, sort of. We know that General Vo used the Emerald Forest hackers to control all the Internet of Things sensors in Taiwan as a pre-attack."

Marcia rubbed her eyes and replied, "Lovely."

Everyone in the room stopped for a moment to process what Marcia had just said.

"AG, if we are going after a known global criminal organization, congress will launch an investigation," Alvin said.

Marcia considered this and then spoke. "Okay, people, here is what we are going to do. Jack and William will handle any issues with the Yakuza. Mr. Wilson, I would suggest you stay far away from this. Alvin, Bill, and Gerald, focus on taking out the law firm and freezing the Chinese funds at the World Bank. Do not mention that any U.S. government employees have been contacted with any members of the Yakuza, Triads, or PLA. Clear?" Everyone acknowledged. She continued with her orders. "Okay, now, no more direct communication going forward until this cyberattack has ended. Copy that?" Everyone agreed.

The video call disconnected without warning. Forest quietly said to himself, "Jack, be careful, Marine."

Li heard the whole story. Jack strongly urged her, "Li, you need to forget everything you just heard." Li slowly nodded.

Jack called Forest. "Forest, thank you for getting on the line."

Forest was still gathering his thoughts when he warned, "Jack, watch your back."

Jack appreciated Forest's concern and responded, "Forest, I will be in touch. Be safe."

Forest hung up with Jack as he stared out the window in his hotel room and prayed, "Take care, Marine."

"Sunny, it's Jack. We are approaching the warehouse." Sunny had a clear view of Jack's video camera on his laptop.

Jack called out to Li. "Li, slow down! Look straight ahead. Do not make any eye contact with the security guards. We need to cycle without looking at the building."

Li acknowledged Jack's instructions. Jack and Li approached the warehouse that was suspected to be Dragon Vault's fiber hub. He saw several men walking around the perimeter of the building.

Sunny advised, "Jack, those are Triads. Do not look at them!" Jack heard Sunny's command. However, his attention was focused on Li who was ahead of him.

Jack ordered Li to look to the right and away from the cameras. Li looked away from the building and pedaled past the harbor.

"Sunny, what's next?" Jack asked.

Sunny looked at his fiber map and directed Jack. "Jack, head north towards Taichung. Follow the coastal path. There, you will find a fiber node that Tang stopped and breached."

Jack relayed the message to Li and instructed, "Keep going north along the coastal path to Taichung."

Li listened to Jack and pedaled faster on her bike.

"Sunny, we are ten kilometers from the vault. Where is the node eighty-six?" Jack asked.

Sunny checked Jack's GPS from his bike, matched it to the fiber vault, and gave directions to Jack to proceed two kilometers north.

"The fiber vault should be next to the light pole on Xua Street and the pier leading to the beach."

Jack motioned Li to follow him. After cycling for several minutes, Jack noticed the steel container box next to the pier leading to the ocean. Jack pedaled faster. He arrived at the box with Li. "I'm in position, Sunny. What do I do?"

Sunny checked his system for the access code and replied, "The code is 67544AA92." Jack entered the code and the door of the secured fiber vault opened.

Jack told Sunny, "Okay, I am in."

Sunny took his notes out to read instructions for Jack. "Jack, pan your camera inside. Look for something new or something that looks out of place." Jack moved his camera phone around the inside of the box to give Sunny the view. "Good, move right, slowly," Sunny directed. "Jack, stop there. Do you see the orange fiber connection? Third one from the right?"

Jack looked inside and reported, "Yes, I can't reach it. My hand is too big."

Li heard the conversation and offered to help. "Let me try. I have small hands."

Jack moved out of the way for Li to reach her hand inside the box.

Sunny addressed Li. "Li, this is Sunny Ho, CEO of ADConnect. Please reach your hand inside. Slowly pull out the orange cable. Don't touch any of the sides."

Li used her steady hand and slowly removed the orange cable. "Done," Li said.

As the cable became loose, Sunny noticed several hub nodes going offline. "Oh shit, that is how she did it, that bitch!"

Jack heard Sunny yell and asked, "Sunny, everything okay?"

Sunny stared at his screen and replied, "Yes. Tang created a maintenance sub-network between a few of the nodes. This was the secret backdoor to get the data out of Taiwan. Once Li removed the cable, my network map showed that the rogue network shut down. Great work, Li!"

Li smiled at the compliment from Sunny and said, "My pleasure, Mr. Ho."

"Jack, great work! I suggest you hide out until the storm blows over."

Jack sighed in relief and agreed with Sunny.

Bao witnessed firsthand the operation fall apart. "Guard seven, this is Bao. Any sign of anyone approaching the warehouse?" he asked the Triad security guard.

The security guard replied, "No sir, just a couple of cyclists and runners."

"Good," Bao whispered to himself. He realized that Operation Dragon Vault had failed.

Bao began to plan his escape from Taiwan. He grabbed his secured communicator.

Message: Encode: Encryption: message to BOSS: recommend we break off the agreement with the PLA, Dragon Vault compromised.

Signed,

Bao

BOSS, better known as the Dragon Head of the Fong Gao Triads, read his encrypted message from Bao, his trusted advisor. "Break off the agreement with the PLA?" BOSS paced in his quiet ocean-view home in Taitung, Taiwan, while considering Bao's recommendation. *Message: encode encryption: message to Bao, will consider options. Stand by,*

Signed,

BOSS

Noah Blake was still hiding out in his hotel room in Naha, Okinawa. He received a flash message on his phone. "What the hell?" Noah screeched as he ran across the hall to Travis Jones's room. "Travis! Wake up! The FBI just raided my law office in Boston!"

Travis was still hung over from indulging at last night's party. "What?" Travis asked. He started reading Noah's phone. "Well, that is shitty news. You're famous pal."

Noah was stunned by Travis's statement. He snapped back at Travis. "I'm famous? Are you kidding me! What am I going to do?"

Travis sat up and accessed his phone. "Look, calm down, no one knows you are here."

Travis got out of the bed and headed over to his laptop to send a message to Bao.

Message: Encode: Encryption: message to Bao, law firm raided in the U.S., partner on the run, Emerald Forest is shut down, confirm if operation is blown.

Signed,

Travis

After waiting for a few moments, Travis decided to message the general directly. *Message: Encode: Encryption: Message to Vo, General, confirm if operation is exposed. A law firm in the US was raided by the FBI. The senior partners on the run. Project compromised. Confirm.*

Signed,

Jones

Travis returned to Noah and said, "Okay, pal, start with the basics. Burn your phone and laptop now. Cancel all credit cards and stop using real money. Use Bitcoin only because it is untraceable."

Noah silently agreed and went back to his room. He quietly destroyed his equipment.

General Wong heard General Vo's phone ring. He attempted to retrieve the encrypted message. "General Vo, what is the password?"

Vo shook his head in defiance. Wong took out his pistol and violently smashed Vo's finger against the table.

"AHHHH!" Vo screamed in pain.

Wong demanded again. "Password!"

Vo looked down at his smashed fingers and replied, "82202#."

Wong entered the password. After reading the message from Travis Jones, Wong showed the message to Hai Ming.

"Hmm... Jones is on the run with the law partner," Hai Ming whispered.

Hai stepped outside the interrogation room. He thought about how to flush Travis Jones out into the open.

"Mr. Adams, welcome to Taiwan. Passport please."

Forest arrived under a diplomatic passport. He cleared customs at Taipei International Airport. He grabbed a taxi line to the Taipei Marriott. On his way to the hotel, he messaged Jack. *Message: Encode: Encryption. Message to Jack, I am in the same jungle, Marine. Stay low and out. Hunting Benedict Arnold. I will be in touch.*

Signed,

Forest

Jack cycled with Li to a hideout in Taichung. He pulled over to check his messages. Jack asked himself, "Forest, what are you doing in Taiwan?" Jack immediately sent a message. *Message to Forest. Be safe. Lots of unfriendly people everywhere.*

Signed,

Jack

Forest read the reply from Jack and smiled.

Hai Ming considered his options for a moment. He decided to message back Travis Jones using Vo's phone.

Message: Encode: Encryption: Message to Jones, mission compromised, exit plan executed. Evac to secondary location, send status once you arrive.

Signed,

Vo

Travis read the reply from General Vo's device and sensed something was wrong. "Evac to secondary location? What is he talking about? That is not the general!" Travis smashed his communicator and his laptop. He concluded to himself, "Christ! Everyone has been arrested."

Travis entered Noah's hotel room and yelled, "Everything is screwed! The general, Bao, and the team—all of them have been arrested. We need to lie low. Pack up! We need to move to another location outside of Naha."

Noah moved swiftly and packed up his room.

Forest checked into the Taipei Marriot and headed up to his room. After settling in, Forest opened his communicator and sent a message to Marcia.

Message: Encode: Encryption: message to Marcia Robertson. In Taipei, making contact. I will update later.

Signed,

Adams

Marcia read the encrypted message and responded to Forest.

Take care, Forest. Please.

Signed,

Marcia

Forest searched his online encrypted data sources for cross-connections with Bao Xu and known associates in Taipei. The data search returned several entries. "Jesus, this guy gets around." Forest discovered that Bao was associated with the Triad's crime boss and local politicians. He also met frequently with several senior political officers in Taipei.

"Congresswoman Zang Fu," Forest whispered to himself. He wrote the address of the congresswoman's office and headed for the elevator.

Forest arrived at the office of Congresswoman Fu and entered the main lobby. "Good day. I am Forest Adams from the U.S. Consulate in Vietnam."

The administration assistant looked a bit confused by the request. "Do you have an appointment with Congresswoman Fu?"

Forest looked sternly at the assistant and insisted, "This is an urgent issue that needs her attention immediately."

The assistant rang the congresswoman. "Yes, Mr. Adams, please have a seat. She will be out shortly."

Zang Fu, a four-term congresswoman in Taiwan's parliament, was one of the most powerful politicians in the country. She was well connected with the president of Taiwan, had close ties to associates of various Triad groups, and was deeply connected with Beijing.

"Mr. Adams, how can I help?" Zang asked.

Forest rose from his chair in the lobby and addressed Zang Fu. "Congresswoman, thank you for seeing me on short notice."

Zang motioned Forest to follow her back to her office. "So, Mr. Adams, what does the U.S. Consulate in Vietnam have to do with the affairs here in Taiwan?"

Forest opened his phone and revealed a picture of Bao Xu. "We need you to set up a meeting with this man."

Although Zang was completely stunned by this request, she calmly asked, "Who is this man?"

Forest closed his phone and explained. "Bao Xu is a lawyer and middle-man between the Fong Gao Triads and the PLA."

Zang sunk back in her chair as the color drained from her face. "Damn it, that is not Bao Xu. That man is Chu Ku, an investment banker."

Forest knew Zang was not telling the truth. "Congresswoman, his real name is Bao Xu. We need to find him."

Zang shook in panic. "I don't know how to find him!"

"Congresswoman Fu, our intel shows you had dinner with Xu several times over the last year. If this gets out that you have been meeting a high-level member of the Triads and PLA, you will be politically destroyed."

Zang was close to tears. "Wait," she said as she walked around her desk. "What do you plan to do with him?"

Forest stood up, approached Zang, and replied, "You will never see him again."

Zang turned away in fear and mumbled, "Oh my God, this will ruin me."

Forest gently put his hand on her shoulder and quietly said, "I need your help."

Zang wiped away her tears and hesitated before asking, "Give me a moment. Where do you want him to meet you?"

Relief flooded Forest as he replied, "In front of the big heart by the 101 building at 7:00 pm."

Zang realized that she had no choice. She composed herself and brought out her communicator.

Message: Encode: Encryption: Message to Bao. I need some release. Meet me at the heart by the 101, 7:00 p.m.

Signed,

Zang

Bao was in between meetings in Taipei when he noticed a message from his favorite politician. "Release," Bao whispered. He smiled with excitement as he headed to his car.

Message: Encode: Encryption: Message to Fu, release? Sounds great. See you at 7.

Bao

Zang looked back at Forest with a sinking feeling. "Done. He is all yours."

Forest faced Zang and firmly delivered his instructions. "Thank you. However, I need you to be there at 7:00 p.m. You will give him a hug and walk him over to the taxi stand. We will take it from there."

Zang reluctantly agreed and showed Forest to the door.

After Hai Ming had been interrogating General Vo for several hours, he ended with, "General, I don't believe I will see you anymore."

Hai Ming left the interrogation room and headed back to his Beijing office. General Wong gave one last punch to General Vo's face. "Vo, you are going to be held here until your trial." Vo laid his bloodied and swollen head down on the table and wept.

Zang tried to keep her composure as she waited for Bao to appear outside the 101 Building in Taipei. She watched him climb out of the cab and approach her.

"My lover, I am here to release you," Bao whispered in Zang's ear.

"Release me, my love," Zang whispered back to Bao.

Bao looked into Zang's eyes when he noticed her shaking. "Cold? My love?" Bao asked.

Zang ignored Bao's question as she looked over to the taxi stand and motioned, "Let's go."

Bao proceeded to the taxi line. "Taxi!" As Bao held the door for Zang, a man came from behind and stuck a needle into Bao's neck. Bao fell into the taxi. Zang walked away quickly with tears welling up in her eyes.

"Bao Xu, I am Forest Adams. You don't know me yet, but you will."

BOOK TWO

Ghost

"Wounds become hemorrhages.
Sicknesses become aches.
Ruining a life without death
forever feeds the anger that fuels the torment."

Gigi Kim Peeling

Chapter 32
Affliction

The sound of bone being crushed came from Bao's hand. He fought to stay conscious through the pain. The tormented suspect could only pray that the interrogation would end soon.

"Where am I?" Bao Xu screamed. The Taiwanese high-powered lawyer had a longstanding history as a deadly power broker. He acted as a middleman between the Fong Gao Triad criminal organization and the PLA cyber forces in China for many years. Now, he was in the custody of an American intelligence agent.

"You are in Okinawa," Forest Adams said. "We have been tracking you since Taipei, Mr. Xu. You ordered the killing of an American several months ago in Portugal. Why did you do that?"

Bao was blindfolded and chained to a desk. He screamed in denial. "What are you talking about? I did no such thing!"

Forest was sitting with two members of the U.S. Marine Corps Intelligence Unit based in Camp Henson Okinawa, Japan. "Bao, listen to me. You have no country to claim for your own. Taiwan doesn't have any record of you and China has a warrant out for your arrest because of some plot you and General Vo cooked up. The scheme created by the general, Operation Dragon Vault, was designed to steal a trove of data from Taiwan while secretly controlling their Internet of Things devices and military data networks."

After hearing the general's name, Bao snarled, "The general will die soon."

Forest, hearing this for the first time, asked, "By whom? Your Fong Gao Triad pals?" Bao did not answer. "Answer me!" Forest demanded.

"I have nothing to say," Bao muttered.

Forest took a deep breath and motioned the Marines to take Bao away. He reached for his communicator and sent a message.

Message: Encode: Encryption: Forest Adams to AG Marcia: Encryption: Bao, keeps silent, will continue to press.

Signed

Adams

The attorney general of the United States received Forest's secured message. "No surprise there," AG Marcia Robertson thought to herself. She realized holding a high-level member of the Triads with connections to the PLA could pose several international security risks to American personnel. She called FBI Director Alvin Ramsey. "Alvin, come see me, please."

Alvin Ramsey arrived in her office. "Ma'am?"

"Sit down, please. Director, our man in Okinawa has Bao in a cell. We will get him to talk at some point. Do you believe he can lead us to Travis Jones?"

Jones, a global lawyer, masterminded several global cyberattacks, including the one that almost brought down Taiwan with operation Dragon Vault.

Alvin explained, "Yes. Travis Jones is the key player in the Taiwan hack. Also, he may have assisted several Bitcoin thefts over the last two years."

"Agreed. Let me reach out to our contact in China and ask him if we can work out a trade. I will make the call this evening. Thank you, Alvin." Marcia ended the meeting.

Jack and Li had been using a Bed & Breakfast in Taichung, Taiwan as their hideout for the past few days. As Jack finished his shower, he mulled over the events of the last few weeks. He was still haunted by the murder of his love, Nella, who was murdered in Portugal by the Chinese Triads. At night, he relived the tragedy of that horrific day in Cascais... the black Audi car, the look on the face of the French hitman, Nella's mangled body being flung from her scooter. Trying to find a way to ease his pain, Jack refocused on getting back to America in time to see the birth of his first grandchild. He couldn't wait to see his son, William, and daughter, Regina, in Virginia. He was desperate to return home to them in Reston.

Li, the cycle guide Forest had hired for Jack, was asleep on the couch. Forest knew Li's husband before he died three years ago due to a tragic explosion. Jack was thankful for his dear old friend connecting him to Li. Her company was a comfort to him. He quickly dressed before waking her.

"Oh, thank you for letting me sleep," she said rubbing her eyes. "I guess I earned it." Li said in a playful manner.

"You sure did. Without your hands, we never would have been able to accomplish the mission. You're amazing, Li!"

"What's our next move?" Li asked.

"I think it's time for you to hear the whole story." Jack explained all that had transpired. He told her about Travis Jones, the World Bank project, and the Frenchman who killed Nella. Li was shocked to hear all that Jack had gone through. She stared deeply into Jack's eyes and spoke with compassion, "So, are you telling me that when we were cycling around Taiwan and disconnecting those fiber optic nodes, this was connected in some way to your fiancé getting murdered in Portugal?"

"Yes, and we still don't know where Travis Jones is. I need to find him," Jack growled.

"Jack, when my husband died three years ago, I also suspected foul play," Li admitted.

Jack looked into Li's eyes as they filled with tears and asked, "What happened to your husband?"

Li wiped away her tears. "My husband was killed three years ago while inspecting an offshore oil rig in Vietnam. There was an explosion on the crew boat carrying him and his team."

Jack remembered reading something about this in the news and asked, "Bio-Trend Global Oil?"

"Yes," Li said. "Bio-Trend hired my husband to audit the rig owned by some Russian holding company. My husband also inspected the production output records."

Jack, not wanting to open too many old wounds within Li's heart, asked, "Where was your husband from?"

Li looked away from Jack and quietly answered, "He was from Budapest."

The wind whipped at Travis Jones's face as he sped north of Okinawa, Japan, in his BMW convertible, accompanied by Noah.

"Bro, where are we headed?" Noah asked.

Travis was still reeling from his Dragon Vault cyberattack failure. He had helped organize the *Hack of the Century* along with the PLA Cyber forces in Beijing and the Fong Gao Triads in Taiwan. The hack failed for unknown reasons. A Japanese hacker group, Rising Sun, stopped the data from being stolen and sent it back to China.

"North. I have a safe house in Nago," Travis answered.

Noah was always on edge. He was especially stressed now that he was a wanted man by Interpol for his role in Taiwan's failed cyberattack. "Trav, look, my fucking face is all over the world by now! I need to lie low."

Travis was annoyed at Noah. "Chill. We will lie low and figure out our next move together. We are safe here on the island." Travis realized that everyone within the Dragon Vault Team had been compromised, captured, or on the run. He needed to find a way to get in contact with someone who may still be active.

"Noah, we need to get to the safe house immediately. I need to find someone from Dragon Vault that will help us move to the next target."

Noah looked out at the shores of Okinawa and its beautiful beaches and trees flying by. "Who?"

"Vulturess."

While finishing her lunch near the airport in Naha, Okinawa, Lilian Tang, aka Vulturess, in the cyber hacking world, began to scan the Darknet for any mention of the Dragon Vault hack. Her hacker tag, *Vulturess*, gave Lilian great power and visibility on the Darknet. She was known for her hacking skills predating her college years at UCLA. Lilian understood how to penetrate computer networks and financial systems. This made her a target for rival hackers and foreign law enforcement, including the American FBI and Interpol. Lilian was on the run from the Chinese PLA security forces and began to consider all her options.

"My cover is blown, damn it!" Lilian muttered to herself.

She scanned the Darknet, home of the most secured global hacker chat rooms. She read about the group, *Rising Sun.* "Fuck, who mobilized these guys?" Lilian wondered. She began to sweat after reading messages from the leader, SwordBitch. "Oh shit!" She knew *Rising Sun* was the San-Hamada Yakuza property, the Fong Gao Triads' top rival.

Message: Darknet: Rising Sun All: Encryption: Message to Darknet, Vulturess IDs as Lilian Tang, a Sea Turtle, hiding out in Taiwan or other locations; San-Hamada paying top crypto for location.

Signed,

SwordBitch

Finishing the flash message into the Darknet, SwordBitch, a hacker leader from the influential group, *Rising Sun,* controlled by the San-Hamada Yakuza based in Tokyo, began to send a message to William Kendall.

Message: Darknet24: Knight2Rouk7: Message, flash sent to Darknet, thanks for the Intel on Vulturess.

Signed,

SwordBitch

William Kendall was spending time with his wife, Tricia, at a Northern Virginia hospital, when he saw a flash message from his Darknet account. "SwordBitch is going after Vulturess. Outstanding," William murmured.

Tricia, waiting to deliver, asked, "Will, did they get that bitch, Poppy, finally?"

"No, this is the other bitch, Lilian Tang. SwordBitch just sent a global flash picture of her on the Darknet."

Tricia stared straight at her husband with a concerned look, knowing what this meant for Lilian. "Oh shit, she won't last long."

After spending the greater part of four hours on the run in Vancouver, Poppy Ledger began to run out of options. Her plan was to hide out after stealing valuable source code and crypto keys from an American company while attending a global fiber optics technology conference in San Francisco. While watching the failure of the Dragon Vault Hack against Taiwan's TAINET fiber optic communication network and Internet of Things sensors, first-hand, Poppy discovered that her team was responsible for the death of an American citizen in Portugal. She learned that the American killed was Jack Kendall's fiancée.

William became a victim of Poppy's data theft at the conference in San Francisco. She stole the codes needed to move the data from Taiwan to China from his computer. Most of her teammates have vanished or have been caught by Interpol, Chinese Internal Security, or the American FBI. She knew it was only a matter of time before one of those law enforcement agencies caught up to her in Vancouver. While hiding out in a corner coffee shop near the Gastown section of Vancouver, Canada, Poppy planned her next move.

Thomas Wilson, CEO of the now merged companies Techline / Cybercom, with the help of his new general counsel, Regina Kendall, had just completed the buyout of all remaining private shares of Cybercom.

"Well done, Regina!" Thomas said.

Regina had assisted the FBI with details about Dragon Vault and helped bring her old firm under federal indictment. After the FBI in Boston raided the offices, they arrested all the significant partners, except her old boss, Noah was still missing. The FBI asked Interpol to issue a global *Red Letter* hoping some countries will see this request and detain him.

"Thomas, I hope they catch Noah and Travis Jones. They need to pay for what they did to Nella and Taiwan," Regina said.

Thomas replied cautiously, "Reg, when you have lived as I have, where there is despair, there is an opportunity. Where there is an opportunity, there is a path to correctness."

Reg smiled through her Cisco Webex video conference. "You are right, Thomas."

Thomas replied, "Okay, kiddo, let's start working on the Smart Country Project between our friends in Taiwan and Japan. Please, take the lead on this and contact our friend Sunny Ho."

Reg nodded as she disconnected from the video chat.

Sunny Ho, CEO of ADConnect in Taiwan, just completed his secured post briefing with the President of Taiwan about the PLA Cyber and the Fong Gao Triads failed attempt to hack the TAINET network. Thanks to his friends Thomas Wilson, William Kendall, and the *Rising Sun* hacker group, they managed to stop the stolen data from leaving the island. After the three hour briefing, Sunny needed a break. He headed out of his office in the 101 Building in downtown Taipei and took some time to walk across the street to the Xinyi District. Sunny loved to walk around, watch the people, and enjoy specialty coffee and dumplings.

"Sunny here," he answered his phone.

"Sunny, this is Regina. How are you?"

Sunny always loved hearing from Regina. "Reg, how are you? Working for Thomas, I see."

Regina replied, "Yes, I am."

"What can I do for you, young lady?"

Regina gathered her notes. "Well, I see you are about to kick off the Smart Country Project with Japan. I understand you are interested in the backhaul QoS software my brother, William, created."

The Smart County Project became an essential communication method between Japan and Taiwan. By leveraging existing underwater cabling, these two countries will be able to directly connect their universities, businesses, and government systems. This will allow them to share information faster and provide a better means of financial commerce.

Sunny decided to have some fun with his friend. "Ah, well, I did get a stolen copy of the software from an old friend at Fiberex in Xiamen. However, I am having a hard time trying to get him on the phone."

Regina heard Sunny laugh. "Oh my God, I am going to tell William!"

Sunny began to laugh and replied, "Just kidding, dear. Yes, I will send over the distance and bandwidth requirements to William tomorrow. Please, tell Thomas if we can work on a site license agreement between Techline / Cybercom and ADCONNECT Taiwan that would help move this project along."

"Okay, let me start working on the legal language of the agreement. I will speak to Thomas about your site license request," Regina replied.

"I am glad you are well, along with your father and brother. That whole Dragon Vault hack could have ruined the country forever. Thanks to all of you, Taiwan was rescued from a major catastrophe. We will forever be in your debt," Sunny declared with great sincerity.

Regina was touched by Sunny's words and said, "Oh, Sunny, you would do the same for us."

Sunny was pleased as he hung up with Regina.

Interpol: internal communique. Encryption: Message to all global members. Red Letter issue: Noah. Citizenship: United States. Age: 42. Height: 1.72 Cm. Weight: 210. Eyes: Hazel. An Arrest Warrant was issued by the United States Government connected to global money laundering, cyber terrorism, and accessory to the murder of a U.S. Citizen in Portugal. Authorize detainment granted. Contact: SAC Gerald Burns, FBI – Boston. Via secured chat.

Signed,

Javier Garcia, Secretary-General. INTERPOL, Milan

Chapter 33
Continuum

Camp Hanson (Kinville, Okinawa, Japan)

Japan's evening air was very humid, unusual for the late hour when Forest Adams stepped out of the integration holding area on Camp Henson Okinawa, Japan. He started to consider the direction he needed to take with Bao Xu. While he paced in the parking lot, thinking about how to get Bao to give more details on the failed hack in Taiwan, Forest remembered his days as a United States Marine shortly after Saigon's fall in 1975.

After arriving in Okinawa in May 1975, Forest re-enlisted in the Marines and asked to be sent back to Vietnam, thinking that maybe someday he could find Bui. Only knowing her for a few moments, he felt deeply connected by her determination to climb to safety, only to be pulled back into the mob. That dreadful scenario traumatized Forest. Being a very young man, he never had deep romantic feelings for anyone. Only then did he feel a deep emotional connection to that beautiful orphan girl. Bui also gazed back at Forest several times while being taken to safety at the nearby Catholic Church. Forest committed his life to finding this girl, the woman of his dreams.

While taking a walk around the secured building on the Marine base, Forest heard his name and was pulled back into reality. "I love you forever my Bui."

"Mr. Adams, phone call, sir." A Marine guard called again.

Forest put out his cigarette. "Coming." He picked up the phone. "Forest, here."

"Forest, it's Jack."

Forest was happy to hear his old friend's voice again. "Well, Marine, how's Taiwan?"

"Beautiful, evergreen everywhere!"

Forest smiled and asked, "And Ms. Cao?"

"Yes, I was going to get to that. Why did you hire her?" Jack asked.

Forest sat down on the chair outside of the interrogation building. "I asked her to look after you, Jack. She is a good person. I knew her husband before he died."

Jack listened to his mentor and friend with gratitude. "Yes, she told me that he died in an explosion. Any truth in that?"

Forest did not want to confirm that information. "Marine, let's chat about that again when we see each other. I am here with Bao and he isn't talking yet."

Jack knew the importance of getting Bao to talk. "Let me call you at a better time."

Forest agreed and hung up.

Attorney general of the United States, Marcia Robertson, read the Interpol *Red Letter* regarding Noah. "Well, this is a good start. We still need Travis Jones," she whispered to herself. Marcia quietly continued maintaining backchannel communication with Hai Ming, head of all finance for the Chinese government. Marcia and Hai had a deep love affair during and after their college days at Harvard. After spending a few years in America, working on Wall Street, Hai went home and worked his way up to the Official in Charge of all Finance for the entire Chinese government.

"Hai? Did I catch you in a bad moment?"

Hai always enjoyed his confidential communication with his past lover.

"Yes, let me tell my wife another woman is calling me!" Hai smirked.

Marcia, hearing that tone from Hai, remembered how easily he could get under her skin.

"Okay, I threw my wife out of the room. What is on your mind, Madam Attorney General?"

Marcia rolled her eyes and spoke, "Look, Hai, official business for a moment. We need to know where Travis Jones is. We believe he is somewhere in Taiwan. After the failure of the Dragon Vault hack against Taiwan, we suspect he is up to something new."

Hai listened to his old friend and replied, "Well, Marcia, you haven't delivered Bao Xu yet. My sources tell me that you are holding him somewhere. You failed to tell me that!"

Marcia didn't realize that the information had been compromised. She spoke hesitantly. "Hai, we have him in a secured location. When we are done with him, we will arrange an exchange. However, we will only exchange Travis Jones for Bao."

Hai didn't know where Jones was. He replied, "Okay, I will lean on General Vo again and see if we can shed some light."

"Thank you, Hai," Marcia replied.

After hanging up the phone, Marcia sent a secured message to Forest Adams in Okinawa.

Message: Red. Encryption: Forest Adams. Secured: China knows we are holding Bao. We will arrange a trade once they acquire Travis Jones, need to expedite interrogation.

Signed,

M

While checking his secured messages, Forest received a secured communication from Marcia Robertson. "Shit, how the hell did the Chinese find out about Bao being taken to Taiwan?" Forest started reevaluating in his head how this could have happened and realized that Taiwan's Chinese Intelligence assets probably found out from Congresswoman Zang Fu.

Fu, a powerful congresswoman in the Taiwan government, helped Forest capture Bao several weeks ago. Fu, one of Bao's assets and lover, agreed to meet him outside the 101 Building. Forest and his team grabbed Bao and smuggled him to Okinawa.

"Shit, she must have talked," Forest whispered.

While driving north from Naha to Nago Okinawa, Travis feared that he could be in great danger. "Fuck, if the Triads or Yakuza find out that I am here in Okinawa, I am dead!" Thinking about his future, Travis knew he needed to find a way to raise the necessary funds required to execute his next attack plan while remaining hidden in Okinawa. In the car, Noah, sitting next to Travis, spent his time admiring western Okinawa's beautiful coastline. The warm air, golden beaches, and cliffs provided Noah with a beautiful view to help pass the time until they arrived in Nago.

"This place, Trav, looks a lot like Hawaii, yet without all the tourists."

Travis stared back at his friend. "Look, Noah, Interpol released your *Red Letter* an hour ago. We need to lay low while we are here in Okinawa. No fucking, no drinking, and no leaving the safe house. Cool?"

Noah looked over at his friend with a sheer look of fear and asked, "Yeah, what about you? Is there a *Red Letter* with your name on it?"

"No, not yet. I suspect there is a reason why the FBI and Interpol haven't issued one yet."

"Oh yeah, what reason?" Noah shrieked.

"Because they want me dead!" Travis replied in an agitated tone.

Noah and Travis didn't speak again until they reached the safe house in Nago, Okinawa. This beautiful coastal city in northern Okinawa was famous for the Nago Castle and its beautiful sea life. Travis followed the GPS until he arrived at the top of a hill to a house that overlooked the South China Sea.

"Noah, here we are. Let's unload. Remember, no fucking!" Travis was serious and terse in his tone.

Noah departed the car with a baseball cap and sunglasses. He didn't look at his partner while heading into the house.

"Your room is upstairs with a great view of the ocean. I will be downstairs over here," Travis said.

Noah began to carry his bags up to his room. After settling in, Noah connected his phone to the Wi-Fi. "Stop! Dumb shit!" Travis yelled.

"What?" Noah shouted.

Travis retorted back, "They will trace that phone, idiot! If you need to connect to something, use the laptop and remote VPN access software I loaded!"

Noah turned away from Travis in fear and shame.

Travis grabbed Noah's phone. "Give me that!" He smashed the phone and placed the broken pieces in the trash.

Noah used the laptop connected into the VPN network Travis established. Noah watched the various layers of connections begin to connect to Tokyo, Moscow, Paris, and Brooklyn, New York. Surprised, he asked, "Travis, how the hell did you do that?"

Travis casually replied, "Oh, I contacted some Russian guys in Brooklyn. We are using their outbound IP addresses to hide our connections."

Noah looked at his partner with great concern and reluctantly exclaimed, "Russians?"

"We are working on something big. That is why I asked you to come to Okinawa," Travis replied.

Noah retorted, "Oh, fuck! Russian Mafia, dude?"

Travis ignored Noah and proceeded down the stairs to his room. He entered his room and logged in as well. "Okay, I need to find Vulturess." After a few minutes, Travis was in the Darknet. He spent nearly an hour checking the various chat rooms. Travis found a message from Sword-Bitch.

Message: Seeking Lilian Tang, aka Vulturess

Travis logged into other secured sources and databases and scanned for any data on Lilian Tang. He muttered, "Fuck me! UCLA, Binarycore, and intern at Qualcomm. No wonder General Vo had her on Dragon Vault."

Travis crafted a secure message in the Darknet hoping Lilian would see his communication. "So, Lilian Tang, where are you?"

Message: Darknet15. Secured chat. Encryption: Message to Vulturess, sanctuary offered in Nago. Signed,

Rambonus

Members of the Russian hacking group, Gorky Park, were monitoring their rogue global network in their warehouse office in Brighton Beach, Brooklyn, New York. They detected a series of new connections coming from Asia. In the Darknet, Ivan Linu, alias *darkhorse34*, started to record the connections to share with the other team members.

Gorky Park was formed in 2002. They became the central team for a global cyber operation for the Russian Mafia based in the Brighton Beach section of Brooklyn. The hacker group protected all cybersecurity assets for the Russian criminal organization. In turn, the group maintained a very shadowy presence on the Darknet.

Vlad called for Ivan. "Come here."

Vlad Zoe was a lead enforcer and Bitcoin expert for the team. He watched the new connections and asked, "Who the fuck is that?"

Ivan started to decode the message traffic but was unable to find a way to break through the encryption. He advised, "I don't know what's going on. I will trace the connections back through the firewalls and see."

Chapter 34
Exchange

Poppy Ledger logged into the Darknet from a café in Vancouver, Canada. She still hadn't come to grips with the failure of the Dragon Vault hack attempt against Taiwan. Her role was to steal the source code from William Kendall and hack and control all the firewalls within Taiwan's TAINET network system.

During the early part of the operation, she successfully maneuvered the firewalls away from the ADConnect engineers. However, once the engineers rebooted the devices, she lost control and never gained access again. Poppy was still trying to determine which members of the Dragon Vault teams were still alive or running loose. She logged into the Darknet, using her hacker callsign, Yellowslayer. During the operation's collapse, *Rising Sun* disclosed her identity as Poppy Ledger of the PLA Cybersecurity to the entire Darknet community. Poppy made the decision to continue to use her compromised hacker nickname. She watched a flash message from SwordBitch appear that disclosed the identity of Vulturess, Lilian Tang.

"Oh my God, that is her real identity!" Poppy was familiar with the history of Lilian Tang during her time at Facebook. "She is a legend, my God; she is Vulturess." Poppy continued to read more chats about the failed hack attempt in Taiwan and the various Interpol Red Letters, including one for Noah. After spending nearly an hour online in the Darknet, Poppy decided to take a significant risk and contacted William Kendall.

Message: Darknet10. Encryption: To Knight2Rouk7. Message: Seeking a knight in shining armor once again. Willing to cross the bridge, need help.

Signed,

Yellowslayer

After finishing sending the message, Poppy accessed her Bitcoin digital wallet.

Access: Bitcoin: Wallet: Pearl Tower Shanghai: Shou: $10,000,000.00 currency: 667 QTY Bitcoin.

Poppy verified that the Bitcoin was in her Blockchain ledger and wallet. "Okay, now I need to somehow convert this to dollars," Poppy mumbled to herself.

William checked his secured communicator with access to his Darknet account, Knight2Rouk7. William's face froze while reading the message from Yellowslayer.

Need a knight in shining armor, willing to cross the bridge.

William had already confirmed that Yellowslayer was, in fact, Poppy Ledger.

William held his phone and stared out the window outside the Virginia hospital. His wife, Tricia, was due anytime with their first child. She looked at her husband and could see he was in distress. She asked with worry, "William, what is it?"

William answered his wife, "Poppy has surfaced; she is asking for help."

Tricia knew she needed to control her emotions and stay calm. She was in the last month of her pregnancy and had some medical complications with her pregnancy. "Well, okay, tell the FBI, honey, so they can arrest that bitch!"

William gently held his wife. "Tricia, breathe baby. I will send this to the FBI." William took several deep breaths and told Tricia, "My love, I want her caught as much as you do."

Tricia tightly hugged her husband.

Travis Jones spent an hour on the Darknet before turning off his secure computer in his safehouse in Nago, Okinawa. He had a connection through the Russian secure private network. While on the Darknet, Travis received a flash message.

Message: Darknet16. Encryption: Rambonus: from Gorky Park. message: deposit 2 Bitcoin to cover your access into our portal.

Signed,

Gorky Park

Travis was aware that using the Russian Mafia's private communications network would be risky. However, this was the only way his communications would not be traced back to his Okinawa safehouse.

Message: Darknet16. Encryption: Gorky Park: Rambonus: Deposit made.

Travis logged into his digital wallet, containing over 300 bitcoins worth $4,500,000.

He selected the oldest mined coins from this blockchain ledger and sent them off to cover his and Noah's internet access.

Lilian continued to scan the Darknet for any updates and messages surrounding the failed Dragon Vault. She saw an encrypted message from Rambonus. *Message: Encryption: Vulturess: safe passage in Nago.*

Lilian stared at her screen in complete shock. "How the fuck do they know I am in trouble?"

Lilian began scanning the callsign, Rambonus, within the Darknet. The secure chat rooms gave very little information. Secure chat rooms gave hackers the ability to operate with extreme privacy. She was very aware of the fact that the PLA, Chinese government, and Japanese Yakuza wanted her dead, not only due to her role in the failed Dragon Vault hack, but also because she stole over 100 million dollars in Bitcoin a year ago. She made the decision to take a chance and reply.

Message: Darknet12. Encryption: Rambonus. message: Offer Accepted, en route to Nago.

Signed,

Vulturess

Lilian sent the message, packed up her laptop, paid her bill, and headed off to the parking lot. Lilian was distracted by all that had occurred and failed to notice the live camera feed in the diner. Lilian made her way to the parking lot and began to look for a ride to Nago. She scanned the parking lot for any male or female traveling alone when she noticed a middle-aged woman sitting in her car.

Lilian approached the woman and politely asked, "Excuse me, I am heading to Nago. Any chance you can give me a ride?"

The woman had just finished a call and answered, "Oh, that's not too far from where I am headed, sweetie. Sure. Jump in."

Lilian smiled at the older lady, "Thank you."

Lilian hopped in the car and quickly became aware that the older woman was stunningly beautiful for her age.

"I am Noki. Nice to meet you," the lady said.

Lilian courteously replied, "I am Suki, a pleasure."

Noki began driving. Lilian could still feel the effects of being in the cargo hold while flying from Taiwan. She was bruised and dirty.

Lilian asked Noki, "Would you mind pulling over into a Japanese public bathhouse? I could use some refreshing."

Jack finished his call with Forest. He decided to stop asking Li any more questions about her husband.

"Jack, was that Mr. Adams?" Li asked.

Jack replied, "Yes, he sends his regards."

Li inquired, "What is the plan for today?"

Jack was going over all that had happened in his mind. He took a few seconds, looked at Li, and finally answered, "Forest asked us to stay low for a couple of days."

Li could see that Jack was preoccupied and asked, "Jack, what are you thinking?"

Jack made a quick decision to tell Li as much as he could. He started by explaining his relationship with Travis Jones and World Global. "His firm placed a lower bid on a World Bank project for Vietnam. Later, we learned that he was protected by General Vo, head of Cyber forces for the PLA."

Li's eyes opened wide in shock. "Jack, it is horrifying to think that one of the world's top criminal organizations is involved. Are we now in the middle of all of this?"

Jack reluctantly nodded back at Li. "Yes, I am trying to find Travis Jones. I am going to punish him for everything he has done."

Li wanted to reach out to Jack and comfort him. Instead, she just kindly warned, "Jack, that won't bring you closure."

Jack knew that she was probably right. He replied, "Maybe so. However, someone needs to stop that guy before he kills more people."

"Jack, listen to me. When I lost my husband, I wanted revenge for his death. Eventually, all the evidence pointed to a gas leak on the boat. I settled with the oil company out of court for millions of dollars. I decided to retire from teaching."

Jack interrupted Li and asked, "How long were you married to your husband?"

Li answered, "We were married for twenty-four years. Boris and I had two children, Nadia and Joseph. Nadia is twenty and Joseph is twenty-three. Both attend school in Switzerland. Shortly after their father died, I sent them off to a prestigious university to continue their studies while I continued to investigate their father's death. In the end, I had to concede that he died from a tragic accident."

Jack recalled his conversation with Forest and asked, "Li, Forest knew your husband well?"

Li was surprised and said, "Yes. He worked at the embassy in Vietnam and the consulate in Singapore. I often visited with his wife, Bui."

Jack's eyes began to tear as he said, "So you knew Ms. Bui?"

Li could see Jack's eyes swell and asked quietly, "Did you know her as well?"

Jack cleared his throat and said, "She was the most wonderful friend to me."

Li and Jack reminisced about their friendship with Bui for a few minutes. They were able to share the good memories they had with her. This comforted them and gave them a momentary break.

Chapter 35
Skeletons

"You are crushing my leg!" The Russian shop merchant shouted. The Brighton Beach business owner was several months late on his protection payments to the local Russian Mafia outfit.

"Look, you piece of shit! We protect you, your family, and your fucking business from those Italian and Chinese assholes!" The Russian enforcer yelled.

Dimi Zosh, a former KGB officer and veteran of the Russian Army during the war in Afghanistan, continued to squeeze harder on the pipe cutter attached to the merchant's legs. He violently placed more pressure on the businessman's leg until the leg broke with a loud snap. The leg was destroyed.

The merchant yelled before he passed out.

Dimi lit a cigarette as he stared outside his Brooklyn office. "Look, Lasky, I will break the other leg and your arm if you don't pay your protection fee. You have twenty-four hours to pay me with interest or I will come back. I will return with my pipe cutter and do the same to your wife!"

Lasky started trembling from shock and fear. He relented in pain and terror. "Okay, okay, I pay!"

Dimi walked over and began to loosen up the pipe cutter from Lasky's broken leg. "Get the fuck out of here!" Dimi lit another cigarette and smiled sinisterly. He was very satisfied with himself.

In extreme pain, Lasky tried to get out of the room, only to fall down the stairs leading to the front door. Dimi got pleasure from seeing Lasky suffer.

Dimi continued to watch Lasky as he called out, "Vlad! Help that piece of shit out the door!"

Vlad rushed to the door and kicked Lasky before helping him. "You piece of shit! I warned you!" After opening the door, Vlad pushed Lasky onto the Brooklyn sidewalk.

Dimi sat back in his chair and cleaned his pipe cutter. He was getting ready for his next victim.

Vlad went to Dimi's office. "Boss, you think he will run to the cops?"

Dimi pointed and ordered, "Open the closet door."

Vlad walked over to the closet and opened the door. He stepped back and yelled, "For fuck's sake!" Vlad found a gagged and bound woman in the closet. "Who the fuck is this?"

Dimi laughed and replied with a snarl, "She is Lasky's wife."

With fear in his eyes, Vlad stared back at his boss and said, "I guess he won't go to the cops then."

Triumphantly, Dimi turned his attention to his e-mails.

Message: Encryption: Shadowbear: network: Secured: Message to Bear-Bone: Rambonus: Need to meet to discuss Crypto-funding source for updated hack.

Signed,

Rambonus

Dimi began to consider if this proposed hacker attack was worth the risk to him and his organization. He ordered, "Vlad, look into this Rambonus. See if he has failed any recent hacking attacks."

Hearing his boss's order, Vlad immediately left the room and headed downstairs to the data center.

Forest Adams entered the interrogation room at Camp Henson Marine Corps, Okinawa Base. "Well, Bao, I am back. Anything you want to share with me?" Forest inquired.

Bao Xu was still chained and blindfolded to the table. He said nothing.

Forest continued. "Bao, here is what we know for sure. The Chinese government wants you. We want to trade you for someone else. You, however, could save yourself a ton of pain and suffering if you helped us out. Do you understand? Are we clear?"

Bao was feeling all the effects of being tortured and isolated. He screamed in pain and anger, "What do you want?" Forest grabbed one of Bao's fingers, and bent it back until he heard a crack. "FUCK! " Bao shouted.

Forest continued to bend Bao's fingers back and demanded, "Okay now that I have your attention, where the fuck is Travis Jones?"

"I don't know!" Bao pathetically screamed.

Forest looked over at the two U.S. Marine security guards and requested, "Hey guys, could you grab me a cup of coffee? Two sugars, please."

Both guards looked confused and alarmed. "Sir, do you want both of us to fetch you a cup of coffee?" Forest nodded and motioned the guards to leave. He turned his attention back to Bao and said, "Don't know, huh? Okay." Forest picked up a fountain pen and stabbed Bao in the arm.

"Ah! My arm!" Bao shrieked as Forest stabbed and pushed the pen deeper into his arm.

Forest continued the interrogation. "Alright, let me try something a bit easier. Did you order the killing of Nella Fiero in Portugal?"

Bao was reeling from the pain from the pen stabbing and broken finger when he yelled, "I never ordered any killing!"

Forest demanded, "Bao, one more time. Why did you order the killing of Nella Fiero?"

Bao insisted, "I didn't order any killing!"

Forest took a hammer out of his bag that was lying in the corner, then walked back to Bao, and pulled back Bao's head. He began to hit his teeth with the hammer. Four of Bao's teeth broke off, dropping onto the table. They made a clanking sound on impact.

"Damn you!" Bao cried.

Forest paused for a few moments to let the pain take over Bao. He then added, "Bao, you killed Nella to keep Jack Kendall in Portugal. Why?"

Hearing Jack Kendall's name made Bao lift his head and turn his face towards Forest. "Do you know Kendall?"

Forest punched Bao's face before answering. "Yes, he is my dear friend. I know you are the one who ordered the killing of this fiancée. Why?"

Bao knew that his punishment was only going to get more severe. He answered, "Yes, I hired the Frenchman to hunt down Kendall and his fiancée."

Forest pounded his fist into Bao's face one more time as he shouted, "How did you know they were going to Portugal?"

Bao cried and spoke through his broken teeth. "An asset from the PLA cyber team, Poppy Ledger, hacked into Thomas Wilson's e-mail account at Techline to steal the Vietnam World Bank project details."

"Why did you want to keep Kendall in Portugal?" Forest yelled in frustration.

Bao gasped before answering, "Travis Jones wanted to inflict as much pain as possible on Kendall for spoiling the Vietnam project."

"Okay, Bao, who else on this Dragon Vault Team is on the run?"

Bao sensed that there might be a possible negotiation opening and asked, "If I give the names and past locations, what do I get in return?"

Forest stood, walked over to Bao, removed his blindfold, stared directly into Bao's eyes, and responded, "You will probably live another day."

Bao looked at his captor and asked, "Who are you?"

"I am the only one keeping you alive," Forest whispered in a very serious tone.

Bao looked at his broken teeth on the table and started to spit out the blood from his mouth as he mumbled, "Whoever you are, I am already dead. The Triads will come for me unless you can protect me."

Forest queried, "Oh, if I keep you alive, will you tell me what I need?"

Bao nodded in complete exhaustion and defeat.

Forest placed the blindfold back on Bao's eyes before he departed the room to make a call. "Let me think about it."

Jack was asleep in the Bed & Breakfast room in Taiwan. This was the first time he was able to really rest. Hearing his phone ring, he picked up and said, "Jack here."

Forest went outside to continue the call. "Marine, this is Forest."

Jack sat up quickly and urgently asked, "Hey, how is it with Bao?"

"Bao ordered the hit on Nella. He found out you and Nella would be in Portugal by one of his hackers. That hacker was able to get into Techline to steal your Vietnam proposal. Does the name Poppy Ledger ring a bell?"

After hearing the name, Jack sank in his chair. "Oh yes."

Forest paused to let Jack absorb the information before continuing, "Yes, Bao hired the Frenchman. Jack, he wanted to give up more people on the run. Outside of Noah, the lawyer, and Jones, who else should we be looking for?"

Jack went over the CONFAB conference call a few months ago in his mind. He recalled how the FBI, Will, Thomas, and Marcia ran all the players in Dragon Vault and replied, "Now that you ask, we need to know if Vulturess is still alive."

"You are right, Marine. Vulturess is the one the Taiwan National Police are looking for. She is a suspect in a double homicide in Taichung."

"Hold on. Li mentioned that two days ago. They had their throats slashed."

Forest carefully listened to Jack speak before answering. "I read somewhere that this Vulturess has a huge appetite for sexual domination and has been known to torture her victims sexually. In some cases, literally draining the life out of them."

"We will start monitoring any other unexplained killings here in Taiwan," Jack added.

"Look, Jack, about Li..." Forest began.

Jack stopped Forest. "Let's have that conversation later. Danger close."

Forest, hearing the Marine Corps term *danger close*, knew what Jack meant. Jack was communicating that Li was near him.

Jack took a moment to gather his thoughts before stating, "Forest, I need to see this guy. I am coming to you."

Forest did not want to expose Jack and Li to any further danger. He responded, "Marine, I would appreciate the company for sure."

Jack acknowledged and hung up.

Lilian and her new friend, Noki, arrived at a private bathhouse near the shoreline just outside of Nago, Okinawa. "Let's enjoy!" Lilian said. Both ladies departed the car and headed into the bathhouse.

"Good evening, ladies. One room?" the manager asked.

Noki responded, "Yes, please."

The manager requested to see their passports. Noki reached into her purse and presented her passport. Lilian knew that her passport would be scanned and sent to the local police system. She hesitated and proclaimed, "Oh, I think I left mine at home."

The manager looked at Lilian and said, "I can't allow you to stay without a passport."

Noki looked disheartened and begged, "Sir, please, my friend had a long day."

The manager liked Noki's presence and relented, "Okay, let me take your picture at least."

Lilian agreed and posed for a picture. "I will be back for that," Lilian whispered.

Noki and Lilian entered their private room, disrobed, and sat in the hot tub. They looked at each other. Noki leaned into Lilian and began to kiss her when she suddenly felt a strong push on the top of her head. Noki began to panic as she tried to raise her head above the water. Lilian got pleasure from watching Noki drown. She continued to push Noki's head under the water. Within minutes, Noki's lifeless body began to float. Lilian pulled herself out of the tub and dried off while smiling at her latest sexual conquest and murder. She sarcastically said, "Babe, you were great! Thanks."

After getting dressed, Lilian rummaged through Noki's bag and took whatever she wanted in her bag. Lilian grabbed her belongings and headed to the manager's desk. She approached the manager. "Hi, remember me?"

The manager replied, "Yeah, you checked in with another woman. Anything wrong with the room?"

Lilian replied, "No. Nothing is wrong with the room."

The manager was in his late sixties and looked at the stunning woman in front of him. "Ummm, well, you do realize that I am a bit older than you."

Lilian swiftly grabbed the manager's throat and stabbed him in his trachea with a pencil. The manager reached for Lilian's hand and tried to sit up. She continued to stab more and more until his body went limp. Lilian got up and took the manager's phone. Covered in blood, she scanned the manager's phone photo gallery. She located and deleted her picture and threw the manager's phone in her bag.

Lilian departed the building and quickly got in Noki's car. She drove the vehicle close to the cliffs and jumped out of the moving car just as it fell into the water. Lilian waited until the car was completely submerged and then walked to the town center to contact Travis Jones.

Chapter 36
Interchange
ADConnect Headquarters (Taipei, Taiwan)

President Yu Chu Fong was in her second term as president of Taiwan. Yu had grown weary of the continued cyberattacks against her people and the island she governed. "If we are planning to connect Tamsui to Naha, Okinawa, I want to ensure that you are taking every precaution necessary to prevent our data from being stolen!" the President shouted.

Sunny Ho was still recovering from the failed Dragon Vault hack. He wearily answered, "Madame President, we will take further steps to protect our connections and data. This Smart Country project with Japan will revolutionize our Internet of Things technology along with our ability to carry near real-time data streams across 700 KM."

The President stared back at Sunny through her video screen and said, "Okay, Sunny, it's your ass!"

Sunny was in his office inside the 101 building in Taipei. He complained to himself, "I didn't even vote for the lady!"

After dealing with the security breach caused by Vulturess during the recent cyber hack against TAINET, Sunny ordered his entire team to recheck all fiber connections and vaults across the whole island. "Yung, Sunny here. Double-check all external firewalls and intrusion detection systems between Tamsui fiber and our TAINET node in Taipei. No surprises!"

Yung was the chief engineer for ADConnect. He assured his boss, "On it, Chief!"

Sunny looked at the additional network connections feeding into Tamsui from TAINET. "Ho Ling!" Sunny called on his intercom. "My office!"

Ho Ling was a recent graduate from George Mason University in Fairfax, Virginia. Ho arrived in Sunny's office and said, "Here, Boss!"

Sunny inquired, "Okay, what is the latest on the Blockchain deployment on our side?"

Ho cleared his throat and began to map out their deploying Blockchain process that supported the new smart city project between Taiwan and Japan. "For starters, the whole concept around Blockchain will give both parties greater security for peer-to-peer transactions. Once a transaction is requested in Blockchain, a cryptographic calculation and hash value will be attached to the block itself sending the new block into the existing chain. The previous block and hash value must match the new block for the transactions to be validated by the miners. Miners validate the transactions in blocks to ensure the integrity of them across the distributed ledgers."

Ho looked at his CEO to see if he understood the concept. "Chief, follow me so far?"

Sunny smiled back at his young engineer and said, "Yes, sport, I am good. Keep going."

Ho was surprised his CEO understood the Blockchain concept. "Well, one of the initial applications for this project will be a new digital currency similar to Bitcoin. The merged digital currency codename, *Green Kyoto*, will be based on the Blockchain platform. The goal for the new currency is to trade in real-time when the people from those smart cities are traveling or using e-commerce with this new digital coin."

Sunny was confused and asked, "Wait, you are telling me that people from Naha to Tamsui and from Tamsui to Naha will be using a custom digital currency based on the activity levels?"

Ho responded to his CEO. "Chief, today, people in Japan are carrying the Yen and will need to convert to Green Kyoto Bitcoin. The people in Taiwan carrying TWD dollars will also need to purchase the same Bitcoin. With this new way of paying for services, each country will be able to stamp out counterfeit currency and reduce the value of the dollar in the exchange process. The more users transact with this digital currency, the more the trade value will be."

Sunny understood the project's value and said, "So, if I am a hacker, how do I steal this digital coin?"

Ho replied, "Well, from a pure transaction-to-transaction perspective, unless the hacker has access to several supercomputers or even the latest quantum computing machine, cracking all ten distributed ledgers at the same time while reversing the hash value calculations of the previous block makes the sheer concept of the hacking the Bitcoin nearly impossible."

Sunny knew that no system in the world was a hundred percent safe. He inquired, "Ho, did our cybersecurity guys run various penetration tests against your Blockchain platform?"

Ho replied, "No, not yet."

Sunny looked concerned. "Report back to me in a week when the tests are completed."

Ho rose from his chair and bowed at his CEO.

After Thomas reviewed the latest legal documents regarding the Smart Country project in Taiwan, he needed more eyes behind the project itself. Thomas picked up the phone to call William.

"William, Thomas here."

William sat in his Virginia home admiring his wife, Tricia, who was due any day with their first child. "Yes, Thomas, how are you?"

"I am well, my boy. Do you have a moment?"

William gave Tricia a kiss on her lips and headed into his home office. "Yes, boss, how can I help?"

Thomas gathered his notes and spoke, "Will, please investigate this Taiwan and Japan Smart Country design. We will be offering ADConnect a site license and in return, we will receive five percent of all transactional values based on commerce across this fiber connection by using our software. This is a huge opportunity for our company and your software is the key. I would normally send your dad into battle here; however, he is in Taiwan lying low."

William listened to Thomas. "Yes, I will contact Sunny Ho in the morning and discuss this with him."

Thomas inquired, "How is Tricia?"

William took a moment to sit back in his chair and replied, "She is great. The baby is due anytime now."

Thomas replied, "Anything else on your mind we need to discuss?"

William closed the door to his office. "Yes, Thomas, I need some advice."

Thomas said, "Tell me, son, what is on your mind?"

William began to lay out the secured message he received from Poppy Ledger via the Darknet chat room. William described the message and the hidden meaning behind it.

Thomas replied, "So, Poppy is on the run, probably in Vancouver. The PLA, China's Internal Security, and the Taiwan government want her."

William acknowledged the truth of Thomas's statement.

Thomas thought for a moment and stated, "Let us consider this for a moment. A cyber hacker working with General Vo and the PLA cyber forces wants to defect to the U.S. She has complete access to every cybersecurity procedure, technology, and location of cyber hackers for the entire nation of China. Our FBI, CIA, and NSA would like to get their hands on her." William agreed. Thomas continued, "So, it sounds like we are on the clock. Someone needs to bring Poppy across."

William considered the options and spoke. "She wants me to bring her across. She probably doesn't trust anyone else."

Thomas was thinking the same thing and said, "Will, you need to stay in Virginia with Tricia. Your baby's birth is the most important mission in your life."

"Thanks, Thomas."

Thomas thought about his options and said, "Let me make a few calls, son, and I'll get back to you."

Per Dimi's instructions, both Vlad and Ivan spent the morning logging into the Darknet, looking for any intelligence around who Rambonus was or any recently failed hacks somewhere in the world. Ivan, better known in the hacking world as Darkhorse24, started scanning various chat rooms. Within an hour, Ivan began to pick up a series of global messages from a hacker group in Japan called Rising Sun. SwordBitch, the leader of this Japanese hacker squad, posted several messages identifying various hack attempts against Taiwan from something called Dragon Vault.

Ivan read more posts from SwordBitch. "Lilian Tang, Vulturess, and Poppy Ledger, PLA cyber, Yellowslayer? Interesting."

Lilian left her latest victim dead in the public bathhouse a few hours before reaching downtown Nago, Okinawa. She spotted a coffee shop across the street. Lilian covered her head with a baseball cap and walked into the café to access the internet. After ordering a green tea on ice, Lilian set up her laptop and logged into the internet hotspot.

Close to her, several United States Marines enjoyed a bowl of beef yakisoba and a Sapporo beer. Most of those Marines were stationed nearby at Camp Schwab and Camp Henson.

Both Marine Corps bases had been in existence since after World War II. One of the Marines looked at Lilian., "Guys, look at that. She isn't a regular geisha!"

Within moments, the rest of the Marines looked at Lilian. "Oh shit, she is not!"

Lilian, noticing the attention coming from the Marines' table, decided to turn to them. "Hey, fucker, watch your mouth. I will snap your dick off and ram it down your throat!"

The Marine was shocked by Lilian's threats, got up from the table, and tried to approach her. Before he could take a step, one of the Marines pulled him down. "Let it go, pal."

One of the other Marines took out his camera phone and took Lilian's picture without her consent. After a few minutes, the Marines finished their food and beers and left the coffee house.

"Keep walking, dickless," Lilian whispered. After checking to see if anyone was watching her computer screen, Lilian logged into Darknet to contact Travis Jones.

Message: Darknet14: Encryption: Rambonus: Vulturess: Come get me, coffee house, Nakijin-son road.

Signed,

Vulturess

Lilian continued to scan the various chat rooms in Darknet when she discovered SwordBitch from the San-Hamada hacker group in Tokyo had broadcasted her true identity. "That fucker, I will kill him!" Lilian screamed.

Chapter 37
Back Channel

Conference Call (Taipei, Taiwan)

"Madame President, good to chat with you again," Prime Minister Ang Yoshi San of Japan said.

President Yu Chu Fong of Taiwan knew how critical this video conference was to her country. "Mr. Prime Minister, the pleasure and honor are mine, sir."

"Yu, we have been discussing our joint Smart Country project. I have concerns about the overall cost and cybersecurity risks," Ang said.

"Yes, Ang, I share the same concerns."

Ang referred to his notes. "Yu, I understand the design architects will be deploying a Blockchain system to ensure a failsafe security plan to protect the data. Your thoughts?"

Yu stopped for a moment and thought to herself, "Dammit, I should have listened more to Sunny!" The president gathered her thoughts and spoke, "From my understanding, Blockchain encryption and the entire distributed ledger strategy will be deployed in many countries in the next five years. We are going to be pioneers, Ang. If I may, leveraging Blockchain to create a new digital currency is a huge leap of faith. We know our currency is being manipulated each day in the open markets. By creating a digital currency based on activity between these two initial host cities in our Smart Country Initiative, we can establish a true commerce reward system based on the approved, verified, and confirmed transactions by the Blockchain system."

Ang nodded in agreement. "Yes, Yu, I agree with you. However, I am not ready to abandon the Yen quite yet."

Yu agreed and explained, "Ang, I am not ready to abandon the Taiwan Dollar either. However, I believe this initial digital currency will establish a trust between our two countries that will lead to other joint ventures."

"I need to ask, Yu, have you spoken to Beijing about this?"

Yu looked away from her computer screen and spoke bluntly. "After the whole Dragon Vault hack, I am not in the mood to have a conversation with them."

Ang nodded. He knew if the Japanese Yukuza's stealth hacker group, Rising Sun, didn't block the connections going into Xiamen, China, Taiwan would have suffered the most significant data breach in history. Ang stated, "Yu, you need to have that conversation. Japan still supports the One-China policy. We recognize Taiwan in private, as you know. However, we currently have many business and knowledge sharing agreements with Beijing."

Hearing this statement made Yu even more determined to change her country's global status in the world. She spoke reassuredly, "Okay, Ang, I will have that call with them."

Ang smiled, then suggested, "Let's chat after your call with Beijing and then we can discuss the next steps in our project."

Yu agreed and exited the video call.

"Coffee house?" Travis Jones mumbled after reading the encrypted message from Vulturess. Travis knew he needed to get Lilian back to the safe house in Nago.

Message: Darknet14: Encryption: Vulturess: Rambonus: Stopping at a 7-11 now to get your coffee. ETA 5 minutes.

Signed,

Rambonus

Lilian saw the notification on her secured communicator. "7-Eleven for coffee? Give me a break." She hid in a small alley near the coffee house in Nago and waited for Travis's arrival.

After sending a new secured message to William seeking help, Poppy Ledger remained hidden in Vancouver, Canada. While walking in the city's Gastown section, Poppy dropped into a local pub for a beer and a place to check her messages. Poppy hoped for William's response as she continued to focus on drinking her beer and scanning her messages.

Thomas sat in his office in Pasadena, California and began to devise a plan to bring Poppy Ledger across from Canada. Based on the message from William, Thomas knew he needed to act fast.

Message: FBI.GOV: Encryption: SAC Burns: Thomas Wilson: Need urgent CONFAB, request yourself, Director Ramsey, SA Parker, and AG. Most urgent.

Signed,

Thomas

Gerald just finished a meeting about the Russian Mafia expansion in his city and he noticed an urgent request for a CONFAB, a confidential meeting with him, the FBI, and the Justice Department leadership.

Message: FBI.GOV: Encryption: Thomas Wilson: SAC Burns: Acknowledged, standby for time.

Signed,

Gerald

Travis arrived at the coffee house to pick up Lilian. "Coffee delivery!"

Lilian, hearing this, couldn't believe Travis was yelling that. "Oh, fuck, would you shut up!" Lilian huffed.

Travis smiled from his car and ordered, "Shut up, lady, and get in the car!"

Lilian climbed into the passenger side of the car and said, "I am Lilian."

Travis playfully replied, "Yes, you are. You are much hotter than your college photos, Vulturess."

Lilian smiled back at Travis and robustly replied, "Fuck you."

After a brief look over his shoulder to see if he was being followed, Travis drove back to the safe house with Lilian.

With the CONFAB time confirmed by all the parties, Thomas moved into his secured conference room and began to connect into the dial and video communications bridge. "Thomas, here."

As the video came on his screen, Thomas recognized Attorney General Marcia Robertson, FBI Director Alvin Ramsey, SAC Gerald Burns, and SA Robert Parker.

"Well, thank you all for joining me here," Thomas said with appreciation.

"Be brief, Mr. Wilson," Marcia said sternly.

"Well, let's get to it. We received a flash from Poppy Ledger, a known global hacker on Interpol's most wanted list and an asset for the PLA Cyber, codename Yellowslayer inside of Darknet. She was the one who stole the Backhaul QoS software from William Kendall. She is also the one who hacked into the TAINET firewalls in Taiwan as part of the Operation Dragon Vault hack."

Marcia looked up at the screen and impatiently replied, "We know Mr. Wilson. What is your point?"

"She asked Willian for help to defect. She is currently on the run somewhere in Vancouver, Canada. Royal Canadian Mounted Police confirmed someone drove their car recklessly out of an expensive mansion last night in the city's upper end. I suspect Poppy is running away from her own people and has asked William to bring her across."

The entire conference room went silent. Gerald spoke up. "Excuse me, you are telling us, Mr. Wilson, that a global hacker for PLA cyber group in China wants to defect?"

Thomas nodded.

FBI director Ramsey questioned, "Okay, back up. How do we know this is really Poppy Ledger?"

Thomas answered, "William confirmed the encrypted message contained keywords from a Chinese Cyber Command standard message format."

Marcia stared back at the screen. "Alright, Mr. Wilson, you have our attention. What do you suggest?"

Thomas paused before he answered. "I think Poppy wants William to come to Vancouver to help her get across. William is staying put. Tricia, his wife, is due anytime now."

Marcia threw her hands in the air in frustration. "Who else then?"

Thomas cautiously replied, "Regina Kendall, his sister."

Marcia rolled her eyes. "Another civilian, Christ." She glanced over at FBI Director Ramsey. "Alvin, what do we know about Regina Kendall?"

Alvin opened his iPad and retrieved a file. "Regina Kendall, ex-Coast Guard, decorated, Harvard Law Grad. She worked at Blake, Wilson, and Todd. Her father is Jack Kendall."

Marcia looked stunned at her FBI director and asked incredulously, "Is this the same Kendall running around on his bike in Taiwan?"

The FBI Director reluctantly confirmed that was the same person.

"Christ, that is some family," Marcia whispered. "Okay, Thomas, please see if Regina is willing to do this."

Thomas nodded and hung up the video call.

"Bill, I need the FBI to send React 5 to Vancouver, just in case something goes wrong."

Bill Parker acknowledged Marcia then got up from the meeting room and left.

"Gerald, please brief Regina on her mission. I am sure she can handle a weapon. Please coordinate with the Canadian authorities. We need them to stay back and let the target get to the border checkpoint," Marcia instructed.

Gerald replied, "Yes, AG."

Marcia then continued with her FBI director. "Alvin, stay close to this one. If we can get our hands on Poppy Ledger, the CIA, NSA, and the DEA all would love to get their hands on her as well."

Travis pulled up to the safe house in Nago. He walked around to the passenger side to help Lilian get out of the vehicle.

"Here we are." Travis proclaimed.

While exiting the car, Lilian looked at the view of the Okinawa coastline and said, "Great view."

Travis smiled and headed into the house. Sitting in the living area was Noah watching a movie. He commented, "Ah, shit man, you said no fucking!"

Lilian was not amused by Noah's comment and angrily replied, "You dickless wonder, I will fucking kill you if you come close to me."

Noah stood up from the couch and coarsely spoke, "Trav, did you bring a whore for me?"

Lilian glared at Noah, strolled over to him, and asked, "Whore?"

Noah smiled while staring into Lilian's eyes and replied, "Oh yeah!"

Lilian drew a sharp object from her back pocket. In a blink of an eye, she slashed across Noah's face. Blood flowed down Noah's cheek as he screeched, "Fucking whore!"

Lilian punched Noah in the throat and knocked him back on the couch. Travis, seeing this exchange, jumped over and pushed Lilian down to the ground. "Stop!"

Noah attempted to get up to go after Lilian and Travis screamed, "Noah! Stop! This is Vulturess!"

Noah froze and yelled, "Fuck!" He then headed off to the bathroom to check the cut on his face.

"You need to control yourself!" Travis yelled at Lilian.

"No fucking way," Lilian playfully laughed.

Lilian continued laughing while walking over to sit down on the couch. After a few minutes, Noah emerged from the bathroom with a five-inch cut on his face. "You fucking bitch. I will fuck you up."

Lilian chuckled at Noah and snickered, "Watch your dick, asshole. I collect them!"

Travis tried to establish a sense of order and commanded, "Both of you shut up!"

Noah sat back down on the other side of the couch from Lilian and said, "Tang, I know all about you."

Lilian looked up at Travis. "You were the one during the Dragon Vault briefing call with all the team members who compared a fiber optic cable to a snake?"

Travis started to laugh, and said with great enthusiasm, "Oh, and don't forget the millions of cyber-bots swimming upstream!"

Lilian started to laugh as well.

Noah was confused. "What the fuck are you guys talking about?"

Lilian looked over at Travis and requested, "Can I have a beer, please?"

Travis got up to fetch a round of beers.

Lilian explained to Noah, "Look, Dragon Vault was designed to hack into Taiwan's TAINET network. General Vo of the PLA cyber forces commanded this project with the help of the Fong Gao Triads—my bosses."

Noah was completely shocked and shouted, "What? Who the fuck said anything about Triads?"

Travis returned with the beers and advised, "Hold on, Noah. Chill."

Travis handed out the beers to Lilian and Noah and said, "Look, operational security required that no one knew everything about the operation except for General Vo."

Noah drank his beer and shook his head.

"So, sport, what was your role in this failed hack?" Lilian asked Noah.

Noah responded, "I was the global lawyer that set up Dragon Vault, LLC along with suing and blocking the American software company from releasing their product."

Lilian took a long drink of her beer and ordered, "Hey Jones, another beer?"

Travis looked sternly at his new accomplice and got up to get more beers.

Lilian continued, "So, you are the lawyer who set up the offshore company in Vietnam?"

Noah replied, "And you princess, what was your role in this shitshow?"

Lilian was amused by the term princess and replied, "Well, I was the one that got hired by ADConnect in Taiwan and cross-connected the underwater fiber from Xiamen to the fiber vault in Kaohsiung, Taiwan. I also created the maintenance network that secretly began to copy the data from the Internet of Things network back to China."

Noah looked at Lilian with respect and said, "So, you were on the ground doing all of that? Who was the one that hacked the firewalls and stole the software from Cybercom?"

Travis took a drink of his beer and replied, "Poppy Ledger, PLA Cyber. She reported to General Vo. She was the one that stole the software from William Kendall at the San Francisco technology conference."

Noah asked, "Who else do you know from the team, princess?"

Lilian answered, "Well, the middleman between the Triads and General Vo, Bao Xu."

Travis knew Bao well and asked, "Where is he now?"

"No clue, the last message from him was when I left Taiwan on a cargo plane to come here," Lilian explained.

"Who else?" Noah inquired.

Lilian thought for a moment before answering. "Abe Yang, CEO of Fiberex in Xiamen... not sure of his status. The general, I heard, got arrested by the Chinese Internal Police. So, Travis, why are you sitting here in Okinawa?"

Travis cleared his throat before replying, "Yes, I got something brewing. I need both of you to help."

Lilian finished her beer and chimed in, "Well, I am free at the moment, sport."

Travis guardingly replied, "Before we get started on something new, we need to close a few gaps."

Lilian glared at Noah and Travis. "Okay, what is it?"

Travis referenced a document on his laptop. "A year ago, someone stole a hundred million dollars in Bitcoin from the Japanese San-Hamada Yakuza outfit—the same outfit that fucked up our Dragon Vault Hack with their Blackhat group called Rising Sun."

Lilian put her beer down because she knew where this conversation was headed.

"According to my sources, Vulturess stole the Bitcoin. The Yakuza has been trying to hunt her down ever since. I guess she killed the number two man and his guards as well," Travis said.

Noah was completely shocked and uttered, "One person did all of that?"

Lilian stared back at Noah and stated, "You were lucky I only cut your face."

Travis looked over at Lilian and said, "We know you are the one that stole the Bitcoin and killed the Yakuza guards and San-Hamada's number two man. However, that is in the past. We have new business to discuss."

Lilian nervously acknowledged Travis' statement and replied, "Agreed. Let's move forward." Noah also nodded in agreement.

Travis glanced at Lilian. "Before we move forward, where is the hundred million?"

Lilian stared at Travis and answered, "I deposited it into several digital wallets controlled by BOSS himself and the Fong Gao Triads."

Noah leaned back on the couch and predicted, "Well, that money is gone."

Travis smiled back at his friend and remarked, "Maybe."

Lilian got up and pushed Travis in the chest. "Look, asshole, don't even think about making a move against the Triads. They are the only family I have ever known. BOSS, himself, adopted me from an orphanage in Taiwan when I was two."

Noah asked, "So, you have been a Triad your whole life?"

Lilian replied, "Yes. It is the only life I know."

Travis reflected on his decision to bring Lilian into the new plan. "Look, love birds, I will brief you guys later. I need to discuss some things with our investor. We need to get two hundred million in Bitcoin to pull off this new heist.

Lilian spoke up. "Before you head out, I am hungry. Let's go eat."

Travis got up and motioned his partners to follow him out the door and suggested, "There is a great seafood restaurant down the street."

Chapter 38
Withdrawn

While finishing the legal language for a site license agreement between Cybercom / Techline and ADConnect, Regina received a message from Thomas Wilson.

Message: Cybercom: Encryption: Thomas Wilson: Regina Kendall: I need to chat with you and your brother.

Signed,

Thomas

Regina called her brother. "Bro, Thomas needs us on the video conference. Are you free? How is Tricia?"

William stepped outside Tricia's hospital room and said, "She is great, sis, thanks. Give me a moment."

Within a few moments, Regina, William, and Thomas were connected on a video conference call.

"Thank you for joining me on short notice," Thomas proclaimed.

"Always, Thomas!" Regina responded.

"Okay, Regina, let me bring you up to speed for a moment. Poppy Ledger reached out to William a few hours ago."

Regina was completely in shock over this development and shouted, "What? That fucking bitch after what she did to William?"

Thomas let Regina blow off some steam, then interrupted, "Hold on, big picture here for a moment."

Regina said, "Okay, I am done. Proceed, please."

"In summary, she asked William to help bring her across the border. I asked William to stay home for the birth of his new baby. Regina, the FBI and the AG request your help to bring her across."

Regina was stunned by the request and answered passionately, "Thomas, I will kill her before she steps over the bridge into my country!"

Thomas took a breath before he replied, "Reg, please. For a moment, if we can sort out how to get Poppy Ledger across, the information in her head could save thousands of American lives."

Regina reluctantly answered, "Thomas, I will kill her if she tries to trick us!"

Thomas laughed loudly and exclaimed, "Spoken like a true Kendall."

Regina composed herself. "Let's get to the point. How is this going down?"

Thomas retrieved the secured email from Gerald Burns. "There is a gulf stream G5 at the airport. Please pack what you need and head over to hangar seven. SA Bill Parker and SAC Burns will be making the trip with you. FBI React 5 will be your backup in case something goes wrong." Regina nodded. Thomas addressed William. "William, take care of that wife of yours and nothing else. If you have a moment, please continue to dig into this Smart Country stuff that Sunny Ho is working on."

Regina heard that comment and remarked, "Oh, I have the site license agreement ready for your review, Thomas."

Thomas said, "Thank you, guys. Let's get this girl over here."

Hai Ming had a busy morning. Being the Minister of Finance for all of China, he had back-to-back calls with the president of China discussing

Taiwan and the possible economic sanctions from the U.S. After finishing his calls, Hai reached over to answer his red phone. Only heads of state and his own president ever used that phone line.

"Minister Ming, hello?"

"Minister, President Fong from Taiwan. Do you have a moment?"

"President of Taiwan, do you mean governor of Taiwan?"

Yu, not taking Hai's comment well, said, "President, thank you, Minister."

Hai made his point. "What can I do for you, Madame President?"

Yu held back the urge to scream at Hai and politely spoke, "Minister, we are considering a new crypto-currency pilot project between two Smart Cities: Tamsui, Taiwan, and Naha, Okinawa."

Hai replied with optimism. "Go on."

Yu proceeded. "We are piloting a fiber connection between Japan and Taiwan along with a new Blockchain architecture."

Hai did not like the direction of this conversation. He commented, "Wait. Are you now connecting a portion of China with another country? Who approved this?"

Knowing the president of Taiwan was within her right to approve this, Yu said, "I did, Minister."

Hai, not happy with the answer he received, stated briskly, "Madame, be careful where you are going with this."

Yu clarified, "Minister, our goal is to eliminate counterfeit money and online transactions by experiencing a digital currency based on the consumption of the digital coin itself. The coins won't be working outside of those two cities. This is only a pilot program."

Hai took a moment to hear the president's plan and said, "Proceed."

Yu detected a disrespectful tone from Hai and replied, "As you know, Minister, my country almost suffered from a data breach that could have resulted in very sensitive Taiwanese data. The data could have been stolen by global hackers working with your PLA forces. Our intelligence sources point the finger at your General Vo, members of the Fong Gao Triads, and some law firm based in the States. Furthermore, without the help of a third party, the data would have been exfiltrated. Beijing has said nothing about this event. I owe it to my people to protect their data and move forward with this pilot project."

Hai, along with the Chinese Internal Security Forces, continued to interrogate General Vo in secret, while trying to find other members of the Dragon Vault hacking group. He replied with restraint, "Madame President, we have General Vo in custody. Once we have valuable information to share with you, we will."

"Thank you, Minister. Now, we plan to launch this project next month. However, the prime minister of Japan asked me to reach out to you to seek your support," Yu requested.

Hai sarcastically replied, "Oh, well. I can look into ways we can offer our support, Madame President!"

Yu hated every word coming out of Hai's mouth. She showed remarkable self-control and calmly asked, "Where do we go from here, Minister?"

Hai sat back in his chair and replied, "Let me get back to you, Madame President."

Hai hung up the phone and made a promise to himself. "Blockchain between Japan and Taiwan isn't going to happen." After thinking for a few moments, Hai thought out loud, "We haven't named a successor for General Vo yet to command PLA cyber." He started to consider a replacement for the general. "Major Vonn, Minister Ming here. Report to me, ASAP."

Major Vonn, executive assistant to General Vo at PLA cyber, replied quickly, "Yes, Minister."

Bao Xu sat motionless in his jail cell on Okinawa. He realized that the Americans had no plans to release him and return him to Taiwan. His only option was to expose everything he knew about the Dragon Vault Hack against Taiwan, his involvement with General Vo of the PLA, and the whereabouts of Lilian Tang.

"Guard, I need to speak to my interrogator," Bao requested.

The Marine guard on duty called to the main exchange line at Camp Henson. "Sir, the prisoner wants to speak to Mr. Adams."

The officer on duty got up from his desk and headed over to the barrack where Forest Adams was sleeping. "Mr. Adams, sir, the prisoner requests to speak to you."

Forest sat up in his bed and replied, "Thank you, Captain." Forest got dressed and headed over to the building where Bao Xu was imprisoned. While walking, Forest decided to call Jack Kendall.

"Jack here."

Forest stopped for a moment and said, "Jack, I need you here, Marine. Bao wants to talk."

Jack was still lying low in Taiwan with Li Cao. He replied, "Okay, I will get the next flight out."

Jack hung up and leaned over the bed where Li was lying. "Li, I need to go. Forest needs me in Okinawa."

Li rolled over in the bed and replied, "Come find me when this is over."

Jack smiled and replied, "I will." He packed his bags and before walking out the door, turned once last time to say goodbye to Li.

While Ang Yoshi finished his morning exercise, he received a call on his private line. "Prime Minister, I hope I am not bothering you?" Hai Ming said.

"Oh, Minister Ming, what a pleasant surprise."

Hai sheepishly smiled at the prime minister of Japan's response and answered, "Prime Minister, I just got off the phone with the governor—I am sorry—the president of Taiwan."

Ang cringed under his breath and said, "Yes?"

"Well, sir, I do ask in the future that Japan please honor the One-China Policy and not deal directly with Taiwan unless Beijing is involved."

Ang knew that the Chinese Central Committee took a tough line with any country that recognized Taiwan as a separate nation. "Noted, Minister. What are your thoughts on the project?" Ang inquired.

Hai realized that he needed to be very diplomatic and spoke slowly in his response. "On the surface, I see great things coming from it. China also is investing in Blockchain and digital currency."

Ang felt a bit relieved and replied, "Yes, we have great plans too, if we can connect these two smart cities."

"Prime Minister, has a bank been chosen to host the digital currency and to be a member of the distributed ledger?"

Ang saw a possible win-win in this conversation and enthusiastically responded, "Well, we are planning to use Bank of Tokyo for the Yen conversion to the Green Kyoto Bitcoin Exchange. I don't believe President Fong has selected a Taiwan bank to handle the Taiwan dollar exchange yet."

Hai sinisterly replied, "That is a good point, Prime Minister. I will discuss these banking and exchange with her. Good day, sir."

Hai hung up the phone and sat back to consider his next move. "I need an expert on cyber currency to take over the PLA cyber forces."

Regina arrived at airport hangar seven. The FBI officer stopped her car and shined a flashlight into her eyes. Regina, stunned, called out to the FBI agent and said, "I am Regina Kendall. I am here to meet SAC Burns."

The guard waved her through.

"Kendall, over here, please," Gerald said.

Regina grabbed her bags and headed to the G5 aircraft. "SAC, Regina Kendall reporting for duty, sir."

Gerald smiled at Regina and enthusiastically replied, "Come on, Kendall, climb aboard."

Jack continued to have nightmares of losing Nella while on the plane ride to Okinawa. "Oh, God, help me!" Jack screamed and broke out into a cold sweat.

"Sir, are you feeling well?" the flight attendant asked.

"I am fine, thanks," Jack weakly answered.

"We will be landing soon. Please buckle your seatbelt," the flight attendant announced.

Upon touching ground, Jack reached for his secured communicator.

Message: Encryption: Forest Adams: Jack Kendall: Landing in Naha. Please secure access to Camp Henson. It has been a while since I have been on base.

Signed,

Marine

Forest read Jack's encrypted message and chuckled. "Been a lot longer for me, Marine!"

Forest left the interrogation room and walked out of the building on Camp Henson. He headed over to the main administration building, retrieved his government ID, then went into the security office. "Captain, Forest Adams, here. I have a man arriving at the main gate within the hour. Please, grant him unlimited access. Here are his credentials and permissions."

The Marine Corps captain reviewed the security documents and proceeded to enter Jack's name into the system. As the captain entered Jack's social security number, he spoke out to Forest, "Sir, this man has been here before."

Forest smiled at the acknowledgment and proudly replied, "Yes, Captain, well before you were born."

The captain looked up and smiled. After a few minutes, the captain created a secured access badge for Jack. The Marine spoke, "Sir, I will take these up to the main gate for you. When Mr. Kendall arrives, the guards will grant him access and give him his badge."

Forest thanked the captain and headed back outside.

Chapter 39
Remembrance

Message: Encryption: Kendall: Adams: Computers have a long memory, Jack; you still are in the system. Your credentials will be with the guard shack at the main gate. No stopping off in Kinville, Devil Dog! That is an order!

Jack laughed after seeing the message from Forest. Kinville, a Japanese town outside of Camp Henson Okinawa, was long known for movie lounges, yakisoba restaurants, and beautiful flowers. Jack arrived at the gate at Camp Henson for the first time in thirty-four years. He couldn't believe all the changes to the base and the town. Glancing across the street from the Marine base entrance, Jack could see the same bars and food stands he saw thirty years ago when he visited the place as a young U.S. Marine.

Jack smiled while remembering 1983 when he was stationed in Okinawa. He allowed himself a moment before entering the base again. After a few minutes, Jack turned to the Marine guards. "Jack Kendall. I am expected."

The Marine guard replied, "Yes, Mr. Kendall. You are cleared. Here is your badge. Mr. Adams is expecting you in Building Five. Please proceed."

Jack looked back at the young Marine. "I remember where Building Five is. Thanks."

The young Marine stared back at Jack and opened the gate.

While heading into the military installation, Jack passed several buildings he remembered from his early years as a Marine: the mess hall, the shopping center, and the main administration building. After a brief ten-minute walk, Jack found Building Five and entered looking for Forest.

"Forest?" Jack called out.

Forest was sitting in the lobby when he rose to meet Jack. "Been a long time, Jack. I haven't seen you since you departed Vietnam in 2015."

Jack nodded at his old friend. "Missed you, too, pal."

Forest walked over and gave Jack a big hug. "Good to see you, Marine."

Both men looked at each other with admiration and respect. "Okay, where are we at with this piece of shit?" Jack asked.

Forest motioned Jack to follow him to the back of the room. "Well, he wants to talk. I am glad you are here."

As Jack and Forest entered the interrogation room, Bao, still blindfolded and chained to the desk, yelled in fear. "Who is there? I have my rights!" After seeing Bao Xu for the first time, Jack picked up a chair and smashed the object on Bao's head.

"Fuccck!" Bao yelled.

Forest stepped aside and let Jack take a few shots at Bao, knowing he was the one who ordered the killing of Jack's fiancée in Portugal several months ago.

"Stop! I want to talk," Bao said.

Jack threw the chair against the wall and removed Bao's blindfold. "Okay, asshole, start talking!"

Bao opened his eyes and tried to focus. "Who the fuck are you?"

Jack reached down and grabbed Bao's ring finger on his right hand then proceeded to bend the finger back until the bone broke.

"Stop!" Bao screamed in pain.

"I am Jack Kendall, asshole!"

Bao looked completely terrified. "Oh. Kendall!"

Jack stared at Bao. "Yea, it's me asshole, in the flesh. Now, start fucking talking!"

Bao tried to wipe the blood flowing down into his eyes from the cut on his scalp, and said, "Yes, I will speak."

Jack took one more punch at Bao directly into his face. "Now!" Jack ordered.

Forest interrupted. "Bao, where is Travis Jones?"

Bao swallowed before he nervously replied, "The last time I communicated with him he was still in Taiwan."

Forest glanced over at Jack. "Hit him again!"

Jack got up and punched Bao in the mouth.

"Stop!" Bao cried.

"Okay, let me try an easier question," Jack said. "Where the fuck is Poppy Ledger?"

Bao looked over at Jack and replied, "Vancouver, BC in a safehouse, Fourteen Mansions Row."

Jack nodded and looked over at Forest. "Okay, good start, shit for brains. Here is another one. Where is Vulturess?"

Bao looked sharply at Forest and replied, "You don't want to know. She is the most protected asset in the Fong Gao Triads."

Jack rose to give Bao another punch.

"Jack, hold on," Forest demanded.

"Why?" Jack asked while standing in place.

Bao took a moment to compose himself and spoke gingerly. "BOSS, the Snakehead himself, adopted her at the age of two. Lilian is his only daughter. If any harm comes to her, there will be no limits to BOSS's revenge."

Forest replied, "Look, Bao, we need to get her now. She is a possible suspect in Taiwan for killing several people, including a couple in Taichung. I guess this chick has a serious kill streak in her. Especially for killing her business associates and partners. I guess we can classify her as a modern-day black lotus!"

Bao took a deep breath while tasting his own blood. "She is here on the island. I flew her there a week ago via cargo plane to Naha. The Triads released her near the airport. She could be anywhere on the island hiding out."

Jack nodded and looked over at Forest. "I bet there is a camera somewhere that caught her leaving that area."

Forest looked over and agreed.

"We probably want to let the Japanese police know that she is here and be on the lookout for any unexplained murders in the last seven days," Jack added.

Getting up from his chair, Jack moved behind Bao and commented, "Okay, Bao, that earned you a few points. How about we get into why you ordered the killing of Nella?"

Bao put his head down and replied sharply, "Part of the deal with Travis Jones was supposed to make you and your children suffer greatly for almost costing him the Vietnam project. General Vo was about to order a kill squad to take him out."

Jack took a moment to hear Bao explain why Nella was killed. "Go on."

Bao answered, "We needed you to stay in Portugal while we stole your son's code and leveraged your daughter's law firm to handle the injunction."

Jack nodded. "So, you kept me in Portugal, and then what?"

Bao looked straight ahead and answered, "Our plan was to kill you a few days after Nella."

Jack punched Bao in the back of the head and screamed, "Why?"

Bao attempted to lift his head. "Benoit wasn't supposed to die that day."

Jack remembered being on the boat in Cascais Portugal with Rico Gomez from the special Portugal Investigation Team, and said, "Yes, the boat had his blood everywhere."

Bao nodded. "Francois was supposed to hide the car and stay in a hotel for a few days, then hunt you down. We didn't expect him to get injured when he ran over your girlfriend."

Jack smacked Bao again in the back of the head and snarled, "When we are done, asshole, I will fucking kill you!"

Forest motioned Jack to sit down and spoke calmly, "Bao, if Vulturess is on Okinawa, then so is Noah Wilson. There is a pretty good chance that Jones is here as well. If so, where would he be?"

Bao looked up at Forest and replied, "I don't know. However, I know he had a safe house somewhere on the island. I bet he is hiding out in Nago."

Forest showed a small grin. "Jack, come with me."

After walking back into the lobby, Forest said, "Jack, the Chinese want him badly; the AG told me to finish up quickly and get rid of him. What else do we need from him?"

Jack took a seat and began to think about what else Bao knew about Dragon Vault that could help them. "How about where is the one hundred million in Bitcoin that Lilian Tang stole from the Yakuza last year in Macau."

Forest began to think as well and replied, "That could be helpful. We could leverage the Yakuza here on the island to track down Vulturess."

Jack and Forest went back into the room to see Bao again. "Okay, Bao, last question. Where is the one hundred million in Bitcoin that Lilian Tang stole last year from the Yakuza?"

Bao looked away from Forest and replied cautiously, "I can't tell you."

Jack rose to hit Bao again. However, Forest motioned to Jack to wait. "Bao, if you want to see the light of day again, we need to know where those Bitcoins are."

Bao considered what choices he had left. "If I tell you, what will happen to me?"

Forest handed Bao a glass of water. "Drink."

Bao drank the water like he hadn't had any water in months.

Forest then spoke to Bao in a direct tone. "Well, honestly, we will turn you over to the Japanese police. You will be charged with murder, extortion, drugs, and human trafficking."

Being a global lawyer, Bao knew the Japanese laws well and nervously answered, "If I tell you, what will you do with me?"

Jack replied, "I will kill you quickly!"

Bao stared at Jack, and said, "I bet you would, Kendall."

Forest laughed. "Okay, Bao, what do you want? If you tell us where the Bitcoins are, I will see what I can do to help you."

Bao pondered for a moment. "Let me go to Vietnam."

Jack looked over at Forest before speaking. "Oh, why Vietnam?"

Bao replied, "I have a house there near Sapa."

Jack eyeballed Bao. "Okay, one-way ticket to Vietnam. Fine. I will even pay for it. Now, where is the Bitcoin?"

Bao started to explain the complexity of Bitcoin and Blockchain security. "Vulturess deposited the Bitcoin into several digital wallets controlled by BOSS himself. All the Blockchain ledgers are distributed and controlled by various miners and reviewers. They became manipulated by the Triads in some way."

Forest peeked over at Jack and asked, "Do you have any idea what he is talking about?"

Jack replied, "Some." Jack scrutinized Bao's explanation. "So, Vulturess had to be in the room with access to a secured communicator linked to the Yakuza's digital wallet, correct?"

Bao analyzed Jack's reaction. "Yes, she killed the number two man in the San-Hamada Yakuza. She used his finger to access the device after he was dead."

Forest took a deep breath. "Jack, we are done here."

Jack agreed. Both men stepped out of the room.

"Forest, we need to turn him over to the Chinese."

Forest reluctantly agreed with Jack. "Guards, please move the prisoner to a VIP cell block, feed him, and give him medical attention."

The guard replied, "Yes, sir."

Forest entered the room. "Bao, we are going to keep our end of the bargain. These men will take care of you. I will arrange for your transport."

Bao looked up with a skeptical look. "How can I trust you?"

Forest turned to Bao and punched him in the face. "You can't."

Jack headed out to the Building Five lobby and asked, "Forest, are we really letting him go?"

Forest stood quietly before answering, "Let me make a few calls. Come on, Marine."

Message: FBI.GOV: Encryption: Marcia Robertson: AG: Forest Adams CIA: Need CONFAB urgently.

Signed,

Forest

At home in her Georgetown townhouse, Marcia Robertson was resting from a long day when she noticed a flash message from Forest. "CONFAB, this should be good." Marcia opened her secured communication terminal linked to her office system and sent Forest a reply.

Message: FBI.GOV.Justice: Encryption: SAC Burns, SA Parker, FBI Ramsey: CONFAB: 30 minutes – urgent.

Signed,

AG

Forest and Jack walked over from Building Five in Camp Henson to the main administration building. After flashing their badges, the Marine guard escorted them to a secured conference room. While Jack and Forest got settled, Gerald Burns and Bill Parker were currently enroute to Vancouver with Regina Kendall to lure Poppy Ledger across the border. The two FBI special agents received the message. However, the G5 aircraft lacked the needed Internet bandwidth to connect to the secured conference.

Gerald directed, "Bill, try to send an email to AG, letting her know we are still in the air."

Bill nodded and attempted to send a message.

Message: FBI.GOV: Encryption: Bill Parker: SA: Marcia Robertson: AG: Still in the air with SAC and the asset, won't be able to connect to the CONFAB.

Signed,

Parker

Marcia saw the message from Bill Parker. Within a few moments, Marcia connected into the video conference with FBI Director Ramsey, Forest Adams, and Jack Kendall.

"Good evening, Marcia," Forest greeted.

Marcia smiled, "Good evening." Jack smiled and kept quiet. "Mr. Kendall, you have an exceptional daughter. You should be very proud of her."

Jack smiled back at Marcia. "Thank you, Madame."

Marcia realized that Jack and Forest weren't aware of Vancouver's upcoming operation and said, "Mr. Kendall, your son received an encrypted message from Poppy Ledger on Darknet. She wants to defect. We sent Regina with SAC Burns and Bill Parker's React 5 team to Vancouver."

This enraged Jack. "What? You sent my daughter to bring Poppy across?"

Marcia expected Jack to be upset. "Mr. Kendall, we couldn't send William. Your daughter-in-law is expecting to give birth anytime now."

Jack looked at Forest before answering Marcia. "Madame, you are putting my daughter in harm's way!"

Alvin Ramsey spoke up. "Look, Kendall, she is the only one we could send in. We have SAC Burns with her and React 5 as a backup."

Jack still looked very upset. "Alvin, pray that something doesn't happen to my daughter!"

The video conference fell silent for a moment.

"Marcia, we have an update on Bao," Forest said.

Marcia sighed. "Please go ahead, Forest."

Forest reviewed his notes. "Okay, Bao couldn't tell us the location of Travis Jones. However, he did confirm that Vulturess is on the island somewhere. He also confirmed Noah Wilson, the fucking lawyer, is here as well."

Marcia continued, "Go on."

"He also confirmed Vulturess killed the number two man in San-Hamada Yakuza last year in Macau and stole one hundred million in Bitcoin. We also know the San-Hamada has a contract out on Vulturess."

Alvin interrupted, "Forest, what is the plan then?"

Forest answered, "Well, Bao wants to go to Vietnam quietly in exchange for this information. We prefer to turn him over to the Chinese and let him rot."

Marcia agreed. "Forest, I will make an arrangement with the Chinese. Any chance you can get him back to Taipei?"

Forest evaluated what options were available and said, "Well, yes, we have a plane here at Kadena Air Force Base on standby."

Marcia added, "Get him to Taipei and I will arrange for the Chinese assets to take him from there."

"Madame AG, what are we getting in return?" Jack questioned.

Marcia looked coldly at Jack through the video screen. "None of your business, Kendall."

Jack stared back at the AG and replied sharply, "Aye, Madame."

Forest disconnected from the call and said, "Jack, don't take it personally; I have known her since high school and college days. Okay, let's get this piece of shit back to Okinawa. You need to stay here, Marine. You need to find Vulturess and Noah."

Jack paused before answering, "Roger that."

Chapter 40
Sorrow

Poppy was still hiding out in Vancouver, not knowing if William ever received her message. She began to consider what other options she had left. She pondered going back to the safe house and claiming it was a mistake to escape her PLA protectors. After concluding that option as a bad idea, Poppy ordered a third beer, hoping her message to William made it through.

As she began to drink her beer, a flash message appeared on her secured communicator.

Message: Darknet24: Encryption: Knight2Rouk7: Yellowslayer: The bridge is down. Move to the jump point two hundred meters from the gap. Help is on the way, ETA for extraction: Two hours and 30 minutes.

Signed,

Your Knight in Shining Armor

Poppy noticed the flash message come across her secured communicator.

Message: Knight2Rouk7: Yellowslayer: Message received. Resources on their way to jump point. Hold your position 200 meters from the crossing.

Signed,

William

Message: Darknet24: Encryption: Yellowslayer: Knight2Rouk7: I will be there waiting for you, Knight.

William read Poppy's message. "She is expecting me to be in Vancouver to help her cross the border. Fuck! I hope she won't be disappointed that I won't be there at the pick-up point," William ruminated.

Message: FBI.GOV: Encryption: SAC Burns: William Kendall: Target acknowledged. She will be two hundred meters from the gap in the next 2.50 hours.

Signed,

William Kendall

Gerald read the encrypted message from William. "Out Fucking Standing!" He rotated in his seat on the plane to address Regina. "Your brother just confirmed Poppy Ledger will be at the pick-up point in the next 2.5 hours."

Regina acknowledged and replied, "Okay, how do we do this, SAC?"

Gerald broke out a mini whiteboard on the plane and said, "Listen up, everyone! Okay, here is the Canadian border crossing near Bellingham, Washington. The target will be two hundred meters here along the road. Regina will cross alone with React 5, a hundred meters to the right of the target. The Royal Canadian Mounted Police will have units twenty-five meters from the target. Regina will approach the target and escort her, here, fifty meters across the border. I will have the SUV ready with Bravo Squad from React 5. Any questions?"

"No, we are good. Let's get this done and go home," Regina said.

Gerald ordered, "Gear up. We will be wheels down in thirty minutes."

Major Vonn, general assistant to General Vo, head of all Cyber forces for the PLA in China, was summoned to the minister of finance's office. "Major Vonn, reporting as ordered, Minister."

Hai Ming looked outside his window and acknowledged, "Come in, Major, have a seat."

"Yes, Minister, what can I do for you today?"

Hai replied, "Major, as you know, we have taken General Vo into custody because his organization financed the Dragon Vault Hack against Taiwan. Were you aware of this secret mission?"

Major Vonn knew there was only one answer to the question. "Yes, sir. I was aware of the mission and I am familiar with all the team members involved."

Hai looked over at Vonn. "Thank you for being honest. Did the general create an alliance with the Fong Gao Triads?"

Vonn was caught off guard, and nervously replied, "Yes, he maintained a relationship with the Triads lawyer, Bao Xu."

Hai nodded. "We know him. Vonn, we need to replace General Vo quickly. Who would you recommend?"

Vonn considered for a moment to nominate himself, then thought of the repercussions. "Minister, I would recommend Poppy Ledger."

Hai snapped at Vonn. "Who is she?"

"Sir, she is the one that stole the American's backhaul software and crypto keys. She also hacked the firewalls within TAINET to create a data channel for the information to flow back to China."

Hai, initially impressed, quickly changed his tone. "Where is she now?"

Vonn urgently answered, "She had been hiding out in a Vancouver safe house after she stole the crypto from William Kendall at a conference in San Francisco. When the Dragon Vault mission fell apart, she stayed in hiding for a few days. Our PLA security forces reported that she smashed through the gate of the mansion while escaping. She hasn't been seen in two days, Minister."

Hai stormed over to Vonn's chair. "What? She escaped and now she is missing?"

Vonn nodded his head violently.

"Find her and bring her back to China!"

Vonn got up and headed back to his office.

Hai was furious at the revelation that one of China's top cybersecurity experts may try to defect. He reached for his phone. "General Voung, this is Minister Ming. Order your guards in Vancouver to capture Poppy Ledger and bring her back to China immediately!"

General Voung, head of China's External Security Forces, was unaware of Poppy Ledger's location or status. "Minister, I have no record of a Poppy Ledger in my system."

Hai remembered that everyone reporting to General Vo had their records hidden from all internal security systems. "General, I will grant you access. Standby." He logged into the central military records database and added the general to the Central Committee Access Administrator Authority list. "Try again, General."

Within a few moments, the general became deeply alarmed. "Minister, I should have been told about this asset before. All matters dealing with Chinese citizens or outside assets working for China are under my authority!"

Hai was not in the mood to talk about internal political decisions. "Shut up, General! Find her and bring her back!" He slammed the phone down and walked over to the window. Hai began to send numerous messages using his secured communicator to various Central Committee members of the Chinese government.

Message: Encryption: Central Committee: members: Minister Ming: External Asset, Codename: Poppy Ledger attempting to defect to the west. I am activating the recovery team now. Stand by for further updates.

Signed,

Ming

Chapter 41
Progression

Travis Jones Safehouse (Nago, Okinawa)

While enjoying the fine food overlooking Okinawa's beaches, Travis Jones, Lilian Tang, and Noah spoke very little to each other. Trying to maintain a low profile, the trio kept their conversations to a minimum.

Noah asked, "So, Travis, I understand you may be considering building a new condo?"

Travis was not amused by Noah's attempt to speak in spy language and snapped back, "Bro, shut up. Not here."

Lilian smirked at the brief exchange between the two men and sarcastically laughed. "You guys are really something."

Travis looked over at Lilian. "What is the problem now, princess?"

Lilian finished her swordfish dinner and answered with amusement, "First off, no one can hear us because of the waves in front of us. Second, no one gives a shit."

Noah beamed at Lilian. "Beauty, brains, charisma… you have it all, princess."

Lilian sneered at Noah. "Oh brother, give it up asshole. You will never have a chance!"

"Enough!" Travis commanded. "Both of you shut the fuck up. Listen carefully. We have something brewing, and I need you guys all in on this one."

Lilian sipped her white wine. "Count me in."

Noah nodded as well.

Travis continued. "Okay, it's about some Russian hacker outfit."

Hearing the word 'Russian,' Lilian interrupted. "Wait, Gorky Park?"

Travis glared over at Lilian in shock and spewed, "How the fuck do you know them?"

Lilian took a breath and replied, "Vlad and Ivan work for Dimi Zosh. He is a real human butcher. Ex- KGB agent, former Russian Army Captain in Afghanistan, runs an outfit in Brooklyn. Same guy?"

Travis became very guarded and replied, "Go on."

Lilian answered, "Last year, Gorky Park hacked into the Fong Gao Triads' digital cloud system. Inside the digital depository held a secured folder system. The folder held our database on all girls worldwide we had working in the pleasure industry. We had girls in forty countries. Dimi's crew stole the database and began to hunt down our girls. Any girl that didn't work for him, the Russian crew would beat them to death. Afterward, Ivan and Vlad would post these pictures all over Darknet." Lilian paused to compose herself before continuing. "Many girls were chopped up. BOSS himself put a contract hit out on Dimi. Each time someone got close, the hitman was killed by one of Dimi's kill squads."

After all the blood drained from Noah's face, he asked, "Then, what happened?"

Lilian responded coldly, "Dimi ordered a hit on BOSS. So far, my father has dodged his share of assassination attempts."

This was the first time Travis heard this story. He was overcome with fear. "I didn't know."

Travis and Noah struggled to process all that Lilian had revealed about Dimi Zosh and his crew. The three sat silently.

Travis broke the silence. "Look, the Russians have a plan and they need our help here in Okinawa."

Lilian and Noah were confused by Travis's statement. Lilian asked, "What part of cutting people up into pieces didn't you get, Trav?"

Travis arrogantly replied, "Like I said, they have a target in mind. Interested?"

Lilian condescendingly replied, "Yes, I am in, asshole."

Travis rolled his eyes in frustration. "Okay, here is how the story begins. Gorky Park hacked into Japan's prime minister's personal email account. He mentioned something about a new cryptocurrency coming out, something called Green Kyoto. The project has something to do with the president of Taiwan. She agreed to create a Peer-Network between a city north of Taipei and a city here in Okinawa."

Lilian listened and replied, "Sounds like they are stealing our Dragon Vault Hack!"

Travis stared back at Lilian. "Not quite. The Russians plan to come here in a few days. I am going to meet them and discuss the plan. Once I have a better understanding of what they want, we will mobilize."

A frightened Noah asked Lilian, "What if they decide to cut us into little pieces?"

Lilian replied with contempt, "These Russian assholes know better than to conduct any business inside of Yakuza territory. San-Hamada has no love for the Russians either."

Travis ordered, "So, lay low guys, stay inside until night-time, eat only in places that don't draw attention!"

Noah mockingly jested at his partner, "Still only into men, Travis?"

Travis coldly stared at Noah with disdain and replied, "Let's try to forget that, shall we?"

Noah became embarrassed and stared at the floor.

Lillian was not aware that Travis Jones was gay and joked, "I know I will sleep easier at night now."

Travis was not amused by Lilian's comment. He impatiently asked for the check and said, "Let's get out of here."

Vlad walked into Dimi's secret office in Brooklyn, New York to update his boss on Travis Jones.

Dimi barked at his lead hacker. "Vlad, what do you have on this piece of shit, Jones?

Vlad was irritated with Dimi's attitude. "I found out that the PLA Cyber and Fong Gao Triads used on outdated fiber connection between China and Taiwan for something called codename: Dragon Vault. Some hacker outfit, Emerald Forest out of Laos, was mobilized by Travis Jones. He was going to use the Dragon Vault mission to hack into TAINET's network and attempt to exfiltrate the data off the Internet of Things network. According to my Darknet sources, someone activated the Rising Sun outfit to assist."

Dimi snapped at Vlad. "Who the fuck are they?"

Vlad disdainfully replied, "They are run by the San-Hamada's Yakuza group in Tokyo."

Dimi answered, "San-Hamada, that Japanese whore! Is he still at war with BOSS, Snakehead of the Fong Gao Triads?"

Vlad rebuffed, "Don't forget the PLA cyber. General Vo personally ran the operation from Beijing."

Dimi despised General Vo.

Vlad continued, "Anyway, the hack failed when Rising Sun executed a denial-of-service attack against the entire city of Xiamen, China. The attack lasted long enough for ADConnect to reboot all external firewalls and disconnect the fiber connection back to China. Our sources tell us that, Vulturess, herself was responsible for creating the backdoor network."

Dimi turned sharply to Vlad. "Vulturess, that fucking bitch!"

Vlad loathed Lilian as much as Dimi did.

Dimi stared out his window admiring the Brooklyn Bridge. "So this Travis Jones has some connection in Moscow? We need to find out what his plan is."

Vlad nodded his head. "I got us booked on a plane to Okinawa so we can meet this guy."

Dimi continued to view the New York skyline while in deep thought.

"Air Force control Kadena, this is Forest Adams, code clearance Alpha176289. Request departure of an asset to Taipei Taiwan. The asset is a high-value target. Permission granted by the United States Attorney General Marcia Robertson."

Captain Tom Neri of the U.S. Air Force was responsible for all VIP transport in and out of Okinawa. He prepared the flight plan and departure orders. "Mr. Adams, the flight plan is approved. We need you on the tarmac in the next sixty minutes, hangar 17A."

"Thank you, Captain. There will be four people in total. Two Marine guards, the VIP asset, and myself."

Captain Neri acknowledged.

"Jack," Forest said, "wheels up in sixty minutes. I am heading to Kadena now."

Jack walked over to his friend and said, "No time for a plate of yakisoba in Kinville?"

Forest smiled at his dear friend. "Next trip, Marine!"

Jack became sentimental. "I wouldn't have gotten this far without you, Forest. From getting me out of trouble in Vietnam to helping me track down Nella's killer. I owe you."

Forest noticed Jack's eyes mist up and spoke, "Marine, I promised Bui that I would look after you."

Jack thanked Forest and said, "Okay, enough mushy stuff. I am going to get these assholes if they are still on this island."

As Jack finished his conversation with Forest, the two Marine guards escorted Bao Xu to a jeep. "Mr. Adams, we are ready."

Forest turned to Jack. "I am off, Marine. I will call you once the package has been delivered."

Before turning in, Jack decided to walk around the old Marine Base again, remembering the last time he was there as a young Marine.

Gerald Burns was enroute to Vancouver, Canada, with SA Bill Parker, FBI React 5 team, and Regina Kendall. They were on the clock to try to lure Poppy Ledger across the border from Canada.

"Team, we are wheels down in five minutes," Gerald said.

Captain Neri informed Forest, "Mr. Adams, we are on final approach into Taipei."

Forest waved at the pilot and acknowledged him. He then addressed Bao. "Bao, hang tight. We will be on the ground shortly. The ground crew will transfer you to another plane and then you will be off to Vietnam. It's been a pleasure doing business with you."

Bao was still in shock that the Americans were letting him go and not turning him over to the Chinese government.

As the plane landed, Forest received an important phone call from Marcia Robertson. "Forest, where are you?"

Forest answered, "We are on final approach into Taipei. Once we land, we will transfer Bao to a flight to Vietnam."

Marcia, with urgency in her voice, ordered, "You need to hold him. The Taiwan National police want him. They want to question him about a double murder in Taichung. To make matters worse, the Chinese want him as well."

Forest looked at Bao and said, "Shit." He knew the Chinese would be waiting for him to land. Forest needed to come up with an idea quickly. "Captain, how much fuel do we have?"

Captain Neri replied, "Sir, we have about two hours of fuel left. Why?"

Forest thought about the next move and gave the order. "Abort the landing. Change your course. Head east twenty-five kilometers and circle the area. We need to buy time."

Captain Neri acknowledged, "Taipei Tower, this is US Air Force Flight 331, Captain Neri speaking. We request a fly-by and a vector please to a holding pattern east of the island."

"Air Force Flight 331, this is Taipei Tower. You are cleared to fly by. Head to vector, 090 degrees twenty-six miles and orbit, waiting for instructions."

"Taipei Tower, this is US Air Force flight 331, acknowledged."

Captain Neri turned to Forest and gave him a two-finger signal. "Two hours, Mr. Adams."

Forest connected back to Marcia. "Okay, we just did a fly-by. We have two hours of fuel. What do you have in mind?"

Marcia knew her options were limited. She decided against her better judgment to reach out to Hai Ming again. "Hai, it's Marcia. Do you have a moment?"

Hai was occupied with stopping Poppy Ledger from defecting at the Canadian border and asked in an annoyed manner, "What do you want, Marcia?"

"We have Bao en route to Taipei. However, we will turn him over to you under one condition."

Hai abruptly stepped away from the crisis center in Beijing while monitoring the developments around Poppy's possible defection. He grew impatience as he asked, "What do you want?"

"Hai, we have a team on the ground ready to assist Poppy Ledger to come across the border. Let her go and allow her to cross the border."

Hai walked further away from the crisis room and headed into a private conference room. "Okay, you give us Bao, and in return, we let Poppy defect to the West."

Marcia was relieved by Hai's deal. "Yes, that is the arrangement. Call off your security detachment, and I will have our people land on Penghu Island. Have one of your helicopters land there."

Hai tried to give the impression that he agreed to the deal. "Okay, I will make the call."

Marcia connected with Forest to pass along the instructions. "Okay, Forest. Tell the pilot to divert to Penghu Island. The Chinese will have a helicopter there to take Bao into custody."

Forest acknowledged, "Captain, divert to Penghu Island."

Hai initiated the arrangement that he had with Marcia. "General Voung, please launch a helicopter to Penghu island. The Americans will hand over Bao Xu to us."

General Voung looked directly at his Minister of Finance and asked, "Sir, do we allow Poppy Ledger to cross the border?"

Hai glared angerly at the general, "Bring that traitor, Poppy Ledger, home!"

After Marcia gave the instructions to Forest, she phoned SAC Gerald Burns in Vancouver to give him the latest update. "SAC Burns? This is Attorney General Marcia Robertson. I cut a deal with the Chinese. They will let Poppy Ledger cross the border and in exchange we will give them Bao Xu."

Gerald couldn't believe the message he just received. "Ma'am, with all due respect, this deal doesn't sound right. The Chinese would never exchange their top cybersecurity hacker for a mid-level broker."

Marcia disregarded Gerald's concern. "I get it, SAC. I don't expect the Chinese to double-cross us."

Gerald disagreed with Marica but replied respectfully, "Yes, ma'am."

With great apprehension, Gerald instructed his team. "The Chinese are expected to allow Poppy Ledger to defect without any resistance from them. However, be on your guard just the same."

The team received and acknowledged the orders from Gerald on their earpieces.

After the plane diverted to Penghu Island, the Chinese External Security Forces landed their helicopter at the airport. "Penghu Tower, this is PLA helicopter 127 requesting landing instructions."

The airport tower on Penghu Island instructed the Chinese helicopter to land near runway seven.

Captain Neri communicated with the airport tower. "Penghu Tower, this is US Air Force Flight 331, requesting permission to land."

The tower replied, "US Air Force Flight 331, put on heading 178 and proceed to land on runway seven."

Forest braced himself for the landing. He looked out the window and observed the Chinese Army helicopter landing.

Poppy proceeded to walk to the US-Canadian border per the last instructions she received. Reaching her pre-positioned jump point near the U.S. and Canadian border, she cautiously looked around for any Royal Canadian Mounted Police and prayed, "Please be here, William." Following instructions, Poppy moved to a tree-filled area two hundred meters from the border crossing where she waited for William.

General Voung, head of all Chinese External Security Forces, became alarmed when he learned how close Poppy was to the U.S. border. He immediately gave the order. "All units, this is General Voung. Apprehend Poppy Ledger immediately. Use all means necessary to stop her from going across the U.S. border. Bring her back to China!"

Captain Ping Yi, head of all Chinese Security Services in Canada, responded, "Yes, sir, this is Captain Yi, acknowledged. We have security teams outside the American consulate in Vancouver along with three units deployed at the border."

The general reacted harshly. "Don't fail, Captain."

As the G5 aircraft taxied to a runway in Bellingham, Washington, the team led by SAC Gerald Burns jumped off the plane, entered the SUVs, and headed to the Canadian border.

"Royal Canadian Mounted Police, stand by. We are approaching the border," Gerald said on the encrypted handheld radio.

"SAC Burns, this RCMP Captain Al Horsestram, the target is spotted."

"Listen up, team. RCMP reported Poppy Ledger is in position; ETA to the border, ten minutes."

"Target moving to the border, sir," the RCMP officer said.

Within ten minutes, Gerald, Regina, and the FBI React 5 team arrived at the U.S. Border. Gerald, seeing Poppy moving towards the U.S. border, motioned to Regina, "Go!"

Regina departed the SUV and moved quickly to make contact with Poppy.

Poppy's heart rate escalated as she approached the border.

Regina yelled, "Poppy, hurry!"

Hearing Regina call her name, Poppy stopped coldly in her tracks.

Regina stopped as well. "Poppy, it's me. Regina. Regina Kendall."

Poppy was confused and angry. "Who the fuck are you? Where is William?"

Gerald witnessed the drama unfolding. "Regina, we need to get her across now!"

Regina pleaded and insisted. "Poppy, please, come across the border. Now!"

A flash message came over the encrypted radio. "Sir, this is RCMP Security Team 4. We have three vehicles approaching from the east."

Gerald spotted the vehicles closing in on the U.S. border.

Bill Parker heard gunshots coming from the vehicles. "React 5 Team, engage!" The FBI React 5 team returned fire at the three vehicles approaching at a high rate of speed.

"React 5, move up and secure the target!" Bill Parker ordered.

Regina immediately drew her 9 mm Glock sidearm.

Gerald was concerned for Regina's safety and yelled, "Regina, get out of there!"

Poppy drew her weapon and began to shoot at Regina as she ran back to the Canadian border. As she attempted to hide in the tree lines, one of the cars spun up next to her. "Poppy, get in!" the driver screamed. Poppy jumped into the vehicle's passenger side as bullets from Regina's gun hit the car.

Regina screamed as she was shooting, "You fucking bitch, I will kill you!"

As Regina went to reload her weapon, she was struck by a bullet in her arm from one of the approaching vehicles. She fell backward and screamed in immense pain. "I am hit!"

Gerald witnessed Regina hit the ground. He swiftly moved to the border to pull her to safety. "Cover me!" Gerald yelled.

Within minutes, Poppy's escape vehicle spun away from the border, heading back east towards Vancouver. She turned to the driver. "Who the fuck are you?"

The driver replied," I am Captain Yi. I was sent to protect you, Poppy."

Poppy grew suspicious and did not trust the Chinese captain. She turned to look out the car window when Captain Yi stuck a needle into her neck. Poppy immediately became dizzy and passed out.

"This is Captain Yi. Poppy Ledger is secured. I am heading to the airstrip now."

While monitoring all communications during the shootout at the Canadian border, the National Security Agency operations team in FT. Meade, Maryland recorded the transmission. NSA Specialist Barney Allen listened to the recording of the shootout at the Canadian border. "Oh shit!"

The shootout continued at the border. A second vehicle contained more Chinese External Forces. They attempted to flee the scene as the shots fired by the RCMP and American agents hit their car.

"Move in and contain everyone in the car," Bill Parker ordered.

Gerald went to Regina's side. "Hold on, help is on the way."

Regina was dizzy from the blood loss. "I am okay SAC. Did I get that fucking bitch?"

Gerald remained calm while looking into Regina's eyes. "No, I think she got away."

Regina pounded the ground in frustration and shouted, "Fuck!"

As the FBI and RCMP surrounded the captured vehicle, the car's occupants began to throw out their weapons. "We surrender!"

"Take them into custody," Bill Parker demanded.

Gerald pulled out a handkerchief and pressed it on Regina's bullet wound. "Hang in there."

Regina grimaced in pain while Gerald pushed down on her gunshot wound.

Bill Parker ran over to check on Regina. "SAC, two vehicles got away. One is heading back to Vancouver. The RCMP had two men hit badly. They are being transported to an area hospital. How is Ms. Kendall?"

Regina was annoyed at Bill Parker's question. "I am fucking great, thank you!"

The EMT team and ambulance from a nearby Bellingham, Washington hospital arrived on the scene.

"Over here!" Gerald yelled.

The EMT dropped down next to Regina. "Okay, miss, I am here to take care of you."

Regina was relieved to see the medical personal arrived. She asked Bill, "How many of our team was hit by those assholes?"

Bill replied, "Three wounds, none of them serious."

Regina spoke directly to Gerald, "Who the fuck were they?"

Gerald sighed. "We are not sure. RCMP has few of them in custody now."

The ambulance loaded Regina and headed off toward Bellingham General Hospital.

The FBI and RCMP handcuffed the Chinese men from the second car and placed them on the ground. Gerald asked, "Okay asshole, who the fuck are you?"

The Chinese officer sneered back and replied, "I am a diplomat from the Chinese Consulate. My team and I have immunity. Fuck you!"

An RCMP officer struck the Chinese Diplomat in the face with his fist. "Immunity? Never heard of it, eh."

The chartered U.S. Air Force plane carrying Forest, the Marine guards, and Bao Xu battled through turbulence while on approach to Penghu Island, off the coast of Taiwan.

"Okay, Bao, the party is over. Time for you to go, pal."

Bao was blindfolded as the Marines led him off the plane. He could feel the humidity in the air. He took a deep breath and said, "Thank you, Mr. Adams."

Forest departed the plane and headed over to the Chinese helicopter. He approached one of the Chinese Army officers. "I am Forest Adams from the American Embassy in Ho Chi Minh City, Vietnam."

The Chinese officer stepped out of the helicopter, briskly shook Forest's hand, and introduced himself. "Wu Shi, Chinese External Security Forces."

The Chinese officer displayed disdain and hatred for the Taiwanese lawyer; he glared at Bao and asked Forest, "Mr. Adams, is this him?"

Forest removed Bao's blindfold and replied, "He is all yours."

Bao was utterly shocked when he recognized the Chinese officers and screamed, "Wait! Who are these men? Are these men escorting me to Vietnam?"

As Forest walked away from Bao, he taunted him. "Oh yeah, there was a change of plans, pal."

With a tremendous sense of satisfaction, Forest walked to the plane hearing Bao scream, "You fucked me!" Forest turned back in Bao's direction and said quietly, "That is for Nella, asshole."

Speeding through several side roads to a secret airfield outside Vancouver, Canada, the Chinese External Security Officer Captain Yi, sped towards the plane before Poppy woke up. The injection he shot into her neck was only strong enough for an hour. Upon reaching the hidden airfield, Captain Yi flashed his lights three times to the plane and waited for the guards to wave through. Seeing the oncoming car, the pilot turned on his bombardier jet and prepared to take off.

Captain Yi slammed the brakes of the car coming to a sudden halt. He instructed his men to get Poppy out of the car.

"Get her on the plane and handcuff her. She will be awake within the hour."

The Chinese Security agents complied with the captain's orders. They lifted Poppy out of the car and carried her on the plane. Once Poppy was strapped in her chair, the security team locked the aircraft's door and motioned for the pilot to take off.

Message: Encryption: PLA: External Forces: Rapid Force Team Vancouver: General Voung: Target captured; the plane is en route back to China.

Signed,

Captain Yi

Chapter 42
Political Interference

Presidential Palace (Taipei, Taiwan)

Dreading the call from the Chinese Minister of Finance, Yu Chu, President of Taiwan, waited impatiently for her nemesis' call. The entire Smart City project hinged on the decision for the location of the distributed ledger supporting the Blockchain framework.

Sitting anxiously in her Taipei office, Yu finally received the call from Hai Ming.

"Madame President, Minister Hai Ming here."

Yu became flustered and angry hearing Hai's voice and stuttered, "Minister, good of you to call."

Hai knew Yu was putting on a show for his sake. He started to provoke Yu. "Well yes, thank you. I've been thinking about our Smart Country project and the development of the new cryptocurrency."

Yu held off asking any questions until her adversary was finished speaking.

Her tolerance for Hai's arrogance caused her to snap. "What do you mean by *OUR* project? Minister?"

Hai laughed, knowing he was agitating Yu. "Ah, well, it is our project, yes?"

Yu picked up her coffee mug and threw it against the wall in frustration. After composing herself, Yu addressed Hai in a direct manner. "Well, Minister, let's come back to that at a later time. What are you suggesting for the project?"

Hai's attitude became humorless as he replied, "I would like to extend an offer for you and the Japanese to leverage our Bitcoin Exchange in Shanghai."

Yu knew that Hai was pressing her to allow China to become part of this project. She considered what options she had on the table before she replied. "Which exchange are you offering?"

"Well, The Pearl Tower Exchange, of course," Hai replied.

Yu reviewed her notes on what she knew about the Pearl Tower Exchange. "Yes, I am familiar with this exchange. I will take your offer up with the Japanese and my most senior advisors in Taiwan and see what we can work out."

Hai became even more determined, "You have no other option, Madame President."

"Minister, let me ring back in a few days so we can discuss this in more detail," Yu replied.

Hai graciously spoke, "Yes, I look forward to your call."

As the phone line went dead, Yu muttered to herself in anger, "Fuck, I hate that guy!"

SAC Gerald Burns logged into his secured phone to contact FBI Director Alvin Ramsey and Attorney General Marcia Robertson to discuss the failed operation at the border.

"Ramsey here," the FBI Director said.

"Sir, SAC Burns, the exchange failed."

The FBI Director roared, "What?"

Gerald was infuriated with Alvin's question. "Sir, the Chinese had assets in the area."

Alvin removed his glasses and began to rub his eyes in frustration. "Hold on, let me get the AG on the line."

Gerald felt the pressure grow in his head as he listened to Alvin calling Marcia.

Alvin spoke, "Okay, SAC, I have the AG on the line, go ahead."

Gerald cussed under his breath. "Shit!" He cleared his throat before he spoke, "Madam AG, the border crossing mission failed. Poppy Ledger allegedly was kidnapped by Chinese External Forces. Regina approached her and tried to get her to come across. Ledger specifically wanted William Kendall to be there. She panicked after seeing Regina, drew her weapon, and began to open fire. After she fired off a few shots, she retreated back to the Canadian side. Three vehicles approached the border at high speed and they opened fire on the RCMP and React 5."

Marcia erupted in a fury. "Wait! Stop! Who fired at us?"

Gerald dreaded answering the question. "Several members of the Chinese External Security Forces, Madam AG. The RCMP has several in custody now. Two vehicles got away. Apparently, Poppy Ledger is in one of the cars."

Marcia was flabbergasted. "That fucking asshole, Ming. He promised that his security forces would back off and let her pass."

Gerald continued with his report. "We have three men wounded, the RCMP has one dead, three wounded, and Regina Kendall took a round in the arm."

Alvin was distraught by this development and said, "How is she? I hate to be the one to tell Jack!"

Marcia was dumbfounded by Hai's betrayal. "SAC, bring the team to the Bellingham FBI field office and await further instructions."

"Yes, Madam."

"Keep me appraised of Regina's condition."

Gerald shook his head in resentment as he walked out of Marcia's office mumbling to himself, "I told you the Chinese would never let her leave."

Marcia attempted to reach Forest in Taiwan to update him on the failed mission in Canada.

"Forest, it's Marcia. Please tell me you have Bao!"

"We just handed him to the Chinese here on Penghu Island. Why?"

Marcia knew her worst nightmare was unfolding. "Our handoff in Vancouver went badly. The Chinese have Poppy Ledger on a flight back to China."

Forest rubbed his head in disgust and unkindly replied, "Oh fuck, you mean the Chinese now have Bao Xu and Poppy Ledger in their custody, and we don't have shit?"

Marcia gasped for air in humiliation. "Yes, I know I fucked up. I trusted Ming."

Forest was mortified for Marcia. "Yep, I am with you on this one!"

Marcia knew that Forest was deeply upset. "I let you down, pops."

Forest was disappointed but felt compassion for Marcia. "Look, we do know that Travis Jones, Lilian Tang, and Noah Wilson are on Okinawa. I am heading there now. I will link up with Jack Kendall and we will hunt down these assholes!"

Marcia hesitated to share additional troubling news. "Forest, Regina took a round in the arm."

"Oh Christ, how?

Marcia responded to Forest, "One of the Chinese agents shot her. She is at a local hospital and is expected to make a full recovery."

"Better let me tell Jack," Forest advised.

Marcia was traumatized by the betrayal and Regina getting shot. She was relieved that Forest offered to break the news to Jack.

Forest was in deep thought while walking back to the Air Force charter plane. "How am I going to tell Jack that his little girl was shot?" He approached and climbed up the ladder. "Captain, turn this plane around and head back to Okinawa!"

The captain acknowledged the order and contacted the airport controller. "Penghu Tower, this is U.S. Air Force flight 331, request permission to depart."

Penghu airport controller replied, "US Air Force flight 331, you have clearance on runway seven for immediate departure."

While Jack was making his way back to his sleeping quarters on Camp Henson, Forest messaged him. "Marine, call me ASAP."

"Forest, what is up?"

"Look, Marine, the handoff in Vancouver went south. The Chinese External Forces showed up and shot up the border crossing. Poppy Ledger escaped. Jack, Regina was hit in the arm."

Jack froze after hearing Forest's voice taper off. "What! Is she alive? Where is she? Who shot her?"

"She is fine, Jack. The doctors expect her to make a full recovery. We aren't sure at this point why the Chinese showed up. The AG had a deal worked out with the Minister of Finance. In exchange for Bao Xu, the Chinese would let Ledger go."

Jack, tormented at the thought of his daughter being shot, said, "Forest, we need to kill these fuckers. They shot my daughter."

Forest let Jack vent his frustrations before he updated him on the status of the mission. "Jack, I know where Noah Wilson and Lilian Tang are, and we have a reason to believe Travis Jones is on Okinawa now."

Jack was alarmed hearing Travis's name. "Jones? Here? Where?"

Forest responded, "He has a safe house in Nago. We believe he is held up there with Noah and Tang."

Jack vividly remembered where Nago was located on Okinawa. "I am heading over there now!"

Forest tried to reason with Jack. "Hold on, Marine, I am enroute now. I will be landing back at Kadena Air Force Base in the next few hours. Let's do this together!"

Jack was still anguished about the news of his daughter and Travis being on Okinawa. He replied in agreement. "Roger that Forest, I will wait for you on Camp Henson."

Forest was relieved that Jack wasn't going to hunt down Travis on his own.

Jack ended the conversation with, "Okay, Forest, I will see you shortly." He tried reaching his daughter on her phone. "Reg, it's Dad!"

Regina was still groggy from the painkillers and replied, "Dad, I am okay. The bullet went straight through."

Jack always admired his daughter for her toughness. "You are so brave, my daughter."

"Dad, I am fine. I will be out of here in a day or two max."

Jack exhaled in relief. "Reg, I don't know what I would do if I lost you. I love you."

Regina began to cry. "Dad, I love you too. I am fine. You need to find Travis Jones and Noah."

Jack knew Regina was right. "I know. We have a lead here on Okinawa. Forest is heading back now to help."

Reg pleaded, "Dad, please stay safe. Vulturess is still out there."

Jack knew that Lilian Tang was a brutal killer. "Yes, I asked SAC Burns to help liaison with the Japanese police."

Regina nervously pondered for a moment. "Dad, ask our Yakuza contact for help. Japan is their turf. They have people everywhere on Okinawa. These guys are killers, however, this is a good time to look past that. The Yakuza will find Tang."

Jack agreed with Regina's logic. "Reg, you are right. Let me reach out to San-Hamada. Please keep me updated. I love you, Reg."

Reg understood her father's concern and tried to comfort him. "Don't worry, Dad, it will be okay. I love you."

Message: Encryption: Sender: Jack Kendall: Techline: William Kendall: Son, please reach out to the Rising Sun. I need help on Oki to find three bad guys.

Love,

Dad

William heard the message notification go off on his phone. He read the message from his father. He responded with a secured message.

Message: Encryption: Reply: Techline: Sender: William Kendall: Jack Kendall: Okay Dad, I will reach out and make contact.

Signed,

William

William logged back into the DarkNet to send a message to the Rising Sun hacker squad. *Message: Darknet24: Encryption: Knight2Rouk7: SwordBitch: Need assistance on OKI, seeking three people in connection with Dragon Vault mission. Our asset is on the ground and standing by for instructions.*

Signed,

Knight2Rouk7

SwordBitch sat in a 24-hour dance club in Shibuya, Japan, nearly passing out from all the vodka and cocaine when he felt his secured communicator buzz. "Message from that fucker Kendall. What does he want?" After reading the message, SwordBitch got up from his bar seat and headed back to his car.

While stumbling back to his car in a darken Tokyo alley, SwordBitch felt the effects of the cocaine. He began to sweat as the lights faded and he nearly blacked out. As SwordBitch approached his car, he began to violently throw up on the street. After a few dry heaves, he sat on the ground completely disoriented. "Fuck, where the hell am I?" SwordBitch began to roll on the ground to a nearby vending machine. "Twenty-five YEN? Fuck that."

He drew out his 9MM weapon and shot the machine with several bullets. "Ha! Charge me for a drink, fuck you!" SwordBitch rose to his feet, headed over to the machine, and grabbed several cans of beer. Leaning against the wall next to the bullet-ridden machine, SwordBitch realized he had forgotten all about the message from William while he was drinking his beers.

"Fuck, what does that asshole Kendall want now?" He staggered over to his BMW, quickly climbed into the car, and reached for his laptop.

Message: Encryption: Rising Sun: SwordBitch: San-Hamada: Knight2Rouk7 request assistance on OKI. Three players from Dragon Vault are suspected to be on the island. Vulturess could be one of them. Request kill order.

Signed,

SwordBitch

Sitting in his private tea house in Taitung, Taiwan, San-Hamada read the message from his lead hacker with great disdain.

Message: Encryption: Rising Sun: San-Hamada: SwordBitch: Permission granted with one condition, we need Vulturess alive.

Signed,

San-Hamada

SwordBitch read the reply from San-Hamada. He hesitated before answering William. "Vulturess alive? No fucking way."

He was well aware of the repercussions that would happen to him if he disregarded a direct order from San-Hamada. "Fuck that old man. That bitch deserves to die. She killed my cousin in Macau!" SwordBitch screamed to himself. He knew if San-Hamada found out that he ordered the killing of Vulturess on Okinawa, he would be killed in a most brutal way. Accepting his own fate, SwordBitch replied to William.

Message: Darknet24: Encryption: Knight2Rouk7: SwordBitch: permission granted; we are at your disposal. The kill order has been approved by San-Hamada. This order extended to all members associated with the Dragon Vault mission.

Signed,

SwordBitch

William became extremely alarmed by the message from SwordBitch. "A kill order on everyone? That is a problem. We need them alive to find out where the Chinese are taking Poppy Ledger." William reached for his phone to contact Jack. "Dad, William, are you okay? Where are you?"

Jack walked outside of the building. "Camp Henson, Okinawa. How is Tricia?"

"Any day now, Dad. I will let you know when you are a grandfather!"

Jack smiled at the thought of being a grandfather. "Thank you, Will."

William retrieved a copy of the message from SwordBitch. "Okay, we have access to Rising Sun on Okinawa. However, San-Hamada has put a kill order out on everyone, including Vulturess."

"I bet they did. She jacked one hundred million in Bitcoin last year. I am sure they want her dead," Jack said coldly. "William, upload what you have on Travis Jones, Noah, and an update on Lilian Tang to them. Any pictures and descriptions. I bet the Yakuza and Rising Sun have access to video cameras all over the island. We know that Jones has a safe house in Nago."

"Okay, Dad, anything else?"

Jack was undecided on how to break the news to William. He began, "Look, son, I need to let you know something. The handoff in Canada failed. I assumed when Poppy didn't see you there, she panicked and ran back to Canada. Three carloads of Chinese External Security Forces showed up and started shooting and Regina got hit in the arm."

William was in shock in disbelief. "Is my sister okay? Who shot her?"

Jack was tentative in his reply. "We suspect either the Chinese agents or Poppy Ledger. She is fine, son. Regina is resting in a local hospital and is expected to be released tomorrow."

William was in a state of shock. "Poppy shot my sister and somehow got away on a private charter plane?"

Jack waited until William finished venting his emotions over Regina getting shot. "Yes, to make matters worse, the Chinese also have Bao Xu in custody. We had a deal with the Chinese and they double-crossed us. Son, Forest is heading back this way. We are heading to Nago to find Travis Jones before the Yakuza and the Japanese police do. Stay close to the phone. I will call you once we have that son of a bitch."

William appreciated his father's update on Regina. "Dad, take care of yourself. I need you in my life to help me become a great father."

Jack held back tears. "Of course, son, I will be there!"

William hung up and headed back to his wife.

Tricia curiously asked, "William, who was that?"

William looked at his wife with deep affection. "It was Dad. He needed help from our Yakuza friends again."

Tricia became concerned and grilled her husband. "What happened with Poppy and the border crossing?"

William was disheartened as he answered Tricia. "It failed. Ledger changed her mind and ran back across to Canada. The Chinese had security teams in the area and captured her. She is on her way back to China, most likely to prison as a traitor."

Tricia felt the pain in her husband's eyes. "Will, are you okay?"

William didn't want Tricia to be worried about Regina being shot. "Baby, I am more than okay. I have the most beautiful wife in the whole world, who, just happens to be giving birth to our first child."

Tricia suddenly felt a sharp pain in her stomach. Following the doctor's orders, she took a deep breath and intensely looked at her husband. In a calm, steady, and stern tone, she said, "William, I am starting to feel contractions."

William's face lit up with excitement as he exclaimed, "What would you like me to do?"

Very calmly, Tricia said to Will, "Get me to the doctor. NOW!"

Willian hurried out of Tricia's room and screamed for the doctor.

"Kadena tower, this is U.S. Air Force flight 331, request permission to land."

The Air Traffic Controller replied, "U.S. Air Force flight 331, you are cleared to land at runway L7. Welcome to Okinawa, Japan."

Captain Neri acknowledged the landing instructions from the tower. "Mr. Adams, we will be on the ground in fifteen minutes."

Forest gave the captain a thumbs up. As the plane made its final approach, Forest reflected on everything that led him up to this moment. He knew Jack wanted Travis dead for the killing of Nella, stealing William's code, and using Regina. However, all of these things were secondary to the emptiness he felt from Bui's passing. "I love you my love, forever. I promised you I would look after Jack. I miss you so much." Forest wiped away a tear from his eyes and continued to speak to Bui. "My love, I will never forget you. Now I must go and help Jack."

Chapter 43

Reveal

"Look," Travis said to Lilian Tang and Noah in a commanding tone, "I need to go to another part of the island to meet with the Russians. They are due here any day now. You know the rules, no fucking around."

Lilian was annoyed by Travis's demeanor and began to mock him. "Or what? Are you going to send me to my room?"

Noah started to badger Travis. "Yeah, are you going to ground me too?"

Travis shouted at his partners in complete disgust. "You know what, fuck you guys. I am the one that is putting my ass out there to get us a billion-dollar payoff. Oh, by the way, I got a Red Letter today from Interpol. The Japanese police found two dead bodies at a bathhouse near here. If someone comes to the door and asks questions, you guys are newlyweds from America, clear?"

Lilian was stunned by Travis's disclosure of the Red Letter. Terrified, she asked, "What bathhouse?"

Travis became suspicious and approached Lilian. "Some remote place outside of town." He began to interrogate her. "Why? What did you do? Did you kill them?"

Lilian was defiant in her answer to Travis. "Fuck yea, I did. They were nobodies!"

Petrified by Lilian's murderess confession, Noah was timid in his response. "Wait. You killed them? Why?"

Lilian felt cornered by Noah's question. She tried to sound nonchalant. "Doesn't matter. They are dead. Let's move on. Travis, aren't you supposed to be somewhere?"

Travis was apprehensive about leaving Lilian alone with Noah. Knowing Lilian was unpredictable left him feeling greatly agitated. As he picked up his bag and headed off to the car to meet up with the Russian outfit arriving from Brooklyn, he yelled, "Don't worry about what I am supposed to do. You, stay out of sight! You blow this, I will kill you myself."

Chapter 44
Habu

Kadena Air Force Base (Okinawa, Japan)

"Mr. Adams. We are here, sir. Please, let me know if you need anything else," Captain Neri said.

"Thank you, Captain." Forest and the two Marine guards departed the plane. He noticed a man standing by their vehicles on the runway.

"Mr. Adams?" the mystery man shouted.

Forest walked up to the man. "Yes?"

The man handed an envelope over to Forest. "Sir, this came for you."

Forest thanked the man for the envelope. The mystery man proceeded to walk toward the terminal and disappeared. Forest motioned to the Marines, "Let's head up to the camp and pick up Jack."

The Marines entered the vehicle and started to drive north of the U.S. Air Force base.

While sitting in the back of the car, he opened the envelope and whispered to himself, "What is so damn important for the agency to send a secured message by courier?"

Message: Classified: Top Secret: Department of Homeland Security: Flash message: National Command Authority: DHS reporting: Suspect Dimi Zosh: Russian Mafia, departed JFK Airport at 2000 hours with a destination to arrive 0830 hours tomorrow in Naha Airport in Okinawa. He is traveling with three members of the Russian outfit, Gorky Park. We believe he is meeting with unknown criminal elements. Japanese SIS and National Police are on high alert. Enclosed is the last known photo of the suspect. The suspect is extremely dangerous and most likely will be armed. Enclosed are documents, photos, and recorded video of the suspect.

Signed,

The National Command Authority

Seeing the photos of Dimi Zosh and his Russian crew jolted Forest. "I thought I killed him in 1984 in Kabul Afghanistan . How the fuck did he survive that car blast?" Forest agonized over the thought that Dimi could still be alive. "I need to find that Russian fanatic and kill him for good.

Chapter 45
Inferno

Naha Airport (Okinawa, Japan)

"Team Alpha – SIS, this is the lead, suspects arriving now," the Japanese Secret Intelligence Service (SIS) Officer said.

"Team Alpha, stand by, Bravo and Charlie units pick up the suspect," Commander Cho, head of all Japanese SIS, ordered.

Dimi Zosh was on the Interpol and FBI's most wanted fugitives in the world list for over twenty years. Known as the butcher of Kabul in the 1980s, Dimi served as a major in Russian Military Intelligence. After the war, he became one of the world's most wanted killers and drug dealers. He has avoided capture by becoming an expert in disguising himself as a tourist in several countries. Dressed in a torn pair of khaki pants, a black tee shirt, and a New York Yankees baseball cap, he strolled through the airport blending in with the rest of the tourists. Dimi's top security detail and hackers shadowed every move he made while he headed out of the terminal.

Dimi spoke covertly into his earpiece and addressed his second-in-command, Vlad. "What have you arranged for us?"

Vlad was a fellow Russian soldier who served with Dimi in Afghanistan years ago. He handled all the travel and security for the entire Gorky Park outfit. Vlad answered, "Boss, just stay on this course and depart the terminal."

Dimi whispered into his earpiece, "We have a thousand eyes on us, Vlad."

Vlad calmly replied, "Boss, everything is in place."

As Dimi made his way through the Naha airport customs, he spotted additional Japanese security teams monitoring every move he made.

"Vlad, tell me you have this."

"Boss, all in hand."

Commander Cho also followed Dimi from a distance at the airport. "Team Bravo, stay with the target."

Term Bravo replied, "WILCO."

Dimi approached passport control and walked up to the airport security office.

"Sir, remove your hat and hand over your passport."

As he handed over his passport, Dimi surveyed his surroundings prior to removing his hat.

"Purpose of visit?" the officer asked impatiently.

Dimi answered casually, "Vacation. I have heard so much about your island."

The officer examined Dimi's documents. "You are from Brazil?" the officer inquired.

Dimi was traveling under a false identity. He often posed as a businessman from Brazil. "Yes, I believe our beaches are better than Taiwan's," he joked.

As the passport was being scanned, a red warning sign came upon the officer's screen. "Allow to proceed, suspect under surveillance."

The officer nervously handed the passport back to Dimi. "You are free to go. Welcome to Okinawa, Japan."

Dimi placed his hat back on his head and collected his passport before heading to baggage claim. After collecting his bags, he followed Vlad's instructions and proceeded to the taxi line.

Vlad continued to whisper instructions to Dimi's earpiece while he walked ten meters behind. "Keep on moving, boss."

Once Dimi headed out to the taxi line, the taxi attendant motioned him to get into the front taxi. Dimi paused and waited for Vlad's instruction before entering the front taxi.

Vlad moved closer to Dimi and instructed him, "Get into the third one, boss."

Dimi ignored the taxi attendant and jumped into the third taxi.

"Ah, sir, you need to get into the first one," the driver said.

"Drive!" Dimi demanded with a dark stare.

Commander Cho tracked Dimi getting into the third cab and ordered his team, "All units converge on the third cab!"

As the Alpha, Bravo, and Charlie security forces ran towards the third cab to apprehend Dimi, an unexpected massive series of explosions rocked the airport terminal sending debris and travelers in several directions. Commander Cho was propelled against a glass window following the blast. Covered in shards of glass, Cho bellowed in pain, "All teams, report!"

Nang, the leader for the Alpha team, reported, "Sir, we have men down. The bombs detonated inside the first and the fourth cabs. People are wounded everywhere! We need help!"

Dimi admired the destruction around him. "Vlad, holy fuck, you are a genius!" He quietly celebrated to himself. As much as he wanted to relish in the chaos caused by Vlad, he knew he had to escape before the Japanese SIS and police caught him. He smacked the back of the cab driver's head and demanded, "Driver, get me the fuck out of here!"

The driver panicked as he drove recklessly to avoid the fiery wreckage.

Following the explosion, rescue teams and airport fire trucks arrived at the scene. Fire and debris were scattered in every direction. The firemen rushed to put out the flames while the rescue teams combed through the debris looking for survivors. Under the debris of glass and concrete, hundreds of bodies lay motionless on the ground.

Rescue workers removed the debris that covered Commander Cho. The minute he was helped to his feet, Cho ran outside the terminal and immediately looked for the third cab. When he realized Dimi escaped, he ordered, "Shut down all roads leading out of the airport. He must be in one of those cabs!"

As the order went out, Dimi's cab had already left the airport. Dimi felt a moment of relief as the cab headed north on Route 58. "Driver, head north to Miyagi Island and do not draw any attention. One false move and I will kill you!" He radioed his team on his earpiece. "Vlad, Joseph, Ivan?"

Vlad replied, "All safe, boss. We will meet up at the safehouse shortly."

Just before reaching Camp Henson, Forest received a flash message on his secured communicator.

Message: National Command Authority: Encryption: Explosion at Naha airport while suspect arrived. Japanese SIS reported multiple fatalities and injuries. Russian suspect Dimi Zosh reported missing from the security team's surveillance.

Signed,

National Command Authority

"Dear God," Forest whispered in complete dismay.

While arriving on Miyagi Island for his meeting with Dimi Zosh, Travis Jones heard the news flash about the Naha airport explosion. This news perturbed Travis. "I bet those Russian fuckers had something to do with this!"

After reaching the safehouse, Travis parked his car under the trees and headed inside. The safehouse was rarely used and it was filled with dust. Travis powered up the house by turning on the breakers. After checking all the power, the Internet access came up. He used his secure communicator to send a message to Noah.

Message: Encryption: Rambonus: Noah: Location Secure. Waiting for the Russian assholes to arrive.

Signed,

Trav

After driving for nearly an hour, Dimi ordered the cab driver to pull over.

The driver complied and pulled the vehicle off to the side of the road. The cab came to rest near the shoreline of the eastern side of the island. Dimi stepped out of the vehicle and began to smoke a cigarette. After he took his last drag, Dimi walked over to the driver's side of the car. "Get out!" he ordered.

The driver was shaken and slowly climbed out of the taxi. Dimi placed his arm around the driver's neck tightly and cynically hissed, "Good Man!" With a quick snap, Dimi broke the driver's neck. The driver died instantly. Dimi lifted the driver and dragged his body close to the shoreline. He pushed the driver over the cliff and into the waves below. Dimi kept his eyes on the driver's body as it crashed against the rocks and was carried out to sea. He marveled to himself, "The pleasure was all mine." He continued his journey in the stolen cab fully satisfied with himself.

Forest and the Marine guards showed their IDs as they entered Camp Henson.

"Proceed," the gate guards ordered.

"Drop me at Building Five," Forest requested. Forest was exhausted from the trip to Taiwan when they arrived at Building Five. He jumped out of the car and headed into the building searching for Jack. "Jack!" Forest called out.

Jack rose from his bed and yelled back, "Here, Forest! What time is it?"

Forest ran over to Jack. "Get dressed, Marine, we have a big fucking problem!"

Lilian and Noah were becoming impatient while waiting for further instructions from Travis. Lilian received a flash message across her device.

Message: Japan News Network: Flash Message: Explosion rocked Naha Airport on Okinawa at 2000 hours local time. Several reports indicated multiple causalities and fatalities. No one has claimed responsibility for the explosion. Japanese SIS is on the scene and coordinating all rescue efforts. More news to follow.

Lilian was deeply troubled by the news flash and sighed, "Oh shit!"

Noah was distressed by Lilian's reaction. He demanded, "What?"

While Lilian was reading the message, Noah grabbed her device. "Who the fuck blew up the airport?" Noah lamented.

Lilian swiftly seized her device from Noah's hand and brutally punched him in the face. "Don't ever touch my fucking device. I have no idea who blew up the airport."

Noah was outraged by Lilian's assault. "You are crazy! Have you lost your mind?"

Lilian vehemently responded, "Shut up! We need to get the fuck out the here. Grab your shit and head for the door!"

Noah was baffled by Lilian's order to leave the safe house. "Wait, what if Travis comes back?"

Lilian was annoyed by Noah's statement. "Fuck him. Grab your shit now!" Lilian stuffed her passport, laptop, and her 9MM weapon into her backpack and headed for the door. She noticed Noah was staring at her. "Look, either stay or come with me. Your choice, Noah. Make it quick. I am out of here."

Noah knew he was out of options. He grudgingly went up to his room, quickly packed his belongings, and rushed out the door. "Where do we go now?"

Lilian, still unsure of what to do, answered harshly, "How the fuck should I know. Let's start walking towards downtown and find a place to lay low for now until the shitstorm blows over."

As Lilian and Noah approached downtown Nago, their senses were filled with smells of fresh fish and ramen cooking in the local restaurants. The locals were enjoying socializing, eating, and drinking beer.

Noah stopped in front of the Kominka Cafe Kiiro restaurant on the main road. He suggested, "Lilian, this looks like a good place to blend in with the locals. How about we grab a table in the corner and order some food?"

Lilian ignored Noah and continued to walk towards a small alley off the main road. She spotted the small local bar hidden in the alley called Yukino.

"Noah! Over here! Let's go inside. We need to stay out of sight. No one will find us in here."

Noah followed Lilian into Yukino. They picked the last table in the back room. The back room was filled with locals and tourists enjoying grilled fresh fish served on skewers and local beers. This bar, like many bars in Nago, was originally a hotel or someone's home containing the original, still preserved, wood. The artwork hanging on the walls were portraits of Japanese families. Lilian stared at the artwork and wondered what her life would have been like if she wasn't adopted by BOSS and the Triads. This triggered her longings for a loving family, not being orphaned, and becoming a member of a global criminal organization.

Lilian's troubled gaze caught Noah's eyes. "Hey, anything wrong?"

She blinked her eyes and shook her head. While very coldly staring at Noah, she scoffed, "Fuck off."

Noah shrugged his shoulders and waved the waiter over to take their order.

A waiter arrived. "Hey, welcome to Yukino. What are you having?"

Lilian realized she was starving. "How about some of the fresh fish on skewers and two shots of Habu."

Noah was perplexed by Lilian's order. "What is the Habu?"

The waiter laughed. "Oh, you don't know about the most dangerous snake in the world that resides here in Okinawa? We ferment the Habu snake in a bottle for a year. The shots are legendary on this side of the world."

Lilian mocked Noah, "What is the matter? Never done anything this crazy in your pathetic little life?"

Noah felt extremely disrespected and lashed out at Lilian. "Look you little fucking Triad, go to hell."

Lilian laughed at Noah's outburst. "Sit down, dickless."

The waiter placed his hands on Noah's shoulders. "Dude, you better sit down or you will be asked to leave."

The waiter became alarmed when he heard Noah refer to Lilian as a Triad. He abruptly left Noah and Lilian's table and headed to the bar to make an urgent call to his boss, Ito. "Ito, yea, it's me. We got a crazy fucking American here and a female member of the Triads. I need backup."

Ito was not only the owner of Yukino, he was also a member of the San-Hamada Yakuza. "Okay, send me a picture of them."

After the food and shots of Habu arrived at the table, Lilian picked one of the glasses and toasted to herself, "Habu, you and I are both soul mates. We both hunt men down and kill them."

Still parked outside of a dance club in Shibuya, Japan, SwordBitch received all the files from William regarding the three Dragon Vault fugitives wanted by U.S. authorities. SwordBitch was high on cocaine as he frantically typed on his keyboard.

Message: Encryption: Rising Sun: Immediate: SwordBitch: Authority: San-Hamada: Seek out and locate three wanted fugitives; Lilian Tang, AKA, Vulturess, Noah Wilson, Lawyer, and Travis Jones, the possible ringleader of the Dragon Vault Hack in Taiwan. Per San-Hamada, kill them all.

Signed,

SwordBitch

Ito read the encrypted message. "Oh fuck, two of these assholes are in my bar."

Message: Encryption: Rising Sun: Ito: Okinawa: Flash: Vulturess and the US lawyer are sitting in my club. Request scratch team now.

Signed,

Ito

Ito knew how important it was to capture Noah and Lilian. He called his head barman. "This is Ito. Do whatever you need to do to keep those two from leaving. The scratch team are on their way."

The barman at the club heard his instructions and called his crew. "Pick up that American and bring him to the back, and don't leave him."

Two of the bar workers grabbed Noah and carried him to the back of the bar building to a private storage room.

Lilian, feeling the effects from the Habu, stumbled around the bar looking for the bathroom. The barman approached her. "What do you need, lady?"

Lilian slurred, "Where is the fucking bathroom?"

"Follow me lady."

The barman led Lilian to the back of the bar as two cars filled with the Yakuza scratch teams arrived. The scratch teams were used only when San-Hamada had ordered an extreme punishment or a painful killing. As the members climbed out of the cars, Lilian took note of those men.

She realized that she could be in danger. "Hey bar fuck, where are we going?"

As the barman turned around, Lilian punched the man in the throat. She quickly spun around and desperately attempted to escape. Several scratch team members grabbed Lilian and pulled her into the private storage area in the back.

"Vulturess, we finally have you," Abe, the leader of the scratch team declared. "We have been looking for you since Macau. You killed our brothers, our women, and our number two leader. You stole from us one hundred million in cryptocurrency. Now, we are going to carve out the hundred million out of your skin."

Lilian backed up against the wall and counted eight men in front of her. Defiantly, she provoked her captors. "Oh yeah, bring it on, baby. Now it's a party for sure!"

Abe walked over to Lilian and struck her in the mouth. "We have orders to kill you. Where is the fun in that?"

Lilian spat blood from her mouth. "You fucking touch me again, and I swear when I get out of here, the Fong Gao Triads will hunt you down!"

Abe smiled at the threat. "This isn't Taiwan, bitch. Welcome to Japan."

By Abe's order, the scratch team members grabbed Lilian and threw her against the wall. Other members of the scratch team grabbed Noah and threw him to the floor.

"Noah!" Lilian screamed.

Three members of the scratch team lifted Noah off the floor and began to punch and kick him. Blood flowed from Noah's nose and mouth. The devastating force of the punches caused Noah to vomit on the floor. While gagging for air, Noah screamed, "Who the fuck are you guys?"

Abe reached over and punched Noah in the face. "Hey, you fucking American lawyer... we have some bad news for you. San-Hamada wants you dead for something to do with Dragon Vault. You know what, I don't give a shit. You are dead anyway."

Abe snapped his fingers and his scratch team members dragged Noah out the back door of the bar. They threw Noah on the ground, gagged him, and tied him to a tree.

The lead barman carried a jar with a live Habu snake. "Hey American? How about another shot?"

The group laughed as the barman placed the jar near where Noah was tied up. He removed the cap. Not more than a minute later, the Habu snake slithered out of the jar and began to crawl up Noah's leg. While shrieking in terror as loud as he could, Noah desperately tried to snap his rope ties. However, the Habu sensed his victim's panic. The deadly snake extended it's vast jaws and bit Noah several times. The group watched the snake bite Noah repeatedly. The team continued to film the entire event to upload to SwordBitch and other Yakuza members. Noah suffered tremendously for two minutes before his eyes rolled backed into his head.

The group hooted and high-fived each other. The barman recaptured the snake and placed it back in the jar. Abe came out of the building and ordered, "Untie him and dump his body into the sewer drain outside of the city."

Abe turned his attention back to Lilian in the storage room. "So, where were we? Ah! The hundred million. Where should I start? Your arms? Or maybe, that pretty face of yours?"

Lilian spat back at Abe. "You put one hand on me!"

Before she could speak another word, Abe grabbed a lead pipe and delivered a crushing blow to her head. The blood gushed from Lilian's head as she collapsed on the floor and lay motionless.

"Fuck, we were supposed to take her alive!" one of the group members yelled.

Abe turned to his team member who spoke. "Oh, really?"

With a swift move, Abe launched an attack on the group member and proceeded to crush his skull with the pipe. "I will explain this to San-Hamada. Get her out of here and dump her body next to the lawyer."

Several of the team members grabbed Lilian's body and carried her outside.

Abe stood over the lifeless body of his group member. "Throw him in the sewer."

Chapter 46
Wolves Den

While Jack was getting dressed, he could hear Forest on the phone talking to someone important.

"Look, Marcia," Forest said, "Dimi Zosh is here on Okinawa."

Hearing Dimi's name after thirty years brought back horrific memories for Marcia. "Forest, Dimi is dead. We killed him in Afghanistan in 1984. I placed the car bomb there myself."

Forest paced the room in distress. "Marcia, the blast today at Naha airport, that was him and his crew making a grand entrance. I need SAC Burns and Bill Parker along with React 5 here in Okinawa. With Dimi here, along with Travis Jones, something big is going down."

Marcia reflected on the request from Forest. "Fuck, I can't believe that killer is still alive all these years. I read somewhere that he was alive and living in Brooklyn. I thought it was a joke sent out by some hacker. This is the last thing we need. We are already in the middle of a major shitstorm with the border crossing in Vancouver and the Chinese hacking Taiwan. The president called for an emergency meeting in two hours. I will discuss this with Alvin. Forest, thanks for being here. We need to get him, once and for all. Whatever you need, just tell me. I will dispatch SAC Burns, Bill Parker, and React 5."

Forest contained his emotions while listening to Marcia. He whispered quietly, "Love you, kiddo." He then turned back to the issue at hand. "That is a great start. Thank you, Marcia."

Marcia was also feeling sentimental. "I know you don't want to hear this, but be careful. I want to see again. It has been too long."

Forest was filled with pride. "Marcia, I wouldn't want to be anywhere else than here with you."

AP Newswire: Explosion rocked Naha Airport on Okinawa today with multiple car bombs at the main terminal. Several casualties were reported dead or missing. The Japanese Security Intelligence Service and Naha Police, along with Interpol, are heading up the investigations. No one has claimed responsibility for the attack. More details to follow.

Reading the news flash from Okinawa, Alexei Rommel, the Russian Ambassador to Vietnam, sat in his Saigon (HCMC) office rubbing his eyes. "Ah, this never ends." After reading the news wire, Alexei grabbed his secure communicator.

Message: Encryption: Russian_Embassy_Saigon (HCMC): Secured: Dimi Zosh: Ambassador Alexei Rommel: Seeing blast on the news, please ensure this doesn't happen in Vietnam. Note: Boris Latcha is presumed dead. He has been missing for several weeks now. We believe an American operative killed him over some human trafficking issue. I raised the issue with the American Ambassador with no results. We believe the operative is either in Taiwan or Okinawa. He goes by the name, Forest Adams.

Signed,

Alexei

Dimi heard his phone vibrate. He received an incoming message from the Russian Ambassador in Vietnam. Dimi immediately pulled over near a cliff off Okinawa's coast in the stolen taxi. After reading the encrypted message, Dimi stepped out of the cab and walked close to the cliff's edge overlooking the ocean. Agitated, he lit a cigarette. "Forest Adams, you fuck! It has been thirty years since Kabul, Afghanistan. I should have slaughtered you years ago, you pig!"

Discovering that Forest killed his friend and mentor, Boris Latcha, Dimi became enraged. Boris Latcha was a Russian military advisor to the North Vietnamese Army in the 1960s and 1970s. He participated in the war against the Americans and was a hero to many Russians. He became famous for his military tactics while assisting the North Vietnamese in shooting down American planes. Boris was also an expert on torturing American pilots. He became Dimi's mentor years later in Afghanistan. Dimi pledged, "Comrade, I will get this piece of shit that killed you."

Dimi still had horrifying flashbacks from his years serving during the Russian and Afghan war in the 1980s. As a Major, he was in charge of all interrogations in Kabul, Afghanistan and he took immense pleasure in torturing captured American spies who supplied weapons and intelligence information to the Afghan rebels. One spy stood out from the rest—Forest Adams. "I remember the day we captured you," Dimi scorned.

Forest smuggled several thousand rifles and rockets into Kabul to help the rebels defeat the Russians while posing as a Red Cross worker. After being in the country for over a year, the Russians finally caught up with Forest trying to flee the country through Pakistan in 1984. Forest was tortured for weeks by Dimi. After receiving a tip from a Russian double agent, Marcia Robertson and the U.S. Army's Delta Force rescued Forest in a remote village south of Kabul. The following day, Dimi narrowly escaped a car bomb planted by Marcia.

"Now, you are here on Okinawa, you fuck!" Dimi finished his cigarette, jumped back into the stolen taxi, and continued driving to Miyagi Island.

The safehouse on Miyagi Island, Okinawa, was a well-hidden single story dwelling rarely used by Travis. It had been over twelve years since Travis used this safehouse. Grabbing a beer out of the cooler, he logged into his secure portal to get caught up on the latest news. "Oh fuck!" He began to read out loud the bombing at the terminal of Naha Airport. "Christ, please tell me the Russians didn't do this."

As Travis continued to read the news, he heard a car pulling up. He stepped outside to see who arrived and noticed a taxi with only the driver inside. "Hey, pal, you can't park here."

Dimi stepped out of the taxi and approached Travis. "You must be Jones?"

Guarded, Travis reached for his 9 mm and hid it behind his back. "And who the fuck are you?"

Dimi gave a death stare at Travis as he scorned with disdain. "Dimi Zosh."

Travis remained apprehensive but tried to appear in charge. "Oh, Zosh, come on in. I will get you a beer."

Dimi cautiously entered the safe house while keeping an eye on Travis. "Beer? Fucking piss water. Vodka."

Travis walked over to his liquor cabinet. "Hey, no vodka. Scotch?"

Dimi looked disgusted. "Scotch? Shit water, Jones. Never mind! So, what is this fucking plan of yours that I had to fly halfway around the world to listen to?"

Travis responded to Dimi's attitude and sarcastically retorted, "Yeah, real awesome of you to make the trip. Now, if you are done whining, let's get down to the specifics. Are we expecting anyone else?"

Dimi opened his communicator. "Vlad?"

Vlad was driving a stolen car with the rest of the Gorky Park outfit. "Boss, we are ten minutes away."

Dimi replied to Travis, "My team is ten minutes away."

Travis arrogantly rolled his eyes. "Make it five, Zosh."

Unimpressed with Travis's demeanor, Dimi asked condescendingly, "So, Jones, tell me how you *almost* pulled off this this Dragon Vault Hack?"

Polishing off his beer, acting all high-and-mighty, Travis said, "With the help of the Fong Gao Triads and secretly with General Vo of the PLA cyber group. We managed to re-enable a fiber connection between Xiamen, China and Kaohsiung, Taiwan."

Dimi found himself unexpectedly impressed. "Ambitious."

Travis discounted Dimi's compliment and continued. "We had a resource inside ADConnect to secretly cross-connect several fiber optic nodes on Taiwan's TAINET network. Our hacker then created a maintenance network to the fiber vault that led back to China."

"Who was this hacker?" Dimi demanded with authority.

Travis was taken back by Dimi's intimidating tone. "Vulturess."

Crushing Travis's beer can, Dimi continued to browbeat Travis. "I assume you know where she is now?"

Travis confidently spoke, "Oh yeah, I know where she is. Instead of discussing the small shit, let me walk you through the whole thing. I am the one that set up the hacker group in Vietnam. I hired the Emerald Forest outfit from Laos to handle the botnet hacking and attacks against the Internet of Things devices inside Taiwan."

Dimi remarked, "Yes, I know of this outfit. They do good work."

Feeling cocky, Travis continued. "Oh yeah, I hand-picked them."

"Arrogant fuck," Dimi noted to himself. "So, Jones, why did this fail?"

The sweat poured down Travis' face as he nervously replied, "The Yakuza's hacking group, Rising Sun, ran a complete denial of service attack against the city of Xiamen. They basically blocked our ability to send the data over the underwater cable."

Dimi raised his eyebrows and cackled, "Oh, impressive for a bunch of Japanese fucks."

While trying to maintain his composure, Travis attempted to appear in control. "After the denial-of-service attack, Sunny Ho, CEO of ADConnect, ordered the external firewall layer to be rebooted and shut down. That broke our hacker connection in Vancouver, Canada, from controlling the firewall rules."

Outraged, Dimi insisted, "What hacker in Vancouver?"

Detecting Dimi's annoyance, Travis attempted to de-escalate the tension in the room. "Her name is Poppy Ledger, a hired gun out of Australia and reports directly to General Vo. She is also known as Yellowslayer on Darknet."

In a heated rage, Dimi bellowed, "I know this hacker! I want her, Jones! Where the fuck is she?"

Trying to get control of the meeting, Travis snapped back at Dim., "Hey, fucking chill out. Let me finish! Yes, the whole fucking thing fell apart. I don't know where many of the Dragon Vault people are. Some may be dead or captured."

Impatient and frustrated, Dimi pointed his index finger at Travis. "You managed to coordinate a hack against Taiwan by using the Triads, General Vo, and PLA cyber?"

Travis added, "Don't forget Emerald Forest."

Three Russians in a stolen Toyota truck pulled up next to Dimi's taxi. Hearing the vehicle stop, Dimi walked outside and motioned his team to come into the house. As the Russians made their way into the house, Travis fetched more beer and handed them out.

Dimi refocused attention on Travis. "My team is here! What is your plan, Jones?"

After finishing several meetings with the World Bank over Chinese financial market options, Hai Ming headed back to his office to get the status of a flight carrying Poppy Ledger. "General Voung, this is Minister Ming. What is the status of Ledger?"

General Voung, head of all Chinese External Security Force, replied, "Sir, she is en route, and the plane should land in Tonghua approximately five hours from now."

"Good, let me know once she is secured in the comfort room and ready for questioning."

The comfort room was inside the Tonghua prison. It was a highly secret prison near the North Korean border that the Chinese used for interrogating essential assets.

"General, I want her alive," Ming stated.

The general smiled on the other end of the phone. "Of course, Minister." Before he managed to hang up, the general asked, "Ah, Minister, I understand you also secured Bao Xu. Is that true?"

Hai, taking a moment to sit down and enjoy his success, answered, "Ah yes, we did manage to grab him as well. I guess our American friends aren't happy now."

"Do you plan to move Xu and General Vo up here to Tonghua?"

Hai, not considering that option now, said, "General, that is a wonderful Idea. Please, make the arrangements."

The general hung up and began to create transfer orders for Vo and Bao Xu to move to the same prison as Poppy.

Poppy woke up feeling pain across her entire body. While opening her eyes, she was unable to focus on her surroundings. "Where the fuck am I?"

A Chinese guard sitting next to her on the plane answered, "You are on a plane heading back to China by orders of Minister Ming."

Poppy could not remember much from the last eight hours. "What? How is that possible? The last I remember—"

The Chinese guard reached over and punched Poppy in the mouth. "Shut up, traitor!"

Poppy's head crashed against her seatrest. "I am not a traitor!"

Another security guard rushed to her and intensely stared into her eyes with hatred. "You are fucking dead. You tried to escape to America!"

Poppy closed her eyes in defeat. Her memory of the crossing in Canada and firing her weapon at Regina Kendall came back. She opened her eyes and attempted to speak.

The guard slapped Poppy in the face again. "Shut your mouth!"

President Yu Chu Fong of Taiwan finished her fourth cup of espresso. She was deeply troubled knowing her options were limited for handling the cryptocurrency exchange issue with China. She contacted her most trusted advisor, Sunny Ho, to deliberate. "Sunny, President Fong."

"Yes, Madame President?"

"Look, Sunny. The Chinese Minister of Finance put me in a corner here. He insists on us using a Chinese Bitcoin exchange to handle the purchase along with several of the distributed ledgers. The Japanese will most likely use their own. What options do we have?"

Sunny was filled with anger and bitterness knowing that the Chinese wouldn't allow Taiwan to host their own cryptocurrency without getting their hands in the pot somewhere. "Madame President, if the Chinese require us to use their exchange, we will lose billions."

President Fong shared the same bitterness for the Chinese. "Sunny, I need you to give me the big picture here. What can we expect if the Chinese control our exchange?"

"Well, for starters, the Chinese will take a transfer and transaction fee of twenty-five percent on all purchases and usage of the Bitcoin itself. Their exchange will have access to all digital wallet users' information. Granted, most of this information is secured. In many cases, the actual identity of the user is hidden behind their wallet ID."

Becoming frustrated with the direction of the conversation, President Yu replied, "Okay, so Beijing makes a fee plus some other revenues along with hosting the money used to back up the value of the bitcoin itself?"

Exasperated by the possible outcome of the exchange issue, Sunny responded, "Yes."

The pounding and throbbing in the back of her head caused President Yu to remove her glasses and rub her temples. "Alright Sunny, I get it. Hai Ming and the Chinese will have an infusion worth billions of dollars of fresh capital once people start purchasing Bitcoin? Correct?"

Sunny replied, "Yes, Madame."

President Yu needed the fresh capital infusion to help support many of her projects across Taiwan including the infrastructure and fiber optics to support her Smart City projects. "Any chance we can host the exchange and give them access?"

Sunny considered how Blockchain worked before answering. "No, Madame President. The whole security model around Blockchain ensures total confidence and integrity of each ledger and validation of all transactions with the previous chain entry. Trying to split access into the same exchange would break that model."

"Sunny, Beijing will try to block this project if we don't use their exchange in Shanghai. Give me a reason to fight this?"

Sunny was a proud Taiwanese national citizen. With great pride, he made an emotional proclamation, "Madame President, I would fight this to the very end! Our own currency, the Taiwan dollar, is secured by the central bank of the Republic of China (Taiwan), not the Bank of Shanghai."

President Yu felt the fire of passion coming from her most trusted advisor. She jokingly said, "Just checking, Sunny!"

Sunny got a great laugh from the president's reply. "Yes, Madame President. We have a Bitcoin exchange ready and available for this project. Our exchange, Codename: Evergreen BTC, has the necessary paperwork and compliance in place."

Feeling relieved that her country had the necessary Bitcoin exchange, President Yu joyfully replied, "Sunny! Thank you! You just made my day."

President Yu sent an encrypted email to Minister Ming in Beijing after she completed her call with Sunny.

Message: Encryption: Republic of China (Taiwan): Peoples Republic of China (China): Subject: Crypto exchange: Message to Minster Ming. Thank you for the wonderful offer to host our cryptocurrency and deposits for Japan's upcoming pilot program. My experts have assured the central banking committee and me that our Taiwan-based crypto exchange meets all the compliance and regulation requirements. Considering this development, we will be using the Evergreen Bitcoin exchange hosted here in Taipei. Thank you for your offer.

Signed,

Yu Chu Fong, President of Taiwan

Hai received a notification inside his email from a message sent by Yu.

Message: Yu Chu Hong, President of Taiwan: Thank you, we plan to use our own Bitcoin exchange.

Hai rose from his desk, grabbed his desk phone, and threw it against the wall. He yelled at the top of his lungs, "That fucking bitch! You want to use your own Bitcoin exchange? Let's see how fucking secure it is!"

Furious, Hai sat back down in his chair in complete anger. He reviewed the latest secure communication from General Voung. Poppy Ledger was due to land back in China in a few hours. Hai remembered how Poppy Ledger was an expert in Blockchain technology. Flustered by the message from the Taiwanese President, Hai began to brainstorm. "Poppy, if you can come back into the fold, I have plans for you," Hai thought out loud.

BOOK THREE

Oval

"To the knights' table they converge.

Disguised in suits of blue,

Old comrades

Armored for battle.

Masqueraded with no costume.

Against old enemies and new foes."

Gigi Kim Peeling

Chapter 47
Oval Office
The White House (Washington, D.C.)

Early morning meetings at the White House have become a very common reality with the current president of the United States. The attorney general of the United States, Marcia Robertson, wasn't a stranger to the highly intense and often toxic White House meetings. Marcia knew the reason for the emergency meeting called by the president had a lot to do with the shoot-out in Vancouver and the bigger mess in Taiwan. The president ordered all cabinet secretaries, the joint chief of staff, and the United States vice president to attend the morning meeting. As each member entered the White House conference room, including Secretary of Defense Mattamore and Secretary of State Hayes, they stared blankly ahead, failing to acknowledge other cabinet members. When all the secretaries were present and seated in their assigned positions at the table, President Taylor looked at each of his cabinet members and military officers with a concentrated glare.

"Good morning, Mr. President," they all greeted.

Alford Wilson Taylor, serving in his second term as the forty-eighth president of the United States, sat in his center seat position with a stern and focused look on his face. Alford, as the former CEO of a defense contracting firm and former governor of California, had seen many crises in his day. Before becoming president, Alford was known as a tough federal and international prosecutor. In this long career as a war crimes prosecutor, Alford successfully brought to justice several members of the Russian Mafia crime family and war criminals from Serbia and Afghanistan.

"Sit," President Taylor began. "I want to thank all of you for a very early start. How this meeting goes solely depends on you, your candor, and your integrity."

Some of the cabinet members didn't agree with the president and his policies. However, most of them still held a deep respect for his efforts to lower taxes, order the killing of several international terrorists, and provide more federal funding to help the homeless with drug rehab and job programs.

"So, let's start with something simple with easy words that we all can understand, shall we?" the president commanded. "I received calls this week from several Heads of State, including China, Russia, Vietnam, and Canada. Not to mention, a sidebar message from our friends in Taiwan."

Marcia knew the president was building to something that could detonate at any moment.

"So, let's start with the easy one first. Taiwan," President Taylor declared.

Secretary of Defense Winston Mattamore spoke first. "Sir, we did pick up several communications that Taiwan almost suffered a huge data hack coming from China. The hack was stopped by a group of third-party hackers."

The president impatiently replied, "Did we have anything to do with stopping the data from leaving Taiwan?"

Marcia, not knowing when to speak up, decided to remain silent.

Valerie Jones, Director of the National Security Agency, spoke up. "No, Mr. President, the NSA tracked several communications both from inside China, Taiwan, Canada, and Vietnam along with several encrypted messages inside of DARKNET, talking about something called 'Dragon Vault.'"

The president was astonished at the revelation from the NSA director. "Dragon Vault? Catchy name... what the fuck does it mean?"

Valerie, the twenty-year veteran of the NSA, had served five presidents. She held a particular distaste for Alford for cutting funding to her agency. "We are still looking into this."

The president, annoyed with Valerie's answer, turned to his old friend and trusted advisor, Skip Saide. " please tell me that the Central Intelligence Agent has something on this one?"

Skip Saide, the first Muslim American appointed as director of the CIA, said, "Mr. President, we have an asset in Vietnam who helped discover the cyberattack."

The president looked a bit relieved and retorted, "Oh, thank goodness, we have intelligence in this cabinet."

Marcia knew where this line of questioning was leading and decided to interject. "Sir, if I may. I have the background you are looking for."

As Marcia rose and began to move towards the big screen in the room, she activated her PowerPoint.

Alford tactlessly replied, "Wait? Do you have slides? This should be great. Let me get some popcorn!"

Marcia held her composure in front of the president and chose to proceed with her presentation. "Mr. President, the Dragon Vault mission secretly orchestrated by the China PLA cyber forces created a coordinated attack against the Internet of Things assets within Taiwan's TAINET network. The Chinese PLA under General Vo, along with the Fong Gao Triads, and a hacker group in Vietnam called Emerald Forest, coordinated a hack against several targets within Taiwan. Their mission goal was to copy stolen data out of Taiwan back to China over an underwater fiber optic cable. A rogue hacker, codename Vulturess, set up a backdoor network deep inside of Taiwan."

Marcia paused to see if the president had any questions.

"Proceed," Alford ordered.

"When the attack started, a hacker in Canada managed to take over all the external firewalls on TAINET and began to copy the data to the underwater cable between Taiwan and Xiamen China." Marcia stopped and took a drink of water before continuing. "The Chinese used stolen software from a U.S. company called Cybercom based on Boston. The Chinese managed to clone and reverse engineer the software package in two days."

The president looked away in total disgust. "Marcia, is this same issue I read about with some Boston law firm getting an immediate injunction?"

Marcia replied, "Affirmative, sir. The attack was stopped thanks to a third-party group that executed a flawless denial of service (DOS) attack against the entire city of Xiamen, basically killing all remote internet access in and out the city. This blocked the ability for the data to flow from Taiwan, giving ADConnect time to reboot the remote firewalls and regain access."

Valerie rudely interrupted, "Excuse me, Marcia, question. Who was the third-party?"

Marcia gestured with a hand to Valerie. "I will address that later, Director, thank you."

The president, curious, demanded, "Marcia, answer the question."

Marcia, offended by the question from Valerie, spoke in a sour manner, "A hacker group tied to the Japanese Yakuza called Rising Sun."

The entire team of cabinet members and military officers took a deep breath, knowing what was coming next. The president stood up from his chair. "Pardon me, Marcia, who interfaced with them to make this happen?"

Marcia found herself cornered and explained, "We had a civilian asset on the ground in Taiwan. He interfaced directly with San-Hamada, the Yakuza group leader in Taiwan, and made the arrangement."

The president walked around the table in the direction of Marcia. "Let me get this straight! We have the United States attorney general coordinating counter-hacking defensive schemes outside of the CIA and NSA?" the President asked incredulously.

Skip Saide spoke up in defense of Marcia. "Sir, for a moment. We activated a retired asset in Singapore to help. He, along with the civilian asset, provided vital information to help stop this attack."

The president moved around the table towards the CIA director. "Okay, Skip, in plain, simple language, who are these mystery assets?"

Skip glanced over at Marcia before addressing Alford. "Mr. President, the CIA asset is Forest Adams, and the civilian asset is Jack Kendall."

President Taylor stopped dead in his tracks. Standing motionless, Alford said, in a soft-spoken tone rarely witnessed in his cabinet meetings, "What did you just say?" Skip started to answer again. However, the president held up his hand. "STOP!"

As the room remained silent, the president moved back to his seat. Alford surveyed the room in deep thought. "I want Valerie, Skip, Marcia, SecDef, the Joint Chiefs, and the VP to meet in the Oval Office, ASAP. The rest of you... this meeting is adjourned."

President Taylor departed the conference room with the secret service agents and headed off to the Oval Office.

Marcia walked over to Skip and gratefully spoke. "Thank you."

Skip gave Marcia a quick wink and answered quietly, "You've been there for me, Marcia. Thank you."

Per Alford's order, the selected members of the cabinet joined the president in the Oval Office.

"Sit, everyone," President Taylor said. "Marcia, any chance you can hold these asses, please?"

Marcia didn't understand what the president meant until the vice president leaned over to her. "He meant assets."

Marcia cracked a smile to help lighten the mood in the room. Collecting her laptop and secure communicator, Marcia headed outside the Oval Office to make a call.

Skip leaned over to Alford for a private sidebar conversation. "Mr. President, we needed to stand arm's length from this."

The president looked over to his CIA director. "I get it, Skip."

Marcia moved back to the cabinet room to contact her FBI director. "Alvin, I need Forest and Jack on the secure video ASAP. The president wants to speak to them."

Alvin sent an urgent message to Forest.

Message: FBI_GOV: Encryption: Director: Forest Adams: Oval Office video, ASAP.

Signed,

FBI Director Alvin Ramsey

Forest received the FBI director's urgent message while heading back to building five on Camp Henson. *Message: Oval Office.* Forest peered over at Jack. "We're fucked!" Forest and Jack ran back into the administration building and to the secured video conference center.

Marcia re-entered the Oval Office to update Alford. "Sir, they are coming up on-screen now."

The president rose from his chair and walked over to the video display. Jack and Forest appeared on the screen while sitting in the secured conference room in Okinawa.

President Taylor took a deep breath and warmly smiled at the sight of Forest and Jack. "Well, Forest. How have you been?"

Forest also smiled at the sight of his old friend and replied sincerely, "Good to see you again, Al."

The entire Oval Office went completely silent. The president's cabinet members were in complete shock over the discovery of the identities of the mystery assets.

Alford remained calm in his reply to Forest. "Been better. I am sorry to hear about Bui. She was a lovely woman." The president looked over at Jack. "Corporal Jack Kendall?"

Jack beamed in pride. "Yes, Mr. President. Good to see you again, sir."

In complete disbelief, Marcia spluttered, "Sir, I didn't know you knew Jack Kendall?"

Alford replied, "Oh, Jack? Well, he ran into a little trouble in Beirut and needed legal counsel. I defended him in 1983 when some Marine officer failed to send back a helicopter to pick up Jack after he saved a bunch of Marines from an ambush outside Beirut, Lebanon. Kendall hiked back to the airport. When he arrived three days later, the same Marine officer ordered Jack arrested for being AWOL (absence without leave). Anyway, Jack drew his 9 mm pistol and shoved it into this guy's face. The Marines arrested Jack, and I offered to defend him at his court martial

Forest stared at Jack in complete confusion. "Oh shit, Jack."

Jack smiled and looked back at the president.

President Taylor continued, "So, fellas, thank you for being great Americans. Now what the fuck is really going on?"

Japanese Network Newswire: Naha Airport still closed at this hour while the Japanese Secret Service along with local Okinawa police units continue

searching for clues surrounding the coordinated bomb yesterday that rocked the airport only hours ago. The police haven't released the names of any current suspects. The casualty total has risen to forty-one killed and thirty-five wounded at this hour.

Commander Cho scoured through the remains of the Naha airport terminal and remained in shock over the blast. Cho, sitting on hold for the prime minister of Japan, moved between the various bomb zones and the car wreckages waiting for his secure call to begin.

"Yes, Prime Minister, this is Commander Cho, SIS."

Prime Minister Yoshi was just coming up to speed on exactly what happened in Okinawa. "Commander! Tell me, was it a terrorist attack?"

Cho sternly replied, "Sir, to answer your question, yes. This was a terrorist attack. An international terror suspect, a Russian warlord and drug trafficker named Dimi Zosh arrived from the United States. He is on Interpol's and the FBI's most wanted list. My agents tailed him to the taxi line. Just as he entered the vehicle, the cars around him exploded. This clearly was a diversion set up by this outfit so he could escape."

The prime minister, still in a state of shock over the blast on Okinawa, replied, "Commander, are we prepared to release a photo of the suspect to the public?"

Cho calmly addressed his prime minister. "Sir, not at this time. We are still gathering DNA and checking to see if any other cabs have explosives. Once we have cleared the second phase of the investigation, we will hold a press conference."

The prime minister approved of Cho's request to withhold the identity of Dimi Zosh. "Okay, Commander, set up a briefing with the upper and lower DIET along with my cabinet in four hours."

Cho acknowledged the order from the prime minster.

"Mr. President," Jack spoke. "We have learned the mastermind behind Dragon Vault is here on the island. Travis Jones and two others are hiding in a safe house. Forest and I are heading over to Nago now to see if we can find any of them."

Alford became alarmed by Jack's last statement. "Corporal, I want you to keep your head on and don't get yourself killed. I hear your daughter-in-law is expecting soon."

Jack appreciated Alford's concern. "Roger that, sir."

Forest raised a critical issue to the president. "Al, more bad news. Dimi Zosh is here in Okinawa."

Alford was petrified at the news that Dimi was alive. "Marcia killed him with a car bomb in 1984."

Forest looked into the video screen directly at Marica before replying. "I know Al, Marcia planted the bomb after Delta Forest rescued me. Zosh must have survived the car bomb."

The president walked back to his chair and replied, "Marcia, any other surprises?"

Marcia finished her water and replied, "Sir, we released Bao Xu to the Chinese last night on Penghu Island. This was a part of a deal we cut with the Chinese. However, the deal went south."

Alford stood up and placed his hands on his hips. "What did we get for him?"

Forest stepped in to reply. "Al, he gave us the location of three suspects hiding here in Okinawa."

The president, who wasn't convinced the trade was worth anything, proposed, "We should have kept him. Let's move on."

Valerie spoke up with a distinctly aggressive tone. "Mr. President, the NSA has an asset in China. The deep cover asset is close to the Minister of Finance, Hai Ming. The asset is willing to give us more intel on Dragon Vault. She may have an idea where the Chinese are taking General Vo, Bao Xu, and Poppy Ledger."

Marcia scorned at the mention of Hai Ming. "Wait! Who is the asset? The fucking asshole screwed us last night over the Vancouver crossing!"

Valerie didn't want to disclose her highly placed source to Marcia under any circumstances. "NSA only, AG."

The president quickly ordered, "Who is it, Valerie?"

"Yung Ming, the wife of the Minister of Finance, Hai Ming."

Marica's eyes nearly popped out of her head in anger. "How the hell did you get to her?" Marcia spouted.

President Taylor interrupted Marcia. "Did she give anything of value?"

Valerie, opening her secured notepad, said, "Yes, she tipped us off that the Chinese deployed several External Security Forces in Vancouver, hoping to prevent a high-ranking member of the PLA cyber force from defecting."

"Well, that explains my call with the prime minister of Canada," the president, in an exhausted tone, declared.

Marica and Valerie glared back at each other in a personal wrath of enragement.

Disregarding the emotional altercation between Valerie and Marcia, Alford continued to discuss the call from Canada. "The prime minister informed me that one of his RCMP officers was shot dead and three wounded. And the Chinese consulate demanded that his country release the captured Chinese agents. The Chinese are claiming those agents have diplomatic immunity."

"Mr. President," General Ike Harold, Chairman of the Joint Chiefs, spoke up. "Sir, we tracked the suspected plane that took off from a remote field out of Vancouver. Our radar station on Midway Island lost track after the aircraft headed towards North Korea."

The president gave a grim look at his staff members. "People, we lost two valuable assets. We have a bombing at an airport in Japan. Now we have a long-lost Russian bad guy on the loose in Okinawa!"

"Mr. President," Marcia interjected, "I am going to send SAC Burns along with Bill Parker's React 5 unit to Okinawa to assist Forest and Jack. They will have more firepower if they are going against Travis Jones. I will also interface with Commander Cho, head of Japanese SIS, to assist. Whatever is going to happen next with Jones, it will happen on Okinawa."

President Taylor looked over at the video screen. "Forest, if you need anything, call me directly. I want Dimi Zosh stopped!"

Forest appreciated the full support of this old friend. "Thank you, Al."

Once the video call ended, Alford turned to the ones remaining in the Oval Office staff meeting. "I want results here, people. I want this Russian stopped, and I want to know if this hacker attack targets any American assets here and abroad."

All the military, cabinet advisors, and staff replied, "Yes, sir," and proceeded to depart the room.

Chapter 48
Trade-Off

After opening his laptop to show his plan, Travis Jones started to give Dimi and his crew a briefing on the proposed operation. "Okay, here is the plan. After hacking the prime minister of Japan's private email, we got intel that he is planning something with our old friends in Taiwan."

Dimi burped from drinking his beer and raised his hand. "You hacked his private email account?"

Travis arrogantly glared at Dimi. "Yes! Our crew in Vietnam pulled it off."

Dimi snarled back showing no respect for Travis. "Interesting, carry on."

Travis took a sip of his beer. "The Japanese and Taiwanese plan to interconnect two cities in a pilot program. I guess those assholes want to show off to the world they have brains. Who the fuck knows."

Vlad threw his empty beer bottle next to Travis. "Which two?"

Travis used his index finger to point on the map attached to the wall. "Tamsui, Taiwan and Naha, Okinawa."

Vlad was pleased with the selection of those two cities by Japanese and Taiwanese governments. "Da, that fits into our plans, boss?"

Dimi nodded in agreement. "Continue, Jones."

Travis felt something was very wrong with how the Russians were reacting to his briefing. He stopped and queried, "What plan?"

Vlad, looking over at Dimi, said, "Ah, nothing, Jones. Just thinking out loud. Get me some beers!"

Travis hesitantly spoke, "Fuck you, get your own. Hey, before we go any further, what do you have going?"

Dimi slurred from drinking the beers. "None of your concern. Continue!"

Travis sidestepped around Vlad and stood in front of Dimi. "Look, come clear or you can just fuck off. I have connections in Moscow, Budapest, and Lagos, Nigeria. I don't your Russian crap."

Dimi sneered back at Jones. "Why don't you tell me where Vulturess is, and we will be on our way!"

Caught off guard by the question, Travis unintelligibility replied, "Fuck off, she is my asset. I will be dammed if I will tell you! Now, pick up the Russian shit you came in with and bail the fuck out!"

Dimi looked over to Josef, and ordered in Russian, "Handle it."

Josef, an ex-Russian Spetsnaz commando, swiftly leaped up, grabbed Travis by the throat, and threw him down to the floor. "Before I snap your neck, Jones, answer him! Where is Vulturess?"

Travis gagged for air while swallowing what tasted like his own blood. "IN ABU NAGO-SHI! Now let me up!"

Dimi motioned to Josef to let Travis go. Before he took his hands away from Travis's throat, Josef gave him another shot to the face.

Josef rose and headed out the door. He entered the stolen SUV and went quickly to the other end of the island to see if Vulturess was hiding there. Dimi turned his attention back to Travis. "Proceed with *your* plan, Jones."

Travis doubled over in pain while still on the ground and stared up at Dimi. "Let's adjourn for now."

Dimi laughed while looking over at Vlad. "Adjourn? We aren't in some fucking courtroom, are we, Vlad? Get up, Jones, you fuck!" Dimi screamed back at Travis.

Slowly, Travis rose from the floor and wiped the blood away from his mouth. As he reached for a beer, Ivan, one of Dimi's top hackers, reached over and knocked the beer off the table. "Ah, no beer for you. Finish your pathetic plan, Jones," Ivan cracked.

Travis moved back toward his laptop to restart his presentation. Still hesitant to continue with the plan, Travis tried to reach under the table in the center room where he kept a 9mm handgun fully loaded. Nervously, Travis reached under the table, only to find the weapon missing.

"Jones, looking for this?" Dimi laughed. "Finish your fucking story or I will use your gun to kill you and make it look like a fucking suicide!"

Feeling dejected, Travis continued discussing his plan. "After Tamsui and Naha become connected via dark fiber, the two cities will launch a pilot program based on Blockchain to start a new cryptocurrency called Green Kyoto."

Curiously, Dimi looked over at his Blockchain expert. "Ivan, what does this mean?"

Ivan served Dimi's hacker outfit, codename: Gorky Park, as a software engineer and hacker. He successfully deployed several Blockchain projects to globally hide financial records for the Russian Mafia from the American FBI, Interpol, and the Japanese SIS. "Well, Boss, this means they are creating a payment method for citizens in those cities. In that way, they will conduct commerce without borders. Using this shared currency and Blockchain for cybersecurity protection, this secured payment platform will prevent counterfeiting."

Dimi rose from his chair to grab another beer. "Ivan, where will the money be stored?"

Travis listened to Dimi and Ivan speak in Russian. "Hey, I don't speak fucking Russian. This is my plan! You are here because of me. Keep going Dimi, and I will be more than happy to drop a dime on you with Japanese SIS and the CIA!"

Dimi took a drink of his beer and without any hesitation, spit the beer out of his mouth and in Travis's face. "You have no plan, Jones, only an idea!"

Travis lunged toward Dimi and screamed, "You need to watch yourself, Zosh. I have people inside of Russia too!"

Dimi swiftly jabbed his thumb painfully into Travis's throat. "Do you, huh? Jones, I believe we are done with you. Get the fuck out of here!"

With a snap of his fingers, Dimi ordered his men to pick up Travis off the floor. Members of the Russian outfit in the room rose from their seats and dragged Travis out of the safehouse. Travis reached for anything he could use to stop the hackers from dragging him outside. He quickly reached for his laptop and threw it at Ivan, striking him in the head. The rest of the team members jumped on Travis and proceeded to punch and kick him for several minutes.

After taking a severe beating from the Russians, Travis passed out from the pain. The Russians dumped Travis into the portal bath on the side of the safehouse.

Dimi extinguished his cigarette as he departed the safehouse. "Vlad, let's go to the other safehouse; we need to find this Vulturess."

Vlad motioned to the rest of the Russian outfit to head out.

After driving for nearly an hour from Camp Henson, Forest and Jack arrived in Nago city. "Okay, Forest, what exactly are we looking for?"

"Jack, let's start with the local police, see if anything has happened." Forest checked his phone for any local police stations. He spotted a local hub two miles ahead and ordered the Marine driver to head there. "Corporal, let's head up this street for two blocks and park."

The Corporal replied, "Yes, sir. I see ahead."

As the Marine SUV pulled up to the spot near the police outpost, Forest noticed a group of people crowding around a sewer drain across the street from the police hub.

"Jack, let's check that out," Forest said.

As Jack and Forest approached the crowd, they noticed several policemen and rescue personnel trying to remove two bodies from a deep storm drain. Jack attempted to move closer to see what everyone was staring at.

He was stopped by a Japanese police officer with a long white stick. "Stop! Turn around, sir. This is a restricted area," the officer ordered.

Forest decided to take a different route to observe the bodies still stuffed in the drainpipe. He moved rapidly to the left of the crowd and worked his way down the drain system. Eventually, Forest was also stopped by a Japanese police official. "Move out," the officer demanded.

Forest reached into his jacket pocket and removed his identification badge. "Officer, I am Forest Adams, U.S. Embassy Vietnam. I need to see those bodies."

The officer inspected Forest's credentials. "Wait here, Mr. Adams."

Forest removed his secured communicator and activated his camera to get a picture of the two victims. As he zoomed in on one of the bodies, it became apparent to Forest that one of the bodies was either an American or someone of European descent. The officer returned the badge to Forest. "Proceed, Mr. Adams. Don't touch anything, just observe only."

Forest thanked the officer and walked in the direction of the two bodies. He motioned back to the officer, "Sir, I need that man with me, please."

The officer signaled to Jack to proceed with Forest.

Forest and Jack moved slowly down the hill leading to the drainpipe entrance. Jack bent down to get a better look at the bodies. "Forest, look at these two faces. That one for sure must be Noah."

Forest knelt to get a closer look. "Yes, that's him."

While Forest examined the body to confirm if the corpse was Noah Wilson, Jack looked up at the crowd and noticed a Western-looking man staring down at them. "Forest, we have a spotter looking at us now. Twelve o'clock, blue shirt."

Forest stood up gracefully and moved away from the bodies, trying to get a good look at the mysterious man. "Yep, I got him. Who the fuck is he?" Forest asked in a guarded voice.

Jack looked again at the man in the blue shirt. "I bet he is Russian."

As the police lifted the second body out of the sewer drain, Jack looked away for a moment to compose himself after he threw up at the sight of the badly disfigured body. The second body the police removed from the drain was a badly beaten woman. Forest, looking a bit closer, said, "Jack, that has to be Lilian Tang, aka Vulturess."

Jack, wiping his mouth, asked, "Let me see again." He took a deep look at what was left of the woman's face. "Yea, that is Lilian Tang."

The Russian man noticed Jack and Forest observing him and started to slip away from the scene.

"Boss, this is Josef. Vulturess is dead."

Dimi rode in the stolen SUV and was heading to Nago to find Lilian. He slammed his fist violently against the dashboard. "Fuck! What the fuck happened, Josef?"

Josef, moving away from the crime scene so no one could hear his conversation with Dimi, replied, "I don't know, Boss. The Japanese police pulled two bodies out of a sewer. Someone really did a number on them. This has the trademark of a Yakuza scratch team hit."

Dimi continued to slam his massive fist on the dashboard. "Fuck!"

Jack looked into the crowd still gathered around the sewer and softly commented, "Forest, the spotter is gone."

Forest finished taking a few photos of Lilian Tang and Noah. "Keep looking, Jack. We need to find that guy."

Jack and Forest started to climb out of the sewer drain and back onto the road.

Looking back down the hill to the sewer drain, Jack reflected on the gruesome discovery. "Got to be San-Hamada's crew that did this."

Forest agreed. "We need to find that spotter.I bet he could lead us to Zosh. Jack, ask William to scan Darknet. If this was a Yakuza scratch team, there sure as shit will have videos uploaded in one of their secure chat rooms."

Message: Encryption: Secured: One-way: Techline: William Kendall: Jack Kendall: Vulturess and Noah found killed on Okinawa. No clue who did the handy work, check Darknet.

Signed,

Dad

While Jack sent the message to William, Forest also sent a secured communication to update Marcia.

Message: FBI_GOV: Encryption: Multiple: Burns, Parker, Ramsey, Robertson: Forest Adams: Two-way: Noah and Lilian Tang found dead. They were found in a sewer drain in Nago Okinawa. Japanese police and SIS are investigating. Please confirm the arrival of SAC Burns and SA Parker with React 5 on Okinawa. Jack has spotted more Russians near the site where the bodies were found. The hit was mostly San-Hamada and his scratch team.

Signed,

Forest

William received a notification on his secure device while sitting in the hospital in Northern Virginia.

Message: Noah and Lilian found Dead.

William placed his hand on his head, and he leaned forward to look at the message again. "Oh my God."

Tricia heard her husband's voice. "Oh, Will, what happened?"

William walked over to his wife's bed. "Noah and Lilian Tang were found dead on Okinawa. Dad is there on the scene with Forest."

Tricia shook her head slowly as she placed her hands on William's chest. "This is getting very dangerous. Be careful, Will, please."

William forced himself to smile. "Let me check something, my love. I will be back in a moment." After he kissed his wife on the forehead, William stepped into the hallway.

"Let me check Darknet."

After booting up his secured laptop, William logged into the Darknet and began scanning anything he could regarding Lilian's or Noah's deaths. After he logged into several secure chat rooms, William discovered the video of Lilian and Noah getting killed. SwordBitch, the lead hacker for the Yakuza, already uploaded Lilian's beating and the Habu snake biting Noah. SwordBitch could be heard laughing hysterically on the video recording.

William continued to digitally move between the various secured chat rooms. He mistakenly landed inside of the chat room, "Scratch team OKI." Once inside this chatroom, the images William discovered brought instant fear into William's heart. He witnessed the video watching Lilian Tang being beaten with a lead pipe. William looked away in disgust as he noticed another video with a man tied to a tree and a snake biting him multiple times. "Noah."

He watched the remainder of the videos in total disgust.

Message: Encryption: Techline: William Kendall: Jack Kendall: Confirmed on DARKNET, It was the Yakuza Scratch team. SwordBitch posted the videos. Looks like five of them tortured and killed Vulturess. The second victim, Noah, was tied to a tree next to a Habu snake. The video shows the bodies being dumped in a sewer. I had seen anything like it in my life.

Signed,

William

Jack read the reply from his son and looked over at Forest. "William just confirmed. Yakuza. It was San-Hamada's scratch team."

Forest motioned to Jack to head back to the car. He made an observation. "If this is a Yakuza hit, what were the Russians doing there?"

After expeditiously moving away quietly from the crowd, Josef continued to hear Dimi screaming and slamming his fist in the car. "Boss!" Josef screamed. "I suggest you don't come here. The place is crawling with

Japanese cops. Also, I spotted two Americans studying the dead bodies. They looked like either FBI or CIA."

Dimi slammed his fist after hearing Josef's account of the situation in Nago. "Are you sure they are CIA?"

Josef was about to reply to Dimi, but instead, slowly turned off his secured communicator when he noticed Jack staring in his direction.

"Josef!" Dimi screamed. He noticed the call with Josef dropped. "Fuck, CIA? Adams, you fuck!" Dimi turned to Vlad. "Turn around and head back to the safehouse."

Vlad spun the car around and began heading back to the safe house on the east end of the island.

"Forest, spotter, two o'clock," Jack said.

Forest nonchalantly looked out the window of the car. "I see him. Jack, let's get him!"

Both men departed the vehicle with great stealth and took off running towards Josef. Josef observed the two American agents eyeball him as they made their way towards him. Instantly, Josef dropped to one knee, drew his weapon, and began to fire. Jack and Forest immediately dropped to the ground to avoid the gunfire.

As shots came from all directions from Josef's weapon, one of the first Marine guard was hit into the stomach with a bullet while the second Marine returned fire towards the Russian.

Josef started to run while shooting widely and he attempted tried to escape down a narrow alley. Jack got up from his position and began to chase the Russian.

Josef, frustrated that he was out of bullets, threw his gun away and ran faster. Jack, giving chase to the Russian, slowly gained ground.

As Jack got closer to the Russian, he dove at Josef's legs, hoping to drag him to the ground. Suddenly and without warning, Josef dropped to the ground. He felt Jack fly uncontrollably over him and crash into a wall. Josef drew a sharp, edgy knife from his boot and lunged toward Jack. Seeing the blade coming towards his neck, Jack dropped down and jammed his fist directly into Josef's throat. Josef countered by delivering a crushing punch to Jack's jaw, sending him backward.

Feeling the pain in his jaw, Jack reached up and stuck his thumbs into the Russian's eyes, forcing Josef to scream and fall back, hitting his head against the concrete ground.

"Fuck!" Josef screamed in pain.

Jack leaped up, dropped his left on the Russian's throat, and struck him in the chest with his fist. After several blows to the head from Jack's bloody fist, the Russian began spitting blood out of his mouth.

"Stop!" Josef yelled.

Forest reached the spot where he found Jack and the Russian bleeding. "Jack! We need him alive."

Before Jack released his grasp of Josef, he delivered a direct kick into his groin. Forest pinned Josef, preventing him from getting away. He placed his elbow on Josef's throat before demanding, "Where is Dimi Zosh?"

Josef started laugh. "You will never find him!" After a few coughs of blood, the Russian turned his head to the right, closed his eyes, and stopped breathing.

Jack, still in pain from the struggle with Josef, sat off to the side, heaving blood from his mouth. He began to shake uncontrollably. Forest watched Jack cough up blood on the ground and calmly said, "Breathe, Jack. Stay calm, Marine."

Jack coughed up the last blood in his stomach and rolled back to the sitting position. He looked at Forest in dismay. "Been a while, Forest."

Forest nodded his head. "I know, Marine."

Forest searched Josef's body looking for any clues. He discovered inside one of the pockets a passport, a cell phone, and a wallet. Forest opened the passport to see the name of the Russian. "Josef Bura."

Jack sat in a state of shock and continued to look away from Forest and Josef's corpse.

Forest observed several Japanese policemen approaching them with their stick weapons drawn in the strike position. "Hands up!"

Jack and Forest slowly rose up from the blood-stained ground and placed their hands on the top of their heads.

Message: FBI_GOV: Encryption: Marcia Robertson: Alvin Ramsey (FBI): SIC Burns: Effectively immediately: SAC Burns will be promoted to the role of SIC for all Organized Crime Global Task Force, effectively Immediately. Gerald, proceed to Nago Okinawa with SA Bill Parker and React 5. Link with CIA station chief Forest Adams and troubleshooter, Jack Kendall. Locate and detain Dimi Zosh and Travis Jones.

Signed,

Alvin Ramsey

SAC Gerald Burns and Special Agent Bill Parker were updating their case notes when a flash message came across their communicators.

"Message: SAC Burns promoted." Gerald looked at the entire message. "I didn't see that coming."

Bill read the same message. "Well deserved, SAC."

Gerald reached over to Bill. "Thank you, Bill. We need to head to Okinawa. Can you get the jet and your team ready? I need to go check on Regina."

Bill replied, "Yes, SAC, we will be ready within the hour."

Gerald got up and headed to the local hospital to check on Regina Kendall.

While heading over to the hospital, Gerald considered the task at hand. Being promoted from the special agent in charge of the Boston FBI office to oversee all the organized crime task forces globally quickly overwhelmed him. "I guess I will be looking for my third wife."

After arriving at the hospital, Gerald departed his SUV and walked over to the guards protecting Regina. As he approached the main entrance, Gerald showed his FBI badge to the security detail. "Congratulations, Sir, on your promotion."

Gerald smiled and thanked the FBI guards for acknowledgement before heading into Regina's room. "Well, Regina, you are looking well."

Regina was using her laptop to answer emails to Thomas Wilson, CEO of Techline. "Well, Mr. SAC of all global bad guys department, well done!"

Gerald became amused by Regina's sarcastic comment. "Hey, watch yourself lady. You may end up like me someday!"

Regina reached over to Gerald as he approached her hospital bed. "Thank you for being here, SAC,. How is my dad?"

Gerald gave a Regina a hug. "Your dad is on the ground in Nago. Bill and I are heading there now with React 5. Can I do anything for you?"

Regina took Gerald's hand. "Bring my dad back alive."

Gerald squeezed Regina's hand in comfort. "Count on it. You get better, lady. We have room for you at the FBI."

Regina smiled back at Gerald. "Interesting idea. Let's discuss later, SAC. What is the status of Tang and her fucking previous boss?"

Gerald sat down next to the bed. "Your father and Forest found Noah and Lilian Tang dead in a sewer. Mostly likely it was San-Hamada and his Yakuza scratch teams that took them out. We confirmed Dimi Zosh and his Russian outfit are also on the island now. Not to worry. Look, things are going to get very serious, real fast. This Russian crew is ruthless. Their hacker group, Gorky Park, is filled with some serious players. I am concerned for your safety and your brother's."

Regina closed her laptop and reassured Gerald. "SAC, I will head home from here and be with my brother. I am going to be an aunt soon."

Gerald smiled. "Ah yes, give Tricia my best."

"I will," Regina said.

Gerald rose and gave Regina a hug before departing. "By the way, the president called you a great American for what you did."

Regina playfully laughed. "I didn't even vote for that guy."

Gerald turned around. "Neither did I."

One of the Japanese police officers kneeled to check Josef's pulse. After feeling no pulse, he rose up and headed over to his watch commander. "Sir, no pulse." The watch commander looked harshly towards Jack and Forest.

"Jack, say nothing," Forest advised.

Chapter 49
Thieves

Travis woke up in a portable bath with a pounding headache and blood on this shirt. "Fuck, my head!"

Attempting to climb out of the plastic tub at his safehouse, Travis stumbled to the ground. Still feeling the pain from the beating by the Russian thugs, he looked around to find the place wholly destroyed. "Those fucking Russians!" Travis ripped his door off the hinges as he re-entered the building. He went into the kitchen icebox and grabbed some ice for his head.

"I can't remember shit!" Then he thought hard about the last thing he could remember. "I told them about the other safehouse. Fuck!"

Travis pounded his hand against the wall until his knuckles bled. "Noah and Lilian, they are fucking dead for sure."

Travis looked around his place to see if anything was salvageable. He tore down a picture from the wall to reveal a safe. Travis inserted his finger into the ID pad, and the secure safe door opened. Inside, Travis removed 10,000,000 in Japanese Yen, $100,000 in U.S. currency, twenty gold bars, several fake passports, and several SIM cards. He started to pack up everything quickly before the Russians returned. Travis poured a bottle of vodka on the carpet inside his safehouse and dropped a lit match on the floor. As the safehouse became consumed with flames, Travis ran to the closest jungle tree line.

Vlad drove the car back to the safehouse and saw large brumes of smoke. "Boss, we are here. What the fuck?"

Dimi and others departed the car and walked back into the safehouse. "Find him!" Dimi shrieked.

Vlad and the other Russians entered the jungle close to the house to search for Jones. Dimi stayed outside and lit a cigarette while watching the safehouse burn up in flames.

Vlad returned from the jungle. "Boss, he cleared out."

Dimi nodded. "He can't be far."

Vlad nodded and motioned to the other men to get back in the SUV to look for Travis.

Travis peered through the jungle tree, seeing Dimi and the Russians climb back into the SUV. After waiting for the vehicle to depart, he headed deeper into the jungle on Miyagi Island. After running for over an hour, Travis found an abandoned cave left over from WWII. As he entered the cave, he could see Japanese writing on the walls and old maps on the ground. He put down his bag and proceeded to open his secured communicator.

Message: Encryption: Darknet 187: Rambonus: Noah: One-way: Russians heading your way.

Signed,

Trav

After sending the message to Noah, Travis opened a and began scanning for any news about the blast at the airport. After studying several secured chat rooms, Travis came across the Yakuza Rising Sun video, "Vulturess death." Travis turned off the video stream because he couldn't bear to watch. After a few moments of seeing Lilian being hit with the lead pipe, he closed the video and began to watch the second one. "Oh my god, Noah." Travis watched the Habu snake attacking his friend.

Travis switched back on his communicator to send out another message to BOSS.

Message: Encryption: Darknet 187: BOSS Fong-Gao: Rambonus: Vulturess is dead. Enclosed is the video of Yakuza handy work on Okinawa.

Signed,

Rambonus

After Travis sent off the message, he laid down his backpack and closed his eyes to rest while he planned his escape.

Staring in deep thought while sitting in the eastern Taiwanese coastline inside his personal tea shop in Taiwan, BOSS, Snakehead of the Fong Gao Triads, heard his phone buzz with a notification.

Message: Rambonus: BOSS Vulturess dead...

BOSS snapped his secured communicator in haste. With an internal rage, he incoherently mumbled, "Oh, my daughter, what has happened to you?"

BOSS demanded his assistant enter the secured tearoom. "Chi, what has happened to my daughter?"

Chi had been BOSS's loyal guard for the last fifteen years. He knew Lilian when she was a little girl. "Sir, we are still getting the facts straight. Our people on Okinawa spotted her in a snake bar in Nago city. The bar is controlled by San-Hamada. She was doing shots with some American lawyer. She later disappeared, and the police found both in a sewer drain outside of town."

BOSS continued in his silent rage while staring at the ocean. He spoke with a quiet yet tense tone. "Where is Bao Xu?"

Chi stuttered in his reply. "Sir, we believe the American's turned him over to the Chinese a few days ago on Penghu Island."

BOSS angerly grabbed his tea kettle, walked over to Chi, and slammed the porcelain container on his head, smashing it into pieces. Chi dropped to the ground while blood gushed from his head. BOSS stood over him and screamed in a frenzy, "Get up!"

Chi attempted to rise to his feet. "Yes, BOSS."

BOSS pulled a pen out of his pocket and rammed the device into Chi's throat. Chi, gasping for air, dropped to one knee, and collapsed on the floor. Several Fong Gao Triads members raced up to the private patio to check on BOSS within minutes.

"BOSS, you okay?"

Still in a rage from the death of his beloved daughter Lilian, BOSS said, "Take me to San-Hamada."

One of the Triad members used his earpiece and proceeded to call the driver to pull up the car. "BOSS is leaving now," the bodyguard screamed.

Forest and Jack arrived at the regional police station near Nago city in handcuffs. The officers led Jack and Forest into a conference room and re-handcuffed them to a table.

"Brings back great memories of Vietnam, doesn't it, Forest?" Jack said. "Remember when you showed up at the police station in Saigon after I got arrested for being with Linh at the hotel?"

Forest grinned for a moment. "Yes, Marine, I think I saved your ass a few times during your time there!"

Jack could not agree more.

A senior Japanese police officer came into the room. "So, gentlemen, you had quite a day. We have two dead bodies found three days ago at a bath outside of town. We had two found in a sewer just a few hours ago, and now we have a dead tourist with his blood on your hands."

Just as Jack was about to challenge the officer, Forest declared, "Sir, I am Forest Adams. I am with the U.S. Embassy in Vietnam. If you can call the ambassador, he will vouch for me."

The Japanese officer stared at the two men. "Mr. Adams, you are in no position to order me around."

Forest patiently replied, "Okay."

The officer started to read their legal rights. "You have the right to counsel of your choice."

Just as the officer finished, the door to the conference room opened. "Officer, release these men," Commander Cho demanded.

"Sir, who are you?" Commander Cho showed the officer his ID. "Oh, yes, sir, Commander Cho." The officer proceeded to unlock Jack's and Forest's handcuffs.

Cho walked over to Forest and Jack. "Gentlemen, I am Commander Cho, Japanese Secret Intelligence Service."

Jack and Forest rose and greeted him. "Great to meet you, sir."

The commander motioned to Jack and Forest, "Come with me." Cho led Jack and Forest out of the room and down the hall. "This way, please." The three men entered a secured hallway, "In here, please. Gentlemen, I know you didn't kill anyone, except for the last man we found. I am sure this was self-defense."

Jack answered with in a calm tone, "Yes, sir."

Commander Cho continued, "I know who you are, Mr. Kendall, and you, Mr. Adams." Cho turned on his laptop and put a series of photos on the overhead screen. "Do you know who this man is?"

Forest picked up a bottle of water from a table. "Yes, sir, that's Dimi Zosh."

The commander nodded. "Do you know why he is here?"

Jack took some water as well. "Yes, he was supposed to be here. We believe he is meeting Travis Jones."

The commander brought another picture on the screen. "Is this is him?"

Jack moved closer to the screen. "That's him."

Commander Cho nodded, "The two bodies we found in the sewer, Noah and Lilian Tang, were taken out by the Yakuza scratch team, not the Russians."

Forest looked at the screen again. "That makes sense. Tang, aka, Vulturess, killed the number two Yakuza leader last year in Macau and stole a hundred million in crypto. I bet the Yakuza wanted her dead and the money back."

The commander took notes. "Yes, we believe the same as well."

Taking another drink of water, Jack asked, "Why do you think the Russians are here, Commander?"

Commander Cho looked up at Jack. "We are not sure. We know several members of the hacker group, Gorky Park, are on the island."

Jack thought about what happened during the Dragon Vault hack. "Forest, is there anything happening regarding that Smart Country thing the president of Taiwan spoke about?"

Forest snapped his fingers. "Jack, you are right! Commander, we need to speak to Sunny Ho in Taiwan. Do you have access to a secured video system?"

The commander pushed several buttons inside the conference to activate the video system.

Message: Encryption: US_Embassy: Urgent: Sunny_Ho_ADConnect_Thomas_Wilson_Techline: Need CONFAB Video now.

Signed,

Forest

Sunny Ho sat in his favorite dumpling bar in Taipei. He always enjoyed pork soup dumplings with a Taiwanese beer on Mondays after work. Hearing the notification signal from his secured communicator, he informed his dinner guest, "I have to take this."

Thomas Wilson, CEO of Techline/Cybercom sat at his desk in Pasadena, California. He picked up the urgent notification to join the video with Forest Adams.

The video call began as Thomas, Sunny, Forest, Jack, and Commander Cho connected into the meeting.

Forest started off the meeting. "Fellas, thanks for jumping on. This is Commander Cho, Japanese SIS."

Thomas and Sunny introduced themselves.

"Jack, how are you, son?" Thomas asked.

"Been a while, Boss, I know."

Thomas showed a bit of concern for his lead troubleshooter. "Son, let's catch up after the call."

Jack nodded and thanked his boss.

Forest started off the call with a question. "Sunny, give it to me straight. Do you have something going between Taiwan and Japan around the Smart Country project?"

Sunny was caught off guard. "Forest, I can't tell you that. That can only come from President Yu Chi Fong."

Forest maintained composure. "Sunny, Lilian Tang was found dead here in Okinawa. Noah as well. We have a Russian hit squad on the island and war that could be breaking out between the Yakuza and the Triads at any moment. Can you please give us some slack?"

Sunny realized how serious Forest was in his request. "Okay, here is what I can tell you." Sunny brought up his laptop and opened a secured presentation file. "We have successfully created underwater cabling connecting Tamsui, Taiwan and Naha, Okinawa. The president and Japanese prime minister have approved the creation of a new cryptocurrency that can only be used in those two cities. The cryptocurrency will be set up in a separate Blockchain architecture with twelve distributed ledgers. The currency, codename Green Kyoto, can be purchased by the citizens in those two cities only. Only commerce between those cities will accept Green Kyoto Bitcoin today."

Jack, following along with Sunny, said, "And let me guess. The Techline / Cybercom Backhaul QoS that William designed will handle the packet transfers across the fiber network."

Sunny replied, "Yes, that is correct, Jack. William's software is critical for this project and many others to follow."

"If I am may," Thomas spoke, "Jack, we are granting ADConnect a site license in exchange for transfer percentage and transaction value cost margin. This will create a massive windfall for our company!"

Jack, being a shareholder of Cybercom / Techline, appreciated Thomas's update.

Forest interjected. "Hate to break up the party, but if what you are saying is true, this is why Dimi is here."

Commander Cho, confused, looked at Forest. "Sir, I am not following."

Jack walked over to the whiteboard and drew out a flow chart. "Commander, the citizen of Naha will take his Japanese Yen currency and purchase a Green Kyoto. Those funds will be handled by a Japanese bitcoin exchange house and a Japanese central bank. In Tamsui, a Taiwanese citizen will execute a similar purchase by using Taiwan Dollars. Those funds will be stored in an exchange in Taiwan and a central Taiwanese bank."

Sunny added to Jack's synopsis. "Yes, Evergreen BTC and Bank of Republic of China."

Jack continued. "Now, when a citizen wants to purchase something from Tamsui, the value of the Bitcoin will be based on the consumption of goods and services between those two cities. The more people spend, the greater the value of the Green Kyoto currency."

The Commander responded, "So, this Russian wants to find a way to either steal the money on deposit in the exchanges or steal directly from the digital wallets themselves?"

Thomas responded to Commander Cho's question. "Or Dimi and his hackers are trying to insert an overhead percentage fee as means to shave money off each transaction." Forest and Jack looked at each other. "That is why he is here. I bet he is trying to discover the location of the Blockchain ledgers."

Sunny spoke out loud, "Oh shit. If he finds them, that could breach the entire Blockchain process and destroy the virtual currency."

Forest gestured to Jack, "Marine, we need to find him."

Forest looked at Sunny and Thomas. "Guys, when is this project supposed to launch?"

Sunny declared, "Ten days."

Jack interjected, "Thomas, I will stay on the ground."

Thomas knew Jack all too well. "I wouldn't have it any other way."

Jack pressed Thomas for an update. "How is my daughter?"

Thomas assured Jack, "She is a Kendall. She is departing tomorrow to be with William for the birth of your first grandchild."

Jack felt a huge gratitude for Thomas. "Thank you, Thomas."

Forest closed the meeting. "Guys, thank you for the update. Sunny, keep us up to date on the fiber connection. We are heading now to get Travis Jones and hopefully Zosh."

Thomas and Sunny gave Forest a thumbs up and proceeded to disconnect from the video call.

Forest remarked with a high sense of urgency, "Commander, we need to find Travis Jones and Dimi."

Cho could not agree more. "Yes, we have their pictures being released to the press in the next hour."

After driving for nearly an hour, Vlad and Dimi couldn't spot Travis anywhere. "Boss, no sign of him."

"That fucking piece of shit! Alright, come back to the safe house. We have a lot of work to do."

Chapter 50
Avenge

PLA Cyber Covert Flight (Tonghua, China)

Still vomiting from the beatings from her Chinese guards, Poppy Ledger felt the pain all across her body as the plane was about to land back in China. She had no idea what life had in store for her. Just now, she realized that her fate had turned dangerously horrendous. Only pain and suffering would be in her future.

As the plane touched down at a secret airfield near Tonghua, China, the security soldier walked over to Poppy and yelled, "Here, traitor!" The guard punched Poppy in the face again before lifting her up.

As Poppy's head pressed back against the seat, she felt nothing but pain throughout her head. As the plane came to a complete stop, the personal security started to blindfold Poppy before taking her off the plane.

Blindfolded, Poppy stepped off the charter plane and into the cold air of China.

"Ah, welcome, Poppy Ledger," Commander Zuh stated. "Welcome home."

The security forces led Poppy back into the trunk. "Get in, you traitor," the guard yelled.

Poppy crashed hard on the floor of the trunk. Unable to get up, she stayed on the bottom of the vehicle to journey to her next unknown.

BOSS had made the long climb up the stairs to the famed tea house in Yilan, Taiwan, several times over the years to come face-to-face with his arch nemesis, San-Hamada. Overlooking Juifen street in eastern Taiwan, BOSS never got tired of the breath-taking ocean view.

While sitting at his private table inside this historic tea house, San-Hamada reviewed the secured messages. He lifted his head slightly to catch BOSS entering this private tea room.

"Ah, BOSS, been a long time."

BOSS, the Fong Gao Triads snakehead, always maintained a distant relationship with his rival leader of the Yakuza. "Yes, San-Hamada, you are looking well."

San-Hamada bowed his head out of a respect for his old rival. "So, is it so important for an old man like you to do this climb up Juifen street?"

BOSS sat across from San-Hamada. Patiently, he placed his secure communicator and pair of chopsticks on the table before he replied. "We have always maintained a peace between you and I, San. Now it seems you have broken that truce on Okinawa."

San-Hamada took a long sip of his favorite dragon well tea. "Here, have a cup, my friend."

BOSS nodded and accepted the cup of tea.

"BOSS, you and I go way back. We both served in Vietnam as allies to the Americans against the communist. We came home to a broken society and helped rebuild our communities. Yet, we have had differences. The bloodshed has been the last thing we turned to."

BOSS reminisced for a moment. He remembered their time in Vietnam. "San-Hamada, we saved each other. I know things have changed, especially with the younger generation."

San-Hamada agreed with his rival. "Yes, the younger members have changed the way we operate for sure."

BOSS finished the tea and placed it on the table. "San-Hamada, your people killed my daughter on Okinawa in a rather disgraceful way."

San-Hamada gracefully placed his teacup down. He reached into his coat pocket and removed a steel pair of chopsticks. "BOSS, your daughter killed my number two man and several of my soldiers in Macau, along with stealing a hundred million in crypto currency. Yet, for over a year now, you have offered nothing in response to this event. Your daughter was an undisciplined killing machine."

BOSS adjusted his pair of metal chopsticks with his smoke-stained fingers. "Your men killed her with a lead pipe. Yet, you offered nothing."

San-Hamada motioned to his security personnel sitting in the room. "Leave us."

The security team hesitated as they rose from their chairs and headed out the door.

San-Hamada showed a brief smile from the corner of his mouth. "Now, BOSS, it is just you and I."

BOSS nodded his head back at his rival. "I guess we never get too old for this, huh?"

With a bold, swift leap, San-Hamada jumped toward BOSS and used his chopsticks to stab him in the throat. Falling back on the ground, BOSS began to cough up blood into San's face. Unknowingly, BOSS managed to shove a chopstick under San-Hamada's rib cage and stabbed directly into his lung, causing him to stop breathing.

"Wheeze!" San-Hamada gasped for air.

Bleeding uncontrollably from the stab wound, BOSS looked into his rival's eyes for the last time. "We are done, old friend."

As the final words came from BOSS's mouth, both men laid still on the floor with no life in them.

Hearing the crashing on the floor, both the Triads and Yakuza security teams rushed into the tea house, only to see their leaders dead from a mutual blood fight that claimed both their lives. Not knowing what to say or to do, the rival gangs drew their knives and began to all-out battle to the death. Several members of the Yakuza began to charge at the Triads, starting with the two under-bosses. After several slashes with the blades and blood flowing, the rival gangs grabbed their crew members who were still alive and ran out of the tea house.

Taiwan_News_Line: Bloodshed today at a coffee shop on Juifen street. Members of the Fong Gao Triads clashed with the San Hamada Yukuza. Several members from each rival gang, including the snakehead for the Triads, BOSS, and the leader of the Yakuza outfit San-Hamada himself. Police are still investigating the motive behind the killings.

The G5 private charter pilot called over the speaker, "SAC Burns, we are on our final approach to Naha International Airport."

SAC Gerald Burns, SA Bill Parker, along with the FBI React 5 team, were sent to Okinawa to link up with Forest and Jack.

Gerald reached for his satellite phone to contact Forest. "Forest, we are on final approach. We will be on the ground in twenty minutes."

Forest looked at his watch. "SAC, good. Once you land, head up to Nago police sub-station."

Gerald checked his map information. "Roger that Forest. We will be there within the hour."

Jack was still horrified by the broken body of Lilian Tang. He couldn't comprehend the pain she must have gone through. Jack bent down over Lilian's lifeless body. "I know your life was hell, yet you brought unspeakable pain and death to others."

Forest walked over to Jack. "She was hell in life, Jack."

Jack wanted to change the subject "Any word on SAC Burns?"

Forest also wanted to look past Lilian's shattered remains. "On their final approach now."

Jack glanced over at Forest and gave him a slight nod. Disturbed by his secured communication notification system, Jack reached down to check his messages. With a cold, blank look on his face and hesitation in his voice, Jack said, "Forest, check your messages. Something just went down in Taiwan."

The cold chill went down Forest's back. "What happened?"

Jack started to read the news flash. *"A clash today in Taiwan leaving several dead in a Juifen tea house. Members of the Fong Gao Triads and San-Hamada Yakuza were found dead, including the notorious BOSS Snakehead and Japanese Yakuza leader, San-Hamada himself. The police and Japanese SIS have cordoned off the area while they conduct their investigation. More details to follow."*

Forest walked away distraught and frustrated. "Let's find Commander Cho."

After completing a very tense meeting with the president and cabinet members to discuss the failed border crossing in Canada and the handoff in Taiwan, Marcia departed the meeting to regroup and figure out a way to get back at Hai Ming for double crossing her. She remembered in the president's Oval Office something about the NSA having access to Hai's wife. Marcia found an empty conference room in the old Executive Building next to the White House. She called Valerie at the NSA on a secured phone inside the room.

"Valerie, I think we need to discuss the issue around your asset in China."

Valerie, who was not a huge fan of Marcia Robertson as he attorney general, said, "Marcia, we have nothing to discuss. You fucked a simple handoff by trusting some guy you fucked in college. Now you want me to give you access to his wife? I got nothing for you, Attorney General."

Marcia let Valerie vent out her anger. Both members of the president's National Security inner circle never saw eye to eye on many issues, especially when it came to China.

"Valerie, she is your asset. However, I am in the middle of something that involves her husband. I need your help."

Valerie remained guarded. "Marcia, you fucked up by letting two assets go. I can't afford to leave my key asset in China, especially someone that is married to China's next president."

Marica knew deep down that Valerie was right. By losing both Bao Xu and Poppy Ledger, the United States Intelligence community lost access to highly placed assets within the PLA and Chinese underworld. "You are right, Valerie. If you change your mind—"

Valerie hung up the phone. "Never in a million years."

Waking up in the cold, damp cave left over from World War II, Travis Jones, with his money, gold bars, and fake passports, still couldn't come to terms with his situation. "How the fuck did this go to hell so fast?"

Travis rose up from the cave floor attempting to depart. With darkness still upon him, Travis hit his head on the low hanging ceiling. He realized the shelter was used by the Japanese in World War II.

Seeing that the sun had settled on Okinawa, Travis exited the cave and hiked towards the main road. He stopped once he reached the road intersection. Travis felt the strain on his shoulder from carrying the money and gold bars. Hoping he could catch a ride back to the Nago safehouse to see if Noah and Lilian were still alive, he sat on the side of the road waiting for some vehicle to stop.

Dimi gathered his team at the Miyagi safehouse and updated his team. "We can assume that Josef is dead, probably by this American operative the ambassador warned me about."

Ivan and Vlad stared at their boss in a silent rage.

"So, what the fuck are going to do about it?" Ivan asked.

Dimi sat in a chair inside the safehouse and replied, "We will get this American in due time. Now, we need to focus on this new plan Jones was speaking about. Ivan? What do we know so far?"

Ivan was an expert hacker and Blockchain engineer. "Well, boss, we don't know much. The Taiwanese and Japanese haven't set up formal bitcoin or Blockchain ledgers yet. However, I suspect they have developed the digital wallet. If I can get my hands on this, I can do something here."

Dimi smiled back at his top hacker. "Mobilize Gorky Park hacking team in Budapest urgently. Tell them to deploy all available hackers from India, South Africa, and Brazil to assist."

Ivan smiled and headed into another room to begin his cyber hacking work.

"Vlad, do we plan to get out of here?" Dimi asked.

Vlad, already working on an escape plan, explained, "Working on it, boss. I have some explosives coming soon."

Dimi answered with an unemotional response. "We arrived in a bang at the airport. I suspect you have something even bigger in mind."

Vlad, staring back at his boss, vowed, "If all goes well, we kill those American operatives as well!"

"Team, let's load up in the vehicles and move on," SAC Gerald Burns ordered. "AG, this is SAC Burns. We are on the ground in Okinawa heading north. We will link up with Forest Adams within the hour."

Marcia replied, "Good work SAC. Keep me in the loop. You have orders to shoot to kill any Russian member of Gorky Park, including Dimi Zosh. The president just approved the kill order."

Gerald bitterly replied, "Roger that, AG."

"Buddy, do you need a ride?" a driver in a passing car asked.

Travis rose up with his backpack and responded, "Yeah, I am heading to Nago."

The driver gave Travis a reluctant stare. "Bro, that is the other side of the island. I can't take you that far."

Travis reached into his backpack and handed a gold bar to the driver. "Will that cover your gas?"

The driver snatched the gold bar. "Hop in, brother."

Chapter 51
Beginning

"Oh, my Tricia, it is a boy!"

Tricia cried from pain and joy. She held her husband's hand. "I love you, William, so much."

William also cried in complete happiness and said with all his love, "I love you more, my darling wife."

The nurse wrapped the baby in a blanket and then handed the beautiful newborn into Tricia's arms. "Here you are, a wonderful and healthy baby."

William became overwhelmed with love. He gently placed his index finger inside his new son's palm. Within seconds the newborn felt his father's finger and squeezed gently. "Oh, I am your father, my son… forever. I love you, Jackson William Kendall."

Tricia cuddled and nursed her beautiful son in bliss.

William stepped outside the delivery room to see his sister and announced, "Reg! It's a boy!"

Regina leaped up from her seat in the hospital hallway. "Bro, I am an aunt now!"

Silvia, William and Regina's mother, who had gone down the hall to get some coffee, came running back. "Am I a grandmother?" Silvia asked, while giving her son a huge hug.

"Yes, Mom, you are a grandmother to a healthy grandson!"

Regina picked up her phone and called her father. "Dad, it's Reg. You are an official grandfather now!"

Jack, who was still in Nago Okinawa, was over the moon with the news of becoming a grandfather. He walked a few feet away to be alone. "Reg, tell me, boy or girl?"

Reg replied, "It is a boy, Dad! Here is the proud father!"

"Dad, he is so beautiful!" William exclaimed.

Jack's eyes filled with tears at the joy of the new life. In a very husky voice, he said, "William, very proud of you. You are now a father! How is Tricia doing?"

William walked back to the recovering room. "Hey, she is fine, Dad."

Tricia took the phone from William. "Jack, he looks like you and William."

Jack felt more emotional as he remembered being there for William and Regina's birth. "Tricia, you are a wonderful daughter-in-law."

Hearing this, Tricia began to cry again. "Jack, I know you can't be here. Please come home safe."

Jack responded to his daughter-in-law, "I will, dear, I will." Trica handed the phone back to William.

"Dad, how are things there?"

"Son, we haven't found Jones yet. However, we have a Russian outfit on the island—"

William interrupted, "Gorky Park?"

"Yeah, do you know them?"

William stepped back out into the hallway. "Yeah, they are real pieces of shit."

Cautiously and calmly, Jack replied, "Son, we think something is up here. I will keep you in the loop. Please take care of your family."

"Come home safe, Dad."

Jack hung up and walked back to Forest. Seeing his friend with tears in his eyes, Forest asked, "What happened, Jack?"

Jack, taking a moment to answer his friend, said, "I am a grandfather now!"

Forest walked up to his friend and gave Jack a hug. "Well done, Marine. Let's get this asshole and head home." Jack and Forest headed back to the police hub to meet up with Commander Cho.

Chapter 52
Synchronicity
Conference Call: Green Kyoto (Taipei, Taiwan)

"Good morning, ladies and gentlemen. Thank you for attending our press conference today," Taiwanese president, Yu Chi Fong, greeted the reporters. "Today, I am joined with my dear friend Prime Minister Yoshi of Japan to announce our new joint venture, Project Green Kyoto."

The audience in the presidential palace in Taipei applauded.

"Thank you, Madame President," Prime Minister Ang Yoshi stated.

Yu continued her opening remarks with extreme pride for her country. "Today marks the launch of our Smart City and Smart Country project. For the first time in history, two countries will now connect digitally, share the same currency for commerce, and reward the citizens with greater spending value. All these transactions will be protected by a new Blockchain architecture co-managed by ADConnect of Taiwan and NTT-Japan."

Ang added additional commentary. "Our cities will be digitally connected to each other. Citizens can order food, medicines, apply for college, and purchase land holdings with this new bitcoin currency."

Yu bowed gracefully at Ang and finished his comments. "Please, for a moment, let me turn over to you, your favorite Taiwanese CEO, Sunny Ho."

Sunny walked proudly up to the podium. He took a deep, emotional breath before this landmark moment that he waited for his whole life. "Thank you, Madame President and Prime Minister Yoshi."

Sunny turned to face the screen to ensure his PowerPoint slides appeared correctly. "Good morning. As you can see from the diagram behind me, ADConnect, in partnership with NTT-Japan, has successfully hooked up 635 kilometers of underwater fiber optic cabling. This cabling will allow a direct connection between Tamsui, Taiwan and Naha, Okinawa. Our two companies have successfully tested this connection, and we are ready to set up the two Bitcoin exchanges."

The audience rose in deep admiration as they gave Sunny a standing ovation that lasted for several seconds. Filled with love for his country, Sunny could not have been prouder to be a Taiwanese citizen. "Thank you, please sit," he said softly and apologetically.

Sunny used his mouse clicker to advance his slides. "We also should recognize that this project would not be successful without partnership with the U.S. firm Cybercom / Techline and their wonderful CEO, Mr. Thomas Wilson."

Thomas joined on via video conference from his office in Pasadena. "Thank you, Sunny!"

Sunny advanced his slide and began to use his laser pointer. "By using software from Cybercom / Techline, we can now push more data faster over longer distance and create a greater user experience. Thanks to Thomas and his team of engineers, we are now ready!"

The audience of reporters, global bloggers, and web content creators rose up in veneration for Sunny's presentation.

Thomas began to receive emails and calls from all over the world.

"Well done, Wilson," Horace Jance, CEO of UK Fiber, proclaimed. "We need to talk about this software. We could use this in the UK."

Thomas removed his glasses and placed them on his computer keyboard. He couldn't be prouder of his company and his partnership with Sunny Ho.

Sunny continued explaining the Green Kyoto project., "Our goal is to launch the Bitcoin exchanges in the next twenty-four hours. In Taiwan, our citizens in Tamsui will be purchasing the new Green Kyoto Bitcoin from the Evergreen BTC. And the citizens of Naha Okinawa will be using MT. Fuji BTC exchange. Sunny stopped for a drink of water. "Questions, please."

In the first row, a reporter asked, "Suk Hong, North China Peoples Media. Why did Taiwan choose not to use a mainland Bitcoin exchange?"

Sunny proudly smiled over to Yu. "Ms. Hong, this is a Taiwanese project, not a Chinese project."

The audience ecstatically rose from their chairs and gave Sunny a heart-felt standing ovation. The president, witnessing the pride in her citizens, attempted to hold back her own tears. Seeing the outcome of emotion, Ang gently reached down and squeezed Yu's hand, showing his deep support for his dear friend.

Composing himself after the standing ovation, Sunny pointed to another reporter in the crowd. "Next question, please."

"Yao Wong, Ningbo Press. Are you planning to use software stolen from a Chinese company?"

Thomas couldn't contain his emotions after hearing the question. "Sir, how dare—"

Sunny, hearing his friend about to say something he may regret later, jumped in. "Thomas, please."

Sunny walked off the stage and stood directly in front of the reporter. "Sir, with all due respect to you and your paper, the software was stolen from Cybercom / Techline by Fiberex. This software was used recently by the PLA cyber group, the Fong Gao Triads, and a rogue hacking group. Thanks to a third party, the hack against our country was stopped, and no data was lost. Sir, Fiberex stole the software."

Thomas sat back in his chair and thought, "I owe that man a bottle of twenty-four-year-old scotch." Sunny continued to stare down the rogue reporter. The reporter broke a brief smile while he packed up his belongings and departed the press conference.

Sunny returned the podium. "Last question, please."

A lady in the third row stood up. "Ming Wang, New China News Outlet. Are there plans to expand this Bitcoin to other cities or countries?"

The president moved forward to the podium to answer. "If I may, Sunny. Taiwan and Japan have forged a unique relationship and bond. We hope that more countries would like to become a digital smart city partner in the future." The audience applauded louder than before. "Thank you." The president smiled at the young reporter. With a slight bow, she extended her hand to thank the reporter for her question.

As Sunny, the president, and Prime Minister Yoshi departed the press conference, Sunny received a call on this phone.

"You old dog, you!" Thomas Wilson chuckled.

Sunny couldn't contain the joy after hearing his old friend's voice. "Thomas, thank you for everything. Your software will make this project successful for years to come."

Knowing Sunny for more than twenty years, Thomas added, "You, my friend, have saved my company."

Sunny gladly replied, "Anytime, my friend."

Thomas sat back and watched the traffic on Colorado Boulevard in downtown Pasadena, California, remembering the day Jack Kendall walked into his office. He knew Jack was still in danger while chasing down Travis Jones and Dimi Zosh on Okinawa. "Jack, be safe, son."

Watching this press conference while enroute to Tonghua, Hai Ming couldn't contain his anger. "You think this is going to work without my help? Let's see how secure Blockchain is!"

"Thomas, Allan Smith is on line four," Arthur, the administrative intern for Thomas Wilson, remarked.

"Allan, to what do I owe this pleasure?" Thomas asked.

Allan Smith, Chairman of the Board and the largest shareholder, answered, "I owe you a huge thanks, Thomas."

Thomas heard this coming from his friend for more than forty-five years. "Thank you for keeping your money here in the company. It is going to pay off big with this Green Kyoto currency project."

"What are we looking at here, Thomas?"

Thomas looked at his revised spreadsheets and revenue projections. "For the initial site license, between Tamsui and Naha, we will get around $42 million upfront, with a two-point-five percent commerce backend each quarter for ten years. That should yield another $125 million per year."

Allan couldn't believe what he was hearing. "Thomas, you are kidding me! That is a five hundred and sixty percent return on investment within five years!"

Thomas rechecked his math. "Yes, that is about right. Those numbers only get bigger if Taiwan and Japan sign up for more Smart Cities."

Allan sat in his Wall Street office in New York celebrating the joyful news. "Thomas, let's have dinner next week in Pasadena. We need to talk about going public on the New York Stock Exchange."

Thomas smiled at Allan's suggestion. "Of course. See you next week!"

While heading back to the office inside the 101 building in Taipei, Sunny Ho, like Thomas Wilson, was very proud of their respective companies. This innovative country project propelled ADConnect to the global technology stage—a dream Sunny had since he started the company thirty years ago. "Taiwan has a lot to be proud of."

"Thanks for the lift, pal," Travis said to the driver.

"Hey, thanks for the gold, pal," the driver proclaimed.

After sitting in the car for over an hour, Travis made his way up the stairs to the Nago City safe house. Once Travis opened the door, he noticed like the safe place in Miyagi Island, the inside of the house was completely torn up. Kicking several furniture pieces, Travis made his way over to a wall that contained a hidden safe. After ripping the picture off the wall, Travis unlocked the safe using a one-time token off his cell phone.

After using his finger ID, the safe door opened. Travis proceeded to remove the contents, including two handguns, one million dollars in US currency, ten more gold bars, and several fake passports. Unaware of the police activity outside, Travis continued to search the house looking for his laptop.

"This is Control Officer Ash, message to Commander Cho. Sir, we have movement inside the suspected safe house."

Cho immediately requested confirmation. "Control Officer, confirm, how many people are in the safehouse?"

Ash moved with great stealth as he moved closer to get a better look inside. "Sir, confirmed. The Canadian suspect is the only person inside. What are your orders, sir?"

Cho instructed his Control Officer, "Ash, hold your position."

Cho walked over to Jack and Forest. "Mr. Adams, we have movement at the safe house up the street. One my officers confirmed Travis Jones is in the safehouse."

Jack, Forest, and Commander Cho ran up the street in the direction of a house under surveillance by Japanese SIS. SAC Gerald Burns, Bill Parker, and the React 5 Team arrived in their SUV's from the airport.

"Adams!" Gerald called out as he departed from the SUV.

"SAC, on me, we have positive ID that Jones is in the safehouse up the road!"

Gerald, Bill Parker, and the React 5 Team quickly departed their vehicles and began running up the street to the suspected safehouse.

Travis continued to pack the remainder of the equipment and his clothes. As he exited the house, he became startled at the sight of the Japanese police and several men running towards the house. "What the hell?" Travis shouted. He immediately slammed the door and began to block it.

"Move around the back. Cover all exits," Commander Cho ordered. The Japanese officers began to split into two groups to cover the house. Jack, Forest, and Commander Cho drew their weapons and positioned themselves in front of the suspected safe house.

"Travis Jones, this is Commander Cho, Japanese SIS. Come out with your hands up."

"Come out? Go fuck yourself!" Travis shouted. Soon after, Travis broke one of the front windows of the house and began firing his weapon.

"Down!" Forest yelled.

Jack and Commander Cho fell to the ground to avoid the incoming bullets. Soon after the shots were fired, Gerald, along with the FBI react team, arrived and returned fire.

"SAC, hold your fire," Forest ordered.

"Check your fire!" Gerald demanded. He crawled up to Jack and Forest.

"Well, glad you made it, SAC," Forest said.

Gerald looked at Forest and spoke. "What do we have, Forest?"

"Commander Cho, this is SAC Burns, FBI Global Organized Crime, SA Bill Parker and FBI React 5."

The commander reached over and shook Gerald's hand. "Glad to meet you, SAC and SA. We have Travis Jones pinned down in the house."

Gerald broke cover from behind the vehicle to get a better look at the safe house. "Do we have units in the back?"

Commander Cho replied, "Yes, I have units covering the back and side."

Panicking, Travis continued to open fire at the Japanese police officers trying to move to the side of the house. "Hey, who the fuck are you guys?"

Jack, hearing Travis screaming, requested, "Commander, we need him alive to tell us where Dimi Zosh is."

Forest, puzzled, looked over at Jack. "Okay, how do you propose that?"

Jack deliberated. "Let me go in. I will talk to him and get the location of the Russians."

Gerald, Commander Cho, and Forest collectively looked stunned. "You are nuts. That guy will kill you."

Jack confidently replied, "Look, he wants me. I will get in there, give me a radio. As soon as you hear the location, take SA Parker and React 5 and go after them before they leave the island."

Forest gave his friend a severe look of doubt. "Jack, I promised Bui that I would look after you. Sending you in there is suicide."

Knowing that he needed to confront Travis Jones again, Jack responded, "I got it, Forest, cover me."

"Travis Jones, this is Jack Kendall. Let me in so we can talk!"

Travis, still shaking from the earlier gunfire, said, "What, Kendall? What the fuck are you doing here?"

Jack stood up with his hands in the air. "I am here, pencil neck. Long time since Detroit!"

Travis nervously laughed, "Yeah, asshole. How is the family? Your daughter-in-law almost die yet?"

Jack slowly made his way to the front of the house. "No, I am a grandfather now, asshole."

Travis smirked. "Oh yeah, your son made an awesome news film. You should be proud of him!"

Jack tried to keep his temper from exploding. "Look, let me come in. We have a ton to talk about."

Travis peeked outside the window and noticed more police arriving and surrounding the building. "Yeah, why not?"

As Jack climbed the stairs, several FBI snipers kept the sights on the window where Travis looked out. "React 5, this is SA Parker. Hold your fire."

Jack opened the door and walked into the house. Travis stood up from his chair armed with an automatic machine gun. Jack stared deep into Travis's eyes remembering that last time they stood in front of each. "Been awhile since Detroit."

Travis gave a quick glance outside of the safehouse to see if anyone followed Jack. "Sit down, asshole. Want a beer?"

Jack moved to an open seat across from Travis. "Sure, I will take a beer."

Travis held his weapon at the ready, pointing directly at Jack's chest. "Over there in the fridge. Grab me one."

Jack got up and moved slowly towards the kitchen, never taking his eye off of Travis. He reached into the fridge and grabbed two Tiger beers.

"Tiger beers from Vietnam. Nice touch, Travis." Jack handed Travis the beer.

"So, Kendall, how have you been?" Travis snarked.

Jack glared with a controlled wrath as he looked straight at Travis. "I have been well, thanks, yourself?"

Travis, unamused by Jack's calm demeanor, asked, "So, why are you here?"

"Answers," Jack replied.

Travis opened his Tiger beer. "Okay, shoot."

Jack took a drink from his beer. "For starters, why did you kill Nella?"

Travis got up to check if any of the police were making their way closer to the house. He replied in a low yet direct tone, "Ah, her, well that was part of the bigger picture, Kendall. I needed you in Portugal so I could make your kids suffer greatly."

Jack took a long pull of his beer. "Go on."

Travis gazed again out the window; he noticed several Japanese officers moving up to the door. "Stay there, Kendall!" Travis lifted his automation weapon and opened fire on the police offers. Jack quickly got up to tackle Travis but before he reached him, Travis demanded, "Ah, get the fuck back, Kendall!" Jack retreated back to his seat.

Travis' threw down his automation weapon and drew out his 9MM handgun and pointed it at Jack. "I needed that Vietnam project, plain and simple. I owed the PLA and the Triads big time. General Vo needed a base of operations in Vietnam, and we needed a home for the Emerald Forest hacking group. Your company got in the way of that plan."

Jack's eyes stayed fixed on the handgun. "So, you bribed Gomez at World Bank to give you the contract. Did you divert the funds to fix the underwater cabling?"

"So far, so good, Kendall, keep going," Travis sneered.

"When Poppy Ledger lost control of the TAINET firewalls, your hack scheme was ruined."

Travis viewed Jack with a sense of appreciation. "Well, look who has figured out the puzzle.

Jack finished his beer. "And now, you are here on Okinawa with the Russian Gorky Park outfit."

Travis leaped in anger from his seat. "Don't ever mention those guys again!"

Jack sense something wrong with Travis at the sheer mention of the Russian hackers. "Oh, problems with Dimi Zosh?"

Travis slammed the weapon's barrel against Jack's head. "Don't ever mention that name to me!"

Jack remained calm even as his head began to spout small drops of blood. "I see I hit a nerve. Where is he?" Jack asked with a forceful tone.

Travis rammed his forehead directly into Jack's head. "You will never find him."

Jack knew he rattled Travis. "Well, we found you, asshole!" Jack laughed.

Travis struck Jack in the head a second time with his weapon and shouted, "You are fucking lucky!"

Jack reeled from the pain from the hit in the head. He shouted, "Tell me where he is, and I will ask the Japanese police outside to let you live!"

Travis stared down at Jack. "I will live, asshole, not to worry. You, however, have lost our little game!"

Travis began to aim this weapon at Jack's head. Reacting quickly, Jack broke the beer bottle in his hand. Travis looked down at the broken bottle in Jack's hand. "What do you plan to do with that, Jack?"

Jack thrusted the broken Tiger beer bottle into Travis's throat. Simultaneously, Travis's weapon fired and hit Jack in the shoulder.

Jack fell to the floor hitting his head on the table, throwing the beer bottles to the floor. In extreme pain from the gunshot, he screamed into his earpiece, "Forest! I am hit!"

Forest, along with Gerald and Commander Cho, crashed through the door to the safehouse with guns drawn. Seeing Jack lying on the floor with blood gushing out his shoulder, Forest grabbed a towel and put pressure on Jack's wound.

"Clear!" SAC Burns yelled.

Cho reached over to Travis and notice the blood gushing from a stab. He quickly removed Travis's gun from his hand. "Travis Jones, you are under arrest."

Feeling the effects of the blood loss, Travis tilted his head toward Jack. "You are dead, Jack, one way or another."

Jack painfully replied, "Where is he, Travis?"

Travis gasped for air while the blood continued flowing out of his body. "You have no idea what he is capable of!"

Forest knelt down next to Travis. "I have known of him since Kabul. Tell us."

Travis began to fade out due to the blood loss. With his remaining breath, he whispered to Forest, "Miyagi Island, forty-two bara."

As the last word exited his mouth, Travis laid dead on the floor. Soon after, Jack, also losing blood from the gunshot wound, began to faint.

"Jack!" Forest shouted.

Commandeer Cho scrambled into the safehouse to find more towels; he grabbed a blanket and pressed on Jack's wound.

Gerald also looked in. "Jack, stay still. Medics are on their way."

Jack looked at Forest. "Get that fucker!"

Forest placed his hand on Jack's chest. "On it, Marine." Forest rose. "Gerald, I need you and SA Parker. We need to move fast."

Gerald and SA Parker loaded up the React 5 team to head out to the island's eastern end.

"Commander Cho, please accompany us. We need you and your men," SAC Burns requested.

"On my way, SAC." Cho waved to his officers and ordered, "Get this man to the hospital in Nago!"

While getting into the SUV with Forest and Gerald, Commander Cho spoke, "That is one brave man you have in there."

Forest, turning around to talk to Commander Cho, said, "You have no idea."

Marcia Robertson sat in her Washington DC office still coping with the loss of two valuable assets to the Chinese. She considered what options she had in front of her. She decided to call the bastard, Hai Ming, to vent out her frustrations and call him out on the double cross.

"Hai, Marcia, do you have a moment?"

Hai Ming had already landed at Tonghua, China and was heading over to the secured prison to interrogate Poppy Ledger, Bao Xu, and General Vo.

"Well, Marcia, nice to hear from you. What is on your mind?"

"Well, for starters, you fucked me, you asshole. I have one dead Canadian police officer and several FBI agents wounded from gunfire from your security forces. You said that your teams would back off. What happened?"

Hai quietly simpered to himself, "I guess the security teams didn't get the word. Sorry, Marcia. My bad. What else can I do for you today?"

Already burning inside from so much hate, Marcia yelled, "Hai, you need to do better than that. I gave you Bao Xu!"

Hai savored the dual strategic win against his American counterpart. "Oh, yes, thank you for that. I owe you dinner next time you are in China."

Marcia got up from her chair. "Where is Poppy Ledger? You need to turn her over to me!"

Hai grinned. "Oh her, well, she is a hero of China now. We are going to welcome her with open arms. She changed her mind and decided to come home. What else can I help you with, Madam Attorney General?"

Marcia slammed the phone down on her desk.

Hai, hearing the phone line go dead, said, "Well, that made my day!"

Hai departed the jeep and headed into the main building after arriving at the secret prison just across North Korea's border. He removed is government ID badge and showed it the security guard. "Hai Ming, Minister of Finance to see General Zhou."

The guard responded, "Please follow me, Minister. The general is expecting you." Hai followed the young solider into the secured prison and main administration building; they headed to General Zhou's office on the fourth floor.

General Zhou, commander of the prison facility in Tonghua and considered the most ruthless general in the Chinese PLA army, ran the secret prison for fourteen years. "Minister, welcome."

Hai replied respectfully, "Thank you, General."

"Minister, please follow me to the observation area. We have all three of your prisoners here."

As the two gentlemen began walking to the observation area of the prison, the general said, "Minister, Poppy Ledger arrived two hours ago. She is currently being received into the prison system. We should see her in about an hour or so. Bao Xu and General Vo are in the same cell."

"Well done, General."

General Zhou led the Minister through a series of steel doors. The minister could hear various levels of screaming and fighting by the prisoners. "Quite the place here, General. Who else is locked up here?"

The general unlocked another door and replied coldly, "Well, we have the most dangerous criminals in all of China here. We are also holding several western spies, including three Americans, two from England, and one from Canada. We also recently captured three Russian spies."

The minister stopped. "Russian?"

The general nodded. "Yes, would you like to meet them?"

Hai thought for a moment. "Next time."

As Zhou and Hai approached the observation room, Hai looked through the various video monitors to see if he could spot Bao Xu and General Vo. "Ah, there they are."

Zhou adjusted the monitors. "Yes, they have been in the same cell now for a few hours. They haven't spoken much to each other. I will move them to the isolation room so we can have a chat with them."

Hai looked at the rest of the monitors. "Who is that prisoner?"

The general smiled. "That is your Poppy Ledger."

Hai glared down at the monitor to better observe Poppy suffering at the hands of the prison guards. After watching Poppy's video feed, startled, Hai uttered to himself, "Oh my."

Handcuffed together, General Vo and Bao Xu were led into a secured interrogation room and chained to a table. As General Vo and Bao started to speak, a badly beaten and bruised Poppy was directed into the same room.

"Oh, Poppy!" General Vo claimed.

Poppy, beaten with multiple black eyes and her mouth bleeding, entered the room. The guards chained Poppy to the same table as Xu and Vo.

"General," Poppy said. When looking over at the other man, Poppy spoke with extreme pain, "Who are you?"

Bao, also severely beaten from his own interrogation, said, "Bao Xu."

Poppy's eyes sharpened. "You were the broker to the Triads. I remember you at the meeting that day in Tiananmen square."

Bao nodded his head slowly.

"Poppy, where did you get captured?" General Vo inquired.

Poppy wiped her mouth before replying, "Trying to cross over to the U.S. side of the Canadian border."

Bao looked over at Poppy and grimaced. "Poppy, who else has been captured from the Dragon Vault Team?"

Poppy took a few breaths to compose herself. "Vulturess was exposed on Darknet; the Yakuza had a scratch team after her. I have no idea about the rest of the team."

Bao looked over at General Vo. "The Americans must have captured Travis Jones."

The general nodded his head slowly. "I hope they kill him."

Watching from a monitor, Hai could not contain his joy seeing General Vo locked at a prison table. Following General Zhou into the interrogation room, Hai took a seat across from the prisoners.

"So, General Vo, Bao Xu, and Poppy Ledger, I am Minister Hai Ming."

Each of the prisoners stared straight at Hai.

"Ming, in this life or next, you are a dead man," General Vo screamed.

Hai reached over and smacked General Vo in the face. "You first!"

Bao tried to look away from Hai before speaking. "Minister, why are you here?"

Hai cleared his throat. "One of you will go free and become a much-needed asset for China. The other two will die by taking these syncline pills." Hai stopped speaking, giving a moment for his words to sink in. "Who gets saved is totally up to you three!"

"Minister," Poppy said in a broken voice, "I will take one of those pills. I don't want to be interrogated anymore."

Hai raised an eyebrow. "Oh, you want to end your life now without even making a case to survive?"

Poppy glimpsed over at the two other men. "These two men have greater access to resources and contacts to help China. I am just a hacker wanted by Interpol. I failed in my mission, and I attempted to escape to the West."

Hai glanced over at Bao and General Vo. "Well, what do you have to offer, Xu?"

Bao eyeballed General Vo before answering. "I can deliver BOSS himself—the snakehead in charge of the Fong Gao Triads."

Hai cracked a small smile. "And you, General, what do you offer?"

Vo looked at Poppy's bloody face and eyes. "I know where to attack Taiwan," the general replied.

Hai smirked at General Vo. "Well, how did your attack pan out?"

Vo stared at the opposite wall across from him. "The plan almost worked. Next time."

Hai raised up from his chair. "Next time, General?"

Vo replied quickly, "Yes, next time."

Hai walked patiently around the room like a shark circling its prey. "I see."

Poppy began to speak. As the first sound came from her broken mouth, General Zhou rose from his chair and smacked Poppy across the mouth. "Do not speak in my presence, prisoner!"

Poppy licked the blood away from her mouth and turned away from looking at Hai.

Hai walked over to Poppy and placed is finger on her chin, lifting it up slowly, "Poppy, you did great work here. China is very proud of you!"

Poppy snapped away from Hai's hand. "Fuck off!"

Hai enjoyed tormenting the prisoners more. "So, Bao, you mentioned that you could give us BOSS? Hmm... interesting. However, BOSS is dead. Killed with chopsticks."

Bao, startled by the news, asked, "Who killed him?"

Hai took out his phone to show Bao some pictures from the tea house in Taiwan. "Well, he met San-Hamada in a tea house in Yuli, Taiwan. San-Hamada stabbed BOSS with metal chopstick in the throat. As he fell backwards, BOSS stabbed San-Hamada in the lung, killing him instantly."

Poppy, hearing this for the first time, asked, "Why did he agree to meet with his rival?"

Hai answered in a low guarded tone, "A Yakuza scratch team killed an American lawyer and some hacker named Vulturess in Okinawa the day before."

A sudden look of fear came over Poppy. "The Yakuza killed Vulturess?"

Hai peered over at Poppy and inquired, "Did you know her?"

General Vo replied, "We all knew her. She was the one who infiltrated ADConnect in Taiwan and changed the fiber optic network to send the data out of the country."

Hai became more interested in who Vulturess was. "I see. What was her name?"

Bao spoke up. "Lilian Tang, daughter of BOSS Snakehead of the Fong Gao Triads."

Shocked by these revelations, Hai said, "I guess this is even a more glorious day for China. The top Triad leader is killed by his Japanese rival and his only child, a known global hacker, is killed!" Hai packed his notebook and headed for cell block door. "I will be back tomorrow to continue our discussion."

As Hai departed the room with General Zhou, Poppy, not wanting to go back to her cell, tried to reach for the suicide pills. Hai looked through the cell door window with an assuming glare and retorted, "We aren't done talking yet, Poppy. I suggest you stay alive."

General Vo and Bao Xu were led back to their cell, still being chained together. Poppy was left in the room by herself. After a few minutes, female guards entered the room. The lead guard took her rubber club and placed it across Poppy's face.

Chapter 53

Redemption

Nago Regional Hospital (Nago, Okinawa)

Control Officer Ash reached down to Jack's head to help him become more comfortable. "Mr. Kendall, we are going to transport you to Nago Regional Hospital. You have lost a lot of blood."

Jack still felt the effects of the gunshot wound from Travis Jones. "What about Jones?" Jack pointed to Travis Jones's body.

Ash replied, "Sir, he is dead."

Jack took a breath and closed his eyes. The emergency medics loaded Jack into an ambulance. While lying in the ambulance, Jack texted William. "Son, everything is fine here in Okinawa. I got Travis Jones. More to follow. Love, Dad."

William read the incoming text from his father. He suddenly had a bad feeling something happened. "Dad, are you alright?"

Jack read the reply from William. Overcome with emotion, Jack texted back. "Yes, having a beer with Forest. Will chat soon, Will."

Jack knowingly lied to his son so he wouldn't worry. He turned his head and wept.

As the ambulance arrived at the hospital carrying Jack, three U.S. Marine Corps Security Guards were waiting for Jack. "Mr. Kendall, we are from Camp Schwab Security Detachment. Mr. Adams ordered us to stand guard, sir."

Jack used the arm that didn't get shot and saluted the Marines, thanking them for their service.

Forest, Commander Cho, Gerald, and the FBI React 5 Team arrived at Miyagi Island where Dimi's safehouse was located on the Eastern coast of Okinawa. The team began to ready their weapons and map out a plan to capture Dimi Zosh. They departed their SUV's and hid in the high grass overlooking the house.

"Okay people, it is go time," Forest spoke with a commanding tone. "When these assholes arrived on the island, they blew up half a terminal at the airport just to cover up their escape. We can expect the same here with this safe house."

Gerald interjected, "Roger that. I suggest we get an unmanned drone in the air to scout the house."

Commander Cho volunteered his drone. "I can help with that." Commander Cho got on his cell phone. Speaking in Japanese, he ordered one of his men to launch a portable drone. "SAC, done, sir. The drone will be in the air, STAT."

"Good," Forest said. Forest and Gerald observed an SUV pulling up to the safehouse. "Ah, people, that is must be him."

As the suspected vehicles arrived, Forest ordered, "Everyone move up to the house and stay low!"

Forest headed to a patch of grass near the side of the road and gave his instructions. "Listen up, these assholes are well armed and not afraid to die.

We need to split into three teams. I will take two of the FBI React 5 guys and one Japanese officer. We'll cover the back near the water. Gerald, take the four React 5 and two Japanese officers to cover the front. SA Parker with Commander Cho take the remaining units and cover the building's left side facing the waterfront. Let's move!"

As each team moved to their position, Forest stopped for a moment, thinking aloud, said, "Dimi, I got you finally."

"Boss," Vlad said, "the speed boats should be here in ten minutes."

Dimi, packing up his laptop and weapons, responded, "Da, set the explosives to go off in twenty minutes."

Vlad motioned with a thumbs up.

"This is Adams, in position at the back of the house."

Gerald acknowledged, "In position."

SA Parker and Commander Cho were in position. "Acknowledged."

Forest began moving up to the safe house. He froze as he heard a sound coming from the water. "All units, stay frosty, speedboats inbound."

Forest turned to the water to see how close the boats were.

Cho whispered into this earpiece, "Mr. Adams, the drone is picking up multiple hostiles on board those boats."

Forest commanded to Bill, "SA Parker, move your team to my position quickly!"

SA Parker rose and motioned to his team to follow through. As the boats began to draw close to the waterfront behind the safe house, Dimi and Vlad made their way out the back door.

"All units, the target is moving to the speedboats. Everyone, move up quietly!" Forest whispered in his earpiece.

Using the drone to monitor Dimi Zosh's movement, Commander Cho reported, "All units, Cho here, drone heat signatures showing targets moving quickly."

Gerald ordered his unit back away from the house and began to shift towards the rear of the house. "Adams, heading to you."

Forest started to feel his hands shake. "I haven't seen this monster since Kabul, Afghanistan in 1984," Forest whispered. He became galvanized in fear as he spotted several blocks of high explosives mounted near the house doors.

"All units move away from the house, ASAP!" Adams ordered.

"Boss, look left!" Vlad warned.

Dimi noticed several men moving quickly.

"Vlad, blow the house!" Dimi yelled.

With a click of his detonator, Vlad set off a series of explosions, causing a massive shock wave.

"Get down!" Forest shouted.

Within a blink of an eye, the entire waterfront exploded into a yellow and red thunder ball, knocking Forest, Gerald, SA Bill Parker, and Commander Cho into the water.

"I am hit!" SA Parker yelled as he crashed into the water. Gerald was also knocked down from the blast.

After hitting the water, Commander Cho spun up out of the water, drew his weapon, and fired at the two Russians.

"Vlad, head for the boat!" Dimi ordered.

Vlad, knocked down from the blast, began to crawl his way to the speed boats. Several of the men on the approaching vessels open fired with their weapons in the direction of Forest and the FBI team. Forest, seeing the speedboats slowing down as they approached the burning safe house, also drew his gun and began to fire.

After discharging his weapon, Commander Cho swam ashore to help the men not moving after the blast. Dimi, along with Vlad, made their way to the speedboats.

"Go!" Dimi shouted.

Commander Cho yelled at one of his officers, "Crash the drone into the boat!"

The Japanese officer controlling the overhead drone turned the unmanned device towards the speedboat. The drone spiraled down, becoming a remembrance of World War II's Japanese kamikaze pilots while trying to protect Okinawa from the American forces in 1945.

Within moments the drone crashed into the speedboat, causing the craft to explode. Gerald ran towards the burning boat with his weapon drawn to capture the Russians. As he approached the burning boat, multiple shots rang out, hitting him in the chest and leg.

"Down!" Gerald shouted. Hitting the ground, Gerald managed to reload his weapon and returned fire.

"Boss! I am hit!" Vlad screamed. Blood gushed from Vlad's throat. Slowly, Vlad leaned over the boat and fell into the water.

"Vlad!" Dimi yelled.

The remaining gunman grabbed Dimi and dragged him to the second boat. "Boss, leave him!"

Dimi drew his weapon off the floor of the boat and started shooting at the men on the shoreline. "Die, you fucking pigs!" he screamed.

Forest moved along the dock area waterline to try and help save Gerald. "Gerald!"

Gerald didn't respond to Forest's voice. Forest looked up to see Dimi Zosh after so many years. The sheer sight of this butcher inflamed Forest. He grabbed Gerald's weapon and ran after the boat. "Dimi!" Forest fired his weapon in a rage.

Dimi, turning to hear who was calling his name, yelled, "YOU!"

Forest fired his weapon at Dimi and noticed his target fell backward. Dimi, who had already been hit with two bullets, ordered his men, "Kill that fucker!"

Several Russian gunmen started to shoot at Forest, hitting him several times in the stomach and legs.

Dropping to the ground in severe pain, Forest rolled off the deck leading to the boat and fell into the water. The Russian boat captain pulled Dimi. He pushed the gas pedal on the speedboat attempting to escape from the American and Japanese police. Dimi looked back to see his safehouse burning along with seeing several of his men floating dead in the water, including his most trusted soldier and friend, Vlad.

With the Russians speeding off into the night, Commander Cho rallied his men and tried to help those who survived. Cho first ran over to SA Bill Parker. Seeing his lifeless body floating in the water, Cho pulled Bill out of the water and dragged him to shore. After checking his pulse, Cho closed Bill's eyes.

Cho ordered Ash, "Get the Coast Guard Air Patrol to track that speed boat!"

Ash waved back to his commander in acknowledgement. He got on his radio and contacted the Japanese Coast Guard Station at Nago.

Cho ran over to the dock to check on Gerald. He quickly noticed Gerald bleeding from several gunshot wounds. "Medic!" He started applying pressure on the various gunshot wounds to stop the bleeding. "Wake up, SAC!"

One of the police medics arrived and began to apply multiple bandages to Gerald. The doctor also gave Gerald a shot of adrenaline to wake him up. After a few CPR presses, Gerald came to life, and moaned, "Oh shit... what happened?"

"Steady on, sir," the medic said.

Commander Cho heard additional splashing in the water. He jumped off the dock to save the man from drowning. As he hit the water, Cho began to swim towards the man. "Mr. Adams!"

Forest floated on his back in desperation and weakly cried, "Cho!"

Cho grabbed Forest by his shirt's collar and started to swim towards the shore. "Medic!" Cho yelled as he came closer to the beachline. Several Japanese officers came running over to get Forest out of the water. "Officers, call in medical air support!" Cho ordered. The officer got on his radio and requested several helicopters to assist with the wounded's evacuation. "Forest, help is here," Cho said.

Forest looked up at Cho and asked, "Did he get away?"

Cho replied, "Yes. We have the Coast Guard chasing the speedboat. He won't get far."

Forest turned his head to the side in pain. He couldn't bear to think about Dimi Zosh getting away from him again.

Cho could hear several helicopters approaching along with two watercrafts from the Japanese Coast Guard.

"Forest, we will get you out of here and to the hospital," Commander Cho reassured Forest.

Passing out from the pain of the gunshot wounds, Forest laid motionless on the shoreline and closed his eyes.

Chapter 54
Aftermath

Nago Hospital (Okinawa, Japan)

"This is Commander Cho, Japanese SIS, speaking. We have helicopters en-route to Nago's Trauma Center. American VIPs on board. Have medical teams standing by on the landing pad."

Nago Trauma Center was one of the few trauma facilities on Okinawa. Forest, Gerald, and several Japanese policemen were being transported by helicopter. Special Agent Bill Parker, along with two FBI agents and three Japanese officers, were pronounced dead on the scene. Their bodies laid together on the shoreline next to the burning safe house.

With the first helicopter touching down at Nago Trauma, the Emergency Medical Technicians rushed to remove Gerald and two Japanese officers from the aircraft. All were listed in critical condition. Once the emergency crews wheeled the men into the hospital, helicopter two landed with Forest Adams and two wounded FBI React 5 team members. Even with suffering several gunshot wounds, Forest was barely alive.

"Take them first into the hospital," Forest ordered in a very weak tone.

The medical staff acknowledged and removed the FBI men first. Once the agents were placed in wheelchairs and rolled into the hospital, Forest was placed on a gurney and wheeled into the trauma center. With helicopter two unloaded, helicopter three landed with Commander Cho and three Japanese officers wounded in the house explosion.

Commander Cho ran into the hospital to check on Forest. "Mr. Adams, I will contact the US Ambassador. Do you need me to contact anyone else?"

Forest removed his oxygen mask and replied softly, "Marcia Robertson." Cho acknowledged.

Message: Encryption: Whitehouse: Attorney General: US_Ambassador_Japan: Commander CHO: Japanese SIS: Flash Traffic: Several US Agents critically wounded in shootout with Russian Mafia on Okinawa. SAC Burns, Forest Adams, 3 FBI React 5 agents in critical condition. 3 Japanese officers KIA. Special Agent Bill Parker, KIA. All victims were transported by air to Nago Regional Trauma Center, under heavy guard, please reply.

Signed,

Commander Cho, Japanese SIS

Marcia couldn't believe what she was reading. Seeing the flash traffic message on her phone, she exclaimed, "Oh my dear Forest, no!"

Marcia reached for the secured telephone. "Alvin, good heavens, who were they chasing on Okinawa?"

Alvin, still collecting the facts, replied, "Ma'am, Forest and Jack found Travis Jones. He disclosed that Dimi Zosh was in Okinawa at another safe house. From what I have been told, Bill Parker and three agents died when the house exploded. Several Japanese personnel were also wounded or killed in the exchange of gunfire."

Marcia's knees gave out. Trying to keep her voice steady, she asked, "How is Forest and Gerald?"

Alvin, checking the last message he received from one of the FBI React 5 Team members, answered, "Ma'am, they are listed as critical."

Marcia couldn't fathom what she was hearing. "Alvin, we need to get there."

Alvin waited for Marcia to finish her statement. "I am going with you, Ma'am."

Within the hour, after hearing about the gun battle on Okinawa, Alford authorized a C17 plane to take off from Joint-base Andrews, carrying Marcia Robertson, Alvin Ramsey, and several FBI members React 12 Team. As the plane began to taxi on the runway, Marcia received an encrypted call.

"Marcia, this is Valerie from NSA."

Marcia moved from her seat to a more secure location on the plane. "Valerie, not a good time."

Valerie already knew about Forest and Gerald's condition. "I know Marcia, I will be brief. We picked up the communications traffic out of Okinawa at one of our listening posts. The Russian thug you were after has headed out to sea. We lost track of him."

Marcia was shocked to hear that even the all-powerful and mighty National Security Agency with all their advanced satellites and technology could still be outsmarted by the criminals. "Submarine?"

Valerie was also in a state of shock that her agency lost track of Dimi Zosh. "Possibly, I will be in touch."

Marcia heard the phone line go dead as she walked back to her seat just before takeoff.

Arriving shortly after 6:00 pm local time on Okinawa, Mary Rogers, U.S. Ambassador of Japan, walked into the Nago Trauma Center on Okinawa. Several FBI agents along with a detachment of U.S. Marines were in the lobby standing guard.

Mary Rogers showed her government ID. "I am Ambassador Rogers. Where is SAC Gerald Burns and CIA Station Chief Adams being treated?"

One of the FBI agents replied, "They are still in surgery, ma'am, on the fifth floor."

Mary nodded and headed to the elevator with her security detail.

"Mr. Kendall. Mr. Kendall, wake up, please," the nurse on duty said.

Jack, who was recovering from the Travis Jones-inflicted gunshot wound, responded, "Yes, what is it?"

The duty nurse replied in near perfect English, "Sir, US Ambassador Rogers is here. Several American and Japanese wounded from a gunfight somewhere on the island were transferred here," the nurse explained.

Before Jack could get up, Commander Cho entered the room. "Jack, please don't get up. I came by to check on you."

Jack tried to sit up in his bed. "What happened, Commander?"

Cho motioned for the nurse to leave. "We arrived at the safehouse on Miyagi just as the speedboats arrived with more Russians. Forest and his team covered the back of the house and got into a gun battle with Dimi Zosh."

Jack observed the excruciating pain on Cho's face. "Is he alright?"

Cho, with a troubled look, painfully replied, "He took four bullets—two in the chest, one in the shoulder, and one in the leg. He is still in surgery."

Pain ran across Jack's face. "Who else got hit?"

Cho took a seat next to Jack. "SA Bill Parker from React 5... he didn't make it. He died when Zosh's man detonated the explosions in the house, killing him and three other men."

Jack asked, "How is SAC Gerald Burns?"

Cho, showing very little emotion, replied back at Jack, "He is also listed in critical condition."

Jack became deeply troubled. "How many men did you lose, Commander?"

Cho looked away from Jack. With great composure, Cho replied, "I lost three men, five are wounded."

Jack reached over to Cho and gripped his arm in support. "I am sorry for your losses."

Cho patted Jack on this arm. "Thank you, Jack. I forgot to mention, the U.S. ambassador is here. She is going to stop in your room for a few moments. The U.S. Attorney General, along with your FBI director, are enroute. They should be landing in nine hours."

Jack thanked Commander Cho. "Please, let me know how Forest and Gerald are doing."

Cho promised he will return later with an update.

Mary Rogers arrived on the fifth floor and headed into the intensive care unit. She looked for the Americans wounded in the shootout. Mary approached the nurses' station in the ICU. "I am Ambassador Rogers. Where are the Americans who came in on the helicopters?"

The duty nurse reviewed her chart. "Ma'am, there are several Americans on the ward. Gerald Burns and Forest Adams are still in surgery. Jack Kendall is resting in room 6A down the hall. The rest of the Americans are in the clinic area on the second floor."

Mary thanked the nurse and headed down the hall. She opened the door slowly and entered to check on Jack. "Mr. Kendall? Mary Rogers, U.S. Ambassador."

Jack sat up in his bed. "Good to meet you, ma'am."

Mary came in, accompanied by her security detail. "I am perfectly safe, gentleman. Please, wait outside."

The security team acknowledged and went outside the room.

"So, Mr. Kendall, I understand you are a civilian. How did you get mixed up chasing Russian mobsters with the CIA and FBI across Okinawa?" Jack explained the back story behind the failed Dragon Vault hack against Taiwan and how the Russians were there to meet up with a Canadian named Travis Jones. Ambassador Rogers continued her questioning. "You came here to find Jones, who ordered the killing of your fiancée in Portugal?" Jack nodded. "The attorney general and the CIA were well aware of this?" Jack again nodded his head in acknowledgement. Mary continued to ask questions around several of the recent events. "How is this connected to the double murder in Taiwan between the BOSS Snakehead of the Fong Gao Triads and the San-Hamada Yakuza?"

Jack took a deep breath and replied, "The triads had a hacker named Lilian Tang. She was a key player in the Taiwan hack. She stole one hundred million bitcoins from the Yakuza a year ago and killed their leaders. When she escaped Taiwan to come here, the Yakuza found her."

Mary took a seat next to Jack and perused her line of inquiry. "So, you got your revenge killing, while the FBI and CIA went after the Russian, Zosh?"

Jack admitted, "Yes, ma'am."

Mary replied, "As you probably already know, the attorney general and the FBI director are enroute."

Jack replied, "Yes."

Mary rose from the chair. "Can I do anything for you, Mr. Kendall?"

Jack smiled, "No, ma'am."

Mary smiled and departed the room to go check out the other Americans being treated.

"Okay, suture him up and move him into ICU," the surgeon ordered. After removing his gloves, the doctor departed the operating theatre and walked to the visitor waiting area. Feeling very tired after a four-hour procedure to remove the bullets from Forest Adams, the doctor went through the door to speak to the officials outside. "Commander Cho?" the surgeon called out.

"Here!" Cho and Mary Rogers walked together to meet with the doctor.

"How is he?" Mary asked.

The doctor, wiping his forehead, said, "For a seventy-eight-year-old man, he is hard to kill. I removed four bullets and stopped the bleeding. He is in the ICU recovering."

Mary took a deep breath. "Thank you, Doctor."

"Excuse me, how is Gerald Burns?" Cho questioned.

The doctor walked over to the nurses' station to check the status of Gerald. "Hmm, he is still in surgery."

Cho nodded and walked over to the ambassador. "Ma'am, I need to go check on my men. I will be on the second floor. Please, let me know if you need anything." Mary thanked Commander Cho for his hospitality. "I will be back shortly," Cho informed her.

"Nurse, another pint of whole blood. STAT!" the surgeon ordered.

After several hours of surgery, Gerald was still in a coma. His wounds were sustained in the gun battle with Dimi Zosh and the Russians. After the surgeon removed several bullets from Gerald, he found considerable damage to his internal organs.

"Suture," the surgeon commanded.

"Nurse, rib spreader."

He separated several of Gerald's ribs to find the last bullet.

"There it is," the nurse indicated.

Using his fingers, the doctor felt around Gerald's rib cage. After several attempts, he finally found the bullet.

"Okay, suction," the doctor ordered.

Several hours passed. The doctor, after checking on all sutures and Gerald's vital signs, completed the operation. He then ordered, "Move him into ICU and place him on around-the-clock monitoring."

"Yes, doctor," the head nurse replied.

Stepping out of the operating theatre, the doctor removed his gloves and washed his hands. The surgeon went out to find Commander Cho. Upon finding him in the waiting area, he spoke, "Commander Cho, I am Doctor Anui."

Cho walked over to the doctor and asked, "How is Gerald?"

The doctor took a long breath and replied, "He is still in a coma. For how long, I don't know. We stopped the bleeding. However, there was considerable damage done to his shoulder and chest area. I moved him to the ICU."

Cho thanked the doctor. Looking around for Ambassador Mary Rogers, he called out, "Ma'am."

Mary was on the phone with someone at the State Department. "Let me call you back." She walked to Cho. "That was the Secretary of State on the phone. She asked about SAC Burns and the team."

Cho was deeply concerned for Gerald's condition. "He is still in a coma. The doctor also mentioned Gerald was badly damaged from all the gun-shots and explosion."

Mary, very concerned with the news, replied, "When did they say Gerald will come out of the coma?"

Cho, unsure, replied, "Doctor doesn't know at this time."

Mary rubbed her forehead. "Thank you, Commander. I need to update Washington. Please excuse me."

Cho shook Mary's hand as he headed back to Jack's room to share the information about Forest and Gerald.

Japan-NT-News-Flash-Massive: A gun battle and series of explosions rocked Okinawa this evening. American law enforcement agents and Japanese police were pursuing several international criminals hiding on the island. We

are getting reports that several men were killed, including one American FBI agent and several Japanese police officers. No word yet on whom they were after, or the present health of the men still listed in critical condition.

After reading the flash message on his secured device, Dimi kept looking back at Okinawa Island while his rescue craft headed out to sea. He thought out loud, "This place has a history of bloodshed; too much blood."

The speedboat headed east of Okinawa. It was scheduled to link up with a Russian submarine operating in the area. One of the Russian men on the boat came over to Dimi. "Boss, where are we heading?"

Dimi, putting out his cigarette, succinctly replied, "Budapest."

Chapter 55
Formation

Nago Regional Hospital (Nago, Okinawa)

The C17 that carried the FBI director and the attorney general started the initial descent into the Kadena Air Force Base on Okinawa.

"Alvin, thank you for coming along," Marcia spoke with deep appreciation for the FBI Director.

Alvin smiled back at his boss. "My pleasure, ma'am. Let's bring our people home."

The plane made several circles around the island of Okinawa to slow downward while landing at Kadena. Marcia and Alvin, along with their security detail, gathered their items while the plane made the landing.

"Marcia, we need to find Dimi Zosh," Alvin insisted.

Marcia looked over at Alvin. "Not this trip. We need to clear things up here in Okinawa first."

Alvin disapproved of Marcia's plan; however, he respected her decisions.

The massive C17 landed safely and began to taxi to a secured terminal.

Marcia opened her communicator to reach out to Commander Cho. "Commander, this is AG Robertson. We have landed. What is the status at this point?"

Commander Cho, still making his rounds at the hospital to check on his men and the various FBI agents, including Gerald and Forest, answered, "Ma'am SAC Burns has been moved to ICU. Mr. Adams is in ICU as well but stable, and Mr. Kendall is stable and moved to a regular room."

Marcia continued to grieve at the news. "How about your men, Commander?"

Commander Cho took a seat in the hospital hall. "I lost three men in the gun battle, one passed away in the hospital... he didn't survive the surgery. Four of my men will recover in a few days."

Marcia replied, "I am sorry, Commander. Any sign of Zosh?"

Commander Cho said, "The last contact was four hours ago when his speed boat headed out to open water."

Marcia looked down in despair and replied in a low tone, "We will arrive at your location within the hour."

Marcia and Alvin departed their SUVs with a Japanese police escort from Kadena Air Force Base to the Regional Trauma Center outside of Nago Okinawa. They arrived at the hospital. The Security Service detail departed the lead SUV and began to form a protective ring surrounding Marcia's SUV. The lead Security Service agent motioned for Marcia and Alvin to depart their vehicle and move swiftly into the hospital.

"Attorney General Robertson, I am Ambassador Rogers. Thank you for being here."

"Thank you, Ambassador. This is FBI Director Alvin Ramsey."

Alvin reached out his hand, saying politely, "Ambassador."

Mary motioned for Marcia and Alvin to follow her. "This way, please."

After entering the elevator heading to the fifth floor, Marcia asked, "Any news on SAC Burns and Mr. Adams?"

"No change in their status," the ambassador bluntly replied.

Marcia felt a deep level of revulsion and pain over this matter.

"Follow me, please." Mary led them down the hall to the ICU ward. "This is Commander Cho, Japanese SIS."

Marcia approached Cho. "Commander, I am sorry for the men you lost. I want to thank you for what you did to save our men."

Cho bowed in acknowledgment of the kind words. "Thank you Madame Attorney General. If you can follow me, Mr. Kendall is down the hall in recovery."

Marcia, Mary, and Alvin followed Cho into Jack's room.

"Jack, you have a few visitors," Cho announced.

Jack sat up on his bed. "A few?" Jack smiled.

"I am Attorney General Marcia Robertson, Mr. Kendall."

Jack stood up out of his bed and shook Marcia's hand. He also turned to see Alvin. "You must be FBI Director Ramsey?"

Alvin nodded and replied, "Yes, Mr. Kendall, an honor to meet you."

Jack looked over at Mary. "Ambassador Rogers, good to see you again."

Mary bowed slightly back at Jack. She placed her hand on Jack's shoulder. "Jack, I understand that Travis Jones is dead along with Noah and Lillian Tang."

"Yes, ma'am, they are," Jack confirmed.

Marcia asked directly, "Where are the bodies?"

Cho spoke up. "We are holding them at the morgue in Naha under federal protection."

Marcia looked back at Jack. "I guess you heard about your daughter getting shot in Vancouver?"

Jack sat back down on this hospital bed. "Yes, I talked to her a few hours ago. I heard Poppy Ledger escaped back to China."

Alvin added, "Yes, the Chinese grabbed both Bao Xu and Poppy Ledger."

Jack added, "Look, Dimi Zosh got away. However, Vlad, Dimi's number two, was killed by Cho and Gerald before he jumped on the getaway boat."

Marcia appreciated Jack's update on Vlad. "Did anyone else from Gorky Park Hack Team escape, other than Zosh?"

"No ma'am. We also took out a Russian crew member while investigating the Noah and Tang murders," Cho replied.

"Thank you, Commander," Marcia affirmed. Marcia circled the room in deep thought. "Jack, I want to thank you for everything you have done. Your work in Taiwan, shutting down those fiber nodes, helped prevent the Chinese from stealing the data and coming here to Okinawa to hunt down the monster that started this whole mess. You and your cycling partner... what was her name?"

Jack replied. "Li Cao."

Marcia nodded. "Yes, where is she, by the way?"

Jack replied, "She headed to Switzerland to see her children. From there, I have no idea."

Jack remembered that he promised Li that he would find her when all of this was over.

Marcia continued, "Jack, once we get cleared up here, we have a seat for you on the C17 out of Kadena. I understand you became a grandfather. Congratulations are in order! The least I can do is get you home safe."

Jack thanked the AG for your consideration. "Yes, ma'am, I could use the ride."

Alvin smiled and said, "Jack, we need to stop in to see how Gerald and Forest are doing along with the other FBI agents. Get some rest."

Jack thanked the FBI director.

As the group headed back to the ICU, the hospital loudspeaker blasted an urgent message. "Code blue, ICU, crash cart, STAT."

The code blue trauma crew rushed past Marcia and Alvin. "Move!" the lead doctor screamed.

Marcia noticed the team entering a secured room following the crash cart. "Who is in there?"

The lead nurse replied, "American VIP."

Marcia joined the room. She noticed an old man lying on the bed with several tubes coming out of this body as she entered.

"Clear!" the doctor yelled. The crash team used a defibrillator to revive the man.

"Oh, my!" Marcia broke out in tears. "Forest! Wake up!"

Forest laid motionless on the bed; he had suffered a heart attack while recovering from the gunshot wounds from the gun battle with Dimi Zosh.

"Recharge four hundred watts. Clear!" the doctor screamed.

"Thump!" the defibrillator sounded.

Watching for the EKG screen for any sign of life, Marcia continued to weep. Praying silently, Marcia thought, "Please, dear God, not him, please!"

The doctor recharged again the paddles for a new attempt. He noticed a new wave across the EKG. "Okay, we are getting the normal rhythm."

Marcia rushed over to the side of the bed and held Forest's hand, pleading, "Please, Forest, wake up!"

Alvin, Mary, and Cho entered the room to see Marcia crying. Alvin walked over to Marcia and placed his hand on her shoulder. "Marcia, it's okay, he is in good hands."

Marcia turned to Alvin. "I know! Oh my God, my dear Forest."

She bent over to look closer at Forest. Marcia whispered, "I can't lose you again, Forest."

Commander Cho walked up to Alvin. "Sir, let's leave her for a moment. We need to check on SAC Burns. He is down the hall."

Alvin nodded and departed with Cho.

Alvin placed his hand on Mary's arm and requested, "Please stay with her. We are going to check on SAC Burns."

Mary tapped Alvin's hand. "I will, Director."

"Forest, please wake up," Marcia continued to cry. Forest didn't respond to her voice or touch. "Forest, I needed you so many times, and you were always there for me. I am here for you now. Please, come back to me." Marcia continued to pray to God hoping Forest would wake up.

Alvin and Cho walked down the corridor inside the ICU. "Commander, how are the rest of your men?"

Cho, pausing for a moment, replied, "I lost some good men tonight, Director. I am sorry for your losses as well."

Alvin asked Cho, "Thank you Commander. I need to see SA Parker's body. Where is he, please?"

Commander Cho informed Alvin the body of Special Agent Bill Parker and the two agents from React 5 Team who died in the firefight were being stored a federal protective facility.

Per the doctor's instructions, Alvin and Cho washed their hands before entering the ICU ward. Gerald Burns, still under heavy sedation from the surgery, woke up as the two men entered the room.

"Gerald, stay still, please," Alvin said. Alvin tried to hold back his emotions. He had known Gerald since they both attended the FBI academy twenty years before.

"Alvin, when did you get in?"

Alvin sat down next to his old friend. "One hour ago with Marcia. She is with Forest Adams."

Gerald cleared his throat. "How is he?"

Alvin looked at Gerald sadly and spoke slowly, "He suffered a heart attack twenty minutes ago. He survived the surgery; however, he is having complications."

Gerald turned away for a moment and queried, "How is Bill?"

Alvin always felt a sense of deep pain when he lost an agent under his watch. "Bill didn't make it."

Gerald lifted his head trying to hold back his tears. "Who else?"

Alvin took a moment to answer. "Gerald, we lost two agents and three wounded."

Gerald nodded with great sadness. "Did Zosh slip away?"

Alvin nodded. "Yes, NSA tracked him heading east out to open water, possibly a submarine."

Gerald started to weep quietly, knowing he lost a great friend and partner in Bill. "How is Kendall?"

Alvin broke into a grin for just a second to change the mood in the room. "Which one?"

Gerald stopped weeping for a moment and began to smile. "The old guy."

Alvin informed Gerald that Jack was recovering well, up and moving around.

Gerald asked, "How is Regina?"

Alvin replied, "Oh, she is fine. She is heading to Virginia to see her new nephew."

Gerald looked over Alvin's shoulder. "Cho, thank you for what you did. You and your men saved us."

Cho bowed respectfully to Gerald and replied, "Thank you, SAC. Get well. We have a fucking Russian to go after."

"Gerald, we have a seat for you, Jack, and Forest on a C17 out of Kadena. We will be transporting you stateside. You can fully recover there," Alvin informed him. Alvin got up from the chair and moved closer to Gerald. "You and I came up together, Gerald. I think it is time I step away from the FBI and retire."

Gerald was startled by Alvin's announcement. "When? Then?"

Alvin removed his glasses "You get to take over for me, pal. I will put in my papers. As soon as we get home."

Gerald looked back at his director and old friend and spoke, "Alvin, you and I came up together. This isn't the time yet. We still have more bad people to capture."

Alvin shrugged off the comment from his friend and said, "Get well, Gerald."

Commander Cho came over to Gerald. "Get well, SAC. We need to discuss this Russian thug."

Gerald nodded.

"Nurse," Forest called out.

Marcia heard Forest's voice and cried out joyfully, "My dear Forest, you woke up!" Marcia moved closer to see her dear lifelong friend and guardian.

"Marcia, how did you get here?" Forest asked with a weak voice.

Marcia wiped away her tears and responded, "C17. I got here as soon as I could."

Forest nodded and turned his head to her. "You didn't need to come all this way."

Marcia stared back at Forest. "I couldn't just sit back and see you suffer again."

The nurses came in to check on Forest. "Sir, please lay back and rest. You have suffered a heart attack," they admonished.

Forest winced in pain. "I felt like a tank ran me over."

Marcia reached for some water to give him and affectionately said, "Here, drink some pops."

Forest took a long drink of water. "Thanks."

Marcia sat down next to Forest and said, "You gave me quite the scare! Shot five times and now a heart attack."

Forest looked straight ahead and inquired, "We missed him, didn't we?"

Marcia looked at Forest and regretfully said, "Yes, Zosh disappeared somewhere out at sea."

Forest looked away and asked, "How is Jack?"

Marcia cleared her throat. "He is fine. He is in the recovery room."

Forest nodded. "How about Gerald Burns and Bill Parker?"

Marcia reached over and touched Forest's face. "Gerald is in the ICU recovering. Parker didn't make it."

A mournful, grief-stricken expression manifested on Forest's face. "How about Commander Cho?"

Marcia brightened up and replied, "Oh, he saved all of you and his men. He is with Gerald now." Marcia's eyes welled up. She whispered, "Forest, I have no one in this life other than you. When you returned to Vietnam so many years ago, I didn't hear from you for a long time. Now that you are here, and I don't want to lose you again."

Forest turned to his old friend and spoke affectionately, "Marcia, I have nowhere else to go. Bui was my life. You knew that."

Marcia remembered the day Forest saved her from being raped as a teenager and reminisced, "I know, you saved me that day, and I thought you would always look after me."

Forest, holding back his emotions, said, "I know, I can't make up for lost time, Marcia."

Marcia cried on Forest's shoulder. "Let's talk about this later after you have recovered."

Forest gripped Marcia's hand. "I love you, kiddo."

Marcia smiled back at her old mentor. "Love you, pops." Leaving Forest to rest and recover, Marcia headed back to see Alvin and Gerald. "Alvin, I need to talk to you in private, please."

Marcia and Alvin found an empty room in the hospital. "Yes, Marcia?"

"Alvin, I need you to take over for me; I am going to call the president and resign my position."

Alvin had known Marcia for so many years and was completely shocked. "Marica, we need you to stay on as attorney general."

Marcia smiled back at her colleague and said, "My time is up, Alvin. I have something more important to do. Would you mind booting up your laptop, please, for a moment? I need to speak to the president."

After resting, Jack felt strong enough to head down the hall to visit Forest. He strolled and used the handrail to maintain his balance. Stopping for a few breaths, Jack still felt considerable pain from his wounds. Taking a few more steps, one of the nurses came over to help him.

"Mr. Kendall-san, please go back to your room!" she insisted.

Jack smiled at the nurse and requested, "Take me to Mr. Adam's room, please."

The nurse reluctantly led Jack to Forest's room in the ICU. Still recovering from the heart attack and wounds, Forest laid in his bed thinking about what was next in his life.

"Well, lying down on the job, Marine?" Jack asked.

Forest looked over at Jack. "Christ, are you still alive?" Forest joked.

Jack walked in and took a chair next to his old friend. "How are you, Forest?"

Forest took a deep breath. "Jack, I had a heart attack."

Jack was shocked at the news. "On top of the gunshot wounds?"

Forest nodded and gloomily said, "Jack, Zosh got away. I don't think I can go after him anymore."

Jack looked back at Forest and quickly replied, "I have no plans to go after him either. We are getting too old for this shit. I need to go home, see my grandson and my children again. I haven't seen them in months—not since Nella and I left for Portugal, after Reg graduated from law school."

Forest envied Jack and shared, "I don't know where I will be, Marine. I haven't been stateside in years. I don't even own a home anymore."

Jack took his friend's hand. "You are going to come home with me. I have a place in Pasadena, next to the Rose Bowl Stadium."

Forest smiled and gratefully replied, "Thank you, Jack." Forest cleared his throat for a moment, then asked, "Jack, promise me you will go and find Li."

Jack stared back at Forest with a look of perplexity. "Why? She is in Switzerland visiting her kids. I suppose she will head back to Taiwan."

Forest turned to Jack, then said, "She is good for you, Jack. Promise me you will try to find her again."

Jack knew about how much Forest cared for Li and her Boris. "Okay, I will try."

Forest thanked his friend.

"Mr. President, may I have a moment, sir?"

The president of the United States had just finished his morning workout in the White House gym. "Yes, Marcia, what can I do for you?"

Marcia sat down and faced the camera. "Sir, we have found SAC Burns, Forest Adams, and Jack Kendall. Gerald is recovering slowly. Forest, a few hours ago, suffered a massive heart attack while recovering from surgery."

The president froze for a moment and replied hastily, "Dear Lord, how is he?"

Marcia wiped her eyes, then said, "He is slowly recovering, sir."

The president still had a look of concern on his face. "Is he getting the best treatment?"

Marcia nodded, "Yes, sir."

The president sat down for a moment, then spoke, "What about Jack Kendall?"

Marcia smiled for a moment and said, "He is better, sir. He will be fine in a few days."

The president replied, "Thank you, Marcia. Anything else on your mind?"

Marcia glanced over at Alvin before continuing. "Sir, I hereby submit to you my resignation as attorney general of the United States."

The president glared back at Marcia. "Oh, what brought this on?"

Marcia took a long breath before responding. "There is something more important I need to do with my life. I request you place FBI Director Alvin Ramsey as acting AG. Alvin has served this country with honor."

The president looked over at Marcia in the camera and commented, "You have it all figured out. Is Alvin there?"

Alvin shot a look over at Marcia and replied, "Yes, Mr. President, I am here."

The president, taking a deep breath, asked, "Alvin, are you up for this?"

Alvin looked back at the president and replied, "Yes, sir."

The president, considering his options, responded, "Marcia, bring our people back here, and we will formalize these plans."

Marcia acknowledged the president's order and disconnected the video call.

"Marcia, thank you," Alvin said.

Marcia hugged and replied, "Alvin, you will make a great AG!"

Alvin smiled as Marcia left the room.

Taking her time walking back to see Forest, Marcia realized that she was now free to do what she wanted for the first time in many years of public service. "The first day of the rest of my life," she thought.

Marcia approached Forest's hospital room. She overheard Forest and Jack discussing plans when they returned to the States. "Jack, I like the idea of California. If you have the room," Forest said.

Marcia entered the room. "Well, look who is up and making trouble already!"

Jack rose, then smiled at the attorney general, while apologizing. "Sorry, AG, I was offering our friend here a place to stay when we go stateside."

Forest looked up at Marcia and shared, "This Marine wants me to bunk with him in Pasadena. I hear the food is great there."

Marcia smiled and announced, "Forest, I resigned today as the AG. I am going to retire from government service."

Forest and Jack looked up at Marcia in astonishment.

"What? Are you kidding?" Jack asked.

Forest looked saddened by his friend's decision to resign. He inquired, "Marcia, what are you going to do?"

Marcia pulled up a chair next to Forest and Jack. "I will take care of you, Forest," she replied affectionately as she held Forest's hands.

Forest was taken aback by Marcia's comment. "You want to take care of me?" Forest asked incredulously.

Marica answered with a soft smile. "You are the closest thing to a family I have left. I have a house on the Chesapeake Bay that I haven't lived in for ten years. There is plenty of a room."

Jack looked over at his friend. "Sounds like a better deal, Forest. I would probably charge you rent," Jack joked.

Forest laughed. "Oh, don't make me laugh, it hurts."

Marcia looked over at Jack and said, "Kendall, you come to visit anytime. Bring that grandson of yours with that daughter. She is one tough lady."

Jack walked over, gave Marcia a hug, and said, "It's a date. I am going to check on Gerald and Cho."

As Jack departed, he looked back at Forest as he smiled up at Marcia.

Forest commented, "Are you sure you want to take care of me?"

Marcia smiled with tears in her eyes. "Until the sun stops setting over the mountains."

Ivan walked across the street, trying to find a coffee shop to use the internet. Within a few short blocks, Ivan found an internet café. After dropping a few yen on the counter, Ivan sat down at one of the open computers and drafted a message on Darknet to the Gorky Park hacker group in Budapest.

Message: Encryption: Darknet 125: One Way: Darkhorse24: Gorky Park: Made contact in Naha with the residence. I will gain access to the digital wallet for Green Kyoto shortly. Contact is the bank manager and transfers approver.

Signed,

Darkhorse24

Standing on the Széchenyi Chain Bridge in Budapest, Dimi Zosh arrived secretly the night before by a Russian military aircraft. After departing hastily from Okinawa by submarine, he began to read the secured message from Ivan.

"Da, Ivan, well done!" Dimi typed back.

Message: Encryption: Darknet 125: one-way: Dimi: Darhorse24: I arrived safely in Budapest, well done on contact in Naha, keep me apprised.

Signed,

Dimi

Ivan, fetching himself a coffee while sitting in the internet café on Okinawa, couldn't contain his emotion that his boss was still alive. "Ah, boss, you are alive!"

Ivan was deeply relieved to see the message. He still carried a lot of guilt that he couldn't warn his boss a week ago about the oncoming raid at the safehouse.

Message: Encryption: Darknet125: one way: Darkhorse24: Dimi: yes, boss, I should have access to a live wallet in a few days.

Signed,

Darkhorse24

Chapter 56
Homeward

"Jack, the doctor has cleared you. You are free to depart," Commander Cho informed.

"What about Gerald and Forest and the rest of the React 5 Team?" Jack inquired.

Cho replied, "Yes, they will be medically transported and released. We are also bringing the remains home."

Jack remembered how many men were lost in the raid at the safe house. He remarked, "Commander, our government has a lot to do in getting things back to normal. Once that is done, I am planning to come back to Okinawa to help in any way I can to find Dimi Zosh."

Cho thanked Jack. "I am glad to hear that, Jack." Cho smiled and shook Jack's hand.

Jack grabbed his backpack and coat and headed slowly to the main lobby of the facility. During this trek, he got to see Forest and Gerald being wheeled out of their rooms.

"So, I understand you guys get first-class seats home!" Jack said.

Forest turned to his friend. "We all have first-class seats, Marine!"

Jack laughed and he began to wheel Forest to the SUVs. "I will take care of him," Jack commented to the nurse.

"Where is Marcia?" Forest asked.

Jack looked around to see where Marcia was. "I think she is downstairs coordinating the transport."

Jack looked over at Gerald in the wheelchair near the elevator. "Gerald, how are you holding up?"

Gerald looked over at Jack. "I am not SAC anymore, Jack."

Jack was surprised at Gerald's statement. "Something happen, Gerald?"

Gerald shot Jack a grim look and replied, "I am now the acting FBI director as of ten minutes ago."

Jack stopped wheeling Forest for a moment and retorted, "Huh? What?"

Gerald replied, "Marcia resigned as AG. The president appointed Alvin as acting attorney general, and Alvin appointed me as acting FBI director."

Jack didn't know if a congratulation was in order. "Congratulations, I think, Director, sir."

Gerald laughed and replied, "As they say, the shit rolls downhill."

As the three men entered the lobby, Marcia had coordinated several secured means of transport for the men to Kadena Air Base. "Jack, you will ride in SUV two. Forest, we will load you in SUV six, and Gerald, you will ride in SUV one."

Jack asked, "Why all the security, Marcia?"

Marcia looked over at Commander Cho. "Cho, show them."

Cho had a yellow envelope with several pictures inside. "Guys, we have surveillance photos from the airport the day Dimi and his crew arrived. According to the photos, there were four Russians that landed that day. We can only account for three."

Jack looked over at Forest with annoyance and said, "Hold on, we have Dimi. Gerald shot Vlad before he got on the boat, then we got that guy who was near where the bodies were found. Oh, shit!"

Forest looked over at Gerald and asked, "Director, are we leaving anyone behind to help?"

Gerald considered all his options. "I will send Bill Parker's replacement back here to help with Commander Cho's search."

Cho told Gerald, "Thank you, Director, be safe getting home."

"Guys, we need to go," Marcia said.

The group waved goodbye to Commander Cho and headed off to the waiting C17 aircraft to take them home.

Shivering on her cell floor, Poppy Ledger didn't know how long she would last in that secret prison. As she fell into a coma, Poppy heard her cell door open.

"Stand!" Minister Hai Ming ordered.

Unable to move, Poppy looked up at Hai. "Kill me."

Hai looked down at his prisoner. "Ah, so you want out of this hell hole?" he sneered obscenely.

Poppy looked up at Hai. "I want to die."

Hai was amused by Poppy's request. "Poppy, that is not possible. I need you in Beijing. China needs you."

Poppy was on the verge of falling into a coma. She cried piteously, "Kill me now."

Hai stood up after gawking and snickering at Poppy, then walked out of the cell.

"What happened to Bao Xu and General Vo?" Poppy asked.

"Oh," Hai said, "they both took the pill."

Poppy looked over at Hai and begged in extreme pain, "Give me one, Minister."

Hai stared back at Poppy. "No. You are the one that will be allowed to live."

Hai stepped out of the cell. "General Zhou. I need Poppy ready to travel in two hours. Clean her up and get her medical attention."

The general saluted Hai and ordered his guard into the cell.

Epilogue
Flight Line - Kadena Air Force Base (Okinawa, Japan)

The C17 carrying the remains of Bill Parker and the three FBI agents killed on Okinawa, together with Forest, Marcia, Jack, and Gerald, landed at Joint Base Andrews outside Washington. Jack didn't sleep a wink on the long flight home. He couldn't believe he would finally get to see his new grandson, Jackson.

"Wake up, Forest, we are here," Jack said jubilantly.

Forest, still under heavy medication, began to wake up. "I am up."

As the plane taxied to a stop, the back door of the enormous plane opened. After several minutes, the ground crew made the plane secure. The honor guard came on board to remove the fallen men's caskets. Forest, Gerald, Marcia, and Jack rose and saluted the soldiers as they took each fallen colleague off the plane. After the last casket was removed, the ground team helped Forest and Gerald out of the plane while Jack and Marcia walked off on their own.

Marcia arranged for several vehicles to be ready on the tarmac. "Jack, that SUV will take you home to your grandson."

Jack stared at the car for a moment. Turning back to look at Forest, he said, "Been a journey to get here, old friend."

Forest stood up out of his wheelchair. "You did well, Marine. Go, see your grandson and those children."

Jack walked over and hugged Forest. "Take care. We will be in touch." Forest smiled back at his dear friend. Jack walked over to Gerald. "Director, let me know if you need me again."

Gerald smiled back and gave a thumbs up. "Absolutely, Kendall. Go back to selling technology. It's much safer!"

Jack nodded at Marcia. "Take care of that one for me, please, ma'am." Marcia smiled back at Jack. Jack entered the SUV and closed his eyes as the vehicle took off for William's house in Fairfax, Virginia.

"Okay, Forest, let's go home," Marcia said.

Forest grabbed Marcia and walked with her to the SUV. After Forest departed, several FBI men came over to Gerald. "Director, we are here to escort you home, sir."

Gerald nodded, rose out of this wheelchair, and got into the SUV.

The black SUV pulled up to William's home. Jack thanked the driver as he grabbed his bags and headed to the door.

After several knocks, William came to the door. "Dad!" William reached over to hug his dad. Hearing the word pater, Regina got up from the sofa and came to the front door.

"Daddy!" she screamed in joy.

Jack tightly held his two children once again after months of being away. He said repeatedly, "You two, I missed you."

Jack, along with William and Regina, began to cry. Tricia, hearing the three of them, said, "Hey, enough of the crying, you three. Come see your new baby!"

Jack slowly walked over to the crib in the living room. Gazing down at his new grandson, he said, "Jackson, I am your grandfather. I will love you forever, to the moon and back."

Jackson moved around the crib and looked up at Jack and gave him a big smile. Jack's heart entirely melted by the sight of this beautiful child.

"Well, Grandpa, pick him up!" Tricia said playfully.

Jack slowly picked up Jackson and held him close to his chest. "Oh, you are a Kendall, my beautiful grandson."

William stood next to his father. "Dad, he has our strength and dashing good looks."

Jack nodded. "He also has Tricia's attitude! What a winning combination of DNA!"

"Hey, Bub, you love that attitude," Tricia joked as she gave Jack a small hit on the shoulder.

Regina came over, placed her arm around Jack, and announced, "We are all home now."

Jack turned and gave his daughter a kiss on the forehead. He slowly took his grandson to the couch and sat down.

William stood near Tricia and said, "Dear, I love you."

Tricia looked at her husband. "I love you, William Kendall." Tricia then turned to Jack. "So, Jack, now that the Smart Country stuff worked in Okinawa thanks to William's software, how rich are we now?"

Jack smiled back at his daughter-in-law. "You have no idea," Jack replied, smiling.

About the Author

Patrick Greenwood, after military service, embarked on a 25-year career in the information technology field, working in various roles in sales, engineering, support, and design. Many of his inspirations for writing came via his business travels to places like Vietnam, China, Japan, Taiwan, and Portugal. A true believer in listening to one's passion, Patrick began writing in early 2020 based on several trips he made while cycling in various countries.

In his debut novel, Forever Our Sunrise in Saigon, Patrick draws upon several non-fictional events that happened in Vietnam including the war with the US, the last days of Saigon falling, and the chaos at the US embassy. Having remembered these events as a young man, Patrick grew up wanting someday to travel to Vietnam and visit these places for himself.

In Patrick's second novel, "Shores of Okinawa," he writes about his time in the United States Marine Corps while stationed on Okinawa in the 1980s. During his 28-year working in the cybersecurity field, Patrick developed his keen interest surrounding global hackers targeting each other.

When Patrick is not writing fictional novels, he is a professional blogger and ghostwriter. Covering the world of cybersecurity, artificial intelligence, and blockchain technology is one of his passions, next to his kids, granddaughter, his bike, and triple espressos.

Along with being a professional writer, Patrick hosts the popular podcast "Writers on Writers over a Triple Espresso," hosted every week on Wednesdays and Saturdays.

Patrick holds a B.S. and MBA in Global Marketing along with completing several post-graduate certificate programs in information security, Internet of Things, and global management from MIT.

Patrick is the father of two boys, John Jr. and Jason, and is a proud grandfather. He resides in Lake Forest, California.

Acknowledgements

Thank you to my publisher, Amy M. Le and Quill Hawk Publishing, for their support in bringing this novel to market. Thank you, Amy, for your friendship, incredible positive attitude, and commitment to the project.

To my book cover designer, Arash Jahani, for making the needed changes to help make the cover become one-in-a-million!

A huge thank you to my editor-at-large and poet-at-large, Gloria Kim Peeling, for her incredible contribution and her works that provided the much-needed book/chapter teasers.

A deep thank you to my proofreader and line editor, Bryn Weber, for the incredible feedback and line editing.

To my dear friend, R. Janet Walraven, for her collaboration on the foreword of this novel.

To my dear friend, Joyce Nwaogazie, for an incredible alpha review.

To all my beta readers, thank you for your patience and time in reading this novel and providing incredible and valuable feedback.

Reviews

"Ranging across the Far East, this fast-paced thriller plunges you into a global cyber heist that will make you think twice the next time you touch a keyboard.

As seen through the eyes of Jack Kendall, a global troubleshooter for a US tech company that is powered by his son's technical wizardry, the story is a riveting portrayal of how big hacker organizations enable both witting and unwitting teams to steal intellectual property and next-generation technology. They target markets, banking, and business systems.

The prizes range from power, influence, and money to outright systematic control. A maverick Chinese general intends to target technologies that will allow his group to effectively seize Taiwan's cyber networks and, thus, control the island nation.

Travis Jones, Jack Kendall's nemesis, is a powerful CEO of a consulting company that has grown rich and powerful, gambling on crooked international deals. The plan is complex, but Kendall and his mentor, CIA Station Chief in Vietnam Forest Adams, uncovered a Russian-built communications array, a critical step in unraveling what is happening.

This incredible story is swift, with short, punchy scenes moving between different characters. Points of view, but with enough backstory about each to make them relatable. The sense ofsetting is terrific, with action moving from the US to mainly China and Vietnam. The climax on the Japanese island of Okinawa is a high-octane page-turner.

Bottom line: reading the book is like watching a breathless Mission Impossible movie, but with global hacker moves instead of motorcycle stunts.

High recommended - 5 Stars!"

—Carmen Amato, a 24-year veteran of the Central Intelligence Agency and Author of the *Detective Emilia Cruz* series

"The Shores of Okinawa by Patrick Greenwood is a geopolitical thriller that explores the China-Taiwan dispute, interconnecting a complicated storyline of international espionage, cybercrime, and politics. The author skillfully presents various characters, including government agents, crime syndicates, and innocent people embroiled in the conflict. The story's extensive geographical scope, spanning Taiwan, the United States, Russia, and Japan, is an exciting backdrop for the unfolding drama.

The book excels in character development, giving each main character plenty of time to demonstrate their motivations, shortcomings, and positive traits. The author's decision to provide brief character descriptions at the beginning of the book is beneficial for readers. Including encrypted exchanges and simplified explanations of complex communication channels adds authenticity to the story without alienating readers unfamiliar with technical jargon.

The plot unfolds across three distinct sections, each building upon the previous to create an excellent storyline of interconnected events. The first section sets the stage with Operation Dragon Vault, introducing key players and establishing the central conflict. The second part expands the scope, bringing new criminal elements and deepening the international ramifications. The final section escalates the tension to a global scale, involving high-level government officials and revealing the complex motivations behind various factions.

A must-read! 5 Stars!"

—Helen Muriithi, Book Editor (London, UK)

"The story is very engaging and very intriguing. It frequently dragged me inside the storyline, and I occasionally wished I could be part of one of the characters so that I could try to concoct a plot to seek revenge on Travis Jones for making Regina's life and her family unbearable!

Excellent piece of work from Patrick Greenwood!"

—Joseph Fagarazzi, Author of *Escaping My Demons*

"The 2nd book in the Jack Kendall Series...here we see Jack Kendall again in a broader character, not just as a loving husband, father, and lover but more of his side in the espionage, where he brings his Marine Background into play, here we meet Travis Jones again his unintended or unavoidable enemy who is set on destroying Jack Kendall and his family as payback for Jack's hand in causing his company to lose a significant deal and millions of Dollars.

Here, we are introduced to cyber espionage with major players on a larger scale, including countries like China, Taiwan, Japan, and the United States.

An excellent book for Non-Tech/Non-Cyber and experienced cyber practitioners.

10/10 and, as usual, hard to put down; each page seems to have a higher climax."

—Olawunmi Afolabi, Cybersecurity Industry Insider
Scrum Master| AGILE | MBA| AI Enthusiast | CEH | CyberSecurity| Women's Society of CyberJutsu SoCal Leadership Chapter | VigiTrust Global Advisory Board